THE LAND OF 10,000 MADONNAS

ALSO BY KATE HATTEMER

The Vigilante Poets of Selwyn Academy

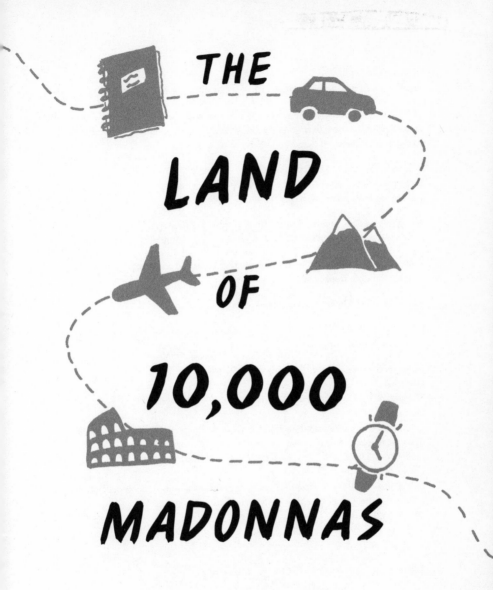

THE LAND OF 10,000 MADONNAS

Kate Hattemer

ALFRED A. KNOPF · NEW YORK

THIS IS A BORZOI BOOK PUBLISHED BY ALFRED A. KNOPF

Visit us on the Web! randomhouseteens.com

Educators and librarians, for a variety of teaching tools, visit us at RHTeachersLibrarians.com

Library of Congress Cataloging-in-Publication Data
Hattemer, Kate.
The land of 10,000 Madonnas / Kate Hattemer. — First edition.
p.   cm.
Summary: "Three cousins take a road trip through Europe to fulfill the mysterious dying wish of their fourth cousin." —Provided by publisher
ISBN 978-0-385-39157-3 (trade) — ISBN 978-0-385-39158-0 (lib. bdg.) — ISBN 978-0-385-39159-7 (ebook)
[1. Cousins—Fiction. 2. Travel—Fiction. 3. Death—Fiction. 4. Europe—Fiction.]
I. Title. II. Title: Land of ten thousand Madonnas.
PZ7.H2847Lan 2016
[Fic]—dc23
2015015899

The text of this book is set in 11.6-point Chaparral Pro.

Printed in the United States of America
April 2016
10 9 8 7 6 5 4 3 2 1

First Edition

THIS BOOK IS FOR SPENCER

When we have found all the mysteries and lost all the meaning, we will be alone, on an empty shore.

—*Arcadia*, Tom Stoppard

An Excerpt from

THE JUVENILIA OF JESSE T. SERRANO

My *dad*!

No one could mistake Arnold for a normal human being.

Let's start with the fact that he's wallpapered our apartment with postcards of Mary. The collection is famous on campus. Visiting luminaries get tours. So does Arnold's senior seminar. The invasion was gradual, of course, but I imagine it happening all at once. Someone whispered, "Go." Ten thousand postcards snapped to attention. In neat and smiling squadrons, they conquered our apartment. They annexed every wall. Our Ladies, Queens of Heaven, Virgins, Mothers: from floor to ceiling, corner to corner, they hoist their standards, blue rimmed with gold. They tilt their heads as if their halos give them cricks in the neck. They smirk. As victors go, they're a little annoying.

Okay. More than a little.

The occupation is ongoing. We've eaten dinner, and Arnold's shuffling through his briefcase. A waxy white envelope falls out. He shows me the painting. Occasionally I feign interest in finding an empty five-by-seven-inch rectangle of wall, but as a rule, I stay at the table.

"Should we allow the overflow Nativities to infiltrate the living room?" he says.

"Meh."

"Maybe I should move this Mannerist sequence behind the armchair."

"Maybe."

"Now, I can't put this Caravaggio next to a Raphael."

"Yeah, that's just unfair."

"Why do you say that?" He steps back into the kitchen, the postcard spanning his fingers. He's still wearing his tweed jacket.

"Because. Raphael's Madonna will look like a wimp. She'll look like she needs to hit the gym."

"Hmm. I was thinking in historical terms. Raphael was a papal favorite, but Paul V practically issued Caravaggio a death warrant—"

He wanders to the dining room. I start my math homework. When he asks, I remind him where we keep the masking tape. Two motherless dudes, me and my dad, living amid an army of Madonnas. I have no idea whether he sees the irony.

Four years ago, on the sidewalk in front of the Eldorado Hotel in Santa Fe, a pudgy pigeon jealously guarded his stale hot dog bun. Cal and I watched him. Arnold watched the time.

"They should have asked the babysitter to come early," he said.

"The *guide*," I said.

Arnold was attending the annual conference of the Society

of Historians of Religious Art, and Cal and I were tagging along. He consulted the emails he'd printed out from the conference organizer. (He says it's barbaric to read on a screen.) "I'll be late to my session."

"Uncle Arnold," said Cal, "we'll wait for the guide. You go ahead."

"And leave you alone in a strange city?"

"We're thirteen," I said.

"Besides," said Cal, "we're not alone. We have each other."

Arnold weighed his options. He hated to be late. "Fine. Don't tell your mother." This was directed to Cal. He hurried back inside the hotel like a traveler who's just checked his bags.

We returned to our pigeon. "Look at his little dinosaur legs," said Cal.

"Gross," I said. But it was kind of sad, imagining a dinosaur who'd been trapped by evolution in the body of a roly-poly pigeon.

"I've got today's Would You Rather," said Cal. We alternated, one a day. "Would you rather be a pigeon or a dinosaur?"

I considered. Pigeons seemed to lead content yet boring lives. Sure, it didn't take much to make them happy, but what kind of life are you leading if you're brought to paroxysms of joy by a stale hot dog bun? Dinosaurs, on the other hand, ruled the world. They flew around and gnashed their teeth and made audacious leaps upon unsuspecting prey.

They'd also gone extinct.

"Good one," I told her. "I'll think about it."

"I'll think too." We took Would You Rather seriously. Our choices defined us.

"Rummy?"

Cal dealt while I leaned back against the adobe. It was August, but early enough that the day clung to coolness. The air had the pleasant smell of hot dogs and dryer sheets. "Your discard," said Cal. We took rummy seriously too. We'd started keeping a lifelong score when we were six. She was ahead by 1,065 points. And she was older by two months, taller by two inches; she was twice as bossy and half as show-offy. I wouldn't have called her my favorite cousin. I liked Trevor and Ben just as much. But Cal was *my* cousin, and I was hers. We were podded peas, a matched set.

We played rummy with utter focus and at warp speed. I drew the queen I'd been waiting for. I slapped down my discard and grinned. No sound was sweeter than Cal's cry of defeat.

But she had stood. She was shaking hands with some woman, who had to be the guide. "Come on, Jesse," said Cal. The woman's back was to me, and all I could see was her long blond hair, floating the way hair floats underwater. It glowed. Next to her, Cal was spider-legged and skinny, all ponytail and blue jean shorts. The guide turned. She smiled down at me. "Thea," she said.

I fumbled collecting the cards. I hoped Cal didn't see me swallow. I introduced myself.

Thea was the most beautiful woman I'd ever seen.

"Shall we head to the museum?" she said.

She checked her watch, and I zoomed in on her wrist because I couldn't look at her all at once. Her forearms were pale, dusted with light hair. The watch was turquoise and silver. I snuck another glance at her face. This wasn't erotic, this wasn't a crush: I just wanted to look at her. Her hair was spun butter, stranded pine.

"Is it only the two of you?" she said.

"Think so," Cal said.

"Hope so," I said. "I've spent way too many art history conferences hanging out with five-year-olds."

She laughed. When she moved her arm, the silver band shimmered. The valet guy smiled at her. Everyone did. A stout businessman with a roller suitcase leapt aside as we started down the sidewalk. "Thank you," she said. Did he *bow*? She didn't even notice she walked in light. The man stood in front of the hotel, beaming as if he'd seen a god.

When I'd stood, I'd felt a wave of dizziness. I didn't tell either of them.

We walked past squat, sun-dried buildings and into the lobby of the Georgia O'Keeffe Museum. We wove through crowds: art students with sketchpads, old people with glasses and guidebooks, children in matching T-shirts who were threaded onto a rope like pearls on a necklace. "I was born in Santa Fe," Thea told us as we waited in line for tickets. "I've come back for the art. But I won't stay long. I don't stay anywhere long."

"All by yourself?" said Cal. "Don't you get lonely?"

Thea paused to think, and I glanced up at her. Her eyebrows were fine and light, and her blue eyes matched her watch. "I might have lost the knack for getting lonely."

We would start, she told us, at the end. "Everyone wants to progress in an orderly fashion through time," she said. "To see

O'Keeffe's life in the order she lived it. But that's one of the beauties of the past. It's not a river. It's a tree. You don't have to be swept up by the current. You can hop from limb to limb."

Behind Thea's back, Cal looked at me. She lifted an eyebrow.

"And I like to watch an artist's work unfold backward," said Thea. "To see the story with the end in mind."

"Do you read last chapters first?" I said.

"I've given up reading novels," said Thea. "But if I did, I would. The future contains the past, and the past contains the future. The ending is born with the beginning."

She meandered ahead of us. "She sounds like a movie trailer," Cal whispered. She affected a deep, portentous voice. *"In a world where time has lost its power—"*

"*—one heroic boy—"* I said.

"*—and one slightly more heroic girl—"*

"*—must—"* I broke off.

"Must what?" said Cal.

Thea stuck her ethereal head back into the lobby. "Follow me!" she called.

And so we followed her into the last gallery.

"I thought Georgia O'Keeffe painted flowers," said Cal. "But these are all about religion."

"She's made of religion," Thea said dreamily, standing before a painting of a southwestern church: orange walls, sharp steeple, deep sky. "Even the flowers. Even the skulls."

"Memento mori," I said.

"Exactly," said Thea.

"Show-off," Cal said in my ear. A memento mori, I'd learned from my dad, is an object that serves as a reminder of death: a skull, a timepiece, a petal falling to the ground.

"But you're used to religious art," Thea said to me.

"Very." Growing up in the Land of Ten Thousand Madonnas, I had believed that art, by definition, was about Mary. In kindergarten, I'd draw myself and Arnold and then I'd add her, hovering between the border of grass and the blue stripe of the sky.

But how did Thea know?

In the next gallery, O'Keeffe's flowers appeared: calla lilies and irises, white though painted with purples and greens and grays. Cal edged to my side. "She's shaking," she whispered.

Thea's watch trembled on her wrist, throwing shards of light to the ceiling.

"Is she okay?" I whispered back.

"Ask her."

"You."

"You."

"Thea," I said, "are you all right?"

"I'm fine." But she'd gone pale, even paler than she had been.

"Are you dizzy? Nauseated? Do the lights seem too bright?"

"You're an expert." She tried to smile, but her voice was weak.

"You should sit down. Put your head between your knees."

"Is that what you do?"

Yes, it was. And now *I* was dizzy, and a bit nauseated, and although the museum had track lighting and muted eggshell walls, I found myself squinting. "Your blood pressure's gone haywire," I told her. "Either too low or too high." My own blood pressure was so messed up it fluctuated between the two. "I'd guess too low. You're having a vasovagal response."

"Show-off," Cal muttered again, but I could tell she was worried, glancing between Thea and me.

"You really should get your head down," I told Thea. "Your brain's not getting enough blood."

"I'll be fine," said Thea, abruptly turning away. I would have responded, but I needed to get my own head down. By the time I straightened, she had left the room.

"Jesse—" said Cal.

"I'm okay. Now I'm okay. I'm not lying to you."

"Do you think you guys have the same thing? Does *she* have a Hole?"

"I doubt it." Thea had to be thirty-five, and there weren't many thirty-five-year-olds with giant holes between the two atria of their heart. "Lots of things cause vasovagal responses. Dehydration. Standing up too fast. Some people get them when they see blood. Or feel some extreme emotion."

"Aren't *you* the expert," said Cal, mimicking Thea. "Do you like her?"

"I don't know."

Thea had drifted into the last gallery, or the first, depending on how you were counting. We caught up to her. She looked stable. I bet she'd taken my advice.

Cal read aloud a placard. *"Blue II."*

The painting was a blue-gray swirl, a black line curling into itself. It was like a snail, or a shell, or a womb. "It looks like a fetus, don't you think?"

I'd meant that for Cal, but Thea stood beside me.

"A baby," Thea said. "A blue baby." Her clear eyes met mine, but as if she were studying the backs of my eyeballs, not the fronts.

"Yes," I said nervously.

"Do you know about Achilles?" Thea roamed the empty

room. Cal looked as uncertain as I felt: her bony knees were canted inward, and her braces flashed as she bit her bottom lip. "A Greek boy. Just a boy. But his mother was a goddess, the sea nymph Thetis, and she knew he had a choice. He could fight at Troy, he could be a hero. He'd die young, but he'd win glory and fame."

"Or?" I said.

"He could stay in Greece. He'd live a long, quiet life. 'For years on years, and long-extended days.'"

I inched closer to Cal. Thea didn't seem ill anymore, but I wondered.

"Thetis did everything to keep Achilles alive," said Thea. "She dipped him in the river of immortality. She gave him god-made armor. But he chose Troy, and he died. All along, she must have known that nothing she did would matter. Nothing."

She looked me in the eyes, the right way, seeing me as I was. "Jesse. I have to leave."

That was it. She left. We gaped at each other. At thirteen, we were old enough to be left alone, sure, but we weren't used to it.

"Did she actually leave?" said Cal.

I checked the next room. "She did."

"I can't believe it. That's against all the babysitter rules. *Now* do you like her? I don't."

"I still don't know." It made me feel uncomfortable to think about her: the beauty, the tremors, the disarming speed with which she'd slipped to a blank despair. "She's too weird."

Cal nodded. Unnerved, we half looked at a few paintings, leafless trees and bleached desert skulls. The museum ended, or began. We spilled out onto the empty sidewalk.

"Should we look for her?" I said.

"Do we even want to find her? She left us." Cal had a point. "Plus, we have twenty dollars. And a map. And your dad's not expecting us till five."

I smiled. Cal smiled. We set off.

On our way to the main square, we stopped at a grocery store, where Cal chose a day-old baguette, a dinged-up package of Chips Ahoy! on clearance, and a two-liter of store-brand root beer. We established a beachhead on a curb in the Plaza.

"You're okay, right?" said Cal.

I was light-headed again. I lifted my head from between my knees. "I'm fine." All that standing in the museum, all that walking in the sun. "I just need a drink."

Cal bared her teeth and attacked the bread like a lioness with a carcass. "My jaw's cramping up," she said after a visibly strenuous swallow. "This is too hard to chew."

I took a bite. Dry as sand. "We should have bought butter."

"Butter's expensive."

"It would soften the bread."

Our curb faced an outdoor café where lazy tourists ate breakfast. Every table had a dish of foil-wrapped pats of butter. I could almost taste it, softening in the midday sun. We *needed* that butter. If I knew Cal, and I knew Cal, we wouldn't be permitted to proceed to the cookie course until we'd finished the baguette, and the baguette was so stale that all the root beer in Santa Fe couldn't wash it down.

Plus, I had to prove myself. Cal had manned the map, chosen the food, picked the curb. I'd trailed behind, feeling dizzy.

I raised my hand to my mouth and spoke into an invisible walkie-talkie. "Mission accepted. Agent Jesse to obtain butter."

Before Cal could respond, I was army-crawling across the sidewalk. I glanced back. How well trained she was! She'd already put on sunglasses. Her face was turned toward the big church, but I knew she was watching me. I hoped I could fit between the potted plants that formed a border separating sidewalk and café. I thought I could. I did.

I was under a table. I huddled in a fetal position, much closer to four pairs of feet than I'd ever wanted to be: loafers with black socks, loafers with hairy shins, ballet flats with cankles, leather flip-flops with yellow toenails. Flip-Flops began to tap her big toes. It was repulsive.

But I couldn't back out now. It was time for action.

Another set of legs approached the table. "More coffee?"

"A little," said Cankles.

"And us too," said Sockless Loafers.

Now. *Now.* I snaked up my hand, groping, unseeing, and I nabbed the first dish I touched. Oh, frick, it was the Sweet'N Low. I set it on the ground and grabbed again. Bingo.

I paused long enough to prod one pat of butter. It was delectable, yielding. My fingernail left a crescent groove in the foil. And I crawled out crab-style across the sidewalk, all the way back to Cal, who—I told you, she knew what she was doing—had already packed up our food. I dared a look back. The waiter, carafe in hand, was departing. The two couples shifted their plates, looking for the sweetener. Giggling like mad, Cal and I speed-walked across the Plaza.

"I thought you might not make it back," she said.

"Cal," I said. "Have some faith. Did you really think I'd let myself get caught?"

That day! We roamed. We got sticky and sweaty and sunburned. We bought cheap souvenirs: a turquoise egg for Cal, a silver-and-turquoise watch for me. We drank root beer and played rummy and found a school playground where she did flips around the monkey bars and I rested on a bench.

I needed another breather on the walk back to the hotel. I leaned against an adobe wall and admired my watch. The silver was plated brass, but I loved it. Cal craned over for a look. "Jesse," she said. "Your fingertips."

They were dark blue. I stuffed my hands in my pockets. "I'm *fine*." I tried to wiggle my toes in my shoes, but they were too swollen to move. The last bout of light-headedness hadn't faded.

I didn't *want* this, damn it. Today of all days—

"We should go find your dad," said Cal, worried.

"Do you think we have that choice?" I said to distract her. "The Choice of Achilles?"

"Maybe."

"Which would you choose? A long, quiet life or a short, heroic one?"

"Both," she said.

"Pigeon *and* dinosaur?"

"Why not?" She quirked that solitary eyebrow.

"I've got to figure out how to do that."

"Practice," she said. "I practiced whenever school got boring. Once, my math teacher thought I was having a fit."

And she grinned. That grin, Cal's wild and wicked grin, contains my childhood. It contains all the Christmas visits, all the summer vacations, all the ageless hours of rummy in the attic, of scheming on the beach. We are training seagulls with a dog whistle. We are hiding to ambush our parents with water guns. Trevor teaches us to play Fly-Kebabs, a game that never ends, since—try!—it is impossible to skewer a live fly upon a toothpick. Intent, we dive around the porch. Ben says, "That's not very humane," and Trevor says, "Here, have a go," and Ben says, "I've got a better strategy, anyway." The four of us plot our adulthood. We will live in one house. Trevor and Ben are older, so they will see to the cooking and the mortgage.

Cal always quit rummy games right as I was about to win, and I couldn't ditch her. I missed the fly and stabbed her leg, and she couldn't decide she'd rather be cousins with someone else. We were stuck. Yet within the cage there was freedom. We chose to grow up together, even though there was no choice. She lived in Chicago and I lived in Berkeley and we saw each other only a few times a year, but when we were together we had the best days of our lives, days I wish I could carve into stone.

We got back to the hotel with a few minutes to spare.

"Rummy?" said Cal, but it was too late.

I'd stopped just inside the doors. I felt it coming. The patches of white sunshine on the floor began to spin, and my head was spinning, and they waltzed, sun and head, world and mind, hand on waist, hand on shoulder, faster, faster.

All light was whisked into a vast golden swirl. I felt my back buckle and saw wings of black and panted, "Cal."

She was already at my side. She grasped my elbow. "There's a bench. A few steps."

I sat and put my head between my knees. All day, I'd hoped that if I ignored it, it might go away. That'd been pure magical thinking. It never went away. My fingers were tinged an inky, purplish blue, and their bulbous tips had thickened.

Couldn't I have one day as I wanted? One freaking day?

"Breathe," said Cal.

Her hands were on my back. I closed my eyes and took deep breaths. That was the only way out. The more I fought it, the longer it would take to pass.

The hotel staff were in a confused bustle. "Give him space," Cal said. She knelt and whispered, "But tell me if you need oxygen."

"No!" I gasped. If they called the paramedics, I'd be swept to the hospital. Cal would spend yet another vacation maxing out the visiting hours. She'd eat my Jell-O. She'd scatter the room with bedpans and we'd throw stuff in them for points.

"He needs space and quiet," she said. She could be imperious. "He knows how to handle this."

My heart thumped so thunderously I could feel it in my scalp. Surely it was strong enough. How could it not be, when the floor shook in time to its beat? I pictured its chambers: two atria on top, two ventricles below. The problem was between the atria. It was an atrial septal defect, an ASD, a Hole.

A heart is a pump, you know, a beautiful pump: the right side sends blue blood, blood without oxygen, to the lungs. When the blood is oxygenated and flush, it returns to the left side. There, the pressure is three times higher than in the right side: high enough to circulate that blood through the body's sixty thousand miles of vessels. That's what happens when your heart beats, once or twice or thrice a second all your life.

But my heart is a beautiful pump with an ugly Hole at its center. The powerful, high-pressure left side pushes blood to my body, but also through the Hole.

"The blood gushes left to right," one cardiologist told me, "and the pressure on the right side of the heart rises. Pulmonary hypertension, it's called." The delicate capillaries are ground out like new grass on a soccer field. "Eventually," the cardiologist said, "the damaged lung arteries are under such high pressure that they begin to force blue blood backward. That's your Eisenmenger syndrome. Blood's shunted the *other* way through the Hole."

I always imagined the Hole like a crowded school hallway, thronged before last period. The well-behaved blood charges over to math class, but the delinquent blood is rushing the other way, to the parking lot to dip out early. I told the cardiologist. She laughed. "Sure." She'd been sketching diagrams, atria and ventricles and arcing lines of vasculature, and she pointed to the left side and said, "The oxygen-poor blood that ends up here? That's the blood that cuts class. It's not supposed to leave—it needs oxygen first—but because it's been shunted left through the Hole, the left ventricle does its job, and circulates it around your body."

"That's why I turn blue," I said.

"Cyanosis, it's called." She gave me the stink-eye. "Now, I know *you* would never skip class."

"Never," I said. "Cross my heart and hope to die."

She thought that was pretty funny. Gallows humor, it's called.

Here's what else the Hole causes:

Increased blood thickness.

Blood clots.

Organ failure.

Death.

That day in Santa Fe, my blood pressure rose too high and my oxygen saturation dipped too low. It happened sometimes. We used to call those episodes *attacks,* and I always imagined frontier skirmishes, good guys against bad. They'd breached the border, they'd inflicted casualties, but in the end they had nothing on us, nothing on modern medicine and my resilience and the sheer brunt of Arnold's will.

I was on the brink of unconsciousness. I felt Cal's hands lift away from my back, leaving two chill and shadowed patches. A pair of strong arms surrounded me. They lifted my limp body and cradled me like a baby.

A blue baby. Thea had left because she couldn't handle it, the painted blue baby that hung on the wall. Not that I blamed her. That was why my own mother left, Arnold had once let slip. I made her too sad.

"It wasn't you," he said, covering his ass. "You were perfect."

No, I wasn't perfect. I was literally defective. "The Hole might close itself," the doctors said. "And if not, we'll fix it as soon as he gets big enough for open-heart surgery."

"Is it my fault?" said my mother. "Did I do something wrong?"

"Sometimes," they said, "these things just happen."

They never chanced the surgery. Eisenmenger syndrome set in too soon. She was right to leave. I was doomed.

But I didn't need my mother and I didn't need Thea. Held tightly, an arm under my shoulders and another in the crook of my knees, I imagined the impossible. Cell by cell, I filled the Hole. I willed the scar tissue to dissolve. I willed the capillaries back to life. My arteries would course with rich red blood. Time passed. Tension ceased. When I opened my eyes, I was in my father's arms.

Thea, of course, was my mother.

I'd never known her name. I'd never asked. Until I met her in Santa Fe, I hadn't cared.

Once everything calmed down, once we'd made it to our room and I'd taken my bosentan, Arnold thought to ask, "What happened to the babysitter?"

He was furious when he found out she'd left us. But that was nothing compared to his fury when we told him that her name was Thea, that she was pale and beautiful, that she was born in Santa Fe.

"She must have figured the chances were good I'd bring you to the conference," fumed Arnold, "and she applied to be the babysitter. She stalked you."

But I say, She found me.

She thought she could try again, even knowing I'll die. And I will. If those were attacks, this is a siege. I'm short of breath even when I go down stairs, and black swoops swan into my periphery every time I move. When I wake up, my hands and feet are blue. My faulty heart will not hold up this body for long.

You know that, Cal, because you're reading this. The inevitable has transpired, as Arnold might say. Translation: shit's gone down. I'm dead and you've got my notebook.

I'd give you all my stories, but I have time for only five. And—I'm asking you, I'm begging you—space them out, okay? Don't read them all at once. I'm not withholding crucial information. There's no master plan. It's just that I know this'll be the last time I say something new.

And, Cal, I want you to know that I'm not often maudlin. I rarely even see the postcards. There's a riot of blue and gold on every wall in this place, but I walk right past it, go to the fridge, make myself a sandwich.

CHAPTER ONE

The package arrived on Saturday morning, two hours before Cal graduated from high school. The kitchen had a festive feel. She'd set her mortarboard on the coffeepot, and Trevor had hung his dress shirt, still unironed, on the oven door. Their dad hummed a never-ending loop of "Pomp and Circumstance" as he cleaned out the fridge. Their mom rustled the op-ed page and stretched her calves. Cal was eating a peanut butter sandwich with her feet on the table. Summer was so close she could see it in the air, in the white sunlight that surged through the blinds. She was almost free. She hadn't felt so good in months.

Maybe tonight she would sleep.

She was arguing with Trevor, her big brother, about which superpower they'd choose. "Flying," he said.

"Invisibility," said Cal.

Trevor tilted his chair onto its back legs. "Anyone who chooses invisibility over flying has a totally underdeveloped sense of fun."

"I do *not!*"

"But we already knew that," said Trevor.

Cal pitched a grape at him. He dove for cover. His chair toppled.

"Children," their mother murmured as she turned the page of the newspaper.

"Besides," said Trevor, righting the chair, "invisibility is a logistical nightmare. Would your clothes disappear with you?"

"Of course."

"So anything you're touching goes invisible?"

"Sure."

"Ah-ah-ah," said Trevor, waggling his finger. "That opens up a whole *host* of complications. I don't think you want that."

He was right. "Fine," said Cal. "I'd strip."

"What about your contact lenses?" He pointed at her, smirking. "Gotcha. That'd be so messed up, two little bits of plastic floating through the air—"

She needed to go on the offensive. "It's not like flying's so easy. The second you got spotted, you'd be trotted off to some lab."

"Only if they caught me."

"So you'd spend your entire life running from authorities?"

Trevor bounced a grape off the ceiling and caught it in his mouth. "Already do."

Their mom went outside to get the mail. Cal felt like a kid, eating peanut butter and arguing with Trevor, the summer arcing to the horizon like an open road. The past ten months had been rough, but she'd put herself together again, just about. She was ready to move on.

"What's the package?" she asked her mom.

"I don't know. It's from Arnold."

Cal frowned.

Her mom sorted through its contents: a thick, padded envelope for Cal; a thin one for Trevor; another thin envelope that she opened herself.

The news must have hit them all at once, Cal thought, because she could feel the shift in the room. The sunlight took on a strained, cloistered quality. Their breaths hushed. Trevor lowered his chair with a muted thwack. "Steve," her mother said quietly. "Come here." Her father closed the fridge.

As salutatorian, Cal was stuck onstage. The ceremony dragged. "You've been versatile and comforting," said the headmaster. She'd lost his thread long ago. "You've provided tremendous support." Was he addressing the parents, or her sports bra? She surveyed the sea of square hats and slick polyester. Her classmates were yawning, fidgeting, glazed over. She hoped her mental state wasn't so obvious. She doubted it. Since Jesse's death, she'd become practiced at holding herself together, at least at school. She'd relied on her image: her cleft-chinned and dimpled smile, her sharp leg muscles, the minor cachet that came with being very good at something that everyone respected but no one really cared about. Last track season, she'd set a school record for the 3,200. She was popular enough to be invited to most parties, and popular enough not to go sometimes. She had a reputation of being bossy and a little mean, a bit of a bitch, they said, but she tried not to let it bother her, because they'd never say that if she were a boy.

"We're so proud," the headmaster said, "of these young men and women, their futures before them—"

If she weren't onstage, she'd have rolled her eyes. The future was always before you. That was kind of the point of the future. On her right, Louis Gumber had his features screwed up, looking constipated. On her left, the dean of faculty swallowed a yawn. Cal's eyes watered with the effort of not yawning herself. She hadn't slept well for months. Twisted in clammy sheets, she'd jolt awake from yet another nightmare. The first day of college cross-country, and everyone was giving her the side-eye. She'd shown up in flip-flops. They began to run and her soles flapped and the pace felt hard from the start.

"This class contains accomplished artists, master musicians, skilled scholars, adroit athletes—"

That damn notebook. She couldn't stop thinking about it. There'd been a Post-it note on top: *It's not without ruefulness that I pass this on, Cal, but I'm following instructions. I'm afraid I don't know any more than you do. Love, Uncle Arnold.*

"Plane tickets," her mother told her father. "One in Trevor's name, one in Cal's. Chicago to Frankfurt, Germany."

Cal opened the front cover: *The Juvenilia of Jesse T. Serrano.* Every page rippled with his fierce, slanted handwriting.

"Departure two weeks from today," her mother said. "With an open-ended return."

The four of them looked up at each other, incredulous. Her mother's face was drawn. Her father's eyes were rimmed with the red that, before last August, Cal had seen only during allergy season. He passed a hand over his face. She felt gutted.

"Jesse's given you a trip to Europe," said her mother.

Cal shut the notebook. Anything could make her cry these days, moldy bread or a stubborn zipper or cling wrap clinging to itself, and she didn't want puffy eyes at graduation.

"Crazy," said Trevor, jumping up. "Crazy! I've got to call Ben."

Now, from the stage, Cal scanned the bleachers for Trevor. It wasn't hard to find him. His hair was the raw orange of construction signs and sports drinks, and he wore it like a thatch. He caught her eye and pantomimed a violent yawn. Trevor was fine with the trip. He was fine with everything. She watched him wrangle his gangly form out of the bleachers, hunched over like an ape. When he saw Cal watching, he mimed smoking, his eyes rolling up in deliverance. Trevor didn't smoke. She didn't think so, anyway. But he'd do anything for a joke.

Louis Gumber's nervous gulps were audible. "Our valedictorian's schedule included fourteen AP classes," Dr. Thornton was saying. Clearly not AP Saliva Conservation, thought Cal. At this rate, he'd be parched by the time he spoke. She nudged him. "You'll be awesome."

Swallow. "Thanks, Cal." He cleared his throat. There, maybe now he wouldn't have to do that into the mike.

"No prob."

Dr. Thornton turned expectantly, and Louis skittered to the lectern. "A wise man once said," he began, "that you should shoot for the moon. Because even if you miss—"

Lucky Trevor, Cal thought. Out there enjoying his fake smoke break. Out there being Trevor. Spontaneous. Fun. Everything she wasn't. "This trip's saved my ass," he'd said, and then refused to explain what he meant. "You excited, Cal?"

"I don't know," she'd managed.

She wasn't. She wasn't sure she was even capable of it. She could imagine herself riding to the airport, teetering as she pulled on a fat backpack, hugging her parents goodbye—but then the reel was zapped off like a television. Would she walk away from them? Could she? Or would she sink to the floor and huddle and rock?

If she wanted to make it through this ceremony, she'd better think of something else. Right now.

"In conclusion," Louis Gumber said, "I exhort you to make the hard choices."

These hats weren't doing favors for anyone, but the way this kid's hair fringed out was ludicrous.

"To boldly go where you would not go before."

Of course he'd make a *Star Trek* reference. Of *course*. Cal tried to find Trevor. Had he returned? He'd catch her eye and snigger, and she wouldn't feel so jaded and alone.

"And remember," said Louis, "remember, on this day filled with both celebration and nostalgia, filled with the bittersweet knowledge that the threshold between youth and maturity is, at this very moment, crossed: remember that graduation marks an end, but also a beginning."

Cal couldn't help it. She rolled her eyes so hard that she didn't see the crouching ninja photographer, who chose that moment to deploy an arsenal of flashbulbs. Damn.

"The world is all before us. Thank you."

There was rousing applause. Cal stood. Louis basked. Finally Dr. Thornton prodded him, and he jumped and returned to his seat.

"That was so good," whispered Cal. She didn't want him to suspect that his speech had been shit. Hers, after all, would have been just as bad. How were you supposed to sum up adolescence in three minutes without mythologizing the whole endeavor?

"Thank you! Thank you!" said Louis in a rush. Up close, Cal

could tell he hadn't yet discovered shaving. His patchy, dirty-blond whiskers were unmistakably rodentian. "I was nervous because my message was a bit countercultural, you know? But—"

Cal nodded along. She hoped Trevor hadn't missed the speech. He was a dead-on mimic, and she was looking forward to his rendition of Rat-a-Louis Gumber.

God, she *was* mean. They were right.

There was Trevor, standing at the back of the gym, down the center aisle. He must have decided not to bother crawling back into the bleachers. Dr. Thornton was speaking again. Couldn't he give them their diplomas and set them free? He introduced the vice principal to read the names and moved to the side with a stack of diplomas.

"Louis—Timmons—Gumber."

Louis twitched. In her mental narration, Cal appended "like a rat" to his every action. He sprang up (like a rat) and grinned (like a rat) as he shook Thornton's hand and accepted his diploma. Mean, she thought. Mean, mean, mean! But no one understood that she was aghast at her own meanness, at the pettiness of her own unbidden thoughts. Louis squeaked, "Thank you, Dr. Thornton!" Click, flash, went the official photographer. The seniors had rehearsed this maneuver ad nauseam. Shake, take, smile down the aisle.

"Callista—Ruth—Rivers."

I'm delighted, she told herself. She wanted a real smile so she'd look good in the photographs. She shook, took, and beamed at Thornton before turning down the aisle.

Shit.

Click, flash.

Was that—

It was.

Thornton must have seen it too. He released her hand. "Congratulations."

"Um," said Cal, "thanks."

"You can tell your brother we're glad he's gone." He seemed weary.

"I will." She hadn't yet caught her breath. That bastard. She couldn't believe him. She didn't dare look again until she had run the gauntlet of congratulatory administrators. There was Trevor, applauding serenely for Lucille—Ann—Abermathy.

She glared at him. He gave her an innocent smile. She glared some more and he widened his eyes, his index finger on his chin: *moi?* She tried her hardest but she felt the laugh rising in her throat.

She'd expected to see him at the end of the aisle. She had not expected, however, that quick as lightning, just as she posed, he'd spin and lower his pants. The audience had been focused forward. She and Thornton were the only ones who'd seen Trevor's tiny, moon-white butt.

CHAPTER TWO

Cal balled up her dress and threw it in the closet. She put on old running shorts and a soft T-shirt from regionals. In her bed, she read the first story of the *Juvenilia*.

It was bad. It was worse than she'd expected. She too remembered that day in Santa Fe, but her memory had dulled like a rock in a streambed, growing as smooth and cold as her turquoise egg. Now the details came back. His crab-like scooch across the sidewalk with that butter dish. His grin, a marvelous and lopsided smile that squinched up the left half of his face. How, when she'd put her hands on his back, she'd felt the panicked thumps of his heart, churning blood through the Hole.

She shoved the notebook under a mess of covers. Those leggy, brace-faced thirteen-year-olds, blithely facing a future they imagined all wrong! They thought growing up meant more days like Santa Fe, not fewer. Growing up meant freedom, and choices, and nobody making you drink water instead of root beer. When you grew up, you could spend your time with whomever you liked best, and she and Jesse, born comrades, mere weeks apart in age, would have chosen each other.

She wished she could find her past self, that girl who skinned the cat on the monkey bars of Santa Fe. She'd beckon her aside and say, Steel yourself. The years ahead do not match your expectations. Her past self would have lifted that single eyebrow. (How obnoxious she'd been!) She'd have said, I don't believe you. Of course I'll keep in touch with Jesse. Why wouldn't I?

Cal tucked her knees to her chest. She had a bundle of excuses, but they were as flimsy as balsa wood. Cross-country, indoor track, outdoor track. Schoolwork, loads of it. Summer jobs pouring coffee and clipping shrubbery. She didn't have time now, she'd always said, but soon, soon. Four years had passed since Santa Fe, four years of infrequent texts and no visits. Last August, he'd died.

Nobody understood how awful she felt. Nobody understood how awful she *was*. She'd abandoned him. And now she was supposed to go on this trip. She felt a surge of anxiety at the very thought. Couldn't she move on? Put her grief and guilt behind her?

She could reach her bookcase from her bed. A Betsy-Tacy book, that was the ticket. She had to stop thinking.

Trevor didn't knock. "What's that *smell*?" he said. "Is this the abode of a Soviet powerlifter? You know, experts recommend you wash your workout clothes every few months."

"Go away."

"This is killing my appetite."

"Well, I lost *my* appetite when I got my diploma."

"Couldn't help myself," said Trevor, testing the bar in her

closet to see whether it'd bear his weight. "It was a golden opportunity."

"Golden?" Cal said. "You'll need a lot more self-tanner if you're calling that golden."

"Excellent. If you're joking about it, I'll consider myself forgiven." The bar creaked ominously and Trevor hopped down. "What's this I hear about Emily Lukas throwing a wild graduation party tonight?"

"Her parents rented a bouncy castle and then went out of town."

"I assume you're going."

"I don't feel like it."

"High school is over! You're free! Celebrate!"

"Maybe this is how I celebrate."

Trevor gave a withering stare to the nest of blankets, *Betsy in Spite of Herself* splayed on top.

"It's a good book!"

"Cal."

"No."

"Come on. I'll go with you. Get out of bed. Take off that shirt and, for the love of God, never put it on again. Find some makeup. Drag a brush through your hair." Trevor preened in Cal's mirror. "Too bad the good looks in this family weren't more evenly distributed, huh?"

The crowd at the party waved at Cal, joyfully shrieked at Trevor. He was rapidly absorbed. Cal scooted through the dim rooms. Music blared. Her classmates—*ex*-classmates, thank God—grasped Solo cups and posed for pictures with open mouths. A few girls swiveled their hips, their eyes closed, their hands lolling above their heads. Guys staggered around and laughed horsily. They were all pretending to be drunker than they really were. It was a mistake to have come.

She got a can of beer and joined a pack of track girls in the brightly lit kitchen. At least the music wasn't so loud back here. She squinted into the dark backyard. She could see the outlines of the bouncy castle. "Gemma Tipping's out there doing handsprings," said Annie. "You want to go watch?"

"Nope," said Cal. "I'm hungry."

The track girls murmured in assent. They were always hungry. Jules found a tub of chocolate frosting in the fridge. They passed it around, taking long swipes with their fingers. A new song started, syncopated drums and an SOS signal, and she heard the crowd chanting in the living room: *Live fast, die young, bad girls do it well—*

They'd have their arms looped around each other's shoulders. The party was still building to its peak, mascara unsmeared, lashes unclumped. No one had yet vomited in front of a solicitous, bleary-eyed friend. No one had begun to think of bed, no one but her, and she was broadsided by a vast wave of loneliness. No one understood.

"This beer is gross," she said to the track girls.

"Seriously," said Annie, taking a swig.

"O little geranium," said Cal, "are you thirsty?" She poured the beer into a potted plant on the windowsill. She should have driven herself. Trevor would want to stay but she wanted to go home and read, to go back to 1907 Minnesota, where life was curlers and essay contests and a sister at the piano. She stood on one foot and stretched her quad as the girls chatted. If only she could run now. She didn't dare, not in Hyde Park at night. She would run as soon as she woke up tomorrow.

But the time between now and then stretched ahead endlessly: this unbearable party, the restless night to come. She shaded her eyes and stared out the window, pretending to look for the bouncy castle. She blinked away tears. She could not go on this trip. If she felt trapped at a graduation party a few miles from home, how could she possibly let herself be trapped overseas, four thousand miles from her mother and her father, from the trails and the track, from her bookshelves, from Netflix, from everything that smoothed her edges and allowed her to present the image of a reasonably okay person? Moody, yes, but not deranged by sadness?

She found herself clutching the countertop, feeling faint. "How hard did you pregame?" said Jules.

"I need to go," Cal said.

She must have looked ill. Annie went right away to find Trevor. He was flushed and smiling. Someone had draped a lei around his neck. "What's up?"

"I think she ate too much frosting," Annie said.

Trevor took her by the elbow. "Come on outside, Cal."

The front porch was quiet, though the steps vibrated with the music's bass beat. They sat and looked out onto Woodlawn. The parked cars were squeezed so tightly together that Cal felt sorry for them. "I'd take you home," said Trevor, "but—"

"I could drive."

"I'm not drunk. Not very. Sit here for a sec. What's going on? I thought your frosting tolerance was pretty high."

"I just don't feel good."

"Is it the trip? Are you worried?"

"Maybe." Oh, why bother pretending? "Yeah."

"Worry tomorrow. Tonight's for celebrating."

It was past midnight. "It *is* tomorrow."

"I know I'm not in full command of my faculties, but that makes no sense."

"Why did he even do this?"

"Who? What?"

"Jesse. Why did he plan this trip? And why is he trying to force us to go?"

"Whoa," said Trevor. "Do I detect some repressed anger?"

Cal scowled. "Can you be serious? For once?"

"I can try," Trevor said obligingly. "Okay. Why do I think he planned the trip? No clue. Bonding, I guess. Ben said, 'More like bondage.' He considers himself very witty. Though you'd think there'd be easier ways to bond. Cheaper ways, for sure. Not that I'm complaining." He barked a laugh. "But, Cal, he's not *forcing* us to go. Even if he could, he wouldn't."

"I think—I don't think—" Cal swallowed. "I'm not going."

"Well." Trevor sighed and twisted the flowers of his lei. "Okay."

"Okay?" She hadn't expected that.

"You've got free choice. Jesse wouldn't make you go. I wouldn't either."

"Mom's going to try."

"*You'll regret this, Callista Rivers!*" said Trevor, his voice a blend of their mother and the Wicked Witch of the West. "Yeah. She'll try hard."

They sat still for a minute, listening to the faint wail of sirens. "Do you really think it's okay if I don't go?" said Cal.

Trevor shoved his fingers through his hair. His eyebrows shot toward his hairline. "Cal, do what you want to do. Nobody's going to blame you."

"Do *you* want me to go?"

He released his hair. "Sure. We'll miss you."

We. That was part of the problem. Ben was fine—Ben was a cousin, Ben had birthright—but why had Jesse felt it necessary to include the others? Matt. Lillian. She'd shaken their hands at the funeral, but she didn't know them at all. "You'll have plenty of company," she snapped.

"Relax! I, your revered older brother, will miss the specific presence of you, my annoying little sister. Okay? And I can see Mom's point. You might wish you'd gone. But I can see your side too. If it sounds like hell, then hell, don't go. No regrets. That's my motto."

Two police cars double-parked in front of the house. Cal was too tired to wonder what was going on, too tired to do anything but stare at the slats of the iron fence, lit in sliding succession by the cars' blue lights. Trevor leapt to his feet. "Now," he suggested, "might be a good time to get out of here."

Cal was running alone on the trails. She hadn't escaped till noon, and summer humidity had already rolled into Chicago, squatting widely and strewing its things like a houseguest who planned to stay for a while. It had to be ninety out here. She didn't feel good. She could hear her stomach sloshing: a murky pond of beer, splotched with oil-slick patches of chocolate frosting. She wiped her forehead with her arm, but her arm was too sweaty itself.

"I can't go," she'd told her parents that morning.

"We know it's been a tough year," her mom said. "You haven't felt like yourself since he died. But this trip could help you break out of that."

"This kind of opportunity doesn't come often," said her dad.

"I can't," Cal said again.

"You'd get to spend time with Trevor and Ben before you go off to college."

"And get to know the other two. His friends."

She waited. They couldn't force her. They could probably get her to the airport, but then she could curl into a ball and simply refuse to move. She'd stay tucked. She'd start screaming if necessary. Eventually they'd give up. You couldn't roll someone onto an international flight.

"It might be fun," said her dad.

"It *would* be fun," said her mom, smiling. "Steve, how many great memories do we have from *our* summer backpacking through Europe?"

"Remember Siena? When we walked an hour uphill with all our luggage, only to discover there was an escalator?"

"Remember Barcelona? The hostel that turned out to be a brothel?"

"And Brussels! Two whole days there, but we couldn't do anything because you were puking."

"Don't forget Amsterdam! Two whole days of *you* puking."

"You'll want to avoid strange meats," her father told her.

"Remember that romantic, moonlit gondola ride in Venice?" said her mother.

They were in gales of laughter. "Just us—"

"The gondolier—"

"And twenty thousand mosquitoes."

"Wow," Cal had said. "You're making this sound amazing."

She was two miles into her run. She took off her shirt and

stuffed it into her waistband. Her arms were sewn over with sequins of sweat. She ran in and out of sunlight, high-stepped over branches, slammed down ravines and across bridges and up the opposite bank. The trail was laced with spiderwebs.

"If someone offered *me* a free trip to Europe . . . ," her father had said.

"I *know*," Cal had exploded. "I know, okay? I'm angsty and privileged and—"

"Honey," said her mother. "Calm down."

A chipmunk darted across the trail. She stopped so abruptly she almost fell. She hadn't remembered till now that she'd dreamt about stepping on a chipmunk. Dusty-rose brains had squirted out of its eye sockets like piped frosting. She hadn't slept for the rest of the night. By daylight, her bad dreams seemed far too inane to block her from something as important and pleasurable as sleep, but once she'd been startled awake, she could rarely lull herself back.

"It'd be too much," she'd tried to explain to her parents.

"Too much what?" said her mother.

"Just—" She couldn't articulate it. She felt choked. She brought her fists up to her mouth. The kitchen walls closed in. "Just—"

Over her, their eyes met.

"Just too much."

They seemed exasperated.

"Well," said her mother finally. Her voice was heavy with disappointment. "It's your choice. But I doubt—"

Waiting, Cal had cringed.

"I doubt this is what Jesse wanted."

She ran faster. Her guilty conscience frolicked alongside

her like an imp. "What Jesse wanted!" he chanted, giving her a gleeful jab with his miniature pitchfork. "What Jesse wanted!"

Of course she should go.

She couldn't.

She should.

The air was thick. She was moving like a spoon through syrup. Halfway up the biggest hill, she walked three steps. She started running again, but she was furious. Her body was betraying her.

She'd charge. She'd run as hard as she could. There was nothing but her quick steps, her pumping arms. Almost there. A few more steps. She threw her foot to the left to dodge a stone, and she slipped. There was a stab of pain. She was on the ground. She slid backward.

Her heel. God. Her *heel*.

She buckled over it. Her face crumpled. The pain was sharp and shooting, radiating up her left leg.

She took five deep breaths. She unclenched her fists. She used a tree to pull herself up, but she had to sink back to the ground. This was no tweak. She was injured. She was seriously injured. She put her hand over her mouth to smother the wail that would have rung through the hills.

It took her more than an hour to limp the three miles home. With every step her heel fired slender silver arrows of pain all the way up to her hip. But this was only fair, she told herself. Every time she'd run in the past year, she'd reveled in the perfection of her legs and lungs and heart. Look, Jesse, she'd thought. Look at me. Look what I can do.

CHAPTER THREE

Trevor should have trusted that it would all work out. It always did. But the prospect of a summer at home had loomed awfully close. Sleeping in his childhood bedroom. Deleting emails from MasterCard. Making the minimum-wage application rounds: *No, I am not a felon. Not yet, anyway.* Fielding texts from Scott, his college roommate and business partner, who remained utterly unconcerned by Plagueslist's free fall, though, then again, they hadn't invested *his* money. Well, no need to pursue *that* line of thought. Upshot was, the summer would have sucked. But hey. It had all worked out. He'd been saved by the skin of his teeth.

Skin on teeth. Huh. Trevor grabbed his phone. Was that a thing? If so, he needed to see photos. And if there existed skin-toothed wretches, they'd have posted photos to Plagueslist. Photo after photo, overflowing their bandwidth, jacking up their webhost fees with no revenue in sight—

"Focus," said Ben. "Choose pants. Two pairs. You can wear them several times without anyone noticing."

Trevor was grateful to drop his phone. He'd accidentally seen Scott's latest texts.

Found a comp-sci nerd who'll help with the quiz section!

Webhost angry, got any cash?

Dude, we need a music video.

He'd been saved, he reminded himself. In a week, he'd be an ocean away from his troubles. Though a music video wasn't a bad idea. He typed Scott a quick *Yes!!!* and added a donut emoji to underscore his enthusiasm.

"Trevor. Unhand your gadget. Pants. Dark-colored, if possible, to camouflage the inevitable stains of traveling."

Ben was Trevor's other cousin. He was eleven months older, and Trevor had never lost the habit of doing what he said.

"Laundry will be undertaken every ten days," Ben decided, pacing the room. Cal was huddled on the floor, her arms wrapped around her knees. She'd dumped her crutches on the bed, which Trevor found slightly disgusting—that was a lot of armpit on his pillow—but she was far too crabby for him to comment. Well, she did have an excuse. Though if *he'd* had an Aircast, he'd totally have let his sibling affix a small, tasteful Plagueslist ad.

Ben stopped by the window, lost in thought. "Why Frankfurt?" he murmured.

This kept happening. With his big toe, Trevor prodded Ben out of his reverie. "Probably just a convenient airport," he said. "Aren't we packing?"

"Right," said Ben. "You'll want five pairs of underwear."

Trevor obediently added five pairs of boxer briefs to the pile. "Wait. Five?"

"You can wear them a second day, inside out."

"No," said Trevor, "I can't."

"Frankfurt. It seems so random."

While Ben was distracted, Trevor swapped the spare pants for five additional pairs of underwear.

"What's the point?" said Ben. "What's our mission?"

"Maybe he wanted us to have fun," said Trevor.

"Fun?" Ben huffed. "I have higher expectations of Jesse than *that*."

"We'll soak in the atmosphere," said Trevor. "Eat the local delicacies. See some art, meet some natives."

Ben harrumphed.

"Bum around Europe," said Trevor.

"I will certainly not be bumming."

"We'll see about that, old chap."

Ben bristled.

Trevor could not bring himself to speak aloud what he assumed was their true mission, Jesse's true intent: they would have to figure out how to be together without him. That would be the hard part. Already, the prospect of a cousins' vacation had Trevor glancing toward the door, expecting Jesse to stroll in. "Sure, I'm all for packing light," Jesse would say, "but I draw the line at inside-out underwear." He'd have them in stitches, describing the PowerPoint he'd had to watch in health class. "You do *not* want those diseases." Even Ben would be laughing. "Cal, I've got today's Would You Rather. Mope at home all summer, or come with us to Europe?" Cal's laugh would trill. She'd once had the easiest laugh in the world. "Of course I'm coming," she'd say. "Good," said Jesse. "We'll all be together."

There were footsteps in the hallway. Trevor started, a firecracker of hope and joy. It was his mother.

"Hey," he said weakly.

Both her arms were full. She flung items toward the to-pack pile. "Money belt, umbrella, antibiotic eardrops—"

"Eardrops?" said Cal.

"Your brother's prone to ear infections."

"That was twenty years ago!" Trevor said.

"Headlamp, collapsible spoon and fork, duct tape, shirt-folding board, clothesline—"

"Mom—"

"Weatherproof journal, universal drain stopper, insect repellent, toilet paper, sewing kit, stamps, spot remover, another money belt for when you lose the first one—"

"This is great," said Ben.

"And an emergency debit card."

"Yeah, I'll take that," said Trevor, lunging.

"Wow, Aunt Debbie," said Ben. "*Thank* you."

"My pleasure. Let me know if there's anything else you need." She left.

"You choose six shirts while I take care of this situation," Ben told Trevor. He swept everything she'd brought under the bed and pulled a notepad from his breast pocket.

"What are you writing?" asked Cal.

"A note to myself. Two weeks from today, Aunt Debbie will receive a postcard telling her how useful we've found the sewing kit." Trevor gave him a high-five.

"Can I have the collapsible silverware?" said Cal.

"Go for it," said Trevor.

"I don't see what use it'll be if you're spending all summer on the couch," remarked Ben.

Scowling, Cal said, "Dr. Monteki told me I could try the stationary bike in a week."

"Only because she has no clue what's going on," said

Trevor. Both an X-ray and an MRI had come up negative for a stress fracture, and the doctor had jabbed and pressed and hemmed and said, "Not periostitis, not a fascia rupture, not an Achilles strain." Cal had come home with a diagnosis of calcaneodynia, which meant "heel pain." Basically, her foot hurt.

"Doesn't your mother have an encyclopedic knowledge of sports injuries?" said Ben.

"Yeah, she's had everything," said Trevor. "That's what running does. Destroys you."

"Yet she couldn't figure it out?"

Cal groaned. "New subject, please."

"You know what?" said Trevor. "You should post it to Plagueslist. I bet somebody would take a whack at it—"

"Shut up."

"No, seriously. You'd be shocked at the medical expertise these people bring to the table."

"Trev. Shut up."

With a flourish, Ben ticked off the last item on his list. "Don't tell me you're still embroiled in that farcical website."

Damn. He had to stop mentioning Plagueslist in front of Ben. Back in October, when it was all beginning, Ben had flipped. "Forgive my language," he'd said, "but that's the shit-tiest website idea I've ever heard of." He got worked up. Trevor had to widen the gap between phone and ear. "Sure, help out with the coding. But don't put any money into it."

Why hadn't he listened?

"Do not invest your money in that website."

Ben gave good advice. (Except when it came to girls.) "You're right," said Trevor. "You're so right."

"Of course I'm right."

"I'll tell him straightaway."

He hung up. His resolve slackened. He'd tell Scott tomorrow. But by the next day, Plagueslist sounded cool again. Anyway, it'd be a dick move to back out. And Scott was here and Ben was there, and Ben didn't understand the Internet. The only sites he ever visited were JSTOR and the *Oxford English Dictionary*.

Besides, the idea wasn't *that* shitty. Eighty percent of Americans looked up health info online. And social media was the Internet's future, right? When Scott explained his Plagueslist dream, Trevor instantly recognized its brilliance. You made a profile with your health problems. Injuries, diseases, weird symptoms: you clicked CONTRACT. You could post updates. How was that rash looking? Any news on the aching elbow? You could stalk your friends' bodies. You could spread the gospel about how pumpkin purée cured your panic attacks, or whatever. CROWDSOURCE YOUR CARE, that was their tagline. It was genius.

Trevor had poured in all the money he had, and then some. But their traffic wasn't growing, and ad revenue was paltry. Scott's ultimate vision was to get advertisers from the healthcare industry. They'd feature a physical therapist on the pages for knee injuries, promote the gastroenterologist on the ever-rumbling IBS message boards. Nobody had bitten.

"We need an advertising campaign, dude," Scott had said.

"I thought we needed—" To be featured on one of the big tech blogs. To be retweeted by a Kardashian. Trevor stopped. There was too much they needed.

"An ad campaign will give us credibility."

Trevor would check their bank statement and discover that another hundred bucks had been transferred to some graphic designer, invariably female, invariably attractive. Now Scott was sure their music video would go viral. He'd found the perfect director.

Is she hot? Trevor texted back.

Irrelevant, dude.

So she was. Their debts built. They ran out of cash even before Trevor left Grinnell for the summer. "That's what a MasterCard's for, buddy," said Scott, filling out an application. "We need one lucky break."

Trevor didn't say anything. Without warning, Plagueslist struck him as—what was the expression? Ah, yes. The shittiest website idea he'd ever heard of.

Aunt Janice and Uncle Terry came over for dinner. "When Benjamin walked out of that airport," Aunt Janice said, "I cried, 'That boy is a *wraith*!' He doesn't eat solid food anymore. Thank you, Arnold."

Trevor had already noticed that Ben had mashed his dinner to a pulp.

"He won't eat a thing I cook," said Aunt Janice. "Though I see he'll eat *your* food, Debbie—but you always were the chef of the family—"

Trevor exchanged a dark look with Cal as he shoved his sweet-potato curry from one side of the plate to the other. Ben looked embarrassed. "Mother, it's just that it has to be mashable. Uncle Arnold and I—"

"Arnold!" said Aunt Janice. "Arnold! It pains me to say it, but Arnold is positively feckless. Have you heard the latest? Has anyone wondered how this trip is being financed?"

Forks halted midair.

"The college fund. *The* college fund."

Trevor saw his parents' eyes meet.

"Can you believe it?" said Aunt Janice. "That Arnold set up a college fund? He's delusional. The child was strong, of course, but by any realistic prognosis—"

"Well, I'm sure Jesse was grateful for the money," cut in Trevor's father. "When I think of that boy, using his last weeks to plan this trip—" His voice was gruff. Trevor fidgeted with his fork.

"Does Arnold know—has Arnold told you—well—" For once, Aunt Janice was at a loss for words. *"Why?"*

Not this again, thought Trevor. They were all obsessed with why. Couldn't they accept the weirdness and move on?

"I assume it's a cousin-bonding thing," said his mother.

"But there are the *others,*" said Aunt Janice.

"I don't get why they're invited," said Cal.

Everyone looked at her. She was alone at the other end of the table so she could keep her foot elevated on the opposite chair.

"I mean," she said, flushing, "they aren't related to him. They didn't grow up with him. Not like we did."

"You aren't even coming," Ben pointed out.

Cal started to cry. She stood, hopped to her crutches, and hobbled from the room. There was an embarrassed silence.

"Was I indelicate?" said Ben.

"Not at all, sweetheart," said Aunt Janice. "Cal's always been touchy."

"She's in a lot of pain." Their mother's voice had an edge. "Her heel is killing her."

"Really," said Aunt Janice.

Trevor felt disloyal, but he too wondered. Coming home

last night, he'd seen her through the kitchen window, and she'd been walking fine. The thought had crossed his mind: was she faking the injury so nobody would blame her for skipping the trip?

No. Cal loved running. She'd never give it up voluntarily.

He'd run in high school too. It was practically obligatory when your mother was the assistant coach. During races, she'd shout, "Be competitive, Trevor!"

"Be masochistic, you mean," he'd mutter. He always had enough breath to mutter. Cal and his mom bragged about how close they'd come to puking, but Trevor always thought, What's the point? He never ran all out. He cruised through mile repeats. His teammates would spend their two-minute rest intervals sprawled on the football field, croaking for water like half-dead soldiers at Waterloo, but when his mother strode through the carnage and barked, "To the line!" they'd haul themselves up to run another four laps. Sometimes they did puke.

"The only way out is through!" his mother would yell.

Now, that was a flat-out lie. You could always find another way out. Look at him. This summer had been shaping up to be grim, but he'd been saved.

He'd told Scott about the trip yesterday. "Who's Jesse?" Scott had said.

"I thought I told you," Trevor lied.

He hadn't told anyone at Grinnell. It hadn't come up. Nobody was like, "Yo, Trevor, how was your summer? Any of your favorite humans bite it?" Nobody wanted to hear about that.

Except on Plagueslist, he suddenly thought. Plagueslisters understood compassion. They could add a button! SYMPATHY

NEEDED, you'd click. There'd be a drop-down menu. DEATH OF LOVED ONE. But they wouldn't all be that harsh. GOT DUMPED. SUFFERED HUMILIATION. MONEY TROUBLES. JUST FEELING BLUE. They could add a slider, so you could rate from one to ten the degree of sympathy you required.

This was a breakthrough. It was brilliant. He opened his mouth, but the table was debating whether Arnold had to pay back taxes on the college fund. This idea! This was *it*! Plagueslist's scope would be widened. Not everyone had mysterious growths, but everyone felt psychic pain. Plagueslist was already a positive community, a community of support, and this was its natural progression.

Trevor was dying to talk up the idea, but the discussion had become heated. Ben was citing the tax law class he'd taken as an elective. Come to think of it, this wasn't the best audience for Plagueslist musings. They'd all scoff. He thought this sympathy system was pretty good himself. It needed to get on the website ASAP. The coding was beyond his capabilities, but they could hire someone. Under the table, he texted Scott.

CHAPTER FOUR

It was early morning at the high school football field. The sun still lurked behind a scrim of trees, and the bleachers were beaded with dew. The boundaries between the grass and the brick-red track, between the track and its white lines, were crisp and unimpeachable. The lanes were numbered in a curlicued font that Cal would have recognized anywhere. All she wanted was to run.

Instead, she was in a lawn chair. Her mother was running 800s. She started each rep gamely. She flew through the first lap and pushed through the second. "Come cheer me on," she'd said.

"Isn't Coach Campbell going to be there?"

"I could use the moral support."

That was a lie. Her mother had done track workouts every week, sometimes twice a week, for years. But Cal still felt guilty about her refusal to go on the trip. She hated to disappoint her mother, but she couldn't go, she just couldn't. She guessed she could manage the track.

Coach Campbell paced with a stopwatch. "Two fifty-two," he called as Cal's mother crossed the line. "Take ninety seconds."

"Okay," said her mother. This was only her second, and she recovered fast. She pulled off her sunglasses and mopped her face with her shirt. "You doing okay, honey?"

"I'm fine."

"I could use some company. Sure wish you could run."

"Not as much as I do."

Coach Campbell wrote the split times on his clipboard. He coached Mrs. Rivers for free in exchange for her help with the high school teams. Forty years ago, he'd been to the Olympic Trials. Now he was wizened and weather-beaten; his body disappeared in the folds of his track suit, but when he jogged to the line, you could see the economy and grace of motion. He ran six miles every morning. He hadn't missed a day in twelve years.

"Ten seconds," he said.

Cal's mother lined up.

"Go."

Her steps, short around the curve, lengthened into the straightaway. Cal watched her. Coach Campbell's face was impassive behind his sunglasses, and she wished she could see her mother through his eyes.

She was on the home straight. The coach lifted his stopwatch. "Eighty-four, eighty-five."

"Woo," said Cal belatedly. Her mother's mouth twitched up as she began the second lap.

"Calcaneodynia," said Coach Campbell.

"Oh. Yeah. It sucks."

"Not a fracture, not plantar fasciitis."

Not this again. Ever since she'd landed the vaguest diagnosis in history, she'd had far too many people weighing in. Walking, she'd recently discovered, didn't hurt at all. The problem was running. She felt queasy at the mere thought, imagining that hot skewer puncturing her heel, impaling her leg.

The sun poked up behind the trees. She had to squint to see her mother finish her third rep. "Two fifty-one," said Coach Campbell.

Her mother briefly set her hands on her knees. She paced, her breath ragged. "All right, Mom, you got this," said Cal unconvincingly. Her mother winced.

"Ten seconds." He cocked the stopwatch. "Go."

Five more reps. Cal was tired. She'd been awake since three, when she'd jolted up from another nightmare. She'd had to traverse a convenience store full of men. They'd grabbed at her body, and they'd laughed when she'd swatted them away.

"Sometimes," said Coach Campbell, "you have to push through the pain. Eighty-seven, eighty-eight, pick it up." Her mother's blitheness was gone. She'd started to suffer.

"Push through, Mom!" said Cal.

"Even when pain means sitting still."

"I hate sitting still."

"I know. I know. Your mom's feeling like death. Lungs flying out of her chest, heart galloping, and you'd change places with her in an instant."

"Yeah." Cal loved track workouts. She felt cleansed by the pain, and comforted by the relentless tick of seconds. What had begun would end. She got blinding headaches every time. "Yeah." Most of her teammates hated the track. Trevor hated it more than anyone. "People bark orders at you," he said.

"Pick it up! One more! On your mark . . . I only like running when I'm free."

It was true, Cal thought: track workouts were exercises in obedience. You obeyed your coach. Your body obeyed you. But you were free to obey, a freedom that grew not on the wide fens of anarchy but within a kitchen garden, colonnaded and kempt. "You just love following rules," Trevor said.

"Two fifty-two," said Coach Campbell. "Nice lap."

Cal's mother bent over, her back heaving like the flanks of a horse. Halfway done, but Cal knew better than to say it. Her mother could think only of the present. "Breathe," she said as her mother straightened. "One at a time."

Her mother took off.

"It's hard to believe," Coach Campbell said, "but you'll run again."

Of course, Cal thought, but her eyes filled with tears. She squinted. The sun kaleidoscoped.

"The time will come when you'll be running and you won't even remember which foot used to hurt."

Her mother flew down the back straight, hamstrings clenching, arms pumping, and all at once Cal saw not her mother but a pack of girls. She was among them. They laughed as they warmed up. The track was bedecked for a home meet, the visiting teams' tents on the field, a smattering of parents in the bleachers. Someone was raking the long-jump pit. The boys jogged along in dynamic stretches, skinny boys in short shorts doing high knees, and Cal's pack split to pass them. "Raise those knees!" Annie shouted.

"Higher!" called Jules.

Cal smacked a couple of her favorite freshmen on their

butts. They yowled. The girls laughed. This very track. She had traced so many ellipses around it, the messy strolls during football games, the tight sharp laps of the 3,200 when she'd jockey for the curb. The warm-ups, the workouts.

"Two fifty-two," she heard Coach Campbell say, and a little later, "Go."

She could still see her team. She found herself. It was junior year, and she was captain. She yelled, "Strides!" and the girls milled around the hundred-meter line, six at once soaring down the straight, jogging back for another. God, she'd do anything to go back. There she went. Look at her. Her ponytail sailed behind her. Look at her run.

"Two fifty-one. That's seven. One to go."

Cal woke from her daydream. Just one left? She'd zoned out. The sunlight was so intense that she could see her mother only in silhouette, hunched over her knees. Coach Campbell jogged toward Cal, offering her something. A pair of sunglasses.

"Debbie, ten seconds," he said over his shoulder.

"For *me*?" said Cal.

"Go." Her mother went. "Yes, you. You want them or not?"

Cal took the sunglasses. She put them on. Now she could see her plucky, fast mother rounding the bend. She would close her eyes on the straightaway, Cal knew. She seemed heroic. She hit the next curve.

"They fit okay?" Coach Campbell gave her a curious look, and Cal realized she was clutching the stems of the glasses.

"They're perfect. Perfect." Her mother was on the home straight. "Thank you."

"An old pair. You can have them if you like them."

"Thank you so much."

"Thank your mother. She's the one who asked me to get them for you."

There was her mother.

"Eighty-four, eighty-five."

"Mom!" called Cal. "I'll go!"

Another weird look from Coach Campbell. But now Cal could see, and she could see that her mother's stride had an extra spring as she made the turn and pushed herself around one more lap.

CHAPTER FIVE

Ben hated a puzzle he couldn't solve, and the maps gnawed at him. He thought about them in the library and at work. He thought about them while blending meals, while packing books, while flying from Berkeley to Chicago. He was thinking about them as he stood among a loose group of kin in the airport, his backpack's stability belt strapped firmly across his abdomen. He'd have preferred to have cleared security by now, but their parents, predictably, were loath to release them.

"Cal, keep using that Aircast," said Aunt Debbie. "Trevor, reassure me. Are you wearing your money belt?"

"I expect weekly contact, Benjamin," interjected his weeping mother. "Via telephone or email. Do not rely on snail mail—"

"Mother, you'd be shocked at the efficiency of modern European postal services—"

"And don't stretch this out longer than six weeks." The tickets were open-ended. Ben had the instructions for scheduling their departure in a plastic sleeve of his logistics binder. "Debbie and I will come fetch you if you're not back by August."

"Speak for yourself," said Aunt Debbie. "The longer, the better, *I* say. Steve and I plan to savor every kid-free moment."

"Partying like it's 1982," said Uncle Steve.

"Never cooking, never showering, never wearing clothes indoors—"

"Mom!" Cal was appalled.

"You oughtn't be cavalier about such matters," Ben's mother said. "Parent-inflicted trauma can have lifelong repercussions."

"So true," said Trevor, who had been pretending to retch into a potted plant.

"And, Benjamin," said his mother, "absolutely *no smoothies*."

"I'm fully prepared to handle my own condition, thank you very much—"

His mother threw up her hands. "Arnold!"

"It's hardly Uncle Arnold's fault that we share a rare esophageal disorder."

"He planted the idea in your head!"

"It's a medical fact, not an idea—"

"Confirmed by a physician?"

She knew perfectly well that Uncle Arnold had diagnosed himself. "Our smoothies, Mother, are far more nutritious than your own diet. Berries, banana, flaxseed, coconut oil, brown rice protein, almond butter. And kale. Mounds and mounds of kale—"

"Smoothies!"

"Smoothies that contain everything a human needs to thrive!"

Ben had planned to stay in Berkeley for the summer, so he'd moved in with Uncle Arnold after he'd graduated. He'd promptly seen the beauty of the all-smoothie diet. It solved humanity's age-old quandary: how to sustain sufficient concentration when so often interrupted by the baying biological imperative to eat? He and Uncle Arnold had formulated an Algorithm that streamlined shopping, automated preparation, and optimized nutritional benefits. Upon their return from the grocery, Ben stacked the produce in the freezer, alphabetizing the bags for ease of retrieval, while Uncle Arnold apportioned the week's bananas into single-serving Tupperware containers. Ben made breakfast and Uncle Arnold washed the dishes; at dinner, the duties were swapped. They ate together in a companionable silence that was broken only by slurps and the sighs of turning pages. Sometimes Ben managed to forget he was eating at all.

The first few days of summer, he'd still attempted lunch, buying tacos from the truck on Telegraph to eat on the library's steps. He'd tried to enjoy the sun, the greenness of the glade, but he could feel his throat closing. "My body rejects it," Uncle Arnold had told him. Ben had the odd sensation that there was no longer a thoroughfare between his mouth and his stomach. He spit the food into his napkin. He swallowed, urgently. He took a sip of water. Fluid was fine, but he couldn't bear to try solid food again. It was as if his esophagus had become a porous mineral. The disorder must be genetic.

Uncle Arnold nodded sagely. "Luckily," he said, "the Algorithm provides a nourishing diet by smoothies alone."

Ben didn't mind. It gave him more time to work. He flitted between UC Press, copyediting academic books, and Doe Memorial, revising his senior thesis for graduate school applications. He tried never to be alone in the apartment, where he felt monitored by thousands of pairs of grieving eyes. Thank goodness Jesse's bedroom was Madonna-free. The only postcards had been sent by Ben himself. He had to be imagining it, but when he pushed his face deep into Jesse's pillow, he could detect the faint scent of his cousin. He hadn't slept so well in years.

Then: the trip.

It had disrupted all his plans. Not that he minded. Not really. He had a few quibbles, but when didn't he?

"The time is nigh," he said now.

"You never told me whether you were wearing that money belt, young man," Aunt Debbie said to Trevor.

Ben managed to complete all requisite embraces before Cal even let go of her mother. He didn't want to hurry her, but the buffer period for the buffer period was elapsing by the second. "Farewell, all," he said pointedly. *"Auf Wiedersehen. Au revoir. Arrivederci. Farväl."* (He wasn't sure which of his European languages he'd need, so he'd been practicing them all.)

"Trevor!" called Aunt Debbie as they walked away.

"Don't look back," said Trevor. He accelerated.

"Do—you—have—"

Trevor, his head bowed, sped through the crowds. Aunt Debbie stood on tiptoes. Her hand was cupped around her mouth.

"Your—money belt?"

The security officials loomed like dragon guardians, the metal detectors like clashing rocks. The line was long. Ben felt fortunate he'd built in time for this eventuality. "Text from Matt," said Trevor. "He and Lillian got in from San Francisco."

Cal groaned.

"You'll like them," Trevor told her. "I hung out with them a couple of summers ago. I like them."

"You like everybody."

"I certainly don't," said Ben, "but he's right. Matt's quite affable. Lillian—"

"Lillian's cool," said Trevor.

"Lillian takes some getting used to."

"Says *you*," said Trevor. "Says the most acquired taste since haggis."

"I'll take that as a compliment. Haggis is a delicacy."

"They're waiting for us past security. I'm excited. The more, the merrier, right?"

"Wrong," said Cal.

Ben nodded. "The more, the louder. The more, the slower. The more, the less likely one is to identify a kindred spirit with whom one can discuss—"

"Somehow," said Trevor, "those don't have the same ring."

"I wish it were just the three of us," said Cal.

"We would be able to move much more expeditiously," agreed Ben. "I prefer to travel solo, myself. Like a bat in the night."

"It's not that," said Cal.

"Nope," said Trevor, grinning broadly at her. "It's that you're a wee bit possessive. It's that you hate admitting Jesse had friends who weren't us. Am I right or am I right?" How, Ben wondered, did Trevor get away with saying such things? He watched him give Cal a playful shove with the side of his shoulder. Yes, the shove said, I think these things are true, and yes, it said, I love you anyway. And look, now Cal was laughing. If Ben had made those accusations, she'd have slugged him.

"You have to be nice to them," Trevor told Cal.

"I'm always nice."

"Ha!" said Trevor. "Good one!"

"I'll fake it."

"That's acceptable."

The line was barely moving. Ben heaved his backpack to the floor.

"What do you *have* in there?" said Trevor. "The Library of Congress?"

"A small portion of it, yes," Ben said irritably. "Do you really think I'd abandon my academic obligations?"

"But you graduated!"

"I've got an entire thesis to revise."

"What's it about?" said Cal.

He dreaded this question. "Michelangelo's *Pietà* sculptures."

"I love Michelangelo!"

"You and the world."

The line inched forward. Trevor, shoving along their backpacks with his knee, said, "Yeah, Michelangelo's always seemed like a weirdly accessible topic for you."

Did he mean to twist the knife? "Well, he is. I'd planned to study the Moorish influences of Guarini."

"Why'd that fall apart?" said Cal.

Because, Ben thought, everything had fallen apart.

But he was capable only of the official explanation. "I spent last summer in Italy, as you know, doing research. I saw Michelangelo's three *Pietàs*. The famous one in Rome, the Bandini *Pietà* in Florence, and the Rondanini *Pietà* in Milan."

"So you liked them?" said Cal.

He'd felt pulled to them. "I was interested in how he got

from one to the other." He'd even thought the word *heart-strings*, although there was nothing he despised more than cardiac metaphor. "It was a period of sixty years. But to begin with that full-bodied Mary in Saint Peter's—then in the Rondanini, she's spectral, a waif." He had stood like a rock in a stream of tourists. His eyes had grown hot with tears. "I was intrigued by Michelangelo's artistic and theological progression."

"Cool," said Trevor.

"I would read that," said Cal.

"Precisely my problem," said Ben.

It was time—well past time—to terminate the Michelangelo phase of his life. Soon, he reminded himself. Soon he would enter a PhD program and embark upon a practical course of study. He would steer his craft far from Michelangelo's gaudy regatta. He would sail the lonely lagoon of Guarini. Never again would someone tell him, "You know that's been done before." Uncle Arnold had said it gently, as if Ben did not know.

Of course he knew.

No one understood.

But how could he bid understanding when he himself did not understand? He knew only that he could not have acted otherwise. Even reproduced on cheap postcards, the marble of the *Pietàs* seemed to glow from deep within.

Matt and Lillian were waiting on the other side of security. Trevor gamboled to them, pounding Matt's fist and thumping his back, hugging Lillian. Ben shook Matt's hand. He'd always had classmates who looked like Matt: easy grins, lean arms, lacrosse socks halfway up their calves, a year-round burnish of California gold. Aftershave wafted in their wake, and girls. Ben never had much to do with them. "It's good to see you again," he said. He held no prejudices; they simply had little in common. Matt surprised him by pulling him into a hug.

Lillian did not escalate his handshake. She shook with only her fingers, and she didn't smile. Her head was still shaved, her black skin gleaming on the curves of her shapely skull. She wore small silver hoops in her ears and Jesse's watch. Her clothes were as wild as ever: a mint-green skirt with a slit up the thigh, a black shirt that had the glint of snakeskin.

Ben felt a slight vertigo. He'd last seen them in August, when he'd flown back from Italy for Jesse's funeral. He'd blamed the jet lag for the haze of unreality that had hung over the day: he had known, but not believed, that Jesse was dead. He was one of the eight pallbearers. They had braced themselves, but Jesse had become so thin that the coffin leapt into the air, unsettling Ben, forcing him into reorientation; it was like taking another step down though you had reached the bottom of the stairs. That feeling, above anything else, had convinced him that what they said was true. Across the coffin, Matt's face had mirrored his own: eyes round, mouth falling open.

The others were looking at him expectantly. He coughed. "We've got a ways to walk." His voice sounded strangled. He needed to compose himself. "Let's get going. The flight departs in less than two hours."

Trevor moseyed along with Matt and Lillian. Ben lagged behind; he was willing to sacrifice speed to reduce the chances of losing any of his charges in the terminal. "Is it too late to go back?" said Cal.

"It would cause a fuss. But technically, no."

Cal sighed.

"I understand," said Ben. "I understand."

"It's not the traveling. I like traveling."

"So do I. Traveling is a true test of mastery. It's a series of trials. Last summer . . ." He'd spent his whole trip elated. Certainly not by Italy—such a slapdash country, beautiful but inefficient; at half the archaeological sites, nobody even cut the grass—but by his own competence. He tracked his budget on a color-coded spreadsheet. He developed a system by which he could, with respectable accuracy, work out the Italian counterpart to any French word. He traveled light, fast, and with all due regard for local customs. "It's the disruption," he said. "We all had summer plans. You did—"

"If reading *People* on the stationary bike and marathoning Netflix with Annie counts."

"Trevor did—"

Cal snorted.

"Well, *I* did. A plan that was difficult to abandon."

"You didn't want to quit your job?"

"Not exactly. Correcting the slipshod punctuation of professors who ought to know better—it's highly amusing, of course, but no, not that."

"Your thesis?"

"I'll be able to finish revisions on the go, or next fall. No—"

"Then what?"

"It's the principle of the thing," Ben hedged.

"I bet I know." Cal smirked. "I bet there's a girl in the picture."

Ben ticked his tongue against his teeth. She took this as confirmation.

"Ooh la *la*!" she hooted. "Ben finds love!"

"Cal. Be reasonable."

"Oh," she said. "No? Darn."

His protest had been almost too effective: so it *was* unreasonable to imagine him with a girl? As much as he hated to admit that he'd fallen prey to romance, Cal was right. There was a girl in the picture: posed on the opposite side of the frame, to be sure, but he was looking at her, and she, he thought, might be looking at him.

He'd last seen her the night he'd found the maps. In the corner of a party thrown by his former roommate, they'd discussed hyphenation, hypercorrection, the delights of sesquipedality. "Could this be a regular event?" she'd said. "Ben and Jean promote prescriptivism?"

He liked the sound of their names together. "I don't see why not," he'd said.

Well, he thought now. No use daydreaming about *that*.

It took far too long, what with Trevor's irksome tendency to dawdle, but eventually they reached the gate. Ben cleared his throat. "Quintet," he said. "Shall we begin?"

He was ignored. Lillian, curled up on the floor, had closed her eyes. Cal was texting. "The angels destroyed the giants," Matt said, and Trevor said, "Totally clobbered them." Ben could not tell whether they were discussing a fantasy novel or a sporting event.

He cleared his throat. "Let's confer, please. Why are we here?"

"I thought we went over this already," said Trevor. "We're here because Jesse wanted us to be here."

"But *why*?" said Ben. "Why Frankfurt? Why us? Why now?"

Cal flicked her eyes and returned to her phone. Matt

concentrated on the squash ball he was tossing from hand to hand. Trevor was quiet, but Lillian, without opening her eyes, said, "He wants us to find his mother."

"*What?*" said Ben.

The gate agent gave him a reproving look.

"His *mother*? He was briefly interested, I know, but he gave up. He told me so."

Lillian straightened. "And you believed him?"

"What sort of mother leaves her six-month-old baby rather than face up to his atrial septal defect?" Ben refused to call it the Hole. "He realized she wasn't worth looking for."

"'Find my mother,'" quoted Lillian. "That's what he told me."

No one spoke. The smacks of the squash ball against Matt's palms organized the noise around them, the clattering televisions and hissing lights and humming footsteps; the ball gave the airport a beat.

"And she's *not* worth looking for," said Lillian. "It's an idiotic idea, this self-styled quest. But that's what he wants, so that's what we're doing."

"I suspected a mission," said Ben. He'd been right all along. He hoped Trevor was paying attention.

"We have to find her," said Lillian.

"We will," Ben assured her. "Let's marshal our evidence. Did he tell you anything else? Do we think she's in Frankfurt, or is that merely a convenient point of arrival?"

"I know nothing," Lillian said with a touch of bitterness.

"Anyone else? Any conjectures?"

Matt was performing a complicated maneuver with the ball, rolling it up his forearm and back to his palm. Cal was still staring at her phone. Trevor glanced up at the television. Ben said, "Anyone?"

"He told you things," Lillian said to the group. "I know he did. There was a folder, and an envelope, and a notebook."

"The folder's mine," said Ben. "Thirty-one maps with no unifying theme. You're all welcome to look, but"—he shrugged modestly—"I've studied them extensively."

"His map collection," said Lillian.

"He collected maps?"

"No idea why. Every so often, he'd go to the bookstore and buy one. He'd leave it on his desk for a few weeks, spread out like a tablecloth. Then he'd fold it up—he was really good at folding maps—and put it away."

"Why did he choose those particular places?" said Ben.

"I don't even know what the places are."

"You never asked him?"

"He never answered." She looked around truculently, as if expecting a challenge. "Look. I know practically nothing." Her words were percussive. *Nothing:* it was a wallop, a blow. "If we want to find her, you have to spill."

Ben narrowed his eyes at his cousins. "The envelope. The notebook."

Trevor nodded genially, but said nothing. Cal didn't even look up.

"We've got to find her," said Lillian. "We've got to do everything we can."

"Agreed," said Ben.

"I should hope so. I hope *everyone* agrees. This was Jesse's dying wish."

Ben winced. Maybe so, but melodrama was never in good taste.

"Got it?" said Lillian.

"Got it!" said Trevor. "Totally. But let's relax now. Enjoy the flight. We'll get to the bottom of this in Frankfurt."

Ben would have preferred to push them further, but Lillian seemed satisfied to curl up again on the floor. He too would have to wait. Nonetheless, he felt an anticipatory thrill. The challenge had been set, and he had no doubt that he would meet it.

His thoughts returned to the night he'd found the folder of maps. Intoxicated by the potent brew of Jean Lin's grammatical know-how, he'd come home late from the party. By the time he was climbing the stairs to Uncle Arnold's apartment, he wished he'd been more gutsy. He could have touched her hand. He could have kissed her.

But he was glad he hadn't, he told himself. He would proceed slowly. They would meet to drink tea and discuss phrasal adjectives. They would play Scrabble, attend lectures, and perhaps, if a summer romance was truly in the offing, select a language to study together. (He would like to improve his Swedish.)

Uncle Arnold would be asleep. Ben tried to mute the tumbling of the lock, to step softly down the hallway. The summer was long. He had time.

He opened the door to Jesse's room. By the streetlight shining through the window, he saw the blue folder on the bed. He held it close to read the Post-it, which said, in Uncle Arnold's cramped handwriting, "My apologies. Following instructions. Will be awake if you wish to discuss."

The folder was stuffed with maps. He thumbed through them. Some were urban, some rural. Some were road maps, some topographical. They had different scales. They were set all over the world.

Then he saw the short letter. "I hope you'll go," Jesse had written.

Ben sat on the bed.

"Yes, but—" he wanted to say. Yes. He would go. He knew at once that he'd go. But. It would foul up his plans. He would have to redo his thesis-revision schedule; he'd have to give notice at UC Press.

He would have to push away the memory of Jean's sleek otter hair, of her small and forthright breasts pressing against her shirt.

Once, in this very room, Jesse and Trevor had ganged up on him. "Mr. Yes But," mocked Trevor. Ben hadn't seen his point.

"You never say an uncomplicated yes," Jesse explained. "It's always *yes, but—*"

"That's a good thing," Ben argued. "I don't think in black and white. My assent is never without qualification."

"Someday," said Jesse, "you should try just *yes*."

"No," said Ben.

CHAPTER SIX

When it was necessary, Matt could slip into a trance on airplanes. "Your father would hold you flat," his mother once told him, "with his hand on your stomach, and he would walk you back and forth like a lawn mower. You'd be asleep in minutes."

Matt couldn't remember this. But now, with his eyes closed, the hum of the engines became his father's low purrs. Like a baby, he would be given a blanket and plied with food and drink. The lights would be dimmed. He would not be afraid.

Before they took off, he'd been able to pretend they weren't on a plane. Trevor was poking at the screen above his tray table. With every jab, the seat in front of him bounced. Matt caught Cal's eye, across the aisle. "How long do you think it'll take that guy to confront your brother?" he whispered. "It's an over-under. The line's takeoff."

"Under. For sure."

"What are you willing to stake?"

She considered. "Dessert?"

"Done."

Ben turned to him as the plane taxied. "Aren't you scared of flying?"

"I used to be. I'm over it."

He wasn't. But he could manage his fear. He could slip into his trance. It'd been much worse when he was little. Usually they'd show up at the airport without tickets, and he'd have to watch Kristen and Molly in the stroller while his mom brandished his father's American Express at the gate agents. "I'll pay anything," she'd tell them. "We need to leave today." Sometimes she'd claim a death in the family. The truth, of course, was that his dad was sleeping around again. It was all so clichéd. The new programmers, fresh from Stanford and Caltech, would start in June, and by September his mom would be trundling the kids to her parents in Boston. She would wait in the station wagon while they said goodbye to their dad. "You're the man of the family when I'm not around," his dad always told Matt.

But Matt never felt so unmanly as when he boarded a plane. His irrational fears were easily quelled, the fears that they'd fly into a river or a field or a skyscraper, because there were precautions to take, seat belts to tighten and masks to inflate, and he knew the chances of disaster were so low that it was solipsistic to believe his plane was the one. But he could not reassure himself about his most basic fear, because it was true: he was trapped. He could not get off the plane. It had always seemed unfair. There had to be a way out, a way to broker the divide between his world and the world of the tarmac, where dollies of luggage were pushed by orange-vested men who seemed unaware of the marvelous luck that left them on earth. But the windowpane seemed as impenetrable as a television screen. Even if he broke it, he would not find their world.

They took off. He was doing fine. He felt languid, his limbs heavy and warm. The flight attendants took drink orders. They were beautiful, these flight attendants, the women and the men alike. Trust Air France to hire based on looks.

He smiled winningly. "What's your red wine?"

"It's a Merlot."

"I'll have that."

"Certainly."

Trevor swiveled when she passed. "Nice! I didn't even try!"

"I'll trade you." He didn't want the wine. He'd asked for Trevor's benefit, and for Cal's. He caught Jesse hovering at the edge of his perception. *Sculpting that image of yours,* Jesse whispered.

Trevor happily handed back his Coke. Matt flipped up his tray table and rested the cup on his knee. "If you don't like the assumptions everyone makes about you," Jesse had once told him, "maybe you shouldn't play right into them."

"I don't play into them." Where had they been? An unfamiliar hallway with prom-court posters advertising unfamiliar faces: toothy girls, boys in midtackle and midswing. Another high school could feel like an alternate universe. All the same, all different. It unsettled him. "I'm not trying to, anyway." An away match for quiz bowl, that was where.

"You do at first. It's that California-boy, frat-boy, golden-boy thing you've got going on."

"That's not who I am."

"*I* know that. Obviously. You can maintain it for about an hour before your true nature emerges."

"What's my true nature?"

But Jesse had only grinned and stretched and said he was starving and was the JV match ever going to end and maybe the team should go out for pho afterward. Matt didn't press him. Why hadn't he pressed him? He sidled his eyes to his right, where a man was sleeping. He'd popped three Benadryl tablets before takeoff and now his mouth had slid slack. Matt half closed his eyes at the blurred form. What, he asked again, is my true nature? Jesse just smiled.

Well. He turned across the aisle. "Jesse told me you're a runner," he said to Cal.

"I used to be." She straightened her injured leg into the aisle.

"She's wallowing," said Trevor. "It's a little heel pain."

Cal ignored him. "You play squash?"

"How'd you know?" said Matt. "Did Jesse tell you?"

"You have 'SILICON VALLEY SQUASH TOURNAMENT,' plus two large rackets, plastered over your chest."

"Oh yeah. Yeah. I do."

"Still?" said Trevor. "Are you playing next year?"

"Yeah." A year ago, he'd have never thought he could make a college team. Chalk one up to Jesse's death. He'd been a solid player, but after August, he'd gotten good. His dad had made him choose between squash and soccer before ninth grade. "It's your choice," his dad had said. "But keep in mind, you're a natural team player. You'll never stand out in soccer."

"But soccer's a team sport."

"Exactly."

He hadn't understood the logic until lately. In soccer, he'd been a midlevel midfielder. He was content to feed the ball up front, to help out on defense. He often assisted but rarely scored. But squash forced him to stand alone. You couldn't give help or get help. You were in a room, and there was one other person in that room, and you had to beat him. It was lonely, and it'd been good for him. Soccer felt like a game. Squash felt like a battle.

This past year, he'd go to the club after dinner and hang out by himself, hitting and hitting and hitting. The way his dad always talked, the ball was the enemy. "You gotta beat the shit out of that ball," he'd told Matt when he'd taught him to play. "Hit it like it's never been hit before." But this fall, something had changed. The guy he was playing, Matt wanted to beat the shit out of *him*. The ball, though, was his friend. He always had one in his pocket, and when things got rough, he threw it against a wall. He liked how it warmed up. During a match, it'd start out torpid, its bounces sullen, but as kinetic energy coursed into it, it'd move faster and faster. The game would move faster too. You had to know the ball. At the end of a match, drenched in sweat, Matt would flip it to his hand and it'd be searingly hot. It felt alive. He almost expected it to pulse along with his heartbeat.

The cabin lights had been dimmed. Matt gave Cal a sleepy smile. "Good night," he said.

She jumped. She slammed shut the handwritten notebook she'd been reading. "What? Oh. Good night. I hope you can sleep."

"I won't have any problem with that." His eyelids slouched. He teetered on the threshold of sleep, and he pulled himself back. One more minute. "You owe me your dessert. That poor guy's never said anything." On cue, Trevor poked his screen. The seat bounced.

"I ate it," said Cal.

"How are you ever going to make it up to me?" He could barely form words. His head wavered on his neck.

"Um. I could substitute. How do you feel about a barf bag and a *SkyMall* magazine?"

"Perfect," he murmured. He closed his eyes, but Ben turned.

"Matt? Are you ready to withdraw money? We're landing in five hours. We'll need euros right away."

"Yeah, yeah, I got the ATM card."

"Do you know where you have it?"

"Think so."

"Fine." Matt let his eyes flit closed. Ben said, "I'd be happy to take care of the money."

"That's okay."

"I've had a lot of experience traveling abroad."

"I can do it."

"But I—"

"Jesse would have wanted us to follow his instructions."

Ben gave up. Matt nodded to the shadowy form at his right. "I've got a college fund, you know," Jesse had casually said one day as they left history class. They were bottlenecked at the door. "Maybe I'll do something interesting with the money."

"And skip college? Your dad's not going to be cool with that."

"You don't think?" Jesse held his backpack open with his chin as he shoved in his notebook. "I guess it would depend."

Matt still hadn't understood. "Your dad's a professor. He's kind of into college."

"Well," said Jesse, "if I can convince him otherwise, I'm putting you in charge of the money."

They popped out into the hallway. They were headed in different directions. Matt said, "Me? Why me? Why not you?"

Over his shoulder, Jesse called, "You're better at it."

Matt had always been good with money; he knew when to spend, when to save, how to save. But he hadn't remembered that conversation until a month ago, when Professor Serrano had asked him to come to his campus office. Matt hadn't seen him since Jesse died. His appearance was startling: the color had washed from his beard, and he had Lincoln-like cavities in his cheeks, deep lines parenthesizing his mouth. He fiddled with a pen as he explained to Matt what Jesse had planned.

"A trip to Europe?" Matt said.

"I'm as surprised as you are."

"I wish he'd told me."

"Yes." Professor Serrano sighed. "I think that's the position in which he left us all."

Now, on the plane, Matt breathed, Your *mother*?

You don't understand, the shadowy figure said. I couldn't tell you. You'd have tried to talk me out of it.

But what about your *father*?

The figure shrugged. He again became Matt's seatmate, an Asian guy with long bangs and curled, sleepy lips. Matt let his vision drift farther, but Jesse would not return.

"Here's the debit card," Professor Serrano said. It was already engraved: MATTHEW LETVIN. "Will you go?"

It hadn't occurred to him that he could refuse. "Yeah."

"Thank you." Professor Serrano glanced around the book-lined cranny of an office. He seemed uneasy. "Whatever he wants you to do over there—"

"You think there's something specific?"

"I have a hunch."

"What is it?"

Professor Serrano fluttered his hands. "It could be wrong. I shouldn't speak it. It's groundless. Utterly unsubstantiated. If there's something, you'll know. And, Matt—"

He paused. Matt's hands were cold. The office was, suddenly, too small. He inhaled deeply but the walls seemed to converge even closer, as if drawn in by his breath.

"His wishes aren't sacred," said Professor Serrano. "You don't have to obey them. You still have a choice. You all do."

Matt imagined the hundreds of books tumbling down. He imagined being trapped under the weight of all that scholarship, the yellowed texts in Romance languages and the shiny color plates. There would be no hope of escape. He had to leave, and fast. "Thanks," he said with a hasty nod. "Thanks."

"Thank *you*," Professor Serrano had said.

Remembering, Matt cascaded into his airplane trance. He could have been anywhere in time, in space. He's on the sidewalk outside Professor Serrano's office. He's queasy. Tanned students rush past and he stares up into the leaves of a eucalyptus. And he's on the same sidewalk, years earlier, Jesse at his side. "The Peace of Westphalia!" Jesse says. "I can't believe we lost on the Peace of Freaking Westphalia!" Which match, when? The memories are in shards. Now he's sitting in Jesse's desk chair. Time has passed. Jesse lies on the bed next to Lillian. Matt is a part of her. He can feel the tension in her back, the looseness of her hips; by the same sort of knowledge that tells him he could drop to the floor and do fifty push-ups, by a deep and interior bodily forecasting, he knows that if she wanted to, she could wrap her leg behind her neck. How strange it is to inhabit another's body. He is a part of Jesse too. To breathe as Jesse is to breathe in humidity, at altitude; what he knows as air is both thicker and thinner. No body feels the same, from within. And he is himself. He's hitting a squash ball now and he's warming up, breathing hard, sweating, slamming into the walls, and he's in the airplane as he was once in the womb, floating and too warm. Cal's long legs are tucked to her chest as she sleeps. Ben reads a German grammar. Trevor cackles at a movie, and Lillian stares out the window, even though the sea and the sky alike are black. He is all of them. His edges have blurred. He is almost asleep.

An Excerpt from
THE JUVENILIA OF JESSE T. SERRANO

In the Land of Ten Thousand Madonnas, the kitchen walls are the most crowded. "The Annunciation has been depicted more often than any other story in human history," Arnold says. It's a Bach fugue played in paint, over centuries: the theme grows ornate and then slender, glides up and down octaves and in and out of keys, turns upside down and inside out before returning home.

If the postcards are any indication, Cal, Mary's not unlike us: she's a teenager who reads a lot. Then an angel appears and says she will bear the Son of God.

Can you *imagine*?

Sometimes, some long afternoons, waiting for Arnold to get home, I tell her, "You could say no." I like the postcards where she's averting her face and holding out a hand to halt the angel. There aren't many. "Just this once," I say. "Tell him no." Instead, she kneels and clasps her hands. She smiles her close-mouthed smile. She never listens to me. Maybe she doesn't have a choice at all.

It was a Friday afternoon in ninth grade, and Matt and I had his whole shiny, silent house to ourselves. In the kitchen, I lay prone on a sleek sweep of countertop. "The marble's all cool," I told him.

He jumped up to the counter opposite mine. "You're right." It didn't seem to grow warm from our bodies. I rested on one cheek. Matt propped his head on his chin, staring phlegmatically ahead like a collapsed sphinx. We heard the garage door open.

"Is that your mom?"

"My dad."

"How can you tell?"

"Sound of the car."

"Should we get down?"

"No need."

Brian Letvin strode into the kitchen, dismantling his suit. His jacket was draped on a chair, his tie slackened, his cuffs unbuttoned, his sleeves shoved up. He opened the refrigerator.

"Boys!" I was startled. I'd started to think we had blended into the countertops. "Who's up for a bike ride? Damn. I *told* that woman to prep me some Gatorade. Matt, get the powder."

"How was Germany?" said Matt.

"Fine, fine. The usual. Business is business." He turned. "Jesse Serrano. How's it hanging?"

"Good," I said lamely.

"Six water bottles, Matt. Now we've got to wait until it's chilled. Could your mother ever lift a finger? Stay here, boys."

He left. Matt said, "Sorry."

"I don't mind." I meant it.

Brian returned in a cycling kit, his laptop under his arm. The jersey—as well as the butt of the shorts, I saw when he turned—was covered with aggressive logos for MooseTech. "Finally got the assholes at the company to sponsor a team," he said. I hadn't been staring at the logos, but at his muscles. He could have been cut of stone. Even his forearms had cords.

"Cool," I said, still staring.

"Push-ups. That's all it takes. Push-ups, pull-ups, and cycling."

He was already on the kitchen floor.

"Don't be a gym rat," he said from his plank. "Do push-ups. They're efficient. They're effective. They've got a million variations. Sure, you can do the standard." He pumped up and down. He wasn't even breathing hard. "If you only want standard muscles. Matt, get your ass down here. Demo time."

I'd almost forgotten Matt was there. When Brian Letvin was around, all I wanted was to be just like him. No: to *be* him. He had a cleft in his calf muscle. A cleft!

"Military!" he called. He and Matt drew their arms straight under their shoulders and did five military push-ups.

"Left leg up!"

"Right leg up!"

"Wide arm!"

"Diamond!"

"Left arm only!" Matt was out of breath. Brian kept bouncing up and down.

"Right arm only!" It was like performance art.

"And the beast. Clappers. Down—and up!" Their hands left the floor, slammed into a clap, and somehow found the floor again. "Who's gonna face-plant first? Down—and up! Jesse, wanna take a guesstimate?"

"Um, I don't know."

"Down—and up! We'll have to ride it out, then. Down—and up!" Matt hit the floor with a thump and a crunch.

"Handstand push-ups can wait." Brian stood and cracked his back. "His mother hates for me to do them inside. She doesn't believe I have total control." He prodded Matt with the tip of his shoe. "Total control, that's my motto. Matt, up and at 'em. Go dig up a couple jerseys and shorts."

Matt's face was red as he left the room.

"And meanwhile, Jesse Serrano, I'm gonna show you Europe." He started tapping at the laptop. "I'm sleep-deprived and overcaffeinated. It's a nine-hour time change. Work with me here."

"Where in Germany were you?" I said.

"Frankfurt. You know where that is?"

I did, thanks to the most interesting postcard Arnold had ever gotten. When he'd flipped it over to see its provenance, he said, "The Städel. Frankfurt am Main. Your mother spent a semester there in college."

"My *what*?"

"Oh dear."

"Tell me."

He left the room.

Most of Brian's photographs were from cycling trips in the countryside. I tried to be enthusiastic.

"They forced some culture down our throats," he said. "A Saturday morning tour. Some old churches, Goethe's birthplace. Ever heard of him?"

"Nope."

"He's a German guy," Brian explained. "But the one perk of going on this tour—in the rain—not that rain is a surprise over there—well, Jesse, you're about to see the hottest tour guide in the history of time. Banging. You're gonna get turned on by the *picture*. You can imagine how hard it was for me to stand next to her. Very, very hard."

Brian clicked, and there she was.

"The best part," he said, "was that cameras were A-okay. We were on a frigging tour."

There she was.

"I got several nice pics. They've already been emailed around the company, I'll tell you that."

Brian, clicking through the pictures, a little smile playing around his lips, didn't notice my shock. "Uh," I said. "Mr. Letvin?"

"Brian. Please. You think I'm old?"

"Brian? Can you email those pictures to me?"

He let out a gigantic guffaw and clapped me on the back. "Jesse! Jesse, my man! You bet. My *man!*" Through the ceiling, we heard Matt's bedroom door close. Brian glanced up. "Sometimes I wonder about him."

"Wonder what?"

Brian grimaced. "Whether he's even. Well. Interested."

"Oh," I said.

"His mother's too easy on him. Plus the limp wrists who teach at that school of yours. It's a bad combination."

"I'm pretty sure he is. Interested." In case Brian got the wrong idea, I added, "In girls."

"You would know." Brian rolled his eyes. "Grab those Gatorades and meet me in the garage."

When Matt returned with an armful of spandex, I was sitting on the floor. "You okay?" he said. I knew he was thinking of the Hole.

"I'm fine."

"What's going on?"

"Nothing." I didn't want to tell him about the photographs of my mother. I would eventually, I thought. Not yet.

"Was my dad weird?"

"Nope."

He got the Gatorade bottles from the fridge. "We better go down."

My cheeks were burning. I rolled one of the bottles against my face. Even in Germany, I thought, she was looking for me. She had decided to work as a guide so she'd meet lots of American tourists. She had put in special requests for Californians, and whenever she ran across groups from Berkeley, she would think, There's *got* to be someone who knows him.

And there was.

A coincidence, or a plan? Impossible, or improbable? I've never been able to decide. It hasn't happened again. Santa Fe, New Mexico. Frankfurt, Germany. There, the trail runs dry.

I guess I knew what Matt would think. I guess that was why I never did tell him. Jesse, he'd think, if she were looking for you, she'd come here. She knows your city. Your street. The number of your apartment. How many stairs she would climb to stand before your door. The sound of the doorbell, and the silence that would follow its ring.

He wouldn't have said it. He'd have said, "She must have been searching for you." But Matt has always been kind. Too kind to say what he thinks, and sometimes too kind to think it.

Brian outfitted us in the garage. He had four spare road bikes. "This heart defect," he said. "Are you gonna keel over?"

Back then, the doctors actually encouraged me to exercise.
"I hope not."

"You hope not, or no?"

"No."

"Good. The last thing I need is a lawsuit."

"My dad's not the suing type."

"Even better." He rooted through the pile of clothes Matt had fetched and tossed me a pair of bike shorts. "Gotta protect your junk."

Matt and I were panting even before we started up Vollmer Peak. "Stay on my wheel, boys," Brian called. "It'll cut the wind." We proceeded uphill in a breathless wagon train. "Power!" yelled Brian. "Watts!" It was a green and golden September, the wind skittering leaves across the road, but I couldn't look any higher than Matt's butt. My breath came in rough, torn gasps. I tried to dissociate as I did during attacks, when I immured my head between my legs and closed my eyes to streaks of orange and purple that warbled like smoke in a breeze. I flicked at my gears, but I'd been in the lowest one since leaving the driveway.

Brian pulled into an overlook. My legs were so wobbly I nearly toppled. I felt better when I saw Matt sucking on the Gatorade bottle like a newborn piglet.

"The view!" Brian said.

Once I'd recovered from severe oxygen deprivation, I could see that we were way up in the hills. The city was nestled into the valley, and, there, far off, was the sea.

"*This* is America. This is why America's the greatest country on earth. You don't find views like this in Germany."

"What about the Alps?" said Matt.

"What about them? You think the frigging Alps could beat this?"

"No."

"No is right. You bet your ass it's right. You feeling good, Jesse Serrano?"

"Yeah."

"You feeling awesome as shit?"

"Yeah."

"Both of you. Fill in the blank. This ride is—"

"Awesome as *shit*," we said.

"That's better. Rears in gear. We got another two thousand feet of elevation."

We continued. Matt fell off Brian's wheel, which was glorious because (a) I wasn't the one who'd succumbed first (though I'd verily been on the brink) and (b) we got to stop while Brian whizzed down and did a U-ie and, still clipped into his bike, told Matt he expected him to suck it up and screw this hill in the ass like a man. I drank Gatorade and looked for animals in the clouds. I found a tortoise, a badger, and a Komodo dragon.

Then the pedals became loose. The road flattened. I dared a glance up and saw there was no more hill to climb.

Matt and I crumpled onto a bench.

"It feels so great to sit," he said.

"Despite technically sitting all the way up," I said.

"This is the life," said Brian. "Get up. Get over here. You gotta see this. That's Mount Diablo across the Bay. Views like this! They feed your *soul*."

This could have sounded ludicrous, coming from a guy whose diaper-like shorts had the image of a moose, whose aerodynamic helmet had the distinct silhouette of a sperm cell. But Matt and I nodded along.

"Why'd we come up here, Matt?"

Matt looked wary. "To get some exercise?"

"Sure, sure. And?"

"To enjoy the view?"

Brian sighed. He took off his helmet and wiped his brow. "I'll rephrase. Why would I bring *you* up here?"

"So I can learn?"

"Getting there."

"So I can learn about biking—"

"Cycling—"

"Cycling? And views?"

I felt so sorry for him that I almost touched his arm. We stood on the summit's edge, where the grass shoulder fell into a sharp ravine. I took off my helmet and peered at the sky. The old animals were gone—you know how quickly clouds change, even when they don't seem to be moving at all—but there was something amphibious, some sort of toad—

"Jesse. Answer me this. Why would a *father* bring his *son* on one of the greatest rides California has to offer? Why would a *father* bring his *son* to the top of a mountain?"

All that came to mind was Moses and Mount Sinai. "To impart some great wisdom?"

Brian laughed. "Sure. Exactly. Matt, I gotta tell you something important."

I should have stepped away. I still feel bad.

"Here's the deal, Matt. I'm moving out."

"I'll be over at that bench," I said.

"Don't bother. This is a two-minute conversation. It's not complicated. I can't take it anymore. *It* being your mother."

Matt hadn't turned to face him.

"I'm moving in with Katie. Katie from the office? You've

met her. I think you've met her. Holiday party last year? Did you go to that?"

Matt didn't respond.

"She's down in Berkeley, not far. I'll still see you and the girls." He slapped Matt on the back. "Who knows? I might be back. Might just need a break. You live with that woman. You understand the concept of needing a break." He grasped the brim of Matt's helmet and rotated it toward him. "You got it? You in a coma? Nod."

Matt nodded and Brian's hand on the helmet went up and down, but I couldn't tell which was making the other move.

"Good." Brian stretched his arms above his head. "Who's ready for a Clif Bar?"

And Matt bolted. Matt grabbed his bike and leapt, a graceful running leap, all his athletic genes on display. He pointed himself down the winding road and he was gone. I didn't have a choice. Did I? Ten seconds elapsed, and he was out of sight. I could have strapped on my helmet, arranged my sore groin on the seat, headed after him. But I didn't. I knew I'd never catch him. He might not touch his brakes the whole way down.

Brian and I stared at the hole in the air where Matt had last been. "He's got some nerve," he said.

"He does."

"Son of a bitch."

I crinkled my nose. I said, "Literally."

We started laughing, Brian Letvin and I. He let me go down first, and I didn't use my brakes nearly as much as I thought I would. I had to squint against the onrush of wind, and I felt like a kid being pushed in a swing, the kind of swing where you're in a bucket, and your dad stands behind you and hums as you're thrown high into the wild, wild air.

CHAPTER SEVEN

Lillian sprawled facedown on the bed. She could not wait to be asleep. Cal's backpack hit the floor with a thud. "I didn't sleep at all on the flight," said Cal.

"Hmm."

"Did you?"

"Some." Her voice was muffled by the pillow. She could be asleep in ten seconds, if only Cal would shut up. "Not enough."

"Would you mind—"

Cal paused. Lillian cocked an eye. "Mind what?"

"Moving over? You're taking up more than your fair share."

Could she be serious? Cal, thought Lillian, was the type to have bisected her childhood bedroom, laying a meticulous masking-tape line between her half and Trevor's. No, she was the type who'd never had to share a room at all. "It's a small bed, okay?"

"Sure, but . . ."

Lillian thickened her breaths. "You're tense," Jesse was

always telling her. She checked. He was right. She relaxed her neck, her hips. She heard another thud as Cal fell into the wooden chair. "I just want to sleep."

I do too, thought Lillian. Drifting into sleep, dark water lapping the keel, she thought, I don't ever want to be out there. Out there was raw: friction and bodies, edges and light.

She felt a hand on her arm. She surfaced to see Cal's face, far too close to her own, and she jerked away. "Look, sorry," said Cal, "but could you just move over like six inches?"

"Don't wake me up," said Lillian. "Don't you ever wake me up."

"I'm sorry," said Cal. Tears glistened in her eyes. Lillian felt a wave of frustration. "It's only—I'm so tired—"

If Lillian was trespassing on Cal's territory, it was by a hair, but she flung her legs to the side. "There. Lie down. Go to sleep. You'll forget all about me." And I about you. Sleep was what they both needed: the human privilege of blankness, of leaving behind the living. Gingerly, Cal lay down. The mattress sagged. They both slid toward the middle. Cal grasped the bedpost. "It's okay," Lillian said wearily. "You can touch me. I don't mind."

"Well, *I* mind."

Lillian wasn't an idiot. She knew Cal was part of Jesse's grand plan, his grand goddamn plan to get her some replacements. To get them all replacements. "You'll like her," he had told Lillian. That vague future tense! It had been almost a year before his death, but already, she now knew, he'd been planning the trip. She had never fathomed how many secrets he held. He started laughing. "I *think* you'll like her."

"How confident you sound," she said dryly.

They were cocooned in the hammock on the rooftop patio of his apartment building. She could feel his whole body shake with laughter. "*Eventually* you'll like her."

She rolled her eyes. "Okay, your Lillian-is-hostile shtick, it's getting old—"

"She's the same way. Except she fakes it more than you do. Sweet Cal, nice Cal, and then you cross her, and she snaps."

"You wouldn't describe me as sweet?"

"Sweet as vinegar," he said, wrapping his arms around her, kissing her neck. "Sweet as wasabi."

She breathed him in. She found his particular scent. The Old Spice hit first and next the shampoo but the trick was to keep breathing, to swirl him like wine in her mouth. "*You're* sweet."

"Why," he said, "I am."

Cal twitched. Lillian rolled over and swung her legs to the ground. She couldn't sleep now. They mugged her, these memories. She needed to stay on broad boulevards, on bright thoroughfares, where passersby and streetlamps would collude to keep the memories far at bay. She needed to whet her weapons and stay wary. Her eyes would flick catlike from side to side. She would tense her neck and her hips. And she would make Cal snap. She had no use for sweet, and certainly no use for Cal. If he thought she'd take a replacement, he thought wrong.

She met Ben in the hallway. He was locking the door to the guys' room with an air of high dudgeon. "They're both asleep," he said. "We were preparing to explore, I look at my map for three minutes, and next thing I know they're conked out. I warned them! Did I not warn them?"

"You did," said Lillian. On the S-Bahn, Ben had explained that when they saw the bed, they'd get tunnel vision. They would come to believe that all they wanted from life was horizontality. The bed was Turkish Delight and they were Edmund. The bed was heroin. It was looking back at Eurydice. It was the Ring. It was— "Jesus," Trevor had said, "it's a *bed*."

"They didn't understand," Ben said mournfully.

"What sloth," said Lillian.

"Precisely my sentiments. Would you like to go out? Or are you going to nap too?"

"Of course I'm not napping. What kind of imprudent, ill-advised traveler do you think I am?"

The cool air outside was rejuvenating, although she wouldn't have admitted it to him. "How are you getting along with Cal?" he said.

"As well as I get along with anyone."

"I commend you for that. She can be extremely moody. Trevor says it's her heel, but I have my doubts."

The river was brown but picturesque, garlanded with bridges like a house trimmed for Christmas. "So," said Ben, peering at the Greek inscription that hung over the pedestrian bridge. "Our mission."

"Right. Our asinine mission." The asinine promise she'd made.

"What else do you know?"

Nothing. As she'd already said in the airport. Not a single thing. "I know Spanish. I know calculus. I know a shitload of Catholic history and theology, thanks to my grandmother—"

"You're Catholic?"

"That's so surprising?" She knew why.

"I haven't met many—er—African American—"

"Ta-da," she said, waggling her hands. "I assure you, we do exist."

"I can see that," Ben huffed. "Back to the *real* question. What else do you know about why we're here? About his mother?"

The bridge leveled out and tipped downhill. Lillian stopped midstep. "Nothing. How many times do I have to tell you? I know nothing. He chose to tell me nothing." And she could kill him for it. She abruptly resumed walking, and Ben jogged to keep up. "What do *you* know?"

"I'm just as ignorant," he said.

"And those cousins of yours?"

"I don't know why they're acting so secretive, but I'm sure they'll come around."

"They better."

"Trevor's easy. Cal can be prickly."

"I've noticed."

They turned onto the promenade on the opposite bank. "I'm glad we've formalized our alliance," said Ben. "We'll attack as soon as they awaken. And in the meantime, might I suggest we visit the Städel?"

The interior walls of the art museum were the colors of jewels and dyes, rich jade greens and Tyrian purples. A teacher lectured a group of German schoolchildren on Jan van Eyck. Ben pretended to look at a painting, but his entire body was tuned toward the lecture. Lillian could practically see quivering antennae. "I can understand almost everything!" he whispered.

"It's directed at seven-year-olds."

The children were set free with crayons and paper. Ben followed Lillian to an Annunciation.

"Daggiù," he said. "Is she giving birth?"

Lillian peered at the angel hovering between the Virgin's legs. "That's a cherub. But she's definitely pregnant."

"Time-lapse Annunciation. Weird. You'd think I'd have seen it all, given how much time I've spent in Uncle Arnold's kitchen."

"Not as much time as I have," said Lillian. "It's on the cupboard with the mugs."

"No way— Wait. You're right."

She pointed at another. "Inside the refrigerator door." Another. "Up near the smoke detector."

Ben goggled. That showed *him*. She knew the Land of Ten Thousand Madonnas better than he did, and she knew Madonnas better than he did too. She turned to cross the atrium.

"I wouldn't go over there if I were you," he said. "That's the modern section. Beckmann. Chagall." He tilted down his chin and raised his eyebrows. *"Ernst."*

"I like modern art."

"Don't say I didn't warn you."

The walls here were a brilliant white. A Franz von Stuck *Pietà*, black and brown and gray like a forest in winter, was tucked into a side room. Christ was laid flat, as if on an autopsy table, and Mary stood upright, her face hidden behind her hands. The figures were as perpendicular as the axes of a plane. Lillian stared at the painting. The hammock had slowly slumped under the weight of two bodies, so that by the end of the afternoon they had felt their backs scrape the ground whenever they were swayed by Jesse's foot or a breeze. It was September. The view from inside the hammock was limited to warm blue sky and a slice of the building next door. "This reminds me of New York," said Jesse.

"Because we can see a building?" said Lillian.

"And we're on a rooftop."

"You've never even been to New York."

"So?"

She giggled. With him, she became someone who giggled. And who held hands in public, which she'd thought she'd never do, but that evening, crossing the bleachers for the first volleyball game of the season, she trailed behind him and minded the footing of her thrifted, treadless ankle boots and thought, Why would I let go? Jesse's friends whistled at them for being late. "Got distracted, Serrano?" "Had something better to do?" Instead of glaring, she smiled. Jesse was smiling too. So what if they were undisguised? So what if the world could see that they were crazily in love? Alicia Dos Santos served an ace and Jesse's friends roared and stomped their feet. The romances of others were forgettable, never as sharp and euphoric as they were from within—which, of course, was part of the thrill, to exist in an emotional space that was created by and for the pair of you. They sat and Jesse turned to greet Matt but kept his grip on her hand. Lillian thought, Haven't you been burned? How can you trust I won't leave? She rubbed his thumb with hers. I won't, she promised. She ducked her head onto his shoulder and let her chunky Senegalese twists spill across both their backs. Never, never, never, she chanted in her head. I'll never leave, I'll never let go.

"We should head back," said Ben, behind her.

She quickly stepped away from the painting.

At the foot of the stairs, he said, "May I make a sortie upon the museum shop?" From the postcards, he chose Vermeer's *Geographer,* Tischbein's *Goethe,* and, after a moment, the Franz von Stuck *Pietà.*

The streets streamed with dapper commuters on bicycles: men in crisp suits, women pedaling in pencil skirts and heels. "I wouldn't have thought you were the postcard type," Lillian said.

"Are you kidding?" said Ben. "I love postcards."

Frankfurt's medieval walls were abraded and landscaped in the nineteenth century, Ben told the group, leaving the modern city with a semicircular belt of parkland. They carried the plunder from their grocery excursion to benches near a small pond.

"One of my favorite travel dinners," said Ben. He'd bought cheap cheese, cheap salami, cheap bread, cheap apples, and a big tub of whole-milk yogurt. Cal had added a bag of salad greens to the conveyor belt but was struggling to eat them, leaves and blades poking in disarray from her mouth. "Appetizing, Cal," said Trevor. Lillian chuckled, and Cal glared at her.

"Ben!" said Trevor. "No."

Ben had pulled a coffee grinder from his backpack. "I must."

Trevor hooted in glee. "Give me that."

"Okay, briefly, but I need—"

"Ladies and gentlemen," said Trevor, displaying the coffee grinder on his palm as if he were starring in an infomercial. "Ben has decided he's got this *problem*—"

"It wasn't a decision!"

"Fine, he's contracted this *disease*—"

"It's a rare esophageal disorder!"

"Which renders him unable to eat solid food."

"How are you going to survive this trip?" said Matt.

"That's the reason for the coffee grinder," said Ben. "In effect, I'll be making smoothies."

"You've had to deal with this your whole life?"

"Well, it's a fairly recent development."

"Is there any cure?"

"Not that I know of."

"Hey," said Trevor. "You know where you'd find pointers for managing the disorder? Where you'd find a brotherhood of fellow sufferers?"

"Don't," said Ben. "Don't."

"Plagueslist," said Trevor, with the air of a magus offering a great boon. "Plagueslist-dot-com."

"What's Plagueslist?" said Matt.

"I am delighted you asked," said Trevor. "Plagueslist is a *community*."

As he explained, Lillian watched Ben fill the grinder with salami, cheese, salad, and a dollop of yogurt. There was a slight whir. "Battery-powered," he told her. He opened the drawer. The sludge was pink with green flecks, and had the consistency of toothpaste. Ben fashioned a spoon from the foil yogurt lid. Lillian had to avert her eyes.

"Wow," she said. "I don't know which of you is the bigger dumbass."

"Lillian," said Matt.

"You've got a made-up disease. And you've got a social network for made-up diseases. Is this a joke?"

Cal put the salad carton on the ground. "You're saying they're lying?"

"I *hope* they're lying."

"You—" Cal clamped her hands into fists. Lillian's interest was piqued. She wouldn't mind a fight.

Laughing, Trevor said, "I wish we were lying too, Lillian. But it's the unfortunate truth. We're dumbasses." He casually slung an arm around Cal's shoulders. "But you should give us a chance. Wait till you hear the latest sector Plagueslist is developing."

Matt glanced at Lillian. "Tell us."

"Online dating. It's a spin-off we're calling Lovesick."

Ben groaned.

"For a small fee, we give you a list of potential matches with compatible symptoms. Say you've got a heel injury—"

"Very funny," said Cal.

"We recommend the asthmatic. That way nobody suggests anything athletic for the first date. What do you think?"

"Ridiculous," said Ben, licking salami purée off the yogurt lid.

"Sure, it sounds weird at first. But as my business partner says, most of these people aren't *sexually* dysfunctional—"

"You signing up, Cal?" said Matt.

"She needs to. You should see the specimens she finds on her own. Guess what her ex-boyfriend said when he first encountered underwire?"

"Trevor!"

"He said, 'Aren't you worried about lightning?' "

"I can't believe you told them that!"

"It's a funny story."

"Ahem," said Ben, looking to Lillian. "Shall we talk about why we're here?"

CHAPTER EIGHT

There was a single boot on the tracks. With the wind of every train, its sagging leather inflated with hope and its broken heel trembled. Cal knew what it was thinking: this could be the one, the train that carried home its lost match. The boot would never be worn again, but nobody had told it that. Or maybe it didn't believe it. The stories had led it astray: Penelope had paced the widow's walk until her husband came back from the sea, Orpheus had stumbled down the rocky path and found his beloved at the bottom. Lost was always followed by found. What fiction.

"Is it almost time?" Cal said. Without thinking, she touched Lillian's wrist to rotate the face of Jesse's watch. Lillian screeched like a tropical bird. Cal yanked her hand away.

"Don't touch that," spat Lillian.

"It's not even yours."

"Now it is." Lillian spun to face the platform.

Cal was horrified at herself, for what she'd done and what she'd said. "You should have asked," whispered Ben.

"I *know.*" He didn't have to rub it in.

"Besides," said Trevor, "we're in a German train station. There are clocks every few inches."

So they were on *her* side. It paid to be aloof. Correction: it paid to be aloof when you were also beautiful. Cal never could have pulled that off. She was sorted as a bitch, while Lillian seemed cool, sophisticated, a snow queen. Cal couldn't have even carried off her clothes. Long skirts and impractical jackets of fabrics you wanted to touch, suede and leather and seersucker. Tops that showcased her collarbones, which arched like the carved wood on top of a love seat. Lillian wore scarves for reasons other than keeping her neck warm. She carried a purse. Next to her, Cal, in jeans and T-shirts, sandals and a ponytail, felt unkempt and chintzy and young.

And what made it worse, thought Cal, was how the boys found Lillian so alluring. They buzzed around her. Even now she was touching Ben's arm and bestowing upon Trevor one of her rare smiles, and look how they glowed. She could be charming. She caught Cal's eye—Cal *knew* she wasn't making this up; it had happened too many times—and smirked. Cal couldn't stand her.

It was their third day in Germany, and they were taking a day trip to Heidelberg. The train seats were bundled in foursomes, one pair facing another. Cal, the odd one out, sat across the aisle. The search for Thea had not progressed. It was all her fault. She felt a stab of guilt every time the topic came up, which, thanks to Ben and Lillian, was frequently. Cal had read the next section of the *Juvenilia* on the plane, and she knew more than anyone, it seemed: that Thea had been in Frankfurt, that she'd been a tour guide here.

Cal knew she should tell them. She bit her knuckle. She

should, and she couldn't. Ben and Lillian became testier by the hour. They believed the notebook held clues, and they wanted her to give it up, to surrender it to the state. Maybe if they were a little nicer, she thought. Maybe if they quit treating her like some shabby suspect.

How immature she was acting! She knew it, and she was powerless to stop it.

Frankfurt seemed to have no suburban sprawl. As if its border had been drawn with a compass, the city gave way to countryside, to hills that receded and grew blue as the train approached the flats of Hesse. Cal closed her eyes. The area behind her forehead felt tight and pinched. She never slept. Not for longer than an hour or two. Five or six or seven times a night, she'd wake up with her heart pounding, her arms bent in strange positions around her chest or head, and her shirt sodden with clean, cold sweat. Nightmares had become rare. Now her body seemed to have been conditioned against sleep itself. Sleep will make you scared, it'd learned. And so, as sneaky as she tried to be, tiptoeing into slumber's house, bribing the guards and disabling the alarms, her body always noticed, and always flushed her out. It woke her up as if doing her a favor.

"Back to Thea," said Lillian. Cal kept her eyes closed. "We need to find her."

"What we need to do," muttered Ben, "is subpoena that blasted notebook."

The lull of the train was broken by the bounce of Matt's squash ball. "I can show you something," said Trevor. Cal cracked an eye. He had half stood to pull his wallet from his back pocket. "I've got a few pictures of her."

"*What?*" said Ben. "Why didn't you tell us earlier?"

"Didn't feel like it," said Trevor, shrugging.

"Utterly irresponsible!" said Ben.

"You guys were being annoying," said Trevor. "So I figured I'd hold out." He winked at Cal. "Are we in that big of a rush?"

Ben, his mouth hanging open, seemed torn between indignation and curiosity. As Trevor extended the photographs, curiosity won. The group leaned in. On top of the stack was a glossy black-and-white senior photo. "We found this one together," said Ben. "In a Berkeley yearbook. He wanted me to help research her. I took him to the library." Cal studied it. Thea's face was fuller than it'd been in Santa Fe, but her golden hair was the same, and her clear eyes, and the luminous quality of her skin.

Trevor shuffled to the next, in which Thea stood beneath a gaudy testudo of umbrellas. That had to be the one Matt's father took. Cal glanced at Matt. His expression was impassive.

The third and last picture was a snapshot. Thea, young and glowing, held an infant in her arms. Cal barely looked. She'd seen enough. She didn't need to see the baby Jesse, regarding her with wondering disappointment: why, Cal, are you transgressing my wishes? Because the *Juvenilia,* she thought, is mine and mine alone. Because you have given me this notebook in recompense for the years I missed with you, and with this notebook I can believe that you missed me too. How could she be expected to share it with the others? With Lillian?

"If anyone else knows anything," said Lillian, and Cal quickly shut her eyes when she saw her turn across the aisle, "it should be shared. We've got to find her. We've got to go all in."

Cal couldn't help it. Her eyes popped open. "I get it, okay?"

she snapped. "You want to read my notebook. Well, it's mine. And you can't."

"No, you don't get it," said Lillian. "This isn't about you. It's about Jesse and it's about what Jesse wanted." Her black eyes glinted. "Though I doubt that matters to *you.*"

I hate you, thought Cal.

"She's right," said Ben. "This has to be a team effort."

Matt slung his ball against the armrest.

"I wish he'd sent me alone," Lillian said.

Out the window lay cultivated fields lined by ruler-straight hedges, but Cal was too gloomy to look past her own faint reflection. She wasn't fooling herself: she knew she was motivated by the lowest of emotions. She was envious of the time Lillian had spent with Jesse, and she was jealous too, jealous of the pair they'd made. There would have been no need for them to flaunt their bond. It would have been as obvious as if a million threads had been strung between them.

Whenever Cal awoke, clammy and shaking, Lillian was asleep. Cal coveted that sleep: deep, dreamless. In the dusky glow of the hours before dawn, Cal watched her; she saw how Lillian's body, tense all day, nestled bonelessly into sleep as if into a mother's arms. She wanted to pummel her. She wanted to dig her fingers into all the soft places of Lillian's body, her palms and her neck and her eyes.

Last night, unable to stop herself, she had brushed two knuckles along Lillian's cheek. Lillian stirred and sighed. Cal felt sickened at herself. Yet she was cheered too: by the object-hood of another's body, by the patent and inadmissible hope that someday she would claw at the cool, smooth skin she had just touched. She withdrew her hand and fell asleep, this time till morning.

They walked across town and climbed up to the ruins of the castle. Cal stood with Matt on the rampart, watching the silver-ribbon river wend through spires and red roofs. French schoolchildren chased pigeons, complained of the weight of their backpacks, and stuck their limbs, and then their heads, through the balusters.

Trevor and Lillian found them. "Ben's reading every German sign in the castle," said Trevor.

"It's going to take a while," said Lillian.

Cal looked pointedly into the distance.

"You want to come get some lunch?" said Trevor. "We're meeting Ben in an hour by the, uh, Jesuitenkirche? That *ch* sounds different when he says it. Like he's scraping his tongue against a rock."

"I'm not hungry," said Cal.

"We'll meet you guys down there," said Matt.

At least she wouldn't have to force down food with Lillian, who literally made her gag. But now she was alone with Matt. She felt gawky and self-conscious around him: probably, she thought with resignation, because he was so good-looking, and she was doomed to feel awkward around such people. Why couldn't she get cool and flirty and fun under pressure? Matt was very nice. He smiled whenever he caught her eye. He verged on pretty-boy but was saved by his chin, which was a bit pointy, and his deep-set eyes. He had to know he was attractive; otherwise, he'd never wear pants that fit so well. (Granted, in Europe they looked positively baggy.) She wished she could be sure about herself. Sometimes she thought she was pretty and sometimes she thought she looked like a

Martian. Her forehead was gigantic and her eyes were so far apart her descendants would evolve into fish if they weren't prudent about the gene pool.

"I'm actually sort of hungry," she confessed once Trevor and Lillian were out of earshot.

Matt laughed. "Me too." They walked toward the stairs. "She's being awful to you."

"No kidding." The stairway was of old stone, canopied by wizened trees. Matt passed through a streak of sunlight and squinted. "But," said Cal, "to be fair, I'm awful to her."

"That's how she works. You should have seen her with Jesse. When she came to our school in ninth grade, he liked her right off the bat. And she acted totally indifferent. Not something he was used to."

She saw Jesse's crooked grin. His ruddy brown skin, his spiky brown hair, the way he'd zoom in on you when you talked. Of course girls loved him.

"He could be a twit." Matt's eyes danced. "God, Cal, the two of them, they were horrible. He dropped his index cards presenting his science fair project, and Lillian started a slow clap. So he told this girl that Lillian had herpes. Herpes! We were fourteen! Fourteen and sheltered! It got all over the school. The rumor, that is, not—"

"How mean." She felt guilty as soon as she'd said it.

"He hated looking dumb. And Lillian always knows the right buttons to push."

That girl deserved herpes.

"We were all on quiz bowl, and she started stealing his history questions. She told me later—okay, don't tell her I told you this—"

"Not a chance—"

"She'd studied his specialties, just to make him mad."

Cal smiled.

"I know. It's funny when they aren't *your* history questions."

"How did they get together?"

"I'll let her tell you."

"We don't exactly speak."

"You'll win her over. You have to be sincere with her. Her bullshit detector is way oversensitive."

"I don't even want to win her over," said Cal, stung.

Matt paused on the bottom step. Cal stayed in the cool shadow of the trees, unwilling to let this conversation continue into the sunny *Platz.* "She's incredible," he said. "She's the toughest person I know. As long as he wanted to be alive, she kept him alive."

Cal couldn't say a word.

"Still hungry?" said Matt.

In the grocery store, they had to follow a prescribed path, like rats in a maze, to reach the cash register. They brought their food to the *Platz* in front of the Jesuitenkirche. "This yogurt!" said Cal. She almost swooned. It was the best food she'd ever eaten. It was creamy and sweet and oddly textured, with small lumps.

"This *yogurt!*" said Matt.

It forced her into happiness, that yogurt. It made her think there was something glorious about sitting on sunny steps with her cousin's best friend, brick and stone spiraling above them. It reminded her of Santa Fe. Five years had passed, and nothing much had changed: the rowdy joys of sunlight, of sneaking off and scrounging makeshift meals outside. And everything had changed. She had heard the shuttering gasp of the old world ceding to the new. In every life there was a zero point, and hers was that day last August. Without knowing, she had always counted down toward that day, and for the rest of her life it would be the point from which she would mark her time: one year, two years, five years, fifty. Nothing important would ever happen without the lancing reminder that it drew her further from the world in which her cousin lived.

Ben strode into the *Platz*, Lillian gliding at his side. Trevor straggled behind with a bag of groceries. "Why are you eating rice pudding?" said Ben.

"It's yogurt!" said Cal.

He took the container. "*Vollmilch*, whole milk. *Kirsch*, cherry. And *Reis*."

"What does *Reis* mean?"

"For Pete's sake, Cal, show a modicum of brainpower."

"Oh," said Matt. "That's why it was so good."

"It wasn't yogurt after all," said Cal.

Ben removed the lid of his coffee grinder with a flourish. "I'm very excited for lunch. It's time to bump up my levels of vital micronutrients." He dumped in a carton of yogurt—labeled *Joghurt*, Cal noticed glumly—and then added an entire quart of strawberries. "Antioxidants, anti-inflammatories, flavonoids!" With the flat of his hand, he jammed the last strawberry into the grinder. "Smoothies are a huge boost to the immune system. They even help prevent the development of wrinkles."

"It's never too early to begin an anti-aging regimen," Trevor said sanctimoniously.

"Mock me all you want," said Ben. "You'll eat your words someday."

"What, when we're in a nursing home together?" Trevor

took on a quavery tone. "'Oh, Trevor, you're so pruney compared to that hot cousin of yours—'"

"Don't be vulgar," said Ben. "Let me see those photographs of Thea again. And you grind my lunch." Amenably, Trevor swapped him. "This has to be the most recent," said Ben, lingering over the tour-guide photo, Thea among the umbrellas. "Maybe we can analyze the architecture in the background to figure out what city she's in. . . ."

Cal put her head in her hands. The architecture was impossibly blurry, but she knew the photograph had been taken in Frankfurt. She should tell them. "This grinder is so high-tech," she heard Trevor saying to Matt. "I was messing around with it last night." Yet now it was too late. They'd hate her. Lillian already did. "It's got all these cool features, none of which Benny uses." This was unforgivable. "You can shake it, even, and it grinds on." She was wasting time, wasting money, contravening Jesse's last wishes. "It works sideways, and upside down—" Yet she could not bring herself to share what Jesse had given her.

Trevor hollered.

Cal jerked up her head. Trevor vaulted to his feet, his arms waving, utter consternation on his face. His pants were drenched with strawberry smoothie. It had splattered down to his knees. His lap was soaked through. Scarlet droplets flew everywhere as he danced about in the *Platz*.

"My smoothie!" cried Ben.

"My pants!" cried Trevor.

"My micronutrients!"

"My *pants*!"

Matt was dying of laughter. Lillian, with a small and incredulous smile, was slowly shaking her head.

"Thanks for screwing on the lid so tight, Ben," said Trevor.

"How was *I* supposed to know my grinder would be subjected to such abuse?"

"Need a tampon?" Lillian said.

Trevor halted his antic jig to consider the state of his crotch. "Apparently."

"Welcome to womanhood."

"I'm honored."

"And *I'm* not sitting next to you on the train home," said Ben.

"A kind cousin would offer to switch pants," said Trevor. "Considering it was the fault of *your* coffee grinder—"

"User error, you mean—"

"And *your* esophageal disorder—"

"Is there a Plagueslist page for rank stupidity?" said Ben. "Or does the whole website function in that role?"

"Ouch," said Trevor. "Too far."

Cal handed Trevor her napkin, and Lillian produced two tissues from her purse. Trevor dabbed.

"I don't suppose any of my smoothie can be salvaged," said Ben.

"Not unless you want me to wring out my pants above your mouth."

"How am I going to meet my nutritional requirements?"

"Look, I'm still mourning my only pair of pants. Your antioxidants are the least of my concerns."

"You only brought one pair of pants?"

"You said to pack light!"

CHAPTER NINE

The stain proved indelible, at least with the tools they had at their disposal: a bidet, a bar of soap. After breakfast the next morning, Trevor put on an impromptu fashion show with his other options. Matt's pants exposed four inches of scrawny, orange-haired calf bone. "Unacceptable," said Lillian.

Next were Ben's pleated-front khakis. "Dude," said Trevor, lying down on the bed to wriggle into them, "I thought I was skinny, but you have the build of a paper clip."

"Careful!" said Ben. "You're going to split the seams!"

Trevor sashayed across the room as if it were a runway. Cal moaned in horror. "Who wore it best?" Trevor intoned. He struck a pose, his hands fig-leafed over his crotch. Cal and Lillian were simultaneously laughing and cringing. Their eyes met, and Cal quickly looked away.

"Looks like my choices are leggings, high-waters, or the aftermath of a chainsaw massacre," Trevor said cheerfully. "What do you guys say?"

"I say shopping," said Lillian.

Cal looked to Ben, hoping he'd propose an alternate activity, but he said, "Well, we've already done the major museums." He just wanted to please Lillian, she thought.

Cal hung back as they entered the mall, six underground stories of chromed, gleaming shops. She could overhear Ben regaling Lillian with tidbits of trivia. "This place boasts the longest escalator in a European shopping mall. Forty-six meters!"

Trevor, on Lillian's other side, said, "You really put in some research for this outing."

"Did you expect otherwise?"

Cal sighed. "Do *you* like shopping?" she asked Matt.

"Nope."

"Me neither."

"I get agoraphobic."

"I thought you were claustrophobic. Aren't those opposites?"

"I'm kind of both."

He was looking studiedly at the store windows. "I see," Cal said.

"This mall seemed so American at first," he said, "but it's not, not really." He was right: the clothes, the lighting, even the poses of the mannequins were different, and all the more disorienting for being slightly, ineffably so. "I know what you're thinking," he said.

"What?"

"That I'm not as cool as I look."

Surprised, she laughed. He looked pleased. "I admit it," she said. "Yeah. That's exactly what I was thinking."

"You can't choose your looks."

"Tell me about it," she said, inadvertently glancing ahead to Lillian. He followed her gaze.

"Do you think it's weird for her?" said Matt.

"Weird? Why?"

"Well." He paused uncomfortably. "To be with her white boyfriend's white family in white Europe, I guess that's what I mean. You see how people stare at her."

"Oh," said Cal. She hadn't considered it. "I thought people stared because she's—you know. So pretty." *Pretty* was not the right word for Lillian, but the words Cal used in her head, *beautiful* and its forceful compatriots, were not ones she could speak aloud.

"I forget that," said Matt. "I guess I'm used to her."

Lillian had one hand on Ben's arm, one on Trevor's. She pushed through the crowd like the prow of a ship, and they fluttered in her wake. Cal dawdled. Matt slowed too. He probably attributed her pace to her heel, she thought with a twinge of guilt, but she'd ditched the Aircast a few days ago. Walking didn't hurt at all.

The gap widened between them and the others. The record-setting escalator came into view. Forty-six meters hadn't sounded especially impressive, but it was a pure, freestanding diagonal, seemingly unsupported as it slanted over six stories, and it looked very long. Lillian, Ben, and Trevor boarded and waved at Cal and Matt from ten feet above the ground. "I guess we're going up," said Cal.

Matt slowed. "Yeah." He looked pale.

"Heights?"

"Heights."

"They have floor-by-floor escalators too. Let's take those."

"Is that okay?"

"I want to see the in-between floors. We'll meet them at the top."

"Thank you," said Matt.

The single-floor escalators were deserted. On the third floor, Matt touched Cal's forearm. "Have you ever run up a down escalator?"

Cal grinned. "Nope."

"Let's do it."

"But what if—"

"There's no one around. Come on. You go first."

Cal hesitated. If they got caught, if they got yelled at in German, she'd probably cry. She didn't even know how to apologize. *Danke,* she'd have to say. Thank you for your scolding. *Danke schön,* thank you very much. But Ben always grimaced when she tried the umlaut. It was gnawing at her, not speaking the language, being surrounded by meaning that she could not divine. It made her feel mute and stupid, arrogant and American.

"Don't think," said Matt. He was already laughing. His eyes were bright. "Just go."

Well, she thought, she'd just go. She charged the first few steps. If she didn't start strong, she'd be stuck. No, she'd never done this, but how well she knew the feeling, the vertigo of stairs slipping from beneath her feet, the realization that all she could do was try to keep up, to run. Her legs moved at triple time. She glanced up. She was making progress, but not as much as she'd thought. Quadruple time now, quick spasms of steps, reminding her of the track warm-up when they'd judder on their toes like windup toys. She was almost there. That last step, it was tricky. She'd have to be unequivocal about it, to take the solid ground as her own. She leapt. She'd made it. Breathless, she leaned over the railing and laughed at Matt's jaunty sprint up the stairs.

"That was *fun!*" He sounded like a kid.

If the trip were always like this, Cal thought, she wouldn't want to go home. "Can I tell you something?" she said.

Matt listened carefully. He didn't interrupt until she was done. "That bike ride," he said. "I thought something might be up. I forgot to ask him, I guess." His face was cloudy. He turned to walk toward the next escalator. "So she's in Frankfurt."

"Or she was three years ago."

"What are we going to do?"

"We should look for her."

"Probably," said Matt. "Yeah."

"I should tell everyone. I should have told already. They'll be so mad. Not that I blame them. What kind of person keeps key information about her cousin's dying wish a *secret*?"

"Hey," said Matt. "You had your reasons. I get it. And everyone else will too."

Cal let out a beat of laughter. "Ben?"

"He'll have a fit for about three seconds. Then he'll get all excited about the mystery."

"*Lillian?*"

"She'll say something mean, sure. But you can handle it. She's taking it out on you, but it's not about you."

Cal blinked away tears.

"She's so angry," said Matt. "She can't believe he left her. She's furious." He gave Cal a glance that was almost shy. "You two should talk about it."

"Right," said Cal. "Right. Next time she says I don't care about Jesse, I'll just snuggle up to her and we'll have a heart-to-heart. Right."

She quickened her pace. Matt said he didn't even see Lillian's beauty; Matt acted all trusty, all confidential, but he always defended Lillian. Always. As Cal stepped onto the escalator to the fifth floor, her heel stabbed her. She grasped the banister and tried to keep the pain from her face.

From behind her, Matt said, "You don't have to tell them about Thea being in Frankfurt."

"Of course I do," snapped Cal.

"Don't you think there's a reason Jesse told only you?"

"I'm sure he assumed I'd tell everyone immediately. I'm sure he assumed I wouldn't be so petty and spiteful and ungenerous and— I wasn't always like this, you know. Such a bitch."

"Nobody thinks you're a bitch."

"Um, my graduating class would beg to differ."

"Why, because you have opinions? Because you're smart and you don't act dumb?"

"Because I *am* a bitch!" said Cal. "Because I'm mean." She felt unhinged. Her eyes were hot with tears and her jaw was trembling. "You've seen me!"

"Hey. Hey." Matt reached out his hand, but Cal jerked away. One touch would topple her shaky walls, and if she started crying now, she would never stop, not on the fifth floor or the sixth floor, not in Frankfurt, probably not for the rest of her life. "Anything Jesse did," said Matt, "he did for a reason. He thought about this trip a lot, Cal."

"Okay," she said. "Okay."

"And he knew that before we could start looking for her, there'd be one thing we'd need to know. That she was a tour guide here. If we don't know that, we don't have a place to start."

The escalator spat them out. They had one floor to go.

"He knew that, and still he only told you. What I think, if you don't want to tell everyone, he'd be okay with that. If you don't want to search for Thea, he'd say, Fine. I think he was giving you a choice."

CHAPTER TEN

Ben was good at writing postcards. Irritatingly good, in fact: he assumed he was destined to fail in all other endeavors, because only an unjust and impossible god would have bestowed upon him more than one talent of such scale. About postcards, Ben felt as Martial must have felt about epigrams, or Montaigne about essays: this was his métier. This was what he had been put on earth to do.

He thought this with some chagrin.

But there was no denying his virtuosity. Take the fact that the postcard reached his correspondent. How many tourists could hack a path through the logistical jungle of a foreign postal service? How many dared wield their machetes against the thickets of regulations, the creeping vines of bureaucracy? Ben vanquished the poisonous dart frog that was governmental monopoly, and he did it with panache. As for the message, there was just enough space. A few trenchant comments on the represented art, a vague sentence about his own journey—and then, where a letter or (ugh) an email might demand a more personal discussion, well, then, the verso was full. One corner remained for his short, self-contained name.

A postcard was like a bagatelle or a haiku, small enough to be perfect. This postcard, he knew, approached the pinnacle of his art: the tasteful photograph of Goethe's birthplace, the dignified profile on the stamp, his own sublime handwriting. He used a fountain pen, and his arches and ascenders, his loops and ligatures, swooped like a bird in flight. It was hand-writing you could fall in love with.

Trevor stretched out a long leg to admire his new pants. They'd paused for a midafternoon cappuccino, much to Ben's exasperation; as he'd told his profligate companions more than once, the hostel offered free coffee at breakfast, and all they needed to do was think ahead and bring an empty Nal-gene. "Whatcha writing?" said Trevor.

"Nothing," said Ben.

Besides, Eis Café Alberto hadn't the slightest Continen-tal ambience. It looked like a trendy frozen-yogurt place in the States. The color scheme was primary, and the furniture would bounce if thrown. Ben forgot to guard the postcard. Trevor grabbed it.

"Seriously? 'Dear Jean,' again? Call her."

"I'm not calling her."

"This café has wi-fi. You can call her free from my phone. Here!"

Ben recoiled. "I'm not calling her!"

"Fine." Trevor flipped the postcard onto Ben's lap. "Good luck with the courtship."

"It's not a courtship," Ben said, but Trevor, ensnared by his phone, didn't respond. And to be frank, *courtship* was exactly the word Ben would use. The word he hoped he could use. He knew he was not the ideal boyfriend. He was slow to catch jokes. He was as crotchety as an aging accountant. He either talked too much or didn't talk at all. He hated sports, and he had never danced in his life. (His only failing grade, ever, had come in fifth-grade gym, when he'd refused to participate in the square-dance unit.) His head was topped by an overgrown briar of curls and his nose was beaky and his posture gave the impression of an unpleasant intensity. Just to be a mumpsimus, he referred to Memorial Day as Decoration Day. He saw no point to fiction; he'd rather read the Internal Revenue Code than a novel. (Tax law was actually quite interesting.)

What upstanding young woman would choose *him*?

Therefore, he'd strategized. He would woo Jean Lin from afar, with his postcards and his intelligence, with his calligraphy: *kalos* and *graphein,* beautiful writing. When he returned, she would overlook the deficiencies and eccentricities of his person. That, at any rate, was the hope.

A phone call would ruin this plan. He had to stick to his strengths. Last summer, he hadn't called Jesse from Italy. Instead, he'd sent postcards, one every day. Oh, there were times now when he felt a turbid mess of regret, when he realized he'd missed his chance. It was difficult to fathom the implacability of it all. He had left California in June, and in August he'd returned to a coffin, to a gaunt and graying uncle. Jesse had propped Ben's postcards on his desk, and when he'd run out of room, he had laid them flat on its surface. "He wouldn't tape them up," said Uncle Arnold. "He wanted to be able to read them."

Ben touched the edge of one he'd sent from Rome, the Caravaggio from Sant'Agostino.

"And he wouldn't give me the Madonnas either."

Le poste italiane wasn't as reliable as he'd hoped: the postcards stumbled back, one by one, all autumn. Uncle Arnold gave them to Ben. They were moon rocks. They were artifacts from another world. Ben felt that he had crossed a threshold, passed through a wardrobe; it was always winter and never Christmas, and in this barren wood he could not find the lamppost that marked the way out. If only he'd called him. If only he'd heard his voice. If only! But he pushed away the thought. He aligned the edges of his postcards, and tightened the barrel of his fountain pen. This was what he'd chosen. This was what he'd been put on earth to do.

"If Cal doesn't bow to interrogation tonight," Ben told Lillian in an undertone, "we'll have to consider harsher measures."

Lillian nodded. Ben planned to convene a summit as soon as they reached the hostel, but Trevor immediately collapsed onto the bed. Now he sat up, popping out of sleep as if it were a shop he'd ducked into to wait out a short summer rainstorm. "You ready?" he said.

"For a discussion?" said Ben.

"For the game!"

"The—" Ben wavered. "The soccer game?"

"Football, you mean."

At least he'd guessed the right sport. "What about our quest?"

"We'll talk about it at the pub."

Ben and Lillian waited in the hallway for the others to emerge from the shared bathroom. "I find professional sports a fantastic waste of time," he commented.

"You know what's a waste of time?" said Lillian. "Hanging around in Frankfurt."

"I couldn't agree more." But he remained stymied. How was he supposed to find Thea when he had only a few snap-shots and a seemingly random set of maps? "Where even to begin?" he muttered.

Another bedroom door opened, and a man tumbled out. Ben prided himself on his ability to pick out Americans from a lineup, and this man was unmistakably so, from the cut of his suit (wide armholes, drooping pants) to his figure (gym-pumped arms, a swollen stomach). He nodded to Ben, and Ben gave him a brief nod back; with luck, he himself would pass for European. "Hey," the man said to Lillian. "Um, *gut Abend*?"

He paused, still looking at her, and she said coldly, "What?"

"Oh, good, English. Would you make sure my room's made up? Fresh towels? *Danke.*" He gave her a jovial salute. "My first German client meeting tonight," he told Ben. "Wish me luck!" He trotted down the stairs before either one of them could respond.

Ben gaped at Lillian. "Did he think—"

Lillian rolled her eyes. "Yes."

"But why?" Ben squinted at her. She was wearing a ruf-fled tuxedo shirt and a tight black skirt. "That outfit hardly screams maid."

"Why?" Lillian repeated. The others came out of the bath-room. She ignored them. "*Why?*" she said again to Ben. "You, of all people, are wondering why? You, with your celebrated analytical skills? Those famed powers of observation?"

"What happened?" said Trevor.

Lillian drew her mouth tight. Ben was forced to explain. "Another guest at the hostel—he seems to have, ah, mistaken Lillian for the maid."

"Oh my God," said Cal. "Where is he?"

"He left."

"Come *on*." Cal was on the stairs. "Come on! He can't have gone far!"

"Cal," said Trevor. "Calm down."

"No! This is an outrage!"

"It was an honest mistake," said Ben.

Cal turned on him. "An honest mistake? You can't be serious."

"Well, she was standing in the hallway," Ben said. "And she *is* wearing black and white, which could easily be a maid's uniform—"

Lillian snorted. "Black, yes. *That* could be a maid's uniform."

"It might not be about race!" said Ben. "We're jumping to conclusions!"

Lillian shook her head slowly back and forth. "Ben, Ben, Ben."

"What?" he said testily.

"*It's not about race.* Do you know why you can say that?"

"Why?"

"Because you're white, that's why."

He sputtered. "That's unfair."

"Agreed."

"An unfair *argument,* I mean. Utterly simplistic."

"You see everything with your white perspective. You can't help it."

"I do not!"

"Oh? Then how come you haven't even *noticed* I'm the only black tourist on this goddamn continent?"

"Look," said Cal. "What are we going to do about this asshole?"

"We're going to watch the football game," said Lillian.

"What if we leave a note under his door?" said Cal. "Like, *You thought I looked like a maid? Because I thought you looked like a racist snot-nose ass-chump*—"

"Let's not engage," said Lillian. "We don't need to bait him. It's over."

"You? *You?*" Cal took a step toward her. "All you ever want is to engage. You've spent this whole trip baiting *me*, trying to get into it with *me*, and now someone's actually wrong, and you want to let him be?"

"Where's this pub, Trevor?" said Lillian. "Can we hit the road?"

"Why can't you let *me* be?" said Cal.

Lillian looked at her with half-closed eyes, with the shade of a smirk. It was a look calculated to enrage her. Even Ben knew that. Cal turned and clattered down the stairs.

CHAPTER ELEVEN

Three pubs in succession turned them away. "Yep, too crowded again," Trevor reported after checking a fourth. "Everyone in Frankfurt's out watching the game."

It was just as well, Ben thought. The extended walk and the evening air would give all the fired tempers a chance to cool. Lillian swerved into an Indian restaurant, which was half empty. "A stroke of genius," Ben told her. She seemed to have brushed off their quarrel, but he was still embarrassed. He wished he could explain. He hadn't been allying himself with that man, as Lillian seemed to believe. Hardly. He'd only been trying to bring nuance into the situation, to avoid the crude identity politics that plagued so many of his fellow Berkeleyites.

"*Wir sind fünf,*" he told the waiter, who led them to a table.

Lillian probably thought he didn't even know the term *white privilege*. For God's sake, he'd gone to school in California. Of course he knew it. But how much, really, did it apply to him? He had always been an outsider too.

Well. Enough stewing. It'd been an unpleasant incident,

but he'd try to put it behind him. "So who's playing?" he said, squinting at the little men scampering about the screen. "Germany?"

"Versus Greece," said Trevor.

"Is this a big game or something?"

"Only the quarterfinal of the Euro Cup," said Trevor, clapping a hand to his forehead. "We're all rooting for the *Vaterland*, correct?"

"I'm on Team Doesn't Give a Hoot," said Ben.

"I'm for Greece," said Matt. "I always root for the underdog."

"Me too," said Cal.

"How clichéd," said Lillian, yawning.

"And futile," said Trevor. "Germany's going to stomp all over Greece. They're not even starting their top three players."

"How do you know all this?" said Ben. "Have you always been a soccer fan?"

"Football. And nah, not really. You just pick up these things."

Trevor could absorb whatever he needed to reach equilibrium with his new environment. The process was thoughtless, natural. Osmotic. Now he was chatting up a man at an adjacent table. They were arguing about Mats Hummels. He'd made a friend, and Ben had completely missed how he'd done it.

"Before the game starts," Lillian said, "we need to talk about Thea."

"Indeed!" said Ben.

"We've been twiddling our thumbs too long. It's time to tell what you know. The envelope. The folder. The notebook."

"The envelope went to me," said Trevor. "The photos."

"And as I've mentioned," said Ben, "I've got the folder, and it contains maps. Feel free to take a look, but they seem randomly chosen to me."

"Are they places Thea could be?" said Trevor.

"Unlikely. How would Jesse have obtained thirty-one worldwide leads?"

They fell silent. Ben sighed. As usual, he'd have to take on the thankless task of giving voice to everyone's unspoken thought. "Cal. If we want to find her, you have to show us that notebook."

"*Do* we want to find her?" Cal said. "She abandoned him. She lost her right to be found."

"Just go along with it," said Trevor.

"Could you please stop bouncing that infernal ball?" Ben said to Matt. "Look, Cal, how will we rest easy with this mystery unsolved? Don't you care about that?"

"Don't you care about *him*?" said Lillian.

"Thea's the one who didn't care about him!" said Cal. "He was her baby! She left him!"

"She's not the only one," said Lillian.

Cal gripped the edge of the table. Ben watched white crescents wax atop her fingernails as the blood beat a forced retreat.

"She's a coward," said Lillian. "She doesn't deserve him. But he wants us to find her, and I'm willing to do just about anything."

She looked around the table. She picked them off one by one. Matt's eyes fell, and then Trevor's. Although Ben was determined to maintain eye contact, Lillian's gaze hit with such impact that he found himself clearing his throat, looking down, adjusting his silverware. But Cal stared back. Her lip curled.

Were these girls about to brawl? It was an undeniable possibility.

"Well!" said Trevor. "It's been a long day. Let's relax and watch the game."

Lillian said, "There is something despicable about each and every one of you."

The game began. Ben had asked for his curry to be overcooked, but he had to press the potatoes through the tines of his fork before he could even think about eating them. He must have mismanaged the German. Did he have any proficiency? The television commentary was like high-speed traffic; most words were a blur, and he could distinguish only the flashy ones.

"Philipp Lahm!" yelled Trevor. "Beautiful. Did you see that swerve?" He looked around. "Dudes. Dudettes. It'll be more fun if you get into it."

If Matt didn't stop bouncing that squash ball, Ben was going to scream. He dropped his fork. He couldn't shove down another bite. "Nobody's even alluded to the political backdrop," he said. "Germany's just given Greece a $174 billion rescue package, and all anyone cares about is which country is better at kicking a ball."

Lillian stood. "I'm going home."

"Stay till the end!" said Trevor. "It's only halftime! It's anyone's game!"

"No. *Home.* California. Screw you. I don't want to be here. Screw him."

She wheeled and marched away. Matt started to stand, but sank down again when Lillian turned toward the back of the restaurant, not the front. She disappeared behind the rust silk that curtained the bathrooms.

An uneasy silence seeped over the table. Cal drained her glass of water. Ben considered reminding her that water didn't come free in Europe, that the two liters he'd ordered had already been drunk, but he anticipated her withering stare and thought better of it.

Cries of anger erupted from the patrons and wait staff. "Jérôme!" yelled Trevor. "You let me *down!*" How, thought Ben, was Trevor already on a first-name basis with *die Fußballnationalmannschaft*? "Enjoy the tie while it lasts," Trevor told Matt. "It'll be brief. Greece is totally outclassed."

Ben cleared his throat. "We've got to start somewhere," he said. "Should we travel to the area shown on the closest map?"

"Magic in his feet!" cried Trevor.

Matt tossed his squash ball from hand to hand.

"Twinkle toes!"

More loudly, Ben said, "Or should we start with the assumption she's in Germany?"

"Yes," said Trevor.

"I have to say I agree," said Ben.

"Yes yes yes—YES!" Trevor high-fived the waiter and his new buddy, an Indian man accompanied by his small daughter. "Sami Khedira with a right-footed volley! Prodigious!"

Ben gritted his teeth.

"We better postpone this conversation until Lillian gets back," said Matt. "I'm a little worried about her."

"She's just taking a breather," said Trevor.

"I would go check on her—" said Matt.

"Just a time-out."

"—but it's the ladies' room."

"Fine," said Cal, rising so roughly that her chair teetered on its back legs. Matt grabbed it. She stormed off and vanished behind the curtain. Ben could hear her knocking on the bathroom door.

"Maybe a third party should be present," he suggested. "For safety's sake."

Again, he was ignored. Trevor, his mouth open, gazed at the television. Matt stuffed his squash ball in his pocket and switched Cal's empty water glass with his own, still full. Ben riffed his fingers on the tabletop. This dinner was emblematic of the whole trip: inefficient, ineffectual, too loud, too emotional. He was the only one willing to put aside trivial personal concerns for the sake of the truth.

The restaurant burst into cheers. "Miroslav Klose!" said Trevor. "Miraculous!" His friend tossed his two-year-old up and down, both of them crying "Deutschland!" every time she landed. "And the girls missed it!" said Trevor. "They'll be so bummed!"

The replays commenced at seven different camera angles, in live speed and slow motion and fancy combinations thereof. Ben watched in disbelief. The sweating, spitting players, the solemn Slovenian referees, the statisticians seeking to quantify a game clearly more suited to narration than to numbers, and the fans, who, though painfully irrelevant to the outcome, watched on tenterhooks nonetheless: they all put so much effort into this game, and so much earnestness! Irony did not play on this pitch.

There were the girls, threading their way through the tables. Lillian, unreadable, walked in her bounceless way with her head held high, but Cal's eyes were puffy and bloodshot, her eyelashes dewy. Ben looked away, wishing he hadn't noticed.

"Three to one," Trevor reported.

Cal wrapped her hands around her glass. "I have something to tell you."

Ben leaned forward as she told what she knew: Thea had been a tour guide in Frankfurt.

"I wish I'd known this last week," he said.

"It was three years ago, remember," said Cal. "So I don't know how important it is."

"Of *course* it's important! Why couldn't you have—"

Matt drew in a sharp breath. "Benny," said Trevor.

Ben relented, but caught Lillian's eye. She lifted an eyebrow, almost imperceptibly, and he gave her a matching tiny nod.

"Come on!" said Trevor, staring avidly at the television.

"I assume you'll lend me the notebook," Ben told Cal. "I'm sure your summary was accurate, but per the dictates of New Criticism, the only true source is the text itself—"

"Come on! Go!" Trevor jumped to his feet. "Yes—and—" He threw up his arms. "GOAL!" The toddler danced on the table.

"A tour guide right here in Frankfurt," mused Ben. "What a lead!"

"I know! Four to one!" said Trevor. He sighed. "Though, yet again, I missed all the groundwork."

"You'll survive," said Ben. Twenty-two grown men trotted around a field in Gdańsk with a polka-dotted ball, and the continent watched with bated breath. He sometimes felt he had been born into the wrong world.

"That's the problem with rooting for the underdog," Trevor told Cal and Matt. "You always lose."

A penalty was awarded to Greece. Dimitris Salpingidis shot right as Manuel Neuer dove left, and the shot scorched the corner of the goal. The air splintered into cries of indignation. "Can I tell you one more thing?" said Cal.

"Need you ask?" said Ben.

"She was here in college too."

Ben felt like adding his own indignant cry to the din. That hoarding girl! Information should be free and public. Her buttoned lips had wasted days.

But he put his hands to the marble block, the material he had been given to work, and his animosity was forgotten. There was a plan in here, and he would sketch its broad outlines with umber crayon and then take his chisel to the block, chipping away the excess, honing and worrying until the shining figure was freed. He knew the first step; the rest would follow. They would find her.

The game ended shortly after the Greek goal. Ben trailed behind the others as they plowed through the crowds. Cars streamed down the main thoroughfare in an impromptu parade. Drivers honked, and girlish torsos, painted black and red and yellow, jutted from open sunroofs like the figureheads of ships. Some people smiled and shouted but some, he saw with shock, were weeping. What had ever affected him so deeply? Was he trapped within marble himself? He felt somehow less . . . less *fleshly* than these people, these fans, who could sense a groundswell and wholeheartedly acquiesce, who could raise their arms and laugh and cry as they were swept away, while he had to remain firm, a statue. But it was just as well. He hated loud noises. When they got back to the hostel, he slammed shut the window, and the screams were muted, if not gone.

CHAPTER TWELVE

On Monday morning, Ben said, "Stage one! I've segmented Frankfurt into five zones. Scour your zone for the business cards and brochures of tour companies. Check hotel lobbies, U-Bahn stations, anywhere you see a big blue *I*."

Out in the city, ricocheting from hotel to hotel, Matt found himself glad to be alone. When he passed a *Tennisverein*, he thought, Why not? He rented shoes, a racket, and a court. The ball, he had.

He hit drives until the ball skipped brightly, and then practiced shots down the rail. Like a chess master, he'd become adept at playing himself. He always won and he always lost.

He felt a little guilty, not so much for skiving off—in the age of the Internet, Ben's plan seemed an absurdly labor-intensive way to compile a list of Frankfurt's tour companies—but for the spurt of relief and glee and numbness that he got with every shot. He'd missed this. How, he wondered, had a confirmed claustrophobic gotten himself addicted to the only sport that was played in a box?

Then he stopped thinking.

The ninety minutes passed slowly and also at full tilt, in the odd custom of focused time: a bat doing loop-the-loops and banking against the brimstone breeze, thoroughly enjoying the road out of hell. He'd called his dad the day before they'd left for Frankfurt. "You want to play?" Matt said.

"I guess I could squeeze in a game."

Matt had never beaten him, but even as they warmed up, he knew this time would be different. His father had never understood that squash was a game of finesse, not of force. Matt spun his racket. "Your serve," he said.

His father served overhand, his body arcing like a fish, his racket coruscating like scales. Matt hopped out of the ball's path and dinked it against the wall: one to zero. His father's strategy worked when his opponent could be scared, but Matt no longer minded the ball bounding off racket and wall with the sound of two rapid-fire gunshots. His returns kissed the side wall, kissed the front wall, died on the floor. His topspin was venomous. His high, curving serves found the back corner and, with a certain lassitude, stayed there. When his father started playing up, Matt lobbed the ball over his head.

By the time they left the court, Matt had grown accustomed to its circumscribed sounds, breaths and footsteps and thwacks and thumps. Out here, it was loud—the chitchat on the bleachers, the clangor as another court's ball hit the tin, the bric-a-brac of his racket bag's zipper—and jarringly so. His dad toweled his face dry and shook Matt's hand. His grip was tense. He hated to lose. He also hated for Matt to lose. "Enjoy Deutschland." His voice was studied in its nonchalance. There was, after all, no resolution to this paradox. "Have a beer for me." When they played, one of them would lose.

Jesse would have understood. In the parking lot, Matt dialed his number and let it ring all the way through. "I beat him," he told the voice mail. "I finally beat him." He was exhausted.

"You want to be like him," Jesse had once said, "and there's nothing you fear more."

"Yes," said Matt.

Both were true. It was impossible for both to be true. Sometimes growing up seemed no more than accepting a series of paradoxes. That you could feel pride you'd won and shame he'd lost. Matt set down the phone without hanging it up. That you could keep living, lacking the person you couldn't live without.

They reconvened for dinner and tossed their collected flyers into a heap. "I still don't see why we couldn't have used the Internet," said Trevor.

"Legwork!" said Matt. "Legwork is crucial!" He grinned at Cal.

"Quite so," said Ben. "Not every tour company has a website. And it's difficult to navigate online in the turbulent seas of a non-native language. Who knows what storms we'd have weathered, what icebergs we'd have struck?"

"On that note," said Trevor, "Ben, do me a favor, would you?"

"Depends."

"We're about to expand Plagueslist internationally."

"No."

"We need a wee smidgen of help translating the menus. It'd take you ten minutes. German? *Ich bin ein Plagueslister?*"

"No."

"French? Italian?"

"No."

"Swedish?" said Trevor hopefully. "When else do you get to use your Swedish?"

"Tempting. But no. Stage two!"

Once they'd visited six tour companies, the proprietors staring at the Thea-among-the-umbrellas photo with no recognition, Matt started to think he would be granted a reprieve: a natural end to the search. He couldn't overcome his sense that Jesse too had felt ambivalent. He had considered bringing it up with the group. "Jesse's telling us to find her," Lillian would say flatly. "That doesn't sound very ambivalent to me."

But Jesse's plan, Matt thought, was too contrived, too convoluted. It was the stuff of fantasy. There and back again, grail in tow.

Ben and Lillian led the charge. Cal gazed at the river path with the same longing Matt had felt toward the squash club. "How's the heel?" he said.

"Walking's fine. Maybe I'll try a run soon. It's such a weird injury."

"Maybe you should consult a panel of self-appointed experts," said Matt. "Crowdsource it."

"Did you just plug Plagueslist?" said Trevor. "Dude, I should hire you." He turned to Cal. "A Plagueslist account is a fabulous idea."

"Don't do it, Cal," said Ben from behind his map, which billowed around him like a small tent. "Have you *been* on Plagueslist?"

"Trevor makes me refresh it when I'm bored. He says they need the hits."

"That's a confidential business practice!" said Trevor.

They trekked through downtown Frankfurt. The morning was overcast. Matt said quietly to Cal, "Does something about this—does it feel off?"

"Looking for her?" Cal stiffened. "Are you saying I shouldn't have told them?"

"No. No." He'd have done the same thing. "It just feels off." It felt like trying to shut a jar when the lid was awry on the threads. "I wonder what Professor Serrano thinks of this. Your uncle Arnold. I wonder whether he feels betrayed."

Cal tilted her head and said nothing.

"But I want to do what Jesse wanted," said Matt.

It'd become a refrain, something to parrot. *Did* he? Did any of them? Matt let Cal float away, let Jesse take her place. With the iron-plated sky and the chill in the air, it wasn't hard to imagine himself on Rodeo Beach, the autumn of their junior year. Matt had driven. Jesse had folded himself into the back but spent the whole ride leaning so far forward that he might as well have been perched atop the gearshift. When the music got good, he drooped his head onto Lillian's shoulder. "I hope you're prepared to swim," he said.

"The water's fifty degrees," said Matt. "If that."

"If you were a kid, you'd get in."

"I wouldn't," said Lillian. With both hands, she adjusted her high, full bun. "I was a smart kid."

"You're both wimps," said Jesse.

The sand on the beach seemed uniformly dark, but when he picked up a handful, Matt saw the grains were motley, greens and deep reds. "Come on, Matt," said Jesse, stripping down to his trunks. "To say you've done it."

Matt took off his shirt and went with Jesse to the edge of the surf. He worked his toes deep into the sand. When a wave caught his feet, he gasped. Jesse waded in and Matt supposed he had to follow. If he were a kid, he thought, he'd have never gotten in. He had spent too much time at their club's swimming pool to like the thought of a bottom he couldn't see, of living things reluctantly tolerating his incursion into their territory, of sharks. The water was arctic. His legs understood it not as cold but as constriction; it was as if they were caught in a vise.

Jesse stopped when they were waist-deep. "Refreshing!" he yelled.

"Uh-huh," Matt managed. He glanced at Jesse. He was shocked. Jesse was thin, beyond thin. How had he not noticed before? There was something deeply disturbing about the sight of his wasted torso rising from the charred water. They were both shivering convulsively. Now Matt couldn't stop noticing: the arms that swelled at the elbow, the skin stretched over the jaw like fabric on an embroidery hoop, the sternum, the ribs.

"I'm girding my loins," said Jesse.

"Don't tell me we're dunking."

Water curled around their waists and spurted in tendrils to their chests. Matt stopped resisting the waves and let himself rock, forward with the crests and back with the troughs. "Look at her," said Jesse. Lillian was a silhouette against the brown hills. She had her arms raised.

"What's she doing?"

"I don't know. Feeling the wind, maybe."

"Oh." Matt wanted to dunk and get it over with, to dry himself with his shirt, to look in the trunk for wool blankets.

"That girl," said Jesse. "I've never felt like this before."

If he hadn't been so cold, Matt thought, he wouldn't have heard his dad's guffaw. Of course he hasn't, his dad said. He's a red-blooded teenager and he's getting laid for the first time.

Dad, Matt protested, I don't even know whether—

"This is real," said Jesse.

Go away, Matt told his dad. "Are you sure?" he asked Jesse.

It was a silly question. Anyone who'd seen him looking at Lillian would have known he was sure. The weak sun sparkled on the droplets of water in his hair and on his shrunken chest. "Yes."

"How do you know?" said Matt.

"It feels right. That's all. It feels right, so I'm going with it." He threw himself under the waves. He came up sputtering and panting. "Holy shit. Your turn." But he didn't stop to watch Matt go under before he dove in again to swim to shore.

Now Matt could scarcely believe days like that had been allowed. Shouldn't someone have warned them? Thanks, he breathed to the ghostly Jesse at his side. Cal had Jesse's laugh. Matt and Lillian had noticed it within minutes of meeting her. Look what you've done to us, he told him. Lillian had spent a year in sleep, Matt in a squash court, and they were no closer to relief. They could not move in this ice-cold water; they could not reach the pebbly beach where Jesse waited, his arms raised. This, Matt thought, was what happened when you went with what felt right.

At the seventh tour company, Lillian took out Thea's photograph and the proprietor replied, "I remember her."

Everyone perked up. Ben responded in German.

"For a short while," said the proprietor in English. "I cannot tell you much. She was a good guide, but not committed."

Again, Ben insisted on German. Matt imagined the conversation hopping from one side of a creek to another.

"Do you know where the Städel is?" English. "The art museum?"

"Allerdings," Ben said bitingly. But outside, he cried, "A lead!" If he'd been physically capable of leaping up and clicking his heels, Matt was pretty sure he'd have done it. Lillian held her bottom lip with her teeth, but he saw her trembling. As he followed her down the sidewalk, even the muscles in the back of her neck looked intent.

They went straight to the Städel. They had no luck when they showed the photograph to the receptionist, but a man thumbing through a Rolodex straightened when he heard the name Thea Vogel. "I am Joachim Abend," he said. "The assistant curator here." He flinched when he saw the photograph. "Perhaps we could have dinner?"

They ate at Zeil Kebap. Behind the counter, a large and unidentifiable cylinder of meat rotated on a vertical spit. "I don't know where she is now," said Abend. "Three years ago, she worked at the museum." He was stocky and soft-spoken, with stumps of eyebrows and a beard that seemed an extension of his gray sweater. He set a sheaf of papers by his plate and handed his briefcase to Lillian, who put it on the empty chair beside her. "I must ask. Why are you searching for her?"

"It's a long story," said Lillian.

"Yes?"

"Yes."

Someone should explain about Jesse, thought Matt. It wouldn't be him. The expectant silence turned awkward, yet no one spoke. At last, Abend said, "I brought you her employment record." He proffered the top sheet, and Ben seized it. "It will tell you little. We once had copies of her passports, numbers you could have run by embassies, but we shred sensitive documents."

"Passports?" said Ben. "Plural?"

Abend looked disconcerted. "I assumed you knew." He glanced at the door. "She is a dual citizen."

"*Really,*" said Ben. "I've been wondering how she obtained a work visa. She has a German parent?"

"Her mother. A Bavarian." Abend's face tightened. "You did not know her at all."

"Did you?" said Lillian.

"To some extent, yes." He put down his sandwich. "Tell me. Why are you looking for her?"

"It doesn't matter," said Lillian. "Someone asked us to find her."

"I see." Abend pushed away his plate, although he had eaten only a few bites. "And have you considered whether she wants to be found?"

They fell silent. Now, Matt thought again. Tell him. But he couldn't. Every time he spoke Jesse's name to someone who had not known him, he felt treacherous. Jesse had lived for seventeen years and died for a moment, but in the telling, the moment became all that mattered. There was a diminishment that came with abridging the story to its final chapter, an ebbing, like a city slipping under the sea, and tonight, Matt could not stand it.

Still the curator waited. Lillian gave Cal a look: was it imploring? Cal looked back levelly, and then turned to Abend. "I met Thea once," she said. Changing the subject, Matt thought, at Lillian's silent behest. "She was beautiful. And she loved art."

Abend visibly relaxed. "Yes. You're right. That was why she took the maid job."

Lillian mouthed thanks to Cal, and Cal nodded.

"Wait," said Ben. "She was a *maid*?"

"A nighttime maid for the museum. She mopped floors, she dusted frames, and then she stayed in the galleries, looking at the art."

Ben was perusing the employment record. "She stayed for only six months."

"And you have no idea where she went?" said Lillian.

"I respected her wishes. She did not want me to follow her. She did not want to be found."

From across the table, Ben peered at the other papers, giving the distinct impression of a turkey vulture examining carrion from a tree. "What else do you have in that stack?" His fingers twitched. "May I?"

Abend gathered them up. Most were torn from a notebook, it seemed, and they buckled around a slender book. "Notes. Personal notes. Nothing of importance." He handed them to Lillian. "Would you mind sliding these back into my briefcase?"

"Not at all."

They watched as Abend wiped his hands: deliberately, finger by finger. He placed the balled napkin atop his abandoned sandwich. "You have nothing to tell me about her?"

"Why would we?" said Lillian. "You said it yourself. We didn't know her."

"Well," he said. "Well. This, then, is where we part."

"Fruitless," said Ben, unbuttoning his cuffs back in the hostel. "Why did he want to meet us if he had nothing to tell?"

Matt flopped onto the bed next to Trevor. "To warn us off," he said.

"Then why did he bring the papers?" said Ben.

Curled on the floor, her arms enveloping her knees, Cal said, "I wish we could go home."

"There must be a next step," said Ben. He rumpled his hair with both hands. "We just can't see it yet."

Lillian was by the windows, looking toward the skyscrapers in the east. She unzipped her purse and tossed a stack of papers onto the bed. "There. There's the next step."

The papers fanned. Matt jerked his leg away from their torn edges. They all stared.

Cal rose to her knees. "You stole his papers?"

Lillian shrugged. "He wouldn't tell us anything."

"You *stole* them?"

"Chill, Cal, they aren't the crown jewels," said Trevor. He gave Lillian a high-five. "Girl! Right under his nose!"

Ben swept them up. "Priceless! His notes! All in German! There'll be clues here, mark my words."

"Hold on," said Cal, standing. "Nobody else is disturbed by this?"

"By what?"

"By the fact that she just committed a felony!"

"A misdemeanor," said Ben.

"What happens when he notices they're gone?"

"He'll think they got left at the restaurant," said Trevor.

"He'll call the police!" said Cal. "The Gestapo will be knocking at our door!"

"Dissolved at Nuremberg in 1945," said Ben.

"Not to mention the *moral* implications!"

Lillian watched the fracas with her arms crossed, one hip thrust out. Matt knew the pose. After ten days her head was laced with a soft burr, but it still caught the oblong panels of light thrown from sun to skyscraper to skull. Lillian had authority. She would make them shut up by waiting for it, by willing it, by flying her heavy eyelids at half mast. There. Cal subsided and crossed her own arms, an unconscious echo. Ben straightened the papers. Trevor lifted his eyebrows and closed his mouth.

"I didn't have a choice," said Lillian. "It was too weird. Why meet with us if he had nothing to tell? Why dig up all those papers? He'd been planning to tell us everything, I think. Then he lost his nerve."

"Because he knew we weren't being straight with him," said Matt. "Because we didn't tell him about Jesse." He felt sorry he hadn't. He reminded himself how impossible it had seemed in the restaurant: he could not have opened his mouth and conjured his friend only to have him die.

"There was no reason he needed to know," said Lillian.

"But we weren't acting in good faith," said Matt.

Lillian dismissed him with a flip of her hand. "Here's what I think. Thea may have told him not to follow her, but he wishes he had. He still wants to find her."

"Solid deduction," said Ben.

"He's still in love with her."

"Don't take it too far. Not all stories are about love."

"I know love when I see it," said Lillian.

Matt watched Cal sink onto the edge of the bed.

"I told you I'd do anything," said Lillian. "I guess you didn't believe me."

CHAPTER THIRTEEN

Her mother would *not* find out that she'd stolen that guy's papers, but Lillian couldn't stop imagining her reaction, the terrifying threats (slap you, flay you, wring you out and hang you out to dry) followed by the threats' fulfillment (yes, no, probably not but you never knew). Her mother had one simple rule: don't do anything. When Lillian got into the ritzy private school, full of the smart-as-shit children of Berkeley professors and Silicon Valley millionaires, her mother had said it outright. The ice you stand on, little girl, is thinner than the ice they stand on. That is the way it works.

But Lillian regretted nothing. She'd had to steal the papers. No papers, no Thea, and she had promised to find Thea. It was as straightforward as that.

The next day, Ben established himself on a bed with Abend's notes and the slim book that had been with them. "These are journal entries!" he said. "From when Abend and Thea worked together at the museum!" He was soon engrossed, lifting his head only to consult his dictionary, making no noise but rustles and hems and the occasional triumphant chirrup. He didn't notice when the other four left. Matt had offered Trevor a squash lesson. "You two could play on another court," he told the girls.

"We're going to an Internet café," said Lillian.

"Then we won't have to talk," said Cal.

Lillian rolled her eyes. Since the theft Cal had heaved a hundred sighs and shot Lillian a thousand recriminatory looks, clearly fancying herself some skulking angel of righteousness. Lillian was on the brink of giving it to her, *really* giving it, unleashing the dogs of hell, her whole fearsome pack of sarcasm and slight and calumny. But every time she came close, someone made Cal laugh. That damn laugh. Spirited away from Lillian's dead boyfriend and right down Cal's throat, and she didn't even know.

Sunshine surrendered to a patch of spitting rain. Lillian and Cal took shelter in the Internet café, a cramped storefront that smelled of fried food, its walls papered with tattered advertisements for lotteries and call girls. For two euros, they each bought an hour on computers whose monitors were so staticky that the air quavered in front of them. Lillian's keyboard was missing its *K*. She cringed whenever her finger landed in the dusty hole; it made her think of the gap left by a decayed tooth.

Momma, she wrote, *I miss zou. Weäre still in Franfurt.* Who'd done this? Switched around the letters, hidden the apostrophe? Not even keyboards were the same abroad. *Iäm oaz,* she wrote, as close as she could get to *I'm okay.* She wasn't about to consider the metaphorical implications of *that.* She tried again. *I love zou. Tell Grandma I love her too.* She had nothing else to say. She hit SEND.

Cal was still hacking away. "You type so fast," said Lillian. Cal didn't look up. "It's a gift."

Lillian returned to her own screen, but what else was there to do? From this distance, social media seemed banal. She started a new email. *Iäm trzing. Iäm trzing as hard as I can. Weäre going to find her. I promise.* When she'd gone to Hawaii with her mom and a few aunts the Christmas before last, Jesse had sent her emails that he'd unself-consciously called love letters. Lillian, perched on a wheeled chair in the resort's business center, would close her eyes while the page loaded and hope for a new one. *Lill! Lill! I miss you! I miss you like the winter sky misses the cry of the whip-poor-will. Isn't that the kind of thing you're supposed to write in love letters? But what the heck[1] is a whip-poor-will?*

He went on. She made herself read slowly. At the very bottom: [1]*That would sound a lot funnier with the F-word, but what if your mom glimpses it over your shoulder? Would she ever forgive me?*[2]

And: [2]*Will you ever forgive me, for putting a footnote[3] in a love letter?*

And: [3]*Two footnotes.*[4]

And: [4]*Actually three.*[5]

And: [5]*Okay, four.*[6]

And: [6]*I seem to have gotten myself in one of those pesky infinite-recursion situations. I'm not going to keep going (if I don't shower ASAP, fungi will colonize my armpits), but, Lill, for you, I would. Lots of maidens have dudes willing to kill dragons— oops, let's skip the heteronormative gender-binary shit—lots of PEOPLE have PEOPLE who'd slay dragons. Who'd bring them soup when they're sick. Who'd laugh at their unfunny jokes. But,*

Lill, the guy who, for all eternity, would insert one self-negating footnote after another: Lill, that guy is a prize.[7]

She'd thought he was done. But she'd kept scrolling, and far, far down, after pages and pages of blank space:

[7]*If I do say so myself.*

Cal sent her email with a dramatic strike of the RETURN key. Their countdown clocks had fifteen seconds left. "You must have written a novel," said Lillian.

"Just about," said Cal. Their timers blared. They both jumped, which made them giggle. "To my best friend from home."

"An update on the trip?"

Cal hesitated. "Not really." They left the café. "I don't really talk to her about this stuff."

Lillian hated euphemisms. "You mean Jesse?"

"Yeah."

"Who *do* you talk to?"

"I don't."

"Your parents didn't pack you into therapy?"

"They kind of suggested it, but—" Cal shivered. "It sounded painful. I figured it'd be easier to get over it on my own. Distract myself and let time pass."

They walked half a block. The weather was unidentifiable, holographic, shifting within seconds between sunshine and rain. Cal added, "I don't think that plan's working too well."

"My mom," said Lillian, "she's always saying, 'Feelings aren't going anywhere. Feelings have to be felt.'" She didn't mention to Cal that her mother said that only when she'd been pushed to the edge of her patience, when a full weekend had passed and Lillian had not left her bed. "Those feelings," her mother would snap, "are going to be there when you wake up."

Lillian would mumble, "So I'll feel them when I wake up."

"Sounds just like my mom," said Cal. "'The only way out is through!' That's her thing. Did *you* get therapy-ized?"

"She tried to make me talk to our priest. No way, I told her. I'm not nodding and smiling to their party line. 'He's in a better place.'"

"I hate that."

"It's stupid. It's stupid even if there's a heaven. I know Jesse, and if he could choose a place, it'd be this sidewalk. This gray sky. Us. Jesse would never think there's a better place than here."

Cal held the hostel door. She'd teared up. She cried if you were mean and she cried if you were nice. At the Indian restaurant, when Lillian had lost it and penned herself up in the bathroom, Cal was already crying by the time she knocked on the door. Furious, yes, but crying. "Matt—we—I just wanted to see if you were okay."

"I'm *fine*," spat Lillian.

"*Fine*," echoed Cal. She spun to stomp back to the table. Lillian didn't know what made her put her hand on Cal's shoulder, but she did, and Cal froze on the threshold.

"Thanks anyway," said Lillian. "Maybe—"

"Maybe what?"

"Nothing. Never mind. Thanks for checking on me."

Maybe, she'd been thinking, we could be friends. She'd almost said it, and now, climbing the hostel's stairs, she thought it again. But it was a big maybe. It wouldn't happen while Cal continued to hoard that notebook. How could there exist a hundred pages of Jesse's writing that Lillian wasn't allowed to touch? She climbed the next flight more heavily. No. It wasn't fair.

They went out to dinner near the Opernplatz, though Ben stayed behind to continue translating Abend's papers. "I'm sustained by language," he said, ferociously thumbing his German dictionary. He had ink marks on his face where he'd scratched with the wrong end of the pen. "I feed on the thrill of text. On the chance of an answer."

"We'll bring you a sandwich," said Trevor.

"Liquid nourishment only, please."

On the way home, Cal said, "I think I'll try a run tomorrow morning."

"I'll go with you," said Matt.

"All right," said Cal, smiling. "It's a date."

Trevor said, "Are you sure that's a good idea?"

The smile soon disappeared. "Okay, overprotective older brother, I didn't mean *date*—"

"No, running on that heel."

"Oh." She flushed. "I'm sure it's fine."

When they got back to the hostel, Ben was exultant. "I've got a theory," he said.

"Let's hear it," said Lillian.

Abend and Thea, he'd discovered, had traveled together to Mittenwald, a Bavarian town near the Austrian border where Thea had spent her childhood summers. They had hiked in the Alps. "Perhaps here," she had told him, "I could be happy."

"Sounds promising," said Lillian.

"The journal entries stop shortly thereafter," said Ben. "Presumably when Thea left Frankfurt. And I think it's possible—nay, *likely*—that she returned to Mittenwald."

"Too bad we can't ask Abend," said Cal, scowling at Lillian.

"Too bad he'd have us arrested the second we set foot in the museum."

Lillian ignored her. "How far away is Mittenwald?"

"By car?" said Ben. "Five hours or so."

"Let's go."

Cal, Matt, and Trevor were silent. Lillian wanted to kick something. Did they feel no pressure to find Thea? Did they even care about Jesse's wishes?

"We'll sleep on it," said Trevor, in his peacemaking mode. Maybe she'd kick *him*. "We can talk tomorrow."

"Should we really make a decision based on stolen evidence?" said Cal. To kick *her*, though, would be the dream. Nail her in the kneecap, grab the notebook while she lay gasping on the floor. "Evidence that's not even admissible in court?"

"Of all the trumped-up—" said Ben.

"Bedtime!" said Trevor.

The girls walked silently to their room. Cal went to brush her teeth. As soon as the door swung shut, Lillian darted to Cal's backpack. She knelt next to it and hastily pulled out T-shirts, jeans, running shorts. She snaked down a hand to feel for the spiral binding. She felt nothing.

Where did she *keep* it?

Lillian removed rolls of socks, stacks of cotton underwear. This backpack was bottomless. A mesh bag of tampons, a sports bra with gray seams. She felt around—and there! Pages! A spine! She jerked it out.

Emily of New Moon, by L. M. Montgomery.

A girl with ridiculous purple eyes gazed winsomely from the cover.

Lillian sank back. The door opened, and Cal gaped.

"Go ahead," said Lillian. "Think the worst of me."

Cal took a step toward her. Lillian didn't bother to stand. She was suddenly swamped by fatigue like a mudslide, fatigue that weighed down her guilty limbs. She was so tired it was hard to breathe.

"I don't even know what to say," said Cal.

"Yeah," said Lillian. "I don't either."

Cal, her hands shaking, began to repack her bag. Lillian hadn't brushed her teeth or washed her face or wrapped her hair, but she lay down. Sleep was so close she could taste it, that sweet void, sweet like cloud candy—no, that wasn't the name—*cotton* candy, that was it. How silly of her. Candy that melted into nothing as soon as you bit it. She was dropping off. She thought, All of Cal's clothing is soft, whisper-soft, even the jeans. It's all been washed a hundred times. She thought, Cal's like a baby. No stiff leather for her. No itchy lace.

CHAPTER FOURTEEN

It wasn't ideal, running with Matt, but Cal was desperate to run. The few times in Frankfurt she'd slept, truly slept, taken a dead fall into a gulch where she could lie unresponsive and unknowing until a dream or fear of a dream hooked behind her navel and jerked her upward, she had, each time, awoken with a childish disorientation—this pillow is not my pillow, this bed is not my bed!—that was, each time, succeeded by a full-hearted longing for home. For her mother, for her father. She couldn't run away, she knew, but maybe it would suffice to run.

She'd risk her heel. Descending stairs, she'd sometimes hear an echo of the pain, but it'd been fine, really. While Lillian slept, Cal slipped into her favorite purple shorts. She felt loose and limber in the brisk morning air. "Ready?" said Matt.

They began. Miss Clavel's thought rang through her head: *Something is not right.* She'd had a nightmare where she'd been running like the nun, pell-mell, tilting more precipitously with every step. Something was not right. What was she supposed to do with her shoulders? Her hips? Her feet slapped the pavement. Her arms felt stiff. Matt was a half step ahead, and she was breathing hard already. What if she couldn't keep up? He was a good runner, fluid, strong, his cadence high and his shoulders serene. What if she tripped? What if she collided with a cyclist?

Then, all at once, it was wonderful. It was like coming home. They reached the path by the river, and they ran in stride. Bridges arched ahead.

"What do you think we should do?" said Matt.

She'd known they'd talk about it. Running opened your mouth, broke down your walls, whether by the clear space or the clear time or the sheer physical pounding. That was why she'd have preferred to run alone. But she'd been doing fine until damn Lillian ruined everything. The other day, hanging out at the Städel, she'd thought, I'm okay with this trip. I'm more than okay. Trevor had made them all Museum Bingo cards. Ben refused to play. "I prefer to show a bit more respect for priceless works of art."

"I'm offering the winner a piggyback ride home," said Trevor. "Tempted yet?"

"Here we are at an art museum," groused Ben, "arguably the pinnacle of human civilization, and you're introducing Bingo—"

"Mutter all you want," said Trevor. "I, for one, have some things to find."

They wandered the galleries. Cal followed Ben. He was unstoppable once he started talking about art, but she liked it. "The Northern Renaissance painters moved from egg tempera to oils," he said, "allowing them to combine extraordinary realism with brilliant colors."

Trevor sidled up beside Cal. "I just got 'Tourist Taking Selfie with Masterpiece' and 'Bored Dad Napping in Guard's Chair,'" he whispered. "I'm so close."

"It only counts if you shout 'Bingo,'" Cal said.

"Don't encourage him," hissed Ben. Trevor disappeared into the modern section. Cal stared at the velvety oils of Jan van Eyck's *Lucca Madonna* as Ben explained how the baby already bore the typology of the Host. "But Mary's face," he said, "has been identified as a portrait of van Eyck's wife."

"What was her name?"

"Margaretha."

Cal peered at the Madonna with interest. The secular and the sacred, the human and the divine, all mixed up in this person, on this canvas. She slid her Bingo card from her pocket and tried not to let Ben see her cross off "Religiously Muddled Dutchman."

Trevor returned, looking triumphant. "'Someone Loudly Proclaiming, "That's Not Art, a Toddler Could Do That"': check! All I've got left is 'Unappealing Flemish Baby.' I'm going to shout 'Bingo' so loud they hear me in Berlin."

Cal and Lillian burst into laughter.

But that, thought Cal, was then. Now she hated Lillian all over again. Skyscrapers shone to the right of the river path. She said to Matt, "What do *I* think we should do? I think we should return Abend's papers."

Matt was silent.

"*She* should."

"I really wish we'd told Abend about Jesse," said Matt. "I feel bad about that. He never knew."

"Well, you could have done it." She herself had been waiting for someone else to speak up. She'd known she couldn't. She had never told anyone. Her mother had told Annie's mother, and it had spread in the swift, muted way of bad news, tilted heads and creased brows, lips drawn flat and sympathetic. How could she have spoken it aloud for the first time in a fast-food restaurant in Frankfurt, in a group whose defining characteristic was his absence? That was the basic flaw of this trip. In his lifetime, they never would have been together without him. How stupid she'd been these past few days to think that the trip might go well. To think that she and Lillian might have something in common.

She still couldn't believe that Lillian had ransacked her backpack for the *Juvenilia*. She hadn't known what to say. But during her fitful sleep she'd realized there was only one significant response: she'd hide the notebook even more securely. She'd ensure that Lillian would never read the *Juvenilia*. No one would.

"Lillian owes Abend an apology," Cal told Matt. Her heel jabbed her.

"It's a complicated situation," said Matt.

"It's not complicated. It's an issue of right and wrong." But did anyone else care about principles, about integrity? Ben, German dictionary in one hand and German grammar in the other, had hit the papers with such speed and force that he could have been slingshot. When he'd reported his findings, Cal had tried to muster the moral fortitude to leave, but she'd succumbed to curiosity. She was no better than the rest of them. *"Thea is sad,"* Ben read from his translation. *"She holds within herself a vast reservoir of sadness. She is ever seeking happiness, something to evaporate that reservoir, some sun fierce enough."* He looked up. "Quite a load of sentiment," he said. Cal and Matt and Trevor were sprawled around the room, listening to Ben's updates but not meeting his eyes. "Then again, Romanticism never died here. Friedrich and Schubert and Goethe, emotion and mysticism and hackneyed metaphor. Give me a stiff British upper lip any day." Nobody responded. Lillian stood by the windows, and despite herself, despite her righteous anger and her contempt, Cal thought, *There is someone sad. There is someone liquid with sadness.*

Now Matt asked Cal, "What do you think about Mittenwald?" The path swelled and then released them downhill.

Cal shrugged. Her shoulders were tight. She straightened her arms and shook them out. "Ben wants to go, Lillian wants to go. We're going."

"What do *you* think?"

"Abend said she didn't want him to look for her."

"But Jesse wanted us to find her."

"So I've heard," she said sharply. She became irritated by the rapport of their steps and breaths, and she changed her rhythm so it was off his. The river path ended. They entered a condo development. She hated this blind, pious resolution to respect Jesse's wishes, to waste time on someone like Thea, someone who couldn't stick around for her own kid—

"I know what you mean," said Matt. "As soon as someone says, 'Jesse wanted it,' all discussion is shut down."

"You're saying we *shouldn't* do what he wanted?" Her voice was shrill. As if in harmony, her heel grated: nails on a chalkboard, knives on a plate.

"It's complicated," Matt said again. "Do you want to turn around? How long's it been?"

"Thirty minutes."

"Four miles? You think we're doing 7:30s?"

It seemed faster. Matt took the lead on a narrow stretch

of sidewalk. He'd sweated through his shirt in a dark gray triangle, and the fabric clung to his upper back and fell gracefully over his shoulder blades. She shouldn't have snapped. Some people had an inner child; she had an inner bitch. It'd risen within her like a snake. She wasn't even consistent. Looking for Thea or not looking for Thea, obeying Jesse's wishes or flouting them: she had no idea where she stood. Why couldn't she be rational? Why couldn't she be *nice*? To Matt, of all people. This kind and sensitive boy, who, because he also happened to be white, attractive, rich, and straight (*was* he straight?), looked like someone to whom nothing bad had ever happened. What would it be like to have a dead best friend? Her grief was all in her head; the details of her life had not changed. But Matt's days were punched not by one hole but by tiny, incessant perforations. Every time he couldn't find Jesse in the hallways between classes. When he had no one's history homework to copy. When he was bored and had no one to text, when he couldn't recap his little sisters' fight because nobody else could tell them apart. When, in study hall, he got two sentences into writing him a note before he remembered. Did boys write notes? Jesse and Matt, Cal thought, had written notes.

"I wish . . . ," she said, and stopped.

"What?" said Matt.

She wished they'd talked in high school. She wished she hadn't lost those years. Those years: *they* would be worth coming to Europe to find. But she couldn't tell Matt. "I wish I'd seen him one last time," she said instead.

Matt waited until they were side by side. Her heel was stabbing her, but she couldn't stop running now. "The last few months," he said, "he was terrible. Complained constantly.

Stayed in bed." It was taking him a while to get the words out. They were running faster, although she wasn't sure who had sped up. "Not that I'm blaming him."

"No."

"Lillian would kill me for saying that." He was focused on the path ahead. "But she got terrible too. She's different. Stealing Abend's papers. She wouldn't have done that before."

Of course. Back to Lillian. Every time.

"All she did this year was sleep. Her mom started answering her phone. 'Sorry, Matt. She's asleep again.' I didn't even want to talk." He was breathless. He was speaking one word at a time. Subtly, Cal sped up. "I just wanted to know someone else was alive. She was always, always asleep."

"I wish I could sleep like that," said Cal.

"Bad dreams?"

"Sometimes. Or I'm worried I'll have bad dreams, so I can't fall asleep."

"Do you dream about him? About Jesse?"

Cal said, honestly, "I wish I did." How she wished it. One dream, that was all she asked. It would break her heart to wake up, but she was willing to find the world newly shattered if one more time she could see it whole. "I dream I'm looking for him." Again and again she found herself on some great plain: a vast dome of evening sky above her, smooth gray cobblestones at her feet. The crowd was immense and expectant. Were they waiting for something, or to go somewhere? No matter. He was there, and she needed to find him, but the crush was too great, and she woke up too soon.

Matt didn't respond. Why had she said anything at all? Now he was the one pushing the pace. Learn her secrets and outrun her, was that his plan? The pedestrian bridge, where they'd turn from the river to the city, was within sight. A half mile, maybe. Her legs churned in tandem with his. Every left step was agony, but the heel pain was more tolerable when the rest of her body was in pain as well. She made her strides one inch longer, and now she set their speed.

"We should probably go to Mittenwald," said Matt, and she couldn't stand that he'd said the whole sentence with one breath.

"Might as well," said Cal. "What else would we do, anyway?" It took effort to sound effortless. She muted her breathing as if she were leading the pack at a race, trying to hoodwink her opponents into believing she could cover any surge when in truth her lungs were ripped open and every step reverberated in torment and her brain was ravaged by civil war. To go on, to stop: no matter how long the first held the line, the second, inevitably, would triumph. Her hamstrings stretched, her knees drove forward, her calves grasped, her feet snatched every inch of pavement they could take.

Matt said, "Good point."

"We're stuck." She made her voice light and carefree. "Stuck together."

He laughed, a snorty exhalation. "It's pretty rough." They had a quarter mile to go. She hated that he could make her feel like this. "Race you to the bridge," he said.

CHAPTER FIFTEEN

"I wasn't made for speed limits," sang Trevor to a tune of his own devising. Nobody was listening to him, but he considered it his sworn duty to liven up the car. It was a bleak morning. The sky looked as though the world had ducked under a gray tarp and refused to come out. *"Baby, I wasn't born for rules."* But the Autobahn was paradise, and Trevor had stumbled in. Imagine! A road that was straight and flat and perfectly groomed, a government that trusted you to go as fast as you wanted to go! Which, this morning, was PDQ, as his grandfather used to say. Pretty damn quick. "Freedom!" he cried. "How do you say 'freedom' in German, Ben?"

Ben, who had rigged up a library carrel in the passenger seat, ignored him. It didn't bother Trevor. Nothing could bother him, not now, now that they were on the road. He hadn't felt like himself in Frankfurt. He'd brooded. Even the Euro Cup had become a source of agitation. Watching Germany lose to Italy last night, watching Balotelli cavort after his first goal and strike a shirtless pose after his second, Trevor had—too late—recognized his anxiety for what it was. He had meant to remain a dabbler, a tourist of passions. But when the second half ended, when the four minutes of stoppage time were decreed, he'd had to step out of the pub. He couldn't deal with desperate hope. A handball by Balzaretti, a goal by Özil. It was brutal, hope. Trevor shaded his face and swallowed fiercely. The clock ran out. The Germans wandered the empty pitch.

He accelerated and swerved left to overtake a lumbering VW. He felt freer with every eastbound minute, with every kilometer he put between himself and Grinnell, Iowa, where his roommate and business partner, Scott, was blithely ruining both of their lives. Trevor wished the Internet were not so pervasive. The World Wide Web: what a ghastly idea. Why hadn't someone realized there was nothing cool about ubiquity, that it was actually downright horrifying that no matter how far away you were, how fast you were going, your phone could still ding its freaking ding whenever you chanced upon an area of unlocked wi-fi? Trevor wanted to ditch Scott, ditch Plagueslist, forget the whole thing.

"You're being tailgated," said Cal.

He tucked back into the right lane. An Audi blew past. Ben, whose mental capacities deserted him when it came to arithmetic, craned over. "One-eighty, Trevor?"

"*Kilometers,* Ben," the rest of them said.

Trevor grinned. "I'd be happy to drive the whole way."

He had almost chucked his phone in the river. He would have if everyone weren't so dependent on it. "Can I check the bank account?" Matt kept asking.

"And I need to email Mom," said Cal.

"Copy mine, would you?" said Ben. "All she needs to know is that we're alive."

Trevor would take back the phone with foreboding. He'd heard the chiming of new email. Against his better judgment, his thumbs would tap their way to his in-box, that cabinet of horrors.

Scott. Scott was out of control. He'd panicked about their finances, at last, and he kept sending distressed emails about shutting down the site, cutting their losses. But twenty minutes later, he'd write, *Scratch that.* He'd discovered the solution to all their problems: a new banner, a new webhost, a new advertising scheme. In fact, he'd already hired someone to help. Trevor only skimmed the emails, but he did know that if their traffic didn't increase a thousandfold by the end of the summer, Plagueslist was kaput. He'd be in serious debt.

Oh, well. What had bugged him in Frankfurt now assumed its proper position: it'd work out, it'd all work out. Meanwhile, these German town names were hilarious. "Cal," said Matt, "let's visit Bad Kissingen."

"Not in a crowded car, please," said Trevor. He didn't need the rearview mirror to know Cal was blushing.

"A joke!" she said.

"Not a very funny one," grouched Ben. "*Bad* means 'bath.'"

"Ben, does your map even show Bad Kissingen?" Trevor said innocently. He could barely believe that postcard rigmarole. When he'd come down to breakfast yesterday, Ben was already hunched at a table, scribbling away. "Another one!" whooped Trevor.

Ben toppled his pile of books in his haste to hide the postcard. "It's just an update!" He opened the book that had been with Abend's papers, Goethe's *Italienische Reise.* "I've been translating all morning. I was taking a brief break."

"May I give a word of advice?"

"I suppose."

"If you want to get in that girl's pants, postcards are not going to pull down the zipper."

"This has nothing to do with pants!"

"Whatever you say, chief."

When Trevor returned from the buffet, Ben said, "Why do you think Abend would have kept this book with his papers?"

"No clue." Trevor took a bite. "This cereal makes me home-sick."

"The *Italian Journey.* I'm sure it's a lovely travelogue—"

"It's Corn Flakey, but it's not Corn Flakes—"

"And Goethe is Frankfurt's hometown hero—"

"The cruel Uncornflake, if you will—"

"But what does it have to do with Thea? Did she go to Italy? Is it so obvious?"

Trevor grabbed the book and flipped to the flyleaf. "Maybe that's why?"

Ben nearly fell out of his chair. "I assumed it had to do with the *text!*"

Smugly, Trevor handed the book back to Ben. It was inscribed.

"*Meinem lieben Joachim,*" read Ben. "'To my dear Joachim.' *Et in Arcadia ego.* Goethe's epigraph for the book. 'Even in Arcadia, there am I.'"

"I who?" said Trevor.

"You know," said Ben. "Death."

Lillian, wearing suspenders and jean shorts and indigo tights, slammed herself into a chair. "Hey."

"Oh. Him. Top of the morning."

"*Deine Thea*," read Ben, angling the book toward Lillian. "'Your Thea.'"

"Her handwriting." With her index finger, Lillian traced the letters of Thea's name. "I wish Jesse could see this." As abruptly as she'd sat, she stood. She filled a glass with water and drank it at the buffet, her back toward them.

"Well," said Trevor into the silence, "I'm taking this opportunity to test-drive German Cocoa Puffs. You want anything?"

"Can't," said Ben, motioning to his throat. Trevor got him some orange juice anyway.

"So we're agreed?" said Lillian. "Mittenwald?"

"*I'm* agreed," said Ben.

"Trevor?"

"Let's talk once Cal and Matt get back from their run."

Lillian fluttered her eyelids. "We've got a majority right here. Let's make the call and get to work on the logistics."

"Excellent point," said Ben. "We'll need a place to stay, and it's peak tourist season. Trevor? Your vote?"

He was getting the gimlet eye from both sides. Go ahead, he wanted to say. I'm cool with that. Whatever you want.

He stirred his cereal.

"Trevor?" said Ben.

"Why can't breakfast cereal be the same?" he said. "One world, one Cocoa Puff. Am I asking too much?"

"Cal and Matt don't even want to find her," Lillian told Ben.

"It's not that I oppose cultural diversity. Hardly. But—just this once—can't we all get along?"

Lillian smacked the back of her earring, a large gold hoop, and it ricocheted forward. "*You* know how long Cal waited to tell us that she'd been in Frankfurt."

"Look," said Trevor. "What are we going to do if we *find* Thea?"

Lillian pierced him with her stare.

"Are we going to demand to know why she left?" said Trevor. "Do we really think she'll have an answer?"

She kept staring.

"She's the goal," Trevor said, "but what's the point?"

The door to the breakfast room opened. "Cal!" said Trevor. The nick of time. "Matt!" The tension had been nearly un-bearable. He would have buckled within seconds. "How was the run?"

"Your sister is crazy fast," said Matt.

Cal, glowering, had gone right for the espresso machine.

"Do you even *care* about what Jesse wanted?" Lillian asked Trevor.

Matt coughed. He was soaked in sweat. "Cal and I," he said, "we're thinking Mittenwald."

Trevor got a bowl of fake Rice Krispies while they worked out the details. His question had been disregarded, which, he realized gratefully, meant that he could disregard it too. It didn't matter what he thought, which meant he didn't need to figure out what he thought. He would drive the car. He would raise morale. He took a bite, chewed, appraised. Finally. The Rice Krispies were exactly as they should be, exactly as they'd always been.

In the afternoon, the beltways and traffic around Munich suddenly gave way to the Alps. "Is everyone still up for Benediktbeuern?" asked Ben.

"No idea what you're talking about, mate," said Trevor, "but I'm up for it."

"The monastery. It's in the Goethe."

Trevor crept along the back roads toward Benediktbeuern. Obeying a speed limit was nearly intolerable. They parked. As they ranged down the path, he picked up a handful of gravel and flung pebbles, one by one, off the back of Cal's Aircast. Plink. Plink.

"Living on the edge," Matt told him.

"Good thing my aim is flawless." Plink.

But he let his fingers go limp, the stones curl to the ground, when the path opened up. They were on a plain that was encircled by the craggy ridges of the Alps. Ben strode toward the sprawling white abbey, hoping to get into the library. Trevor and the others walked to the cemetery. Nobody spoke. The stones were kempt and upright, although the dates were long since past. Trevor kept looking at the mountains. They surprised him every time. Their irregularity, their austere mass, the bent and weather-grayed strata, the tree line, the snow line: he could not look at them long enough. Lillian and Matt went to the garden beyond the cemetery. Cal, all her weight on her right leg, studied the quatrefoil windows of the abbey. Trevor put his arm around her. She turned her face into his shoulder and wept.

An Excerpt from
THE JUVENILIA OF JESSE T. SERRANO

I'm starting to hate writing the *Juvenilia*, Cal. I wish you could see the way it was in my head before I started. It was a gossamer confection, a silk-spun dream of a notebook. I'd immortalize myself in these stories. Flesh would become word.

Then I picked up a pen.

I hadn't done five words before I realized it's not possible to write down what it's like to be me. It is too complicated; there are too many details. You know that, because it's the same with you. But when you read this, there won't be someone around to remind you, and that's why I have to give you this solemn charge: don't think this is all I was. I don't want a mythology. I don't want to live in this spiral binding. And I know I don't have much of a choice.

Two years ago, when Trevor visited for Memorial Day weekend, Arnold suggested a hike. We agreed before he dropped the real plan: we'd drive to Yosemite on Saturday, hike thirteen miles from Tuolumne Meadows to Virginia Canyon, camp, and hike back Sunday. "Sure," said Trevor.

When Arnold was out of earshot, I said, "You're really okay with this?"

"I love camping," said Trevor. "There's a secret ingredient that makes camping fun."

Ben, who had come over for dinner, groaned. "You're the clichéd college freshman."

"Alcohol," Trevor told me.

We left at four. Trevor and I slept the entire drive. When we began to hike, we saw flat green meadows that suddenly gave way to snowy mountains, streams whose water padded up onto smooth, sandlike rocks, pines so straight and tall they could have been scaffolding for a cathedral. I stopped being cross with Arnold two miles in, when he dispensed handfuls of his homemade trail mix. Pistachios and dark chocolate chips, raw almonds and Michigan cherries and crystallized ginger: Arnold loves good food.

He went ahead. "Trev," I said, "will you help me with something?"

"Anything," he said casually.

"How do you make people like you?"

"You don't."

"But everyone likes *you*."

"You're asking for the secret to my universal popularity? Impossible. If I told you, I'd have to kill you, and then nobody would like me."

"Say there's a particular person—"

"Ah!" Trevor turned with an expression of unfettered glee. "I see right through you, Jesse T. Serrano."

"What?" I said, trying to cover up.

"You're in love."

"I am not!"

"You are. Deeply. Passionately. Obviously."

"I am *not*."

"What's twenty-six minus two?" said Trevor.

"Twenty-four," I said suspiciously.

"Correct. Which happens to be the number of miles that remain for me to extract this story from you."

"I'll only tell you if you help. Because I think she abhors me."

"No way."

"It's a definite possibility."

"Hmm." Trevor turned again, and the light shone right through his eyes. Have you noticed that, Cal? How his eyes are like sea glass, that diffused pale green, and they turn to stained-glass windows in the sun? "We'll see what we can do."

I can never decide whether I love or hate how much backpacking makes you appreciate things like sitting down, and taking off your boots, and eating. On the one hand, the euphoria is real: there is truly no greater feeling than perching on a rock and taking that first bite of rehydrated chili. On the other, you kind of suspect it's putting one over on you.

The moon was a sliver, a fingernail's fine indentation. Outside the circle of firelight, it was ink-dark. "Time for my famous hot toddies," said Trevor. He stirred milk powder and cocoa into boiling water, and when Arnold ducked into the tent to look for his sweater, Trevor dumped in whiskey.

"Won't he be able to taste it?" I said.

"Too late now," said Trevor.

"Rats," said Arnold. "I must have left my sweater in the car."

"This'll warm you up," said Trevor.

Disgruntled, Arnold downed his entire cup in one go. "Thanks, Trev."

"Want some more?" Trevor winked at me.

"Oh, why not?" Arnold said. This time he sipped. "Is there something *in* this?"

"A tiny bit," said Trevor. "It's a Grinnell tradition."

"I should hope it wasn't much. Jesse's underage." He sipped again. "In fact, you're underage yourself."

I was close enough to the fire that my skin felt stretched over my face, but it was a cozy discomfort, like being tucked into bed too tightly. The sky was ringed with the dark silhouettes of the pines, a gauzy gird of blackness around the stars. I drank slowly. Matt and I had recently had an unpleasant run-in with his father's liquor cabinet, and I'd decided that I got enough of light-headedness and nausea from the Hole.

"Uncle Arnold," said Trevor, "how'd you get into outdoorsy stuff?"

I'd never wondered, but it was a good question. Arnold didn't like dirt. He was fastidious: his white china, his gourmet food, the intricate golds and blues of Madonna paintings.

"Years ago," he said, "I had a friend who loved hiking—"

"Wait," said Trevor. "A friend, or a *friend*? Are you talking about Thea?"

"Yes, Thea," said Arnold, as if he hadn't noticed the breach of propriety or tradition or whatever it was that made us never mention her name. I held still.

"Want some more hot chocolate?" said Trevor.

He told me later he'd been curious. He'd wondered what

would happen if he got Arnold drunk, so he did. He poured the rest of the saucepan into Arnold's outstretched cup, and mixed more.

"She worked in your department?"

"She was my colleague's research assistant, my first year at Berkeley."

"So how'd you get things going?" He waggled his eyebrows at me. "Any tips for kick-starting a successful romance?"

"Well. I don't know about *successful*." Arnold laughed. "It was pure chance. She invited the whole department on a Memorial Day hike. I figured I'd go. Why not?"

Everyone else flaked at the last minute. When Arnold got to the trailhead, Thea was leaning on her car. "You don't have to come," she said. "I hike alone all the time."

But Arnold had borrowed boots from a neighbor. He'd made trail mix. He hadn't been in the woods since he was a kid, and even from the parking lot he could see how the shanks of sunlight alternated with the trees. "I'll still go," he said. "If you don't mind."

"Not at all."

They started. Walking behind her, Arnold kept staring at her braid. He would turn to the sunlight, to the sunburnt grasses and the leaves strewn on the path, but all the yellows drew him back to her hair. It was the color of bread.

When the single track widened, they walked side by side. "She had the compass she'd bought during her year abroad," he told us. "She couldn't stop using it. She checked our direction every few minutes. I think that's what did me in. She was acting the cosmopolitan, the scholar. We were discussing her PhD applications. She wanted to study Michelangelo's three *Pietàs*, she said. 'I'd like to investigate his artistic and theological progression.' Yet there she was, enamored of a compass. She was so young." He sighed. "I was young too. That's the strangest thing about growing up, I think. Realizing how young you used to be. You were always young." The campfire gave his eyes and forehead a sheen. He wasn't right, I thought. You're always young in the same way you're always old: it's relative, it's born of the way we insist on imagining time as a river, not a tree. At any given moment you're younger than you'll ever be, yes, but you're also older than you've ever been.

"I decided I was in love with her," said Arnold. "And even now, even after everything that happened, I cannot regret that decision."

I squirmed.

"Hand me my wallet, would you?"

He showed us a folded snapshot. A glowing Thea held me. She was beautiful, and, Cal, he *was* right: she was so, so young.

Then I thought I understood why he liked hiking. He liked to remember that day, that first day, a day as golden as my mother's hair. Look into the sun and squint, so your lashes smear the light all over. It's a Byzantine mosaic; it's dust through the amber spyglass. There was no afterward once he had seen that. There was no possibility, I thought, that he could ever look away.

"Are you ready for the secret?" Trevor asked. "Nobody cares how smart you are. Nobody cares whether you're funny or cool or how good your hair is. Even mine, which, I must say, is remarkably good."

We were hiking back.

"Think about him and Thea," said Trevor, lowering his voice. "Do you think she was attracted to his fashion sense? To his dance moves? Nope. She liked him because he's really, really nice."

"That's the secret?"

"In the long run, people just want you to be nice." He reached over and rubbed my hair. He looked a bit embarrassed. "That's kind of my life philosophy, anyway."

Lill's birthday, the Tuesday after Memorial Day, was the day of our final away match for quiz bowl. I skipped my last class and met Trevor in the lot where the school parked its minibuses. "You've got to imagine what she'd most like for her birthday," he had said on the hike.

"World dominion."

"Failing that."

"Um—"

"You can't go wrong with a party bus." Trevor nodded sagely. "That's my other life philosophy."

We devoted Memorial Day to preparations. "What should the banner say?" said Trevor, on his knees on the kitchen floor, a paintbrush poised over an unfurled length of butcher paper.

"'Happy Birthday, Nemesis.'"

"You call her Nemesis?"

"We get competitive about the history questions," I explained. "And all the other questions."

Trevor shook his head. He filled out the *H* in lurid stripes of green and orange. "Nemesis?" He'd bankrolled the whole endeavor, going crazy at the art-supply store. "You might want to rethink that."

We put party hats on the bus seats. We hung garlands. The

crowning touch was a piñata that we'd made of papier-mâché. When Arnold wished us good night, we were just beginning. He eyed the mountainous heap of newspaper strips. I'd cut up the entire Sunday *New York Times*. "Is that this week's?"

"I thought that since today's Monday—"

"For future reference," he said, sighing, "I stretch the Sunday through the whole week." He paused at the threshold. Trevor, gripping a large balloon between his teeth, was adding flour to the paste while I kneaded it in, both hands wrist-deep. A ghostly cloud rose from the bowl and misted all three of us with a thin scrim of flour. The Annunciation postcards calmly looked on.

"Quite a production," said Arnold.

Trevor nodded vehemently, the balloon bounding up and down like a second head.

"You've spent all day on this."

"One of my teammates," I said. "A friend."

A strangled noise escaped Trevor.

"I'm sure she deserves every minute," said Arnold.

At midnight, Trevor surveyed our handiwork. "What a lovely gray blob."

I rested my chin on the table. "Is this even going to work?"

"The night is young, dude! Don't lose heart! What's her favorite animal?"

"I don't know. But once we had an argument about whether skunks deserved all the bad press. She was pro-skunk. Very pro-skunk."

"A skunk it is. We're supposed to let it dry before we paint it, but time and tide and sixteenth birthdays wait for no man." Trevor prodded the oozing piñata. "I'm sure it'll be fine."

"Maybe we should put it in the oven," I said.

"Brilliant man."

"What temperature?"

"I don't know, 350? That's what you do for brownies."

I wasn't sure I followed his logic, but I set the dial while he put the soggy gray mass in a casserole pan. We waited while it baked. "It'd be a shame if this extra papier-mâché went to waste," mused Trevor. "What do you say to a papier-mâché leg?"

I leapt away. "Papier-mâché your own leg!"

Trevor roamed the kitchen. He had dried bits of flour-water paste all over his face, and a strip of newspaper fluttered from his hair. I had another vision, another glimpse through the golden filter: how young Trevor was, what a gift this time was. It wasn't as much time as I wanted, but when you're with a guy like Trevor, when you're in your Annunciation kitchen late at night, a papier-mâché skunk in the oven, how much time would ever be enough?

"What would your dad do if we papier-mâchéed the whole kitchen?"

"Trevor! No!"

"Can you *imagine*?" His eyes were starry. "The world's most legendary prank. Not just the walls, not just the furniture, but, like, *every spoon*."

"I think the piñata's probably done cooking." This was partly to divert him and partly because I'd gotten a whiff of something acrid, a smell I'd never encountered but assumed was that of a charred Sunday *New York Times*.

Trevor removed it with a flourish. "Now, what does a skunk look like?"

We hit some slight bumps in the course of painting, but I thought it looked pretty good once we got it hung in the center of the bus's aisle. "She better like me after this," I said.

"Remember," said Trevor, "you're doing this out of the goodness of your heart. It's not transactional. Keep faking that until it's real." He jogged out to the car. "One more touch," he said, climbing onto the bus with a box behind his back. "Ta-*da*!"

It was a cake, a cake from Berkeley's swankiest bakery. *For Lill*, it said. "If you keep calling her Nemesis, she'll never come round."

This was turning into the best birthday ever, and it wasn't even mine. "Trevor—"

"I don't get credit for this one. It wasn't even my idea. I spent all my money on paint, anyway."

The last bell rang.

"Well," said Trevor, handing me the cake, "have fun."

The piñata was still soggy. When Lill hit it, it collapsed with a sort of squelching noise. She'd teared up when she'd stepped onto the bus. Or something happened: her face had broken open, her eyes had gone wide. "Is that a skunk or an anthropomorphic soccer ball?" she'd said, giving her sheet of hair a scornful flip. Then she looked more like herself.

And she said yes. Maybe it was the party bus, maybe it was the good feelings after our victory, during which she got significantly more history questions than I did, but I contravened Trevor's advice—"Don't you dare say a thing today; it'll be like you think she owes you"—and in the cinder-blocked hallway of MacDonald Prep, I asked her. "Are you *serious*?" she said. "Go out with *you*?" She shrugged. "I guess. Sure."

But on the bus ride back, when everyone was tired and quiet, I noticed she kept smiling out the window.

"Thanks for the cake," I told my dad when I got home. I'd stopped at the bookstore, and I tossed him a bag. That evening, once we'd dropped Trevor at the airport, I flipped through my history textbook on the couch while Arnold rustled behind his fresh Sunday *Times,* all the sections he'd been saving for the week.

CHAPTER SIXTEEN

Cal had a monstrous headache, a Monday-morning headache that had crept into the pension's breakfast room, eyed her, and pounced. The others filled their plates at the buffet, but she could barely move.

"*Möchten Sie ein Ei?*" said the woman who ran the pension.

Cal nodded, although she could have been agreeing to anything: a bowl of sardines, her own execution. She was served a single soft-boiled egg upon a pedestal. She closed her eyes and smelled coffee: black, bitter, how she liked it. "Drink up," said Matt. "It'll make you feel better."

She sighed in thanks. Now she needed time, a few minutes for the caffeine and the cunning egg dish to tackle the headache and remove it from the premises. But Ben officiously shuffled his papers. He licked the nib of his fountain pen and wrote the date at the top of his yellow legal pad. "Today," he said, "we'll continue to canvass Mittenwald." They'd had no luck on Saturday, and yesterday they'd given up when they'd realized all the natives were attending Mass, eating Sunday dinners, taking Sunday naps.

Trevor took a large bite of cereal. "Snap, crackle, pop," he said. "Can't wait."

Cal rested her head on her hand. Ben said, "I know it's drudgery, but she has family here. Someone will recognize her." He opened Abend's notes, which he had festooned with parti-color Post-its, and cleared his throat. "*She knows these mountains well. She grew up in the States, in Santa Fe, but spent summers here in Bavaria with her mother's big German Catholic family. 'I would like to see my family,' she said, 'but I'd rather see you—'*"

Cal couldn't take it. "Don't you feel like a voyeur? Using his personal papers as evidence?" Ben fancied himself a modern-day Hardy Boy, she thought, or perhaps a Sherlock, surrounded by a team of trusty though dull-witted Watsons. "We should have given them back."

"Come on, Cal," said Trevor, giving her ponytail a conciliatory tug. She winced. "It's much better that he thinks they were lost at the restaurant."

"I can't believe I'm a party to theft," she said.

"Girl," said Lillian, "you're about as far from a party as it gets."

Trevor laughed. Cal smarted. "Her family nickname is the Grinch," Trevor said. Now Lillian and Matt were both laughing.

"It's not!" said Cal. "It's *not*. It's just this game we used to play." Jesse was her dog, Max. Together they would throw all the toys in the house into their laundry-basket sleigh and traipse around glowering until Trevor, as Cindy Lou Who, convinced them to reform.

"Remember when Mom officially banned the Grinch game?" he said.

"It made a giant mess."

"And she was sick of hearing *Fah who foraze! Dah who doraze!* in July."

"God," said Lillian. "Your poor mother."

Cal downed the dregs of her coffee to avoid seeing Lillian's face. Everything she said had an edge, a subtle blade that went over the boys' heads and hit Cal squarely in the chest. At least they no longer shared a bed; the pension room had six bunks, dormitory-style. Cal was counting down toward Friday, when their reservation ended. They had to return the rental car on Saturday morning at the Innsbruck airport. Then, she hoped, they could fly home.

The pension was on the outskirts of town, where the railroad tracks bordered the foothills of the ridge. "Mittenwald ho!" cried Ben. The road was not meant for foot traffic, but he insisted they walk. "They'd gouge us on parking."

A truck careered around a bend. They dove into the underbrush.

"I too prefer death to parking fees," said Lillian.

Ben brushed twigs from his hair. "We're hardly in mortal peril."

"From now on," said Trevor grimly, "we drive."

Once they reached Mittenwald's business district, Ben and Lillian took the lead. "Have you seen this woman?" they asked. "Her mother? Her family?" As the shopkeepers pursed their lips and studied the photographs, Cal could see the whole dreary path stretching before them. The sun would beat down, the mountains would tower. They would have no success. The shopkeepers pitied them, she knew, these young

Americans who thought the world was small and pliable. "I don't *think* I've seen her," they would say. "But from now on, I will look."

She hung back. "How's the heel?" said Matt.

"Oh, fine." It wasn't fine. Every few minutes, she'd land wonkily on the cobblestones and feel a thrill of pain.

It was difficult to resume after lunch. *"Karibu Ausrüstung,"* Ben read from a white stucco building. "Something Equipment."

"'Caribou,' perchance?" said Trevor.

Ben hastily thumbed his pocket dictionary. "Wait a sec—"

"Hold, please, for the official translation."

"Caribou," said Ben.

"I should take German," said Trevor. "I'm a natural."

On the exterior walls were the frescoes they'd seen throughout the *Altstadt,* the ones Ben called *Luftmalerei.* They showed hardy, outdoorsy Germans doing hardy, outdoorsy things: hiking, climbing, hunting, fishing. "We should go on a hike," said Trevor, gazing not at the building but at the mountain ridge beyond.

The door opened. They leapt aside. Two young men carried out a canoe, followed by a crew with life vests and paddles and a squat wooden box.

"Let's get this over with," said Lillian.

From the wall behind the counter, a moose head leered at them. "May I help you?" said a woman with thickly muscled arms. Bristling, Ben replied in German. "Let me see," she said. "Beautiful, but I do not know her. Mitzi? Kaspar?"

Mitzi and Kaspar joined her, but Cal could already tell it was fruitless. Recognition happened in a flash. Studying and squinting were the hallmarks of pity.

"But we haven't lived here long," said Kaspar. "We're from Berlin."

"Is anyone here a local?"

"Andreas, yes. But he's just left on a trip." Kaspar suddenly remembered his purpose. "Karibu offers guided trips into the mountains. Hikes, climbs—"

A tall man loped into the store. "Andreas!" Mitzi called.

Up close, Cal could see that Andreas's beard was uneven, lush only on his chin. He grabbed another paddle. "I have to go—"

"Quickly," said Mitzi. "Show him."

He peered at the photographs. He leaned the paddle against the counter. "Do you know who this is?"

"That's *our* question!" said Trevor.

"Of course I do," he said. "She's my mother's cousin."

"Andreas!" yelled someone from outside the store. "*Sofort!*"

"We return Thursday. Meet me here at five-thirty. Yes?" They watched him jog out. When he opened the door, the gusting sunlight illuminated the dust in the air, and the spilling breeze made it whirl.

That evening, they lolled in the pension room. Ben propped himself on a stack of pillows to continue translating Goethe's *Italienische Reise*. Every so often he'd let loose a slew of German and then say, "Fascinating!"

Trevor produced a deck of cards. He and Cal and Matt sat on the floor to play rummy.

"Lillian?" said Matt. "You want to join?"

"Nope." She was in her top bunk.

"Then you want to DJ?" He tossed her his iPod, and to

Cal's surprise, she began to scroll through the songs. The air was celebratory. Cal wouldn't have expected herself to be so cheered by the lead, but she supposed she'd always been susceptible to the charms of obedience. No matter what she thought about Thea, it was a relief to do what she was told.

"And two full days off!" said Trevor. "Amazing!" He scooped up the whole long discard pile just to lay down three twos. "I'm bold," he said when Cal hooted at him. "I'm gutsy. It'll pay off in the end."

They sat in a tight cross-legged circle. There wasn't much room, and Cal's knee bumped Matt's for a while before lodging there permanently. "I feel like a little kid," she said. She should sit on the floor and play games more often.

"Didn't you and Jesse always play rummy?" said Trevor.

"For years." And when it wasn't rummy it was some other game. As long as there was a winner and a loser. They raced to take showers and unload their halves of the dishwasher. They had their parents rate their sand castles like figure-skating routines. One whole family vacation Jesse had carried a bundle of pick-up sticks in his pocket for fear they'd be caught somewhere with no contest. They both hungered to win even though winning was unimportant. The game mattered only because of the end, but the end was nothing compared to the game. It was a paradox she could not have explained to anyone but Jesse, who had understood, who had been born to it.

She played four aces and slapped down her last discard. "I'm out."

Trevor groaned. He had half the deck in his hand. "Zero points for me."

"Nice try. You've got to go into negatives."

Matt whistled. "You take your rummy seriously."

Cal noted the score on the Post-it she'd taken from Ben's annotation stash.

"Ben, distract me from this drubbing," said Trevor. "How's that *Italian Rice*?" They'd all started mistranslating the title to annoy him. "Unearthing any clues?"

"I've just discovered that Goethe went from Frankfurt to Mittenwald."

"And?"

"*And!*" sputtered Ben. "So did we! Unbeknownst to our very selves, we followed his path!" Peeved, he slammed the book shut. He riffled through his folder of maps.

"Are you ever going to tell us what those places are?" said Cal.

"Well," said Ben, "I'd be glad to, but since I've recently heard I can be a *bore* with *details*—"

"Dude," said Trevor, "you're taking that way too personally—"

"And given how much time I've spent studying the maps, to no avail, I highly doubt anyone else will be able to shed any light—"

"That was just a small tip for your social life."

"But if you insist. Mexico City. Rome. Akita, Japan." He was listing them from memory. "KwaZulu-Natal, South Africa. Ephesus. Lourdes—"

There was a rustle and a thud. Lillian had leapt down from the top bunk. "Seriously? No wonder he never let me look at his stupid map collection. I'd have seen through him in an instant."

"What?" said Ben. "Are we supposed to go to all those places?"

"Hold up." Lillian was pacing. "I bet I can name the others. Fátima. Medjugorje. Zaragoza. Walsingham."

"How are you doing this? I'd never heard of Walsingham."

"Are you Catholic?" she said.

"No, but—"

"Yes or no. Were you taught by nuns?"

"No, but—"

"*No but* is neither yes nor no. Were you raised by wannabe nuns?"

"No."

"Look, he's learning. Is there a twee little statue of Mary in your front yard?"

"No."

"Do the coffee-table books in your living room all feature great shrines to the Virgin?"

"No."

"Is Jaroslav Pelikan your grandmother's personal hero?"

"I don't even know who—"

"I rest my case."

"So they're places—"

"Where Mary's appeared. Or shrines, sites of icons, stuff like that. I can't believe you didn't notice. Why didn't you google them?"

"Please. How tawdry. And with the smaller villages, the maps encompass the surrounding region as well. It's hard to tell what's featured."

"Of course." Lillian crashed onto a bed. "Well. This tells us nothing. Just more evidence he's an idiot."

"He's not an idiot," Cal said sharply. Trevor put a soothing hand on her knee.

"Look, I'm not impugning your family's honor, no need to get all riled up. The fact is, he's an idiot. You know that thing he has about Mary."

"What thing?" said Cal.

"He secretly believes Thea is Mary. Not really. But sort of. He can't untangle them. The apartment covered with her face, the woman his dad loves—"

"You're right," said Ben. He sounded impressed. "You're absolutely right. Did he tell you that?"

"You think *he* knew?"

Cal won the rummy game. She allowed herself the tiniest and most interior of smirks. She had also won when she and Matt had raced to the bridge. He had slammed into the pier a half step behind and she'd put her hands on her knees, feeling worse than any workout had ever made her feel, any race. Her heartbeat rang dully in her ears.

"Nice," he said.

Once she could speak, she said, "You let me win."

"I did not!"

"You did." She'd flounced and turned back to the hostel. She couldn't draw a deep breath without wanting to cough out her lungs.

But tonight was different. She swept up the cards, laughing at Trevor's spasms of woe. "Have I ever beaten you in a card game?" he moaned.

"Maybe War." Cal handed him the deck. "Maybe once."

She fell asleep quickly. She was back on the plain, her heel aching on the cobblestones, the sky a deep, crepuscular blue. She caught a glimpse of stark white column through the crowd but the gap soon closed. The crowd was as great as before. They chattered and swarmed in silk and purple, velvet and black. Whatever they were awaiting, they had dressed for it, dressed to the nines. She felt a terrible urgency. She touched the arm of the woman closest to her. "Have you seen him?" The woman frowned, shook her head, turned away. "Have you seen him?" Nobody would pay attention to her. "Where is he? Do you know where he is?" The plain was endless.

Awake, she pulled the sheets tight around her neck and slowed her breaths to match the breaths of the others. It was no use. She tiptoed down the ladder and slid open the door to the balcony. It faced the ridge, which loomed black.

"Hey," said Lillian.

Cal jumped.

"You can come out."

"Sorry—I didn't know you were—I'll just—" She took a step back, but Lillian gestured to the spot beside her on the iron-filigree bench. Cal didn't know how she could refuse. She self-consciously smoothed her hair. The elastic of her shorts was shot, and she gave them a yank. Lillian wore a mod-style shift, satin or something like it, embroidered down one side with spidery vines and flowers. Yes, Cal thought, it's official. Lillian's pajamas are chicer than my prom dress. She glanced down at her T-shirt and grimaced: FUTURE ENGINEERS OF AMERICA CITYWIDE MARBLE RACE. She was starting at a loss.

But Lillian didn't dole out her usual once-over, the flick from head to toe that said, Oh, I have noticed your clothing, and out of the goodness of my heart I will spare you my feedback. Instead, she faced the mountains. "You have to stay out until your eyes get used to the dark."

"How long have you been out here?"

"You won't believe how many colors *gray* can mean."

"You couldn't sleep?"

"Of all people, you should know," said Lillian, and there was the edge again, "I can always, always sleep."

"So why are you out here?" It sounded like an accusation. Cal tried again. "You figured the mountains were worth it?"

Lillian didn't answer. That was enough to send Cal back to her dream, to the crush of people ignoring her questions on the cobblestoned plain. The crowd was infinite and infinity was dreadful. It hit her, for a moment, what *never* meant, a full-body slam of a realization that even in time's endless tromp there would not come a point when she would see him again. She drew her knees up to her chest. Her eyes were full and she tried hard not to let them spill over.

"I woke up," said Lillian. "And I thought, Maybe I'll try feeling some feelings."

"What a novel concept," snapped Cal, swiping at her eyes. "Don't let *me* interrupt."

"Oh, you're quite helpful," Lillian shot back. "You're salt to my wound."

Cal fumbled for a retort. "I haven't even told anyone how you searched my backpack."

"How vastly noble."

"You think they'd like you if they knew that?"

Lillian guffawed. "You think I care whether they *like* me? I'm doing what I want to do. What I have to do. Screw them. You'd rather not admit it, Cal, but you and I, we've got something in common. We don't care whether anyone likes us. We're supposed to care, right? Because we're girls, because we're women. But we don't give a single solitary shit."

"*I* do."

"You do not. If you cared, you'd show us Jesse's freaking

notebook. And I hate that you won't, and I'm going to fight you every step of the way, and if these enormous mountains hadn't put me in my place, I'd never have told you this—but I respect you for it. You know what we are, Cal?"

Cal found herself suppressing a smile. "What?"

"Bitches."

"*You,* maybe—"

"Bitches with hearts of *stone,*" said Lillian with satisfaction.

"We've got feelings. Lots of feelings."

"Well. Okay. Just plain bitches."

Cal giggled. She couldn't help it. Lillian, her chin jutting out, had been facing the gray crags of the Alps, but she turned and caught Cal's eye, and they collapsed into laughter. They couldn't stop.

"This isn't funny," Cal managed in a lull.

"Nope," said Lillian.

This set them off again. Cal's stomach hurt. She couldn't breathe.

"If we ever joined forces," said Lillian, "we'd be formidable."

"Don't hold your breath," said Cal.

"Bitch."

"Bitch."

CHAPTER SEVENTEEN

"Fun!" said Ben. "*Fun!* What happened to edification? What happened to self-improvement?"

"Have you ever *been* to a club?" said Trevor. "And I don't mean Chess Club."

"There's Goethe to be read!"

"We can't spend another evening in Mittenwald. This town shuts down at eight p.m."

"So do I!"

"And that," said Trevor, clapping Ben on the back, "is our problem."

Cal volunteered for the middle seat, though she regretted it when she realized how difficult it was to keep her knees pressed together. She wasn't used to wearing skirts. "Needless to say," Trevor had said, "I've eliminated all the venues with a dress code that says, 'Look cool.' But Lillian and I can't pull all the weight. No T-shirts, Cal. No jeans."

"I've got a dressy T-shirt," she said. "And I just washed my jeans."

"Absolutely not," said Trevor.

Lillian was lounging on her top bunk, flipping through Ben's guidebook. "You can borrow something."

"Thanks, but no thanks."

"Did you *bring* anything besides T-shirts and jeans?" said Trevor. He peered into Cal's backpack with the face of someone sniffing milk to see whether it'd gone bad. "Do you *own* anything besides T-shirts and jeans?"

"I'm not borrowing clothes."

"You have to, Cal," said Trevor.

"You don't have to," said Lillian. She swung her legs over the side of the bed and hopped gracefully to the floor. "But come take a look." She unzipped her own backpack and began pulling out slippery handfuls of chiffon and shot silk and lace. Cal thumbed a sleek striped dress. "I don't think that'd work," said Lillian. "You need a chest to hold it up. But here, take these."

Cal supposed she might as well try them. She wouldn't have before last night. Once they'd finally stopped laughing, Lillian had yawned and said, "I move we go to bed."

"Seconded," said Cal. "The Bitch Club is hereby adjourned."

She'd slept through to morning. She'd forgotten how bright-colored and hopeful the world seemed after a night of sound sleep. At breakfast, she and Lillian had chatted like—well, like friends. They were so hungry! The bread was so good! When had America settled for bad bread, anyway? Was it some sort of Faustian bargain, twentieth-century puissance in exchange for soulless bread that was nothing but a vehicle for margarine and peanut butter and marshmallow creme?

Now Lillian said, "We need to showcase those legs of

yours." She shook out a handkerchief. "You have amazing legs."

No, that wasn't a handkerchief; it was a skirt. Cal felt a smile trip onto her face. "I'm not into displaying my body as a collection of parts."

"Whatever. Follow me, ill-garbed Padawan." Lillian led Cal to the large, dimly lit bathroom. She tossed her a leather skirt wider than it was long and a turquoise shirt. Cal managed the skirt but she couldn't figure out the shirt. Its back was lined with slits and it was twisted like a Möbius strip. Where were the armholes? *Were* there armholes? Lillian untwisted it with a deft flip. Her fingers spread, she held it out like a skein of yarn, and Cal, still wearing her sports bra, ducked in.

Lillian stuck out her lower lip and considered the look. She hummed. She handed Cal another shirt, a white drapey thing that was translucent as a lampshade. This one Cal could puzzle out. "That's better," said Lillian. "Spin."

Cal spun.

"You know?" said Lillian. "The right shoes, and you'll look good."

In the mirror, Cal watched herself flush. It was like a rainstorm on a radar map. It arose in the tight skin on her breastbone and swept over her neck. "You sound surprised."

"Well," said Lillian. "Um."

The moment hung, the girls looking at each other in the mirror, and then Cal laughed.

It was deep twilight by the time they'd driven the half hour to the town of Garmisch-Partenkirchen. "I hear the scene's pretty happening here," said Trevor. "For a mountain resort town, anyway."

The club was called Ü. "They named it for a smiley face?" said Cal.

"Cal," said Ben, disappointed, "it's a nasalized *oo*." He protruded his lips, pinched his nostrils, and made the sound of a disgruntled hippopotamus. "A very standard vowel here."

They joined the line. High-heeled women stalked down the street with determined expressions and knee-first gaits. Men cruised in packs. That much was familiar. But the scene was unmistakably foreign: the timbered latticework of the buildings, the fountain with its bronze sculpture of naked women wielding tree branches, the clothes, though Cal had neither the eye nor the vocabulary to explain what made them so exotic, and, always, the shadow of the Alps.

Trevor, his hands on his lower back, arched to gaze at the mountain ridge. "We can't hang out in Mittenwald and not hike."

"We're not here to enjoy ourselves," Ben said cuttingly. He pulled his English-German dictionary from his breast pocket. "Who wants to quiz me while we're waiting?"

Trevor snatched the dictionary. "No books allowed. Tonight you're living in the real world."

"Give me back my dictionary. And books, I'd posit, are in many ways *more* real—"

"We're clubbing in Europe, dude. Soak it in."

"—than the gaudy trappings of leisure. *Sic transit*, etc. And I want my dictionary."

"Only if you promise not to open it."

"But—"

Trevor dangled the dictionary over the basin of the fountain.

"Fine."

Trevor muttered something about teddy bears and blankies. Ben returned the dictionary to his pocket with a proprietary pat. "I have to say, I'm impressed by this orderly line. If only Americans could be so rule-bound!"

"You'll have to take your girlfriend out," said Trevor. "Dazzle her with the sociocultural implications of standing in line."

"She's not my girlfriend."

"Ooh," said Cal. "Who's not your girlfriend?"

"No one," said Ben. Flushing, he chugged water from the Nalgene he had carabinered onto his belt. "Let's discuss something of general interest. How did you find out about this place, Trevor?"

"Oh, I asked around," Trevor said breezily. "Asked some people who looked cool."

"You don't even speak German."

"I can cobble together the essentials," said Trevor. *"Guten Tag. Wo ist der Party?"*

Ben choked on his water.

"They were happy to help."

They inched to the front of the line. Matt paid, and their hands were franked with passport-like stamps. They entered. It was a different world. The music was almost too loud to hear. Blue and purple light, from sources Cal couldn't see, gleamed on the floor and the walls. Orange globes hung from the ceiling. She brought up the rear as they threaded single file through the crowd. They passed the bar. Two women in strappy sandals danced on top of it. Cal did a double take:

they were not wearing shirts. Nobody else seemed to care. She quickly looked away. Everyone in the crowd seemed to have dressed to harmonize with the space: shiny hair, shiny clothes, smoky makeup. Some men wore sunglasses. Cal was washed with relief that she was not wearing her black T-shirt, the one with no holes and fancy edging around the neck. She slipped to Lillian's side and whispered, "Thanks for the clothes."

Lillian nodded. She glided along, her eyes sultry and half closed. From beside her, Cal could see how Lillian made heads turn. Was it because she was beautiful, or because she was black? Or both? The lights gave pale skin a clammy, sickly tone, but they made Lillian's face and arms an inky deep blue. They highlighted the knobs of her cheekbones, the delicate puzzle of her skull. She had put something in her hair that defined its tiny curls, and she had deepened the black of her eyebrows and the red of her lips. She met no eyes but her carriage made it clear that she was aware of the stares, and amused by them: watch me, if you must. Cal tilted her own head, arranged her lips somewhere between a purse and a smirk, and tried to assume a knowing, jaded gaze. Trevor glanced back over his shoulder and grinned. Embarrassed, Cal gave up.

They headed to an area with low tables and plush couches, where the music, though still pounding, was slightly quieter. "I'll get drinks," said Trevor. "What do you guys want? Never mind. I'll choose."

"First decision you've made all trip," said Ben.

"For *that*, good sir, you have to come help me carry them."

Cal, Matt, and Lillian sat side by side on a curved couch, looking out into the club. Lillian said, "Drunk white boys. My favorite human beings."

"Really?" said Cal.

"Oh, yes. Really. I love it when random guys grab my ass. I'm so grateful for the attention."

"Okay," said Cal.

"And when they expect me to dance like Nicki Minaj. That's the best."

"God. Just asking."

Matt said, "My dad would have been pissed if he'd heard I backpacked through Germany without getting off-my-face drunk."

"So you're planning on it?" said Cal.

"Well, no."

"He's scared of alcohol," Lillian told Cal.

"I'm not *scared*."

"You are."

"I just don't like it."

"Same thing."

"Yeah," said Matt. "Probably." He gave Cal his shy smile. "I don't like the thought of blacking out. I'm scared of what I'd do."

"Dance?" said Lillian. "Cry? Spill secrets? Make out with someone? How bad could it be?"

Matt shrugged. "You've never had the feeling you don't know what's inside you? And you're sort of scared of what it might be?"

"Yes," said Cal. "Yes."

"That your outside doesn't match your inside?"

How did he know? She knew what she looked like: normal, nice, a girl who turned in her homework and ran her 400s. She looked like a girl who had it together. Nobody knew it was only a surface, a lid on the raging cauldron from which a hint of her true self—undisciplined, angry—would escape every so often like a wisp of smoke. Lillian had gotten a glimpse, but had no idea of the extent. "I don't like feeling out of control," Cal said.

"You like control?" said Lillian. "I never would have guessed."

"Lillian," said Matt. "Give it a break."

"She knows I mean it nicely," said Lillian, not sounding nice.

Cal nursed the drink that Trevor brought her, but she felt loose and liquid, anyway. She was drunk off lights, she thought, and noise, and the lateness of the hour: usually by midnight she was insomniac and terrified and lonely. She'd gotten tipsy from showing off her pretty legs and from laughing at Trevor's stories, from the way Ben, whose esophagus seemed to have no trouble with dark German beer, leaned close and confided to her and Matt his situation with the not-girlfriend. "Maybe you should call her," said Matt.

"But I'm a crackerjack correspondent. You've received a postcard from me, Cal, have you not?"

"I have."

"And was it not wondrous to behold?"

"It was."

Ben stumbled up to get another round. Matt raised his eyebrows at her. Cal leaned into his side. "This is so great," she said. "I don't like you at all." All this time, she realized, she'd been braced for a crush on him, on his crinkly eyes and the easy swing of his arms when he walked. "I mean, I like you. But not that way." She nuzzled her head into his shoulder.

"What's going on here?" said Trevor, looming.

"Cal's telling me how I'm like a brother to her," Matt said dryly. He shoved her upright.

"Well," said Trevor, "Cal's brother was just dancing with an extremely good-looking *Fräulein*. So you've got big shoes to fill."

Ben returned. Having taken a wrong turn from the bathrooms, he had discovered a karaoke room in the back. "Come *on*!" he said, his cheeks in high color. "It'll be *amazing*!"

"I happen to know you consider karaoke second only to Dutch elm disease in terms of all-time worst imports," said Trevor. "What's the deal?"

"The songs are *German*! A true test of my language skills!"

"Yep," said Trevor, immediately rising to his feet, "it's fair to say I'd trade my firstborn to see this." All five of them skirted the dance floor to reach the back room. Ben got in line while Trevor thumbed to his phone's video camera. "Just in case he thinks public office is still an option," he told the others. They cheered as Ben strode onstage. He had not deviated from his travel uniform: khakis and a blue button-down with sleeves rolled up to the elbows. The beat started, industrial and metal. Ben gripped the microphone and peered at the screen. *"Du,"* he growled, *"du hast, du hast mich . . ."*

"My God," said Trevor, dropping the phone.

Ben moved in a way Cal might have called a shimmy, if his limbs had bent. *"Du hast mich gefragt, du hast mich gefragt."* The crowd was whooping, jumping up and down, pumping the air with their fists. Trevor appeared incapable of speech.

"Und ich hab nichts gesagt. . . ." Ben spun to one side, and

the other. When the room screamed in glee, he did a full pir-
ouette, his arms in a dainty oval above his head. The crowd
went wild.

Trevor, pale and shaken, gripped Cal's shoulder. Ben
finished the song to tumultuous applause and cries for an
encore.

"It's time to go," said Trevor.

Matt drove home. If she hadn't been dopey with fatigue, Cal
thought, she'd have been scared by the underlit switchbacks,
but Matt seemed alert, perched over the wheel, his hands at
ten and two, and she let him do the worrying. Trevor had insisted on sitting in the middle, and he slung his arms around
both Cal and Lillian, although Lillian shrugged him off after
a minute. He and Ben were singing the fight song of the university they'd founded as children for their Lego guys. A lusty
number to the tune of "O Canada," it concluded with several
measures of harmonized vibrato. Cal clapped.

"Remember when our football team won the champion-
ship?" Trevor said to Ben. "*My* team, I should say. Your guys
considered football barbaric."

Cal had forgotten about the collegiate-Lego phase. She
and Jesse had the crosstown rival. They played football games
against Trevor and filled interlibrary loans for Ben. But she'd
never been interested in building stadiums or landscaping
the quads with twigs from the backyard. She'd left that for
Jesse. Her interest had been walls. Trevor and Ben's college
was sprawling, rec centers and laboratories placed haphaz-
ardly through the basement, but the Jessicaliton campus was
neatly circumscribed by her walls. They were works of art,

those walls, bricks overlapping in careful patterns, monochrome and sturdy, built to last. They had crenellated tops and checkpoints where the students could enter and exit, though why would anyone want to leave? Within her walls they lived trim, safe lives. They forever traversed Jesse's paths, arrested midstep, yellow faces frozen into perfect half smiles, stiff of limb and staunch of heart. Nothing could hurt them, not even when Trevor, bored by the intricate departmental politics that consumed life at Benjevor College, got into his plastic animals and brought out the pterodactyls. They had walls. They were safe from all invasions, all attacks.

And now, in the tidy box of the car, leaning into her brother's side, she thought, Here. Here we are. This is right. "That was fun," she said.

"You're welcome," said Trevor modestly.

"I think he'd have been glad to see us having fun," said Cal. "He would have liked it."

"I hate that phrase," said Ben. His words were slurred. He turned from the front seat to press the point. *"Would have liked."*

"Benny," said Trevor.

"It's a stupid hypothetical. It's as stupid as debating where Raphael would have taken Italian art if he'd lived past thirty-seven—"

"You've founded whole friendships on that debate," said Trevor.

"Would have liked. It's meaningless. It's something to say when we feel good, so we don't feel guilty for feeling good."

"You're drunk, Ben," said Trevor. "Stop talking."

"You stop talking. You're drunk too."

"But I can keep my shit together." Yet Trevor's words too

were sloppy. Matt slowed to a crawl around the hairpin turn. All of them seemed to hold their breath. He made the turn and accelerated.

"I hate it too, Ben," said Lillian.

"*Thank* you."

"But only when it's said by people who don't have any business saying it. How would *she* know what he would have liked?"

CHAPTER EIGHTEEN

Nobody was talking much at breakfast, which was fine by Lillian. She got herself a glass of water and a hunk of bread. She was furious.

"Last night," said Ben, groaning. "Did I do what I think I did?"

"Depends on what you think you did," said Trevor. "And there didn't seem to be a lot of thinking involved."

She had let down her guard, and she'd slipped right into Jesse's scheme. Lending Cal clothes! Laughing with her! Talking about *feelings*, for Chrissake! She wished she could tell Jesse off. What were you thinking? That you could make everything okay with a wave of your hand, that you could beckon Cal from the bench as you blithely jogged off the field? Do you really think it's that easy?

"If I eat this egg, I'm going to hurl," said Ben. "Who wants it? Trevor?"

Trevor's face was gray. "Get that away from me," he moaned.

Hanging out with your cousin, she'd say, only reminds me how much better it was with you. Cal is not you. She isn't like you. She cries if fingers get snapped in her general direction, and she never fights back.

"Whoever gave me all that *Doppelbock* should be publicly flogged," said Ben.

The afternoon was overcast. The frescoes on the walls of Karibu Ausrüstung seemed older, more sallow, and Andreas too looked far grimier. When he noticed Lillian staring at his hands, he said, "It's mostly soot, I promise." She nodded, but she had been looking at how smooth they were, how despite his beard and his corded, deeply tanned forearms, his hands had the tendonless, artless appearance of a boy's.

"How old are you?" she said.

Matt elbowed her, but Andreas was unfazed. "Nineteen. About your age, I think?"

He had an accent, but not much of one. As they followed him down the street, Lillian stared at his browned neck, his sun-bleached hair. He knows Thea, she thought. He might know where she is. Only a straining vestige of politeness kept her from interrogating him. By the end of the night, she told herself, they would know.

"Are you going to steal *his* papers?" Cal whispered. Lillian ignored her. Cal had burst into tears last night in the car. She'd been on the offensive ever since, or her wimpy version of the offensive: nasty comments, raised eyebrows. "I wonder what Jesse would think if he knew."

"He'd think his cousin needs urgent surgery," said Lillian. "She's got a stick jammed up her ass."

Cal, for once, was too shocked to cry. Lillian was a bit shocked herself. Maybe that was a step too far. But as Cal hurried ahead, her left foot dragging in a slight limp, Lillian couldn't hold back a tiny giggle. I'm sorry, Jesse, she thought, but she does. And what *would* he think? It didn't matter. She'd stolen the papers because she'd promised to fulfill his last wish. If he didn't like it, he could think harder about the crap he asked her to do.

She could overhear snatches of Andreas's conversation with Trevor. He was in university, but reluctantly; he liked this job better, leading trips for Karibu, hiking and climbing and canoeing. "I was born with a love for the mountains," he said.

"Me *too*," said Trevor.

Andreas nodded. "You have it or you don't. Some people love the sea, some the forest."

"Or the indoors," said Ben.

"You may believe you like the indoors, but you're wrong."

"It's not a belief."

"Then," Andreas said with a laugh, "modern life has warped you." Lillian, prowling alone at the back, saw him sling an arm around Ben's shoulders, saw Ben instinctively stiffen. She put her hands in her pockets and twiddled a euro coin. She was wearing culottes, a paisley-printed, lavishly cut pair she'd found in a vintage shop in San Francisco. The pockets were magnificent, tailored not for hands but for whole arms, not for coins but for treasures.

"You okay?" Matt asked Cal, who was shading her eyes as if the cloud-strained sunlight were enough to hurt her head.

"Just tired."

"Another bad dream?"

Cal winced and nodded. Behind them, Lillian raised her eyebrows. Cal with her jaunty ponytail, Cal with her friendship bracelets: what could she know of bad dreams? Did she dream that she'd misplaced a flip-flop? That she'd lost some thoroughly inconsequential footrace? Lillian never dreamt. She fell asleep as soon as the light was flicked off, and often before. She fell asleep perched in the middle of the cramped backseat. Sleeping let her forget Jesse was dead, and in the dazed scrabble of waking up, there was always a slivered moment when she still didn't know. She hoarded those moments. Put end to end, how long would they last? A half hour, maybe. In the thicket of this past year, that half hour was as coaxing as a smooth, flat rock, a place to rest her aching feet.

At the edge of town, Andreas stopped in front of a small house, its white walls segmented by a tidy lattice of timbers. A low hedge surrounded the garden, and the geraniums and petunias lining the balcony dribbled red-petaled strands over the front door. "I wish I could introduce you to my family," he said, unlocking the door, "but they're traveling in France this month."

"You throwing any parties?" said Trevor.

Andreas grinned over his shoulder. "Does this count?" Lillian felt as if she'd been kicked in the stomach. She glanced around sharply. Had anyone else seen it, seen Jesse's grin flash out from this German teenager? Matt, massaging his squash ball, was blank-faced. Ben's nose was in his dictionary. Trevor, in a deep backbend, was giving the mountains one last look before they went inside. But Cal's eyes were wide and startled. Lillian twisted away.

"We'll rummage for food, but I've got to shower first," said Andreas. "My mother wouldn't even let me inside. She makes me stop at the garden hose."

"Can we help?" said Trevor.

"Sure, if you can figure out something to cook."

The kitchen was spacious and high-ceilinged. Someone with an eye for color had furnished the room, Lillian thought. Even the cookbooks caught the yellow of the hardwood floor and the warm red of the table. Evidence of Andreas's month alone overlaid the room like dust: the sink full of dishes, the chairs piled with mail and a half-strung guitar, the solitary hiking boot in the drying rack.

Cal went about closing all the drawers while Trevor investigated the food. "Eggs, cheese, yogurt—some very droopy lettuce—decomposing broccoli, a positively flaccid carrot—potatoes, these seem relatively edible—"

"I'd be happy to make everyone smoothies," offered Ben.

"Or," said Trevor quickly, "I could make scrambled eggs and boiled potatoes."

"Sounds good," said Cal.

"If unimaginative," said Lillian.

"*You* have a better idea?" said Cal.

"Of course." She skimmed to the refrigerator, her pants billowing around her. "How about an omelet with potatoes and Gruyère?"

"I'll be your sous chef," said Trevor. "Just tell me what to do."

She'd taken control only to nettle Cal, but it felt good to assemble her ingredients, to set a pot of water to boil. She didn't know much about cooking, but she'd helped her grandmother with Sunday dinners for years. She knew enough.

That was her childhood, her grandmother's kitchen and her grandmother's stories: Medjugorje, Lourdes, Guadalupe. When she and Jesse lay on his twin bed and she curled into the crook of his arm and he said, "My dad read me all those books, Lill, right here, right in this room," she always thought of her grandmother's stories. Their favorite was Fátima. Lillian, nine years old, is learning to crack eggs. "Lúcia saw a woman brighter than the sun," her grandmother says. She puts a hand over Lillian's, slippery raw-silk skin over denim. "Be bold. None of this timid tap-tap-tap."

"Then what?"

"Then people came from all over Portugal, from all over the world. A fast, clean break, Lily. Seventy thousand people saw the sun dance in the sky." Lillian's hair is in micro braids, and her grandmother picks them up and lets them fall through her fingers. "And Our Lady gave Lúcia three secrets." All it took to remember what it was like to be nine years old was to imagine the pitter-patter of the braids on her back. They sounded like raindrops on the hood of a car. Lillian took the potatoes off the stove and set Trevor to slicing them. She would crack the eggs herself.

By the time Andreas came in, she was browning the omelet under the broiler. Trevor put a green salad on the table. "This is splendid," said Andreas. "I've been eating nothing but bread and sausage all month." He had shaved, she saw, the ghost of his beard white against his tanned face. Yes, his entire jaw was Jesse's. "I leave on another trip tomorrow, so this is my only meal not cooked over a campfire." He lifted his glass. *"Prost!"*

They ate quietly. "Where is Thea?" Lillian wanted to shout. Andreas took another helping of salad. Be patient, she told herself. Let the evening unfold. They *would* find her. And for now she would look at Andreas's jaw until she could not bear it anymore. She would not have guessed that the genetically determined silhouette of one single bone could make her feel this way, both hollowed out and full. Cal was doing the same thing: looking, looking away.

At last, Andreas crossed his silverware. "Thea," he said. "My mother's cousin. We have not seen her for three years. She departed very suddenly."

"Do you know where she went?" said Ben.

"She left a note telling us not to search for her. But I wish we had." He stretched his long arms behind his head. "She was here for only a few months."

"Did you know her well?" said Lillian.

"I thought I did. My sisters were babies, and neither Thea nor I wanted to be inside with them. And so we spent the summer in the mountains." He gestured behind him at the picture window, though at this angle there was nothing to see but garden, hedge, a slice of foothill. "We hiked the whole Soiern ridge. Day after day. Yes. I knew her." He shoved back his chair and exited the kitchen. When he returned, he held a mountaineering compass. "She left this for me."

He passed it around. It was well used, the base plate battered, the thin leather lanyard soft and worn. The bezel was marked with degrees and directions: *nord, est, sud, ovest*. "I use it every day," said Andreas. "And I think of her every time."

Ben, with one eye closed, peered through the bezel as if it were a monocle.

"No clues there," said Andreas, amused. He set the compass in the middle of the table. "It was one of her most valued possessions. She'd had it since the year after college. You should know what direction you're facing, she told me, even if you don't know what direction to go."

"Where *did* she go?" said Ben. "Do you have any ideas?"

Andreas gave the compass a tap. Lillian watched the needle sashay. "Berlin? Perhaps Berlin. But she also mentioned Portugal, Bulgaria, Sweden. She has her dual citizenship, and she is facile with languages. She could be anywhere." The needle, at last, had fallen still. "If I had to guess, I would say Berlin."

"But would she be there now?" said Ben.

"Probably not," Andreas said. "This is the smallest lead. This is nothing." He shrugged and gave an apologetic grin. Lillian drank it in. "Why are you looking for her?"

Nobody answered. Matt took a deep breath. "Our friend," he said, "their cousin—" Lillian stared at the compass while he explained.

"Once," Andreas said quietly, "she told me I was like the son she never had. I didn't know she meant a son who'd actually been born."

"You resemble him more than any of us," said Cal.

"What was he like, your Jesse?"

Again, they were silent. Lillian bit her lip.

"I'm sorry," said Andreas. "You don't have to—"

"He was funny," said Cal, blinking rapidly. "He was sweet and funny."

"Smart," added Ben.

"Kind of goofy," said Trevor.

"And nice," said Matt. "Does that sound boring? He wasn't boring. He was the opposite of boring."

"Perfect," murmured Andreas.

"Not perfect," said Lillian. Her Jesse, her sweet and funny

boy. How she longed to touch him. Would she shake him or kiss him? Probably both. That was how it had always been. He was her ally and her rival, her closest enemy and her most intolerable friend. Her undoing and her savior. "Not perfect at all."

"I understand," said Andreas.

But this lineup of adjectives, Lillian thought, is the smallest lead. It is nothing. Andreas, you will never find him from that.

"Shall I see what we have for dessert?" he said.

As Andreas rifled through the freezer, Matt put his arm around Cal's shoulders. Lillian seethed. Was she envious? She was. She wanted an arm around her shoulders. She wanted evidence of that most shocking fact of all: that others were others, that you were not hobbling alone through this world. When she left her baby, Thea had given that up. Lillian would never understand it. To have seventeen years to spend in the fullness of his body and his genius—and to give them up? How had she done it? His infant head would have wobbled until she cupped it. As a toddler, he would have hurtled across the room to grab her around the knees. He would have asked her to help him put on his socks. Running off the field, his golden forehead shining with sweat, he would have been running to her. When he was sick and sleeping, she could have held his hand.

All that, she had given up. And for what? For traveling in Europe without him? I've had both, Lillian would tell her, and I would trade this whole summer for a day with him. For an hour, for a minute.

In the freezer, Andreas had discovered a cache of meals his mother had frozen for him. The others were laughing. "All those sausage sandwiches!" he cried. "When I could have been eating like a king!" Lillian placed her hand over the compass and slid it across the red wood. The needle barely moved, it was so smooth a ride from table to hand to pocket. She didn't know where she'd go, she thought, but at least she would know which way she faced.

"It's hopeless," said Matt in the car. "She could be anywhere."

"We should go to Berlin," said Ben.

"*Bear-leen*," mimicked Lillian. "You *must* be a native speaker."

"We have a lead, flimsy though it may be. We'll follow her trail one orderly step at a time."

"What do you think, Cal?" said Matt.

"I think I'm tired." She was draped against the window, her head vibrating with the road. "I think we're all tired."

"We have to find her," said Lillian. "None of us will have any peace till we do."

"Shall we drive to Berlin, then?" said Ben. "Tomorrow? Tonight's the last night we've reserved at the pension."

"Let's go home," said Cal.

Adjusting his mirror, Trevor said casually, "I think we all know stuff we're not telling."

"That notebook," said Ben.

Lillian said in Ben's ear, "Imagine how many clues that text holds."

He drew in a breath, incensed. He swiveled in his seat and said to Cal, "Do you realize you're basically banning that book from us?"

"I told you what's in it."

"You're as bad as any tyrannical regime."

"I *told* you! I told you everything!"

"Soon you'll be in the pension's kitchen, preheating the oven to 451 degrees—"

She was close to tears. "He gave it to *me*!"

"Cool it, Ben," said Trevor. "We should go somewhere peaceful. And once we're up there, we'll be able to talk."

"Up where?" said Ben.

"There." Trevor craned toward the windshield and pointed straight up.

"You want to climb a mountain?" said Ben.

"It's generally called hiking. The tallest one on the range to the left."

"You want to climb *that*?"

"Hike it. Andreas said it's not too arduous."

"Andreas climbs mountains professionally."

"I say we go tomorrow. We can stop by Karibu in the morning and rent boots. At the summit, we can decide what to do next."

"A summit at the summit," said Ben. "Despite a certain homonymous charm, I'm not tempted."

"My heel hurts," said Cal.

"Sorry," said Matt, "but I really, really hate heights."

Through the fabric of her pants, Lillian traced the compass's square edges, its raised bezel. "I'll go," she said.

"Great," said Trevor. "Lillian and I will go. You lot can hang around in the room."

"I'll hardly be *hanging around*," said Ben. "I'll be working out where we're sleeping tomorrow night. As the responsible member of this party."

"Good for you." Trevor took a swinging left into the

pension driveway and bumped along to the gravel lot in the back. He turned off the car, but no one moved.

"One question," said Ben. "Do you intend to bring a map?"

"A map?" said Trevor. "Nope."

"You're climbing a mountain with no topographical map?"

"Is that the kind with the squiggly lines?"

"Trevor! Look how big that thing is! You'll get lost. You'll be stranded, forced to subsist on roots and small woodland creatures. And all for the lack of a three-euro topo map, which I'm *sure* they sell at Karibu, but no, couldn't plan ahead—"

"Gosh," said Trevor, "it's like we need someone to take care of logistics for us."

"Have you *read* the accounts of Edmund Hillary? Fine. I'll buy you a map. And what about *die Proviant*? Food for the journey? Viaticum, if you will?"

"We can hit the grocery in the morning—"

"*And* rent boots? *And* choose a map of proper scale? Trevor. You wouldn't start till noon. I'll go buy food. I guess I'm climbing after all." He sighed, got out of the car, and headed for the grocery down the street.

"He was looking for an excuse," said Trevor, grinning.

Ben reappeared at the window. "You talk to the pension office about extending our reservation through tomorrow night," he told Trevor. "They'll be closed by the time I get back."

"I'm on it," Trevor said airily.

"I'll hike too," said Cal.

"What about your heel?" said Trevor.

"It's only walking."

"Strenuous walking," said Trevor, but he didn't argue further.

"Wait," said Matt. "So I'll be alone?"

"Looks like it," said Trevor. They piled out of the car. Matt stuffed his hands in his pockets and looked up at the mountains that rose sharply behind the pension.

"I'll come."

"Excellent! All five of us!" Trevor had gotten exactly what he wanted. He slapped Matt's back. "You'll do fine."

After dinner, Ben apportioned peanuts and raisins into plastic bags he'd filched from the produce department. "I can't wait to get ahold of that map," he said happily.

"You know," said Trevor, "we could just follow the signs."

"What makes you think there'll be signs?"

"Oh," said Trevor, "there are always signs."

CHAPTER NINETEEN

It was cool but sunny. The sky was a bold, unbounded blue. The hike to the summit of Soiernspitze began on a gravel road that wound past thick stands of firs, white-frothed waterfalls, ravines of wildflowers, and meadows of lackadaisical cows.

Everyone was very grouchy.

Matt had broken a sweat within ten minutes. The grade was ceaselessly, humorlessly uphill. He became grateful for all the lunges and single-legged squats he'd done that spring, for the cycling intervals he'd pounded out with his dad in the basement, when the details, his burning quads and the sweat sizzling off his hot skin, rose up to dominate the pain instead of serving as its handmaidens. They were overtaken, though slowly, by a peloton of cyclists, grinding their gears and panting. He and Jesse must have looked like that going up Vollmer Peak. His dad had been spinning his legs. He could have sprung up the hill like a jackrabbit.

Trevor pointed up to the left. "That's where we're going."

The ridge surged behind the trees. "Anyone spot the summit cross?"

"Nope."

"Guess that's not the summit, then." So the summit was even higher? Trevor didn't seem perturbed. "Who wants water?"

They passed around one of their liter bottles. Matt's hand bumped Cal's. He noticed, but she didn't. Well, he thought, no different from usual. He remembered playing Horse with Jesse in the driveway. "You kissed her?" said Jesse.

"And then she was like, 'You know what I like about you?'" Jesse flipped the ball into the basket. Matt caught the rebound. "She said, 'I can *talk* to you. Really talk.'"

"The kiss of death," said Jesse. "So to speak."

Matt took aim. The ball poised on his fingertips, he said, "Our friendship, apparently, is too dear to be spoiled by making out." He flicked his wrist. The ball teetered in.

"Damn," said Jesse.

"I know."

"I'm referring to you making that shot."

"Either way."

"Do you mind?"

Matt tossed the ball to Jesse, who set up at the three-point line. "Honestly?" said Matt. "Not really."

"That's what I thought." Matt watched him home in on the basket. He watched his square shoulders, his slim arms, and when the ball took flight, Matt kept his eyes on Jesse. He heard the ball bank and swish. "Don't worry," said Jesse. Was this in the Lillian era? It must have been, because Jesse had the smugness of the happily coupled. He passed the ball to Matt. He gave him his ducking, lopsided grin. "You'll find someone."

What if, thought Matt, I already have?

Trevor gestured expansively to the southwest. "I told you this would pay off." Either the air had thinned, or it was a matter of perspective: there were mountains where there had not been mountains before, smoothed by distance, their summits mantled in cloud.

"Austria," said Ben.

"It always gets me that there's no actual border between states," said Cal. "That all those lines are imaginary."

"Remember how you believed me when I told you colors on the map corresponded to real-life colors?" Trevor turned to the rest of them. "She burst into tears when we went to Indiana and it wasn't pink."

"Typical," said Lillian. "Always crying. Never fighting back."

Matt caught the black look Cal shot her. Trevor, unaware, said, "Once a baby sister, always a baby sister, true?"

They hiked on. To their right was the neighboring ridge. Matt kept his eyes on the sudden frontiers of its timberlines, the glaciated limestone crags, the peaks as jagged as broken plywood. They denied visual logic. Surely they ought to be close enough to touch. Jesse would have liked this, he thought. He didn't dare say it. Jesse had always gotten a high from being outside, more than seemed normal. It *is* normal, Jesse whispered to him. Look around. Look at this extraordinary world.

The gravel road ended at the base house. They mopped their foreheads and waited at the water pump behind the cheerful cyclists. Matt didn't envy them the steep spin down, but neither was he happy at their own prospect. The ridge loomed above them as if they hadn't made any progress at all.

Ben peered at the sign on the pump. "*Kein Trinkwasser,* it says. We can't drink this."

"That's just there for liability," Trevor assured him, refilling their bottles.

"I'd really rather not be infested by parasites."

"I'll take all the blame."

"I don't think your remorse is going to help when I'm incapacitated by explosive—"

"Dude!" said Trevor, cringing. "Every time I think I've succeeded in socializing you, I'm proved wrong."

They drank, rested, and continued upward. They were threading through forest, zigzagging on single-track switchbacks. Ben, walking with the map fully unfurled, moved slowly, and Cal passed him. "How's the acrophobia?" she asked Matt.

"Not as bad as I expected. As long as I don't look back." He had once, and regretted it; at the sight of the miniature, red-roofed base house, far below them in the valley, he'd felt an instant ooze of nausea.

"That's good," said Cal absently. She was looking up at Lillian, who cut the corners of the switchbacks, skipping straight uphill and waiting on the path for Trevor to catch up.

"She's like a mountain goat," said Matt.

Cal nodded. She didn't smile.

"Ignore her," said Matt. "Don't let her get to you. I know she's being horrible, but you've got to imagine what it's like for her. She was really in love with him—"

Cal sped up. Matt hastened to catch her. Her lips were tight. He knew it'd be better to stay quiet, but he had to finish. "She *is,* Cal. She is."

"Who *are* you? Her freaking apologist?"

"I—"

Cal wilted. "Sorry. I'm just tired."

They walked in silence. Ben put away the map when it became clear that the only direction they needed was up. The forest had given way to a rocky scramble. What had once felt difficult now seemed a warm-up for this four-limbed clamber. Matt's shirt was soaked through, but they passed slicks of ice. All conversation ceased. There was no cross in sight even when he craned straight up.

Trevor halted. "We need a chocolate break."

"Finally," muttered Cal.

"What's that?" said Trevor.

"Finally!" she said again. "A Defense Against the Dark Arts teacher who knows his remedies!"

Trevor groaned. Lillian looked at Matt, and in the second before she turned away to slam a rock into a snowbank, he knew what she was thinking: Jesse would have made that joke. Cal and Jesse didn't look alike, but it was clear they'd grown up together. The strands of their allusions were coiled as tightly as a double helix. Trevor handed out slabs of Milka and they kept hiking, though now it was more like climbing a crumbling, treacherous stone staircase. Matt hated when Cal's words or laughter winged midair into Jesse's. He let his mind drift out of focus. He slid into the state where he could sense him by his side. I'd rather have you, he mouthed. I'd swap any of them for you.

I know, said Jesse. You all would.

There was the cross. They heaved up their last few steps. "We made it," said Ben, surprised.

"Dare you to kiss the ground," Trevor told Cal.

"Gross. You."

Trevor belly flopped into a passionate embrace. The summit was nearly a moonscape, whipped by wind, with only a few grass stems sticking through the rocks. Matt would have frozen in his sodden T-shirt if Ben hadn't told them to bring jackets, but Ben, consulting the sports watch he'd borrowed from Cal, missed his nod of thanks. "Three hours, thirty-two minutes," he reported.

"That's a marathon time," said Trevor, wiping grit from his lips.

"I think it'd be easier to run one," said Cal.

"Plus," said Trevor, "after you run a marathon, you don't have to go back." Matt peered over the steep crag they'd just climbed. He'd have to keep his footing down *that*. It wasn't physical pain he dreaded, but the moment of falling: the moment when he'd realize he couldn't stop himself, when the authority of his position in space would cave to that awful freedom. But he could not be scooped into the palm of some giant or god and gently placed in the parking lot. The others gazed far into the majestic panorama of the Karwendel: lakes of an improbable teal, clouds, a raptor pitched on one wing, and mountains, mountains, ridge after ridge, all the way to the horizon.

"*Ge denke auch seiner, der diese Berge gemacht,*" said Ben, reading the inscription on the summit cross. "'Think also of Him who made these mountains.'"

"Think also of lunch," said Trevor. "Think also of him who carried lunch all the way up." He gave them butter-and-cheese sandwiches on coarse, seedy bread. They ate greedily. "I'll make seconds. Then we're talking." The five of them were ranged in a circle, looking beyond each other at the grandeur of the view. Matt ate his second sandwich more slowly.

Trevor passed out apples. He laid his three photographs

on a flat rock and weighed their corners with pebbles. "For inspiration," he said.

Matt leaned in for another look at the baby Jesse. The photograph had surprised him. Jesse was staring curiously at the camera, but Thea had eyes only for her child. "How could she ever have left him?" Lillian whispered.

"I was just thinking that," said Matt.

Lillian turned away.

"Anyone else want to share?" said Trevor.

"You sound like a kindergarten teacher," said Cal.

"I'm declaring Soiernspitze a blame-free zone. It's okay if you've been a tad secretive so far. No judgments will be made."

"I got the maps," said Ben flatly.

"I got the money," said Matt.

Disdainfully, Lillian shook her wrist. The face of Jesse's watch caught the sun.

They turned to Cal.

"I've told you everything important," she said.

"But it's a symbolic thing, don't you think?" said Lillian. Her tone was icy. "You don't trust us. You aren't committed to the search."

Cal's chin was trembling. Matt caught Trevor's eye. "Okay," said Trevor, "okay, everyone—"

"It's not *everyone*," said Cal. "It's *her*."

"Just let us read the goddamn notebook," said Lillian.

"Fine," said Cal. "Fine. Have it."

"We can read it?" said Ben.

"You can read it."

"Yes!" Ben closed his eyes and pumped both fists. "Yes! Yes! Now? Did you bring it?"

"Of course not." Matt saw Cal's eyes flick to her day pack. It's in there, Jesse breathed. It's with her wherever she goes.

"I can't wait to get back to the pension," said Ben. He looked to Cal for affirmation. She said nothing. There was an uneasy silence.

Trevor clapped twice. "Well! Good progress, folks!" He looked around hopefully. "Are we going to figure out where to go next?"

Matt felt sorry for Trevor, but he didn't have anything to say. Cal attacked her apple. Lillian gazed to the north. Ben kowtowed above his topographical map, his face inches from the ground, his scrawny butt pointing to the boundless sky.

"Anyone?" Trevor bore a feeble air of desperation.

"I could have told you that climbing this mountain wouldn't magically solve all our problems," said Cal.

Lillian tossed her apple core into their trash bag and briskly brushed off her hands. "Well, *I've* been thinking. And I've got a theory about Thea. She grew up in Santa Fe, right, with summers in Mittenwald? She did her undergrad at Berkeley, and studied abroad in Frankfurt."

With a rustle, Ben sat. "Then she went back to Berkeley to work as a research assistant."

"She goes back," said Lillian. "Look. In the past five years, she's gone back to all those other places too. Santa Fe, Frankfurt, Mittenwald."

"Solid observation," said Ben.

"Though kind of obvious," said Cal.

"The only time we haven't accounted for," said Lillian, "is the year she had after college."

"A key year," said Ben. He paced the summit, ruffling his

hair. "Right before Arnold, right before Jesse. Where was she?"

"It was a whole year," said Matt. "She could have traveled all over."

Trevor shrugged and nodded, but Ben was caught up by their theory. "Wherever she was," he said, "I bet she went back."

"That's what I'm thinking," said Lillian.

"I bet she's there still," said Ben.

"I wouldn't give you very good odds," said Matt.

Ben didn't hear him. "That was the year she got the compass. She must have been in a mountainous region."

"Compasses work all over," said Matt.

"It said *nord*, didn't it, in German? Another point for Berlin, *ja*? I wish I could inspect it further—"

It was so unexpected, Lillian unzipping her backpack and pulling it out and tossing it forward, that no one realized what was happening until the compass sat on top of the photographs. Its lanyard sprawled untidily across the rocks. With a leap that was almost acrobatic, Ben was upon it. "*Nord*, yes, but *est*, *sud*, *ovest*—"

"You stole his compass?" Cal was on her feet.

"—those are Italian!"

Cal advanced on Lillian, who sat nonchalantly, her legs crossed. "You stole from our *cousin*?"

"She must have been in Italy!"

Cal's fists were clenched. "You—you—"

Trevor caught Matt's eye and made a throat-slitting gesture. They both stood.

"Now the only question is *where* in Italy!"

"I can't believe it," spat Cal. "I can't believe you. I'm—I'm speechless."

"A dream come true," said Lillian dryly.

Cal's whole body seemed to be stuttering. She snatched a rock. She wound up, a coil of fury and intention, but when Trevor flung out his hand, she spun away and hurled the rock to the ground. It bounced off the edge of the summit. Matt imagined he could hear it, its faint clacks and tinkles, tumbling all the way down.

From behind him on the path, Trevor said, "Those girls! They loathe each other!"

Matt nodded.

"What should we do?"

"There's not much we *can* do." Matt was leading the descent. His fear had been dismissed. He felt the way he had when he'd bombed down Vollmer Peak on his bike, when he'd ticked up the gears and pedaled as hard as he could, even on the blind curves.

"Maybe we could call in a professional arbitrator," mused Trevor.

"This isn't a salary dispute," said Matt.

The group was falling apart. And no wonder, he thought: they were on a fool's mission. He skidded on the scree, but he was moving fast enough that his footing didn't even matter. Jesse was a fool to send them, and they were fools to be sent. He'd never say it aloud, but that was the truth. They weren't detectives or knights errant or even adults. They were kids, foolish kids, searching a continent for a woman who didn't want to be found.

What did Professor Serrano think of all this? Matt wished he'd asked him. Professor Serrano would have listened, and he would have told him the truth. He'd always been about as far from Matt's dad as a person could get. He wore his cargo pants hitched up and his sweaters inside out. "He hates the feel of seams on his skin," Jesse said. Jesse railed against him. But Matt also remembered that he'd finish the rants—"My *dad*!"—and start laughing. *"Arnold!"* he'd say, and he wouldn't be able to stop smiling. Jesse would show up at school holding an egg sandwich bundled in tinfoil. They'd sit with their backs to their lockers, and Jesse would say, "He's stuck on this breakfast kick. I'm not allowed out the door without it."

"Poor you," Lillian said.

The sandwich steamed. Jesse extracted a soggy Post-it note. *"Egg Taste Test,"* he read. *"The left egg is cage-free, the right is organic. Which one's better?"* He inspected the sandwich. "How the heck does he expect me to tell which is left and which is right? My *dad*!" He cracked up.

Matt stopped at the tree line and waited for the others. "Water break!" said Trevor. "Drink as much as you want. We'll refill at the base house."

Ben spread his arms. "We're going to sleep well tonight."

"That's for sure," said Trevor. "Let's see the map. This next part through the forest is tricky."

"So you *do* need it. Told you so."

Trevor gave a good-natured laugh. The two of them inspected the map.

"I think I've got it," said Ben, "but I'll consult again when we're a bit farther, just to be sure." He arched his back and massaged his hamstrings. "You know what I'm excited about? A hot shower."

Matt was caulked with dried sweat, wet with new sweat, muddy from the ascent, dusty from the descent. A shower! He couldn't wait. A shower and a bed.

"You talked to the pension lady, right?" said Ben.

Nobody responded. Trevor shaded his eyes to look at the peak of Soiernspitze. "Amazing we were up there, huh?"

"Trevor," said Ben, and Matt knew what Trevor was going to say. Ben knew too. Matt could see his eyes darkening. "Did you ask the woman at the pension to add another night to our reservation?"

"Me?" said Trevor.

CHAPTER TWENTY

Cal was almost running down the switchbacks. Her heel was killing her. She wanted to get ahead, to shake off the sound of Ben haranguing Trevor, but everyone else was moving quickly too.

"We'll talk to her once we get back," Trevor said when Ben paused for breath. "I'm sure it'll be fine."

"We left our luggage in there!"

"She'll assume we want the room another night—"

"She'll *book* that room! It's a Friday in July. The entire district will be flooded. Mark my words, no room will remain."

"Andreas—"

"Andreas is in the mountains."

"We've got the car—"

"The car! The car! That'll do for a bed and a shower."

Trevor stopped replying.

"I handle every detail. Every one. You sail along. It'll be fine, you say. Sure, we can float up a massive Alp with no map. And who needs a room? We'll just pile into the car—which, may I remind you, we're supposed to return tomorrow in Innsbruck—and Ben can deal with the logistics. It'll be a funny story one day, right? Well, Trevor, I think it's sick. Maybe it's an actual illness. Call it fecklessness-itis. Post it to Plagueslist. God, Trevor. Can't you do *anything* right?"

Cal came to an abrupt stop.

"SHUT UP!" she yelled, so loudly it echoed off the opposing ridge.

Ben stopped. Everyone stopped, but Cal started hiking again at full tilt. What was *wrong* with her? She was snapping. She was losing control. On top of the mountain, and now again. She suddenly understood how seemingly normal people could shake babies and pull triggers. She felt crazed.

She took deep breaths. She had to get herself under control. If only she were alone. She was furious with each one of them. Trevor, her own brother, conniving to get her to relinquish the notebook. Ben, superior and single-minded and emotionally moronic. And Matt! Matt faked concern, but if pressed, he'd always defend Lillian. Lillian. Lillian. Her name made Cal's shoulders stiffen. She'd worn her *clothes*. She'd caught her eye and laughed and laughed. Cal kicked a cluster of wildflowers. She hated her. She had never hated anyone like this.

After some time, she slowed, her heel aching. Lillian brushed past. She was the only one who'd spoken in the past hour. She seemed perky, even. Feeding off the strife, Cal thought. Balm to her soul. She skipped down the switchbacks, leading the sullen train.

The trees thinned. Lillian stopped. "I can see the Soiernhaus down there," she said. "But we didn't come up this way. I think we took a wrong turn. Wait here—"

She darted down a trail to the left, and the rest of them stood still, not looking at each other. Cal shaded her eyes. Yes, there was the base house, and there was the meadow of cows that abutted it. But it was hundreds of feet below, separated from them by a steep scoop of a ravine.

Lillian reappeared. "We've got two options. We could go that way, but it's not really a trail. We might have to bush-whack, and if we lose track of the Soiernhaus, we're really up shit creek. Or we could go that way." She pointed straight down the ravine. "Which is what I suggest."

"What about the map?" Trevor said to Ben.

Ben crossed his spindly arms. "I thought you didn't need a map."

"I was wrong."

Ben did not take his eyes from the opposing ridge.

"We *don't* need a map," said Lillian. "Follow me." She stepped off the path. At once, she was engulfed to the waist in grass and weeds. Cal followed, not because she thought it was a good idea but because she could see no other choice.

She was immediately staggering, moving too fast. The ground was steep and slick and invisible, and all she could do was throw one leg after the other. She made it six or seven long strides before she stepped on a hidden rock and fell backward. She was seated, sliding pell-mell down into the valley, buried stones jangling against her tailbone.

She screamed. She saw Lillian go down. Cal grabbed at grasses but clumps came away in her hands. Lillian was sliding just ahead. Would they ever be able to stop? She dug her fingers into the ground but found no purchase.

They were already halfway down the ravine. They were still gaining momentum. Cal was terrified.

Then Lillian grasped a bush with one arm and flung out the other and Cal grabbed it and skidded to a halt.

"Jesusmarianjoseph," said Lillian in a rush.

"God," said Cal.

They were breathing hard. "That was scary," said Lillian.

Cal maneuvered sideways so she could hold on to the shrub rather than Lillian's arm. She forced her heels into the soft ground to brace herself.

"We were going *fast*," said Lillian.

Cal craned to see down the steep hill. She didn't even want to try standing; she'd only fall again. How were they going to get down?

"Look up," said Lillian. "Look at the guys."

Reluctantly, Cal twisted. Ben, Trevor, and Matt were far above them, high up the slope; they'd covered maybe a couple of yards. They were hunched, mincing, like old men who'd lost their canes. Ben still had his arms crossed.

Cal and Lillian snorted with laughter.

"Telling, isn't it?" said Lillian.

"Of what?"

"Of how each one of them is a tight-ass."

Cal almost laughed again.

"Frankly," said Lillian, her lip curling, "they're all dicks."

That was it. It rose within Cal, a scarlet flood of rage. She slapped Lillian across the face.

Lillian gasped. Cal found herself smiling. Lillian smiled too. "Girl finally grew a backbone," she said, and she slapped Cal.

The stinging pain lasted only a moment. At once, Cal felt a surge of exultation. Always crying! Never fighting back! This was her redemption. She grabbed Lillian's shoulders and shook her. Her skin was warm through the thin, glossy shirt. Oh, it was good to feel those collarbones under her hands, to squeeze that flesh. Lillian wrestled her off and kicked her, hard, in the knee. So many hours sleeping next to her, eating next to her, sliding into her every time Trevor hung a turn too fast. So many biting comments. So many scornful looks. They had both let go of the bush, and Cal forgot to brace her legs, but all that mattered was twisting her arm free of Lillian's grasp so she could hit her again. She was vaguely aware that they were sliding down the mountain, that Trevor and Matt were yelling at them from above, but the only important thing in the world was hitting this girl, and shaking her, and crushing her warm, hateful body.

They picked up speed, the double organism they had become, rolling and skidding down the valley. Cal was on top of Lillian. She kicked and punched but then Lillian was on top of her. The straps of Cal's pack tightened around her shoulders, and her shirt was rucked up and the rocks and sharp weeds scratched her back as they tumbled down the slope. Lillian's hand came toward her face. Cal wrenched away but her head hit a rock, and now Lillian's fingers were in her mouth. She bit down. Lillian yowled with pain and clawed at the roof of Cal's mouth. Cal bit harder but Lillian forced her mouth open with her wiry fingers, and then she ripped them out and pummeled the side of Cal's head. Cal tasted blood, sweet and metallic. She writhed away with all her might.

Her foot was suddenly cold. Cold and wet. As she beat at Lillian's chest, she craned away to see it. That was why they had stopped rolling: they were on the bank of a creek. Her entire foot was submerged. She heaved it out and tried to shift her weight uphill, but Lillian seized her shoulders and pressed her down. "Wait," said Cal, spitting out grass and blood. "Wait—"

"Can't handle it?" Lillian's face was inches from Cal's. Her teeth were bared. "Giving in?"

"No! No—wait—" The muddy bank was canted and slippery. Cal's leg, up to her knee, was in the water. She clawed at the ground but Lillian's arm was splayed across her body, holding her down while she reared back for a punch. "Lill—"

It was too late. They were both sliding down the bank. Now to the thighs—now to the armpits—and they were underwater.

Lillian let go instantly. Cal surfaced, sputtering. It wasn't as deep as she'd feared; with her boots firmly planted on the bottom, she could stand, the water only to her waist. She shoved a ruff of hair out of her face and furiously looked for Lillian. How well she remembered the tactics of fights in the swimming pool. The names of the teams varied—sharks versus shipwreck victims, sea monsters versus the *Dawn Treader*—but it was always Cal and Jesse versus Trevor and Ben, and the point was always the same: catch them, take them down, leap onto their shoulders or buckle their knees.

But Lillian was feet from her, gulping and flailing. Cal took a step but slipped on a rock. She fell toward her and caught her under the arms. "Stop kicking!" she said. "You can touch bottom!"

Lillian clutched at Cal's neck. Cal lost her footing again. "Damn it," she said, coming to the surface, her vision blurred by the water in her eyes, "calm down!" The creek was neither wide nor deep, but if Lillian kept thrashing, they'd never get out. "Hold still!" Lillian took a shaky breath. "You can walk—take it easy, nice and slow, we'll go to that side—"

Lillian took her hand. Slowly, step by step, they waded to the opposite bank. Cal dropped her hand as soon as they were in the meadow. Lillian rubbed her eyes while Cal thrust hanks of wet hair behind her ears and ruefully considered her sodden jeans, her squelching boots. "Thanks," said Lillian, facing away. "I panicked. As I guess you noticed."

"I don't think the deepest part was more than four feet." Wincing, Cal moved her arms in circles. All her ribs seemed to be intact.

"I don't think I've freaked out like that in front of anyone before."

Cal made a hmming sound.

"Anyway. Thanks."

"Let's get to the base house," said Cal. The meadow was small, the grass shorn by cows. She walked briskly, without checking to see whether Lillian was keeping up. Her entire body ached.

They stopped at the pump. Cal drank deeply and splashed water on her face while Lillian fumbled to take off a bracelet. "You can tie your hair back with this if you want," Lillian said. "It's stretchy. Can I tell you something?"

Cal wrapped the bracelet around her ponytail.

"He didn't ask me to find her. He made me promise. That's why I took the stuff. That's why I went through your backpack. I promised I'd find her and I promised I'd do everything I could."

"Oh," said Cal. "Oh."

"Yeah," said Lillian. "Can I tell you something else?"

"Sure."

"You have his laugh. You sound just like him. It's the weirdest, saddest, best thing I've ever heard."

There was a blade of grass clinging to Lillian's cheek. "Well," said Cal. She eyed the grass. She couldn't resist, and she brushed it off. "I keep dreaming I'm looking for him. And it's awful, Lill. I feel like I'll never find him."

"What'd you call me?"

"Lill?"

"Nobody calls me that now."

"It's from the notebook."

"I know."

Cal rubbed her upper arm. She could already see bruises forming. "I haven't been in a fight for years. Since I was a little kid, and those barely count."

"Sweet Cal, nice Cal," said Lillian. "Until you cross her, and she snaps."

The words gave Cal a rush of déjà vu. They were a nursery rhyme, a playground chant. She glanced again at her bruises, four smudges like fingerprints, and felt a brimming joy. It filled her up. It threatened to run over. "All right," she said. "Let's find her. Let's do everything we can."

CHAPTER TWENTY-ONE

Trevor! That pea-brained ignoramus. That no-account joke-ster. Thanks to him, they were sleeping in the car. The *car*. They had parked in a decrepit lot near the Innsbruck airport, and at any moment Ben expected Austrian policemen to pop up à la *The Sound of Music* and wave their guns until they got a satisfactory explanation for why five scruffy Americans were sleeping in a BMW sedan. And who would have to explain? Ben. He was always the one to explain. And he was always the one who looked like an ugly American. A blight on the Euroscape. The idiotic student who had to sleep in a car. A *car*.

The hike would have been a fiasco if he hadn't taken over. His groundwork had been superb—and on only thir-teen hours' notice too. His topographical map had led them straight up that godforsaken mountain, and it would have led them straight down if he hadn't been too angry to consult it. But he'd made one mistake: entrusting the smallest, the sim-plest, of tasks to Trevor.

And did Trevor feel guilt? Did he feel contrition? Evidently not. He was so carefree he'd drifted off to dreamland, draped over the steering wheel. And in the rear seat, they'd fallen asleep like puppies: Lillian curled into Cal's side, Matt's head on Lillian's lap, an indistinguishable tangle of legs. Ben sighed. He propped his foot on the dashboard. On that horrific slide down the mountain, he'd stepped into a hole, a trap laid by some sadistic Alpine marmot, and he'd twisted his ankle. By the blue-white glare of the parking lot's lamps, he could tell it was swollen. He ought to ice it. But did they have ice? Of course not. If they'd been in the pension—but he had forsworn reproaches. He would be the silent martyr of his companions' stupidity.

When they'd returned to the pension, the others waited in the car while he went inside. *"Der Amerikaner!"* the woman cried. She let off a torrent of Bavarian-accented German. Ben got the gist. They'd left their room in a reprehensible state. They hadn't given back the key.

"I didn't know—"

They hadn't even packed.

"I don't suppose—"

"Yes?"

"I don't suppose we could stay here one more night?"

The woman actually laughed in his face. "You should have asked last night. Now? No. I wouldn't rent to you even if we *had* a vacancy. I doubt there's an empty room in the entire district. Take your bags and leave."

"Let me get my friends to help—"

"No. Now."

Ben put two packs on his back and one on each arm, and used his good foot to kick the fifth—Trevor's—all the way to the car. He reported the news. He was the model of tact. He said nothing to accentuate Trevor's incredible negligence.

"How would she know all the rooms are full?" said Trevor. "She wants to keep our business from her competition. Let's take a turn through Mittenwald."

They drove through Mittenwald, and Krün, and Wallgau. Every inn had an AUSGEBUCHT sign: all booked up. The sun sank.

"Savor this moment," said Cal. "We are living our parents' worst nightmare."

"I thought that was the time we bought cocaine from the pedophiliac school nurse," said Lillian.

"Fine," said Cal. "Second-worst." They giggled.

"Anyway, Mom's going to think this is a great story," said Trevor.

Ben would not grant him the courtesy of an eye roll.

"So I'm allowed to tell her?" Cal asked Trevor.

He would stare out the window.

"Go right ahead. Incidentally, I think I lost that fake ID I said I'd give you. Let's try for a room in Oberammergau."

He wouldn't even delight them with facts about the famed Passion Play of Oberammergau.

"Ben?" ventured Cal. "Directions?"

Silently, he handed her the map. He would no longer navigate. In fact, he would resign from all leadership. Or had he been deposed? He hadn't even wanted to be in charge; he'd just been the best one for the job. But now that he'd lost power, he would retire gracefully. Like Romulus Augustulus, he would accept the new rulers, barbarians though they might be, and live out his life in peaceful seclusion, in a villa in southern Italy—

"Scratch Oberammergau," said Trevor. "Too small. Let's suck it up and go to Munich. No need for the map, Cal. I'll use this."

Any dimwit could fake competence with a smartphone.

"What does it mean if the entire route is highlighted in red?" said Cal.

"Oh. Traffic."

Ben could have told them that. On a Friday evening in July, the A95 would be horrendous.

"We have to return the car tomorrow at the Innsbruck airport," said Cal. "Let's go there."

Two hours later, they'd swung through the circuit of airport hotels. *Ausgebucht,* as Ben had forecast. They settled for the parking lot.

"Will we be a security concern if we're here all night?" said Cal.

"We can explain," said Trevor.

We? Ben took out the accoutrements of postcard writing, but when he saw Trevor grin, he put them away. He wasn't in the mood to have his courtship ritual razzed by his dolt of a cousin. And what would he say? *Dear Jean, I write you from my night's lodging, the passenger seat of a rented sedan. . . .* She'd lose all interest.

For all he knew, she already had. Maybe it was politeness that kept her sending those pithy, witty, ravishingly attractive emails. (Ben hadn't even known an email *could* be attractive.) Unfortunately, he had also been reading the gossip sent by Liam, his effusive former roommate. *Guess who's been hanging out with Jean?* Liam wrote. *Maria Kopawalski.* Ben had once dated Maria Kopawalski, a relationship that had not begun, middled, or ended particularly well. And now she'd befriended

Jean Lin? This made him feel peevish about all females. When they sensed trouble brewing for one of their kind, they drew in the troops, banded against the hapless male, formed alliances where there had been none before. Look at Cal and Lillian. Womankind!

Oh, he was being unfair. He knew that.

They had stopped at a supermarket in Seefeld. Cal's heel hurt, so only Trevor, Matt, and Lillian went in. Nobody even inquired about his ankle, Ben thought darkly. And nobody asked him what he would be capable of eating.

In the parking lot, Cal said, "I'm fine with being arrested as long as we eat first. I'm starving."

So was Ben. He rummaged for his coffee grinder. He knew his esophageal disorder would not allow him to eat solid food tonight. Sometimes he could get by with lots of chewing and water, but now his throat felt tight, as if closed by hives. He took some Emmentaler cheese, a hunk of bread, and a few slices of suspiciously discounted lunch meat. The choices were nutritionally inadequate—Trevor clearly had no idea how fast scurvy could set in—but at least there were bananas; the coffee grinder balked without a good deal of moisture. It would be a passable meal. A ham-sandwich-and-banana smoothie. It wasn't up to the standard he and Uncle Arnold had set in Berkeley, with their kale, their coconut oil, their Algorithm, but one had to grant some accommodations to traveling.

But when he pressed the GRIND button, there was a faint whir, a dying and accusatory whine. He pressed it again and the whir was fainter, and he pressed it again and there was no sound at all. His batteries were dead. That was fine. He had backups. He felt around in his pack. But he'd lent them to

Trevor for his electric toothbrush. He turned to ask for them back.

Trevor sat cross-legged in the driver's seat, facing the rear. "So *then* the goose hid between the two cases of beer—"

The other three howled with laughter.

Well. He didn't need batteries. He didn't need food. So what if he'd hiked for seven hours? So what if he hadn't eaten since lunch? If this was how they wanted to treat him, this was what they'd get. Gently, he set down the coffee grinder. He zipped his blue pullover and closed his eyes. Maybe he wouldn't sleep, but he was certainly a competent fake.

"Ben. Ben."

"Hrg." His mouth was too dry to form words.

"Wake up."

"Ugh." He could barely crack his eyes.

"Come on. Wake up."

"Hurr." He was ravenous. He could smell the abandoned ham-banana smoothie.

"You've got to look."

With a screech from his neck muscles, Ben twisted to see out the window. He hadn't realized last night how close they were to the mountains. But of course they were. Innsbruck was situated in a valley between two high Alpine ridges. It'd twice hosted the Winter Olympics: 1976, and was it '68 or '64? Then he refocused on the mountains, he actually looked, and to his surprise—he did not characterize himself as one affected by beauty—he gasped.

They were looking west, where the rising sun clarified the dark-teal pines and reflected from the snow on the peaks.

Ben could not take his eyes from the snow: it was pink-gold, a warm, rosy gold he'd never seen in nature. It was the color of the flesh of a Raphael Virgin, of pale skin beginning to blush, and he thought, I'm just as affected by beauty as anyone, and his ankle twinged, and his throat clenched, and he had to look away. It had been a long time since he'd cried.

Cal pulled the blue notebook from her backpack. "You guys really should read this," she said, as if they'd been refusing for months. She opened the cover and Ben craned toward Jesse's economical, forceful letters. *My* dad*! No one could mistake Arnold . . .*

"We could read it aloud," said Lillian.

"We've got time," said Trevor. "It's not like we have somewhere we need to be."

They laughed. How could they consider that funny? Ben's irritation roared back.

"But I have to get out of this car," said Lillian. "It smells revolting."

"Yeah, it smells like meaty banana," said Trevor.

"Enough," said Cal.

"Like a monkey let rip a big one—"

"Enough!"

Outside, Ben let loose a convulsive shiver, but he resolved to suffer in silence. Perhaps the cold air would provide his ankle a sort of poor man's ice pack. They sat in a circle on the torn-up concrete and took turns reading aloud. Ben hesitated when Cal handed the notebook to him. He'd planned to extend the silent treatment a while longer. (At least until someone noticed.) But he supposed he could make an exception. These were Jesse's words, not his.

As they read, Ben remembered his cousin's winning humor,

his social grace, all the traits he'd never had himself. He didn't want them, he reminded himself. He'd long ago renounced wanting them. But it overwhelmed him, the longing for Jesse. To be with him and to be him. To have that sweep of hair, to be good at sports, to know what to say and when. He had to shake it off. He would adhere to New Criticism: the text was all there was. He would consider neither reader nor writer. The *Juvenilia* would be accorded a close reading, and the unity of style and subject would be revealed. Then, they would know where to go.

"*Arnold rustled behind his fresh Sunday* Times," read Matt, "*all the sections he'd been saving for the week.*"

Cal cleared her throat. "We stop here. That's the last story I've read."

Ben's fingers were poised at his temples.

"I guess the logical next step is Berlin," Lillian said slowly. "As Andreas said."

Ben felt the distant surges of understanding, of plates beginning to shift. He held still. The forms were shadowy, the sun lingering behind the horizon in the last moment before clarity—

"But—" said Lillian.

"But—" said Ben.

"That year after college—"

"If she's returned there, wherever she was—"

He thought of the Italian compass. The maps of Catholic shrines. Abend's papers, Goethe's *Italienische Reise,* and the photograph where Thea gazed upon her baby as if he were the Christ child himself. "How," Lillian had asked, "could she ever have left him?"

The earth spun, the light fell.

Ben said, "Rome."

This certainty, this was the best feeling he ever had. This was why he wanted to write papers all his life. His task now was to convince his reader, to draw his argument's threads together and forward to their inevitable, perfect end. Usually he'd be scribbling with his fountain pen, his supple handwriting looping and dashing like a nineteenth-century novelist's, but here, he'd have to talk it through.

"All the clues point to Rome," he said.

"This isn't a book," said Matt. "There aren't clues."

"Think of Goethe. '*Ja, ich bin endlich in dieser Hauptstadt der Welt angelangt!*'"

"We speak English," said Lillian.

"'Yes,'" translated Ben, "'at last, I have reached the very capital of the world!'"

"Goethe went to Rome?"

"He did. Frankfurt to Mittenwald to Rome. A secular pilgrimage. 'I now see all the dreams of my youth, coming to life. . . .'"

"And that's where the *Pietà* is," said Lillian. "The real one."

"Other *Pietà*s are as real as Michelangelo's," said Ben. Or so he was told by basic ontological pragmatism. He didn't quite believe it. He hated when his thoughts didn't line up with his beliefs. This was his senior thesis all over again. He'd known Guarini was a better subject, but instead he'd obeyed his contumacious heart. Michelangelo! Lillian was right. That statue *was* more real than all the others. They were dreams and it was morning. They were fog and it was sun.

"She's gone to Rome," said Lillian. "I'm sure of it. It's a pilgrimage."

"For us, maybe," said Matt.

"No. For her. She has to make amends. She has to forgive herself for leaving him."

Ben nodded at her. She understood.

"I'm with you," Cal told Lillian.

"Rome's cool by me," said Trevor. "I love gelato."

Matt frowned and tossed his squash ball from one hand to the other. "We've got some flaws in our logic, guys."

"You don't get it," said Lillian.

"These so-called clues, they're all trumped up. There's no real reason to go to Rome."

"Imagine what it's like to *be* her."

"How?" Matt said reasonably. "We don't know her."

"*Imagine,* I said."

"Matt, come on," said Cal. "The compass, the Goethe—"

"All the textual evidence," said Ben.

"I'm outnumbered," said Matt. "Fine. Rome. We won't find her there but we won't find her anywhere."

"Who *are* you?" snapped Lillian. "I thought you were his best friend. Well, four to one. We win. Should we drive or fly?"

"Doesn't matter," said Trevor.

"Of course it matters," said Ben. A pro-con list was begotten in his head. Which would be more expensive: last-minute plane tickets, or the fee for returning the rental car in Italy? What about gas? How far away *was* Rome? Italy was very long. Too long, as Napoleon had complained. Perhaps it would be better to fly.

"I know we should get moving," said Cal, "but I think we could read the next section of the *Juvenilia* now."

"Yes," said Lillian.

"Hold on," said Trevor. He got the bag of food from the car. "Breakfast." The other three were heedless, already tugging apart bread and slapping on cheese, eating without a single worry that their esophagi might not collaborate, but Trevor showed Ben his electric toothbrush. "You should eat." He pried open the battery case. He'd gotten the coffee grinder too. Ben wished he could say he didn't need them, that solid food would go down just fine, but he felt his throat stiffening and he could do nothing but mutely accept the batteries and the grinder, the tokens of Trevor's regret.

An Excerpt from
THE JUVENILIA OF JESSE T. SERRANO

Cal, I've been thinking about why I'm writing this, why I've sent you on this trip to nowhere, this grail-less quest, a chase after a wild-goose woman whom you don't know and I don't know.

I used to believe in the Choice of Achilles. I used to think you could choose between a short, glorious life or a long, boring life. Take my father: a boring life that likely will be long, given that his riskiest activity is unicycling with no mouth guard. Compare him to that guy who's plastered all over our apartment. Clearly, there's a negative correlation between longevity and glory.

But here's something I've realized, and although it sounds obvious, I bet it hasn't yet forced itself upon you: we are shackled by time. *Chained.* We should have power over it, right? We can fly across the ocean and travel to the moon, so why can't we control something as mundane as time? A few months ago I took the SAT. (Yeah, Arnold had me take the SAT, even though we both knew I wasn't going to make it to college. Cheap shot, huh?) They told us to open our booklets and I thought, This is going to be so so so freaking boring, and there is nothing I can do but live through it. I felt as if I were in a straitjacket. Which I was, and am.

To do glorious deeds, you need time. I do not have time. Nobody's going to publish my biography. Maybe some wunderkinder like Achilles and Jesus and Raphael can manage to be awesome in twenty or thirty or forty years, but most real people who accomplish real things get their biblical allotment.

It was a lie. There is no Choice. Here are the facts: it's a sunny day in May, it's the most beautiful month in the most beautiful state in the Union, and I'm seventeen, lying in bed, about to do absolutely nothing.

Ben never picked up his phone, but I left an urgent voice mail. He called that evening. "I'm vastly busy, Jesse. Finals are nigh."

"I just need help with a little"—I paused before dropping the magic word—*"research."*

"I'm on it." Twenty minutes later, he knocked. "Research?"

I led him into my room and shut the door.

"Is it for school? AP Euro, perchance? I was fantastic at AP Euro."

"Your life peaked in AP Euro."

"You jest, but it may well have."

"It's not for school. And you can't tell Arnold. Okay?"

"Well—"

"I want to find out about my mother."

Ben blanched. He started jabbering. "This isn't academic

research, which is what you made it sound like, and I'm hardly some cousinly gumshoe—"

"Hold up. She was a student at Berkeley." He nodded. "She must have left a trace. We could start with the yearbooks. I'd look myself, but"—another word to dangle like bait—"I don't know how to use the *library*."

"The library," said Ben. "I do know my way around the library."

We met after school the next day. It was early December, and he looked windswept in his blue pullover. He told me all about his coursework as we walked into the Bancroft Library. "All but three of us dropped Akkadian, can you believe it? The verbs conjugate with infixes. Entertaining, but complex. Good afternoon, Marcus, how are you?" This last was to the security guard, who waved us through without requesting Ben's Berkeley ID or, crucially, mine. "I can only dream of achieving fluency in an infix-based tense system."

I could tell he was nervous. He consulted his notebook. "We'll need to go to the UC Archives."

"You pre-searched the research?"

"Naturally."

He found the shelf that held the yearbooks from the eighties and nineties. "Unindexed, as I expected. We'll have to search manually. Check the seniors' headshots first." Ben's fingers seemed to sense the exact spot to open the book. He was like a blackjack dealer with a pack of cards. I watched him work instead of working myself. He didn't seem to mind. I was still short of breath from the trip up the stairs.

After some time, he closed a yearbook. His thumb held his place.

"You found her."

"I found a *picture* of her."

Her chin spiked the camera. Even in the black-and-white photo, you could tell how golden her hair was. Cal, do you remember how we'd study your parents' old yearbooks? I'd always thought there was something tragic about senior portraits, and now I knew what. It was all that hope. All that forthright, youthful gleam.

"Let's photocopy this," said Ben.

"Yeah."

"You okay?"

"Yeah, yeah."

"Now I know what year she graduated. I can find professors who knew her."

Ben took research even more seriously than I had imagined.

"I have to say, this was a difficult project."

"Sorry."

"No, no. The more difficult, the more rewarding. I couldn't sally forth into the art history department with that photograph. Anyone who recognized her would doubtless know of her connection to Uncle Arnold. He'd be notified, and you'd be in hot water."

"I didn't think of that."

Ben preened. That is, he preened Ben-style: he ruffled his hair and grimaced. "Fortunately, I'm well apprised in departmental politics. You know Professor Ferston?" He didn't wait for an answer. "She loathes Uncle Arnold."

"Why?"

"I *had* suspected it was born of a rough-and-tumble brand

of feminism. That he shouldn't study Mary because he's a man. I'm simplifying, obviously. But now I have a new theory."

He paused. "Do tell," I said.

"Her research assistant"—another dramatic pause—"was one Thea Vogel."

"Her?"

"Her."

"Until—"

"Yes. Until you were born. But they had almost two years together. Having concocted an elaborate backstory, I took notes as Ferston reminisced."

The sheet was full. I snatched it, but it was all about art history.

"Remember," said Ben, "this was a professional relationship."

"But didn't Ferston tell you what she was *like*?"

"Look, sorry. I wish I could bring you notes like 'Thea loved strawberries and sea kayaking and Hercule Poirot.' But I know only one person who could tell you those things."

Arnold.

"This is what I *do* know," Ben continued. "On her own time, she was researching—well, to be frank, a rather hackneyed topic. Uninspired. Pedestrian. The *Pietà*s of Michelangelo."

"There's more than one?"

"Jesse! Are you not the scion of a world-renowned art historian? Michelangelo lived to be eighty-nine years old." Ben marched me into the study, the *Pietà*-slash-*Deposition* room. "This is the famous one, in Rome." Arnold owned so many postcards of this statue that he had to stack the shots taken from the same angle. "But there's also the Bandini *Pietà*." It was unfinished, the figures struggling to burst from the stone. "And Michelangelo's very last sculpture. The Rondanini *Pietà*."

I'd never had such a visceral reaction to a postcard. "I hate it."

"Mary looks like she's about to break, doesn't she?"

"What *happened*? How did he go from a beautiful, young, strong Mary to—to *that*?"

"That's what Thea was writing about."

"Oh." Her notes, her drafts: they existed somewhere. I had to know whether she hated the Rondanini *Pietà* as much as I did. "Let's look through my dad's papers."

"What? Jesse! No! I'm not prying into Uncle Arnold's files!"

"How is that any worse than interrogating his colleague behind his back?"

"I regret it. It was unethical."

Oops, wrong tack. "I'm going to do it either way. But it'll be much more efficient with you." I didn't mention that I couldn't imagine snooping alone. A partner would dilute my guilt. "Ben, he's got this byzantine system of file organization—"

"Well—" He looked pained. "Fine."

I had him at the word *byzantine*. Thank you, Arnold, for making me study for the SAT.

On Wednesday, Arnold had office hours all afternoon. "I can't believe I'm doing this," Ben groused as we entered Arnold's bedroom, the dump for the miscellaneous postcards: the Visitation, the Wedding at Cana, the Marriage of the Virgin. Four file cabinets lined the wall. I sat on the bed while Ben thumbed the folders, pulling ones that looked likely.

When he had an armful, I said, "Let's do this at the kitchen table." It was too weird to be in Arnold's bedroom; I'd dart in to steal socks or fetch him his glasses, but that was it. Arnold had spent a lot of time in *my* bedroom. He used to read aloud to me every night. Sometimes I think all those words sank into the walls. When I'm almost asleep, I can see brave Reepicheep leaving the *Dawn Treader,* and I can taste the red fruit that Lyra gives Will. I can hear Ollivander's wispy voice: *He-Who-Must-Not-Be-Named did great things—terrible, yes, but great.* The stories you hear as a child take hold. They change everything because they change how you see everything. Your world gains narrative. Your days are quests and your quests have grails.

I guess it's not my bedroom that's suffused with stories. It's me.

"The kitchen is fine," said Ben.

Arnold's filing system, we discovered, was about as organized as Mrs. Basil E. Frankweiler's. "This file's labeled 'Very Personal,'" I said. "And look what's in it."

Ben had stopped moving, which was odd. He wasn't often able to resist the allure of stacks of paper.

"Come on, Ben, take a look."

He shook his head.

"Gas and electric bills from 1992," I said, but it didn't seem funny anymore. "Ben? What's wrong?"

"What's the greater meaning to this, Jesse?"

"Huh?"

"That's what my adviser says. I'll pitch a research idea, and he'll ask, 'What's the greater meaning?' And if I can't answer, he'll say, 'This paper should not be written.'"

"You mean, why am I doing this?" I said.

"Yes."

"Let me think."

Ben's a bloodhound when it comes to his questions being answered. He waited.

"She's been missing a long time," I said finally. "I need to find her."

"Jesse, you're not going to find her this way."

I think I knew that already, but it was different being told. "If I find out what she used to be like—"

"No."

"That makes sense," I insisted. "The future is contained within the past. I can predict what you'll be doing in seventeen years. You won't be working in a fish cannery. You won't be an astronaut."

Ben looked wounded. "It's still possible—"

"And look at *her*." Of course I turned to her. I'd been surrounded by her all my life. I found the Simone Martini Annunciation altarpiece. "Look how sad she is. The whole story's contained in the beginning. You're not the only one who knows about typology, Ben." Now I was angry. I starting jabbing at postcards. "Passiflora, she's holding. A symbol of the Passion. The beams of the loggia make a cross. And she's got her finger in the book because she's reading the prophecies. She knows her son will die."

"Your mother isn't Mary."

"Of course not."

Ben stood and leaned into me. "Your mother is *not Mary*. This is human life, not a story. That girl in the yearbook? You could stare at her face for hours and you wouldn't know anything, because the fact is, Jesse, she didn't know anything either."

"But—"

"Look at Mary. Look harder. Maybe the passiflora just grew in her garden. Maybe there's a cross because a building won't stay up without a cross. Maybe she stuck her finger in the book to mark her goddamn place." Ben grabbed the files. "I'll put these away because I know you need help, but I'm leaving and I'm not seeing you again until you ditch this project. Jesse. Jesse. This paper should not be written."

He had exams that week. He texted me and asked whether I'd given up, and I texted back *no*.

"We should have Ben over for dinner before he leaves," Arnold said one evening. I was coloring a map, which was a totally appropriate assignment for juniors in AP history, and he had brought home a stack of journals. "I've run across a few articles that might interest him."

"He already left."

"Oh! Is it really that close to Christmas?"

I wished we were going to Chicago. We used to spend Christmas there, but now airplanes were too much trouble: the oxygen for emergencies, the stares. Though, to be fair, that stuff didn't bother Arnold. It was our mutual inertia that kept us home.

I almost said it. "I wish we were going to Chicago." It would have been so easy. I should have said it. Arnold would have been on the phone within seconds. Oh, Cal. I wish I had. I lay on my stomach and scribbled with crayons. The last time I did that, I was probably with you. I longed for that time so hard that my sigh got stuck and came out a groan.

"Everything all right?"

Arnold would want to stay in California. He would read a lot, write a little, interact only with me. He'd go on solo hikes and avoid campus. On Christmas morning, he would make me a special holiday smoothie. He'd just gotten into smoothies. The berries and the greens would eventually merge into a scatological brown, but in the blender, they'd look awfully pretty. Like holly.

I had to be careful what I wished for, because I'd get it. He'd have given me the moon.

A few days later, I got a postcard from Ben. *Dear Jesse,* he'd written. *I apologize for my churlish comments regarding your quest. Press onward. Everyone here in Chicago misses you and Uncle Arnold. My spare time of late has been devoted to a perusal of* Garner's Modern American Usage *(a classic of our time), and thus I shall leave you with this festive tidbit: the X in* Xmas *is a Greek* chi, *as in* Christos, *and therefore the prejudice against it, per Garner, is "unfounded and unfortunate." Happy Xmas! Yours, Ben.*

I flipped to the front and smiled. I'd been expecting Mary, but instead it was the Art Institute of Chicago's sculpture from Brâncuși's Bird series: a silhouette, a streamlined, golden silhouette, a three-dimensional arrow pointing to the sky. In the white margin, Ben had written:

"All my life, I have sought to render the essence of flight."
—*Constantin Brâncuși*

Ben adored diacritical marks. I adored the fact that Ben had not sent me a Madonna to add to Arnold's collection. I took the postcard to my bedroom, where the walls were white, and propped it on my desk.

All my life, I have sought to render the essence of flight.

The writing gave me a sudden idea. I had to sit down, it struck me so sharply. All those postcards, all those Marys: they had *backs*.

Some of the ten thousand must be inscribed.

What if the essential clue was in my own apartment? What if I'd been living my life within walls that were made of the words of my mother?

Arnold was at his campus office. I had to start. I wanted to proceed from the first story to the last, but the kitchen overwhelmed me; Annunciations had invaded the cabinets, occupied the refrigerator, and crept onto the ceiling. I went to the dining room, the Nativities and Madonna-and-Childs.

I chose a wall and took down the bottommost, leftmost postcard. We put the ones we didn't like down in the corners, and this was that nasty Raphael, the *Cowper Madonna*, where Christ is about twice as long as your standard human infant. It was blank. I stuck it back onto the wall. I tried another.

But I was too impatient. I wanted to see my mother's handwriting, to hold something she'd held. I started processing sets of ten at once. Even that took too long. I could see at a glance they were blank, but I had to reaffix them, straighten them, make sure the ancient tape held. All the reaching and shifting and bending was giving me the swoops.

I took a break in a dining-room chair. I was furious. Why couldn't I wave a wand and have the postcards snap around? Hermione could have done it. And I knew there'd be clues. There were clues in *The Westing Game* and *Looking for Alaska*. The Hardy Boys got clues, and even though I spent formative years spurning books with girls on the cover, I bet Nancy Drew got clues. What was the point of all that reading if it'd taught me wrong? There were always clues.

I believed in clues just like I believed in the Choice.

I gripped the table until the light-headedness faded, and then I began anew. I didn't worry about the postcards' original positions or slide my nails under the tape. I ripped them off and flung them to the floor. I almost forgot to look at the backs. When I pulled over a chair to reach the top rows, postcards crumpled under its legs. I didn't care. I had only one left. I pulled the topmost, rightmost postcard from the wall and glanced at its back and threw it down.

They had all been blank.

I guess I heard his breathing. He stood in the doorway. I opened my mouth and he shook his head, not censoriously, just telling me that I didn't need to say anything. I stepped down from the chair. Yellowed tendrils of masking tape clung to the wall. It was a shock to see that wall empty, like when you've moved a mirror but still expect to see yourself instead of dead space. The floor was splashy and golden with Madonna-and-Childs.

Arnold bent to pick up a postcard that had wafted to the doorway. "The Lippi from the Uffizi."

"I'll get the tape."

"One of my favorites."

This is how we spent that evening. I made tape curlicues and fixed one on each corner. I handed the postcards to Arnold, and he put them on the wall. We didn't talk, we barely even looked at each other, but the wall bloomed, and I stopped envying all those babies on their mothers' laps because being in there, hushed, with my dad: it felt like being held.

CHAPTER TWENTY-TWO

"Wahoo!" said Trevor, launching himself down the aisle of the airplane. "This thing is a ghost town!"

Matt had never seen a jumbo jet so deserted. It was as eerie as a mall after a late movie. The walls and seats were a uniform, pale mint-green that made him feel as if he'd stumbled inside a tube of toothpaste.

"This is uncanny," said Cal from behind him.

He nodded. Supposedly it was the last leg of a long-haul flight from Singapore that had dumped most of its passengers in Innsbruck. Supposedly. Who really knew? He felt sick to his stomach. The only other passengers, a mother and a father and two children, were conked out in the manner associated with either heavy narcotics or multicontinental travel. Matt forced himself to breathe. He'd never heard of Royal Viennajet, but he'd assumed it was just another European budget airline, a Ryanair knockoff that crammed passengers into refurbished planes and bopped around the Continent, tickets for ten euros and onboard Cokes for five. He hadn't expected this.

"Festival seating, I assume," said Trevor. He scooched down a middle row, flipping up all the armrests, and then reclined on his back. "The flight attendants literally outnumber us. What should we ask for? Peeled grapes? Foot massages?"

Ben buckled his seat belt and rolled his eyes. Trevor looked hurt. "Duck confit," Cal said abruptly. "Sweetbreads. Or sweetmeats? Whichever's the not-nasty one."

Trevor grinned. He kicked off his shoes and propped his long legs on the ceiling A/C vent. "Twelve drummers drumming. A personal yoga class. Lullabies."

"A bubble bath," said Cal. "I'm dying for a bubble bath. How is this airline possibly profitable?"

"I'm wondering the same thing," Ben said darkly.

"Peanuts," said Trevor with a dreamy expression. "Pretzels. Or maybe those delicious little cinnamon biscotti—"

"What's this a front for?" said Ben. "That's what I want to know."

Matt felt worse. He headed back and took the window seat he'd been assigned. Why couldn't he be more like Trevor? Laugh at fear, take life as it came? Cal paused in the aisle. "May I?" she said a bit shyly.

"Of course."

She sat. "Don't listen to Ben. He's just ticked that you're the one who found the deal."

It had seemed a great idea at the time, but now Matt regretted trying the deserted Royal Viennajet desk. "Tickets for this flight are no longer for sale," the agent had said. Glancing around, he had added in an undertone, "Two hundred euros."

"Wait, they *are* for sale?"

"Two hundred."

For five last-minute tickets? Matt gladly handed over the bank card.

The agent shook his head. "Cash."

They'd had a hurried conference by the ATM. "Go for it," said Trevor.

Cal stood on one leg and bit her lip. "Do you think it's legal?"

"Girl," said Lillian, "we're bribing a ticket agent to get on an international flight. It's not legal."

To Matt's surprise, Cal laughed. "Whatever. Let's do it."

The agent slid the money under the keyboard and printed five boarding passes. "At the gate," he said, "board with Florian. *Not* with Theresa. Understood?"

Matt watched two of the flight attendants snap shut the overhead bins. They were all women, and they wore flowing turquoise blouses, stiletto heels, and green eye shadow that matched the interior walls. The door would close soon and they'd be locked in, heading to Rome on this apocalyptically deserted jumbo jet. Rome: the most illogical decision in a long trail of illogical decisions. They were going to Rome because Thea had once read about Goethe going to Rome, because she'd once owned a compass manufactured in Italy. These clues, Matt thought, meant nothing. For all his talk about textual analysis, Ben had missed the only important sentence in Jesse's notebook: *I believed in clues just like I believed in the Choice.*

Matt looked across the plane. Lillian was asleep. With her legs tucked under her billowing white skirt and the hood of her white sweater pulled up, she looked like a baby in an old-fashioned christening gown. In the parking lot, when he'd dared question her logic, she'd spat, "Who *are* you?" He had seen, suddenly, the new down burring over her head, the smudges of makeup and fatigue beneath her eyes. He had seen that she was gone, the sharp-edged and oak-paneled Lillian he'd known. To replace her had come this little girl—or had Matt just now caught sight of her, the little girl who'd been Lillian all along? He felt a swooshing collapse, a softening. He thought, Who *am* I? And who am I to judge? They were going to Rome because deep down, in a way that was beyond words or logic, Lillian needed to go to Rome. He could not argue. It was not a matter for argument. And he could not leave. He would not leave. Until she was ready to give up, until Cal and Ben and Trevor were ready to give up, Matt would stick by their side.

From ten rows ahead, Trevor called, "Do you think this airline has a frequent-flier program?"

"For whom?" Ben said acerbically. "The cocaine mules in the cargo hold?"

Matt gritted his teeth. Cal said, "Ignore him."

"But he might have a point," said Matt.

"I'm sure this is fine," said Cal.

What the hell. He'd tell her. "Honestly? I'm scared of flying under any circumstances."

Cal smirked. "Heights, crowds, confinement, getting drunk, *and* flying?"

"I know. I'm a wimp."

"What else? Spiders?"

"Yup."

"Sharks?"

"Check."

"Snakes?"

"I actually had a pet python as a kid, so no. Ernie, I called him. He slept in my bed."

Cal looked impressed.

"Just kidding. Yeah. Snakes. I'm freaking terrified of snakes."

"I thought you *liked* flying. The way you zone out. You seem so serene."

"It's a defense mechanism."

"Ah. Well, if you need to zone out, don't mind me."

"Talking works. As long as I'm not thinking about flying."

"It *is* weird, right? To be trapped in this huge hunk of metal that's somehow levitated hundreds of miles above—"

"Talking about flying, yeah, that's bad too."

Cal laughed. "Sorry. I'm horrible."

"You're not horrible."

She fell silent. They still hadn't taxied away from the gate. He could hear the low hum of the flight attendants' conversation.

"Matt?" said Cal. "Can I ask you something?"

So she suspected. He should have seen it coming. While they were reading the *Juvenilia* in the parking lot, his face, he was pretty sure, had told its own story. All those memories. Jesse prone on the countertop. Jesse on his borrowed bike. Jesse jittering his foot as Lillian walked to the quiz bowl bus, his expression so hopeful that Matt felt a confused rush of protectiveness and embarrassment and anger: don't be so exposed, he wanted to tell him; veil your hope. But sharpest of all were the memories that hadn't been Matt's. Jesse and Matt's father, alone in the kitchen. *"Sometimes I wonder."* Matt knew exactly the expression on his father's face. *"Whether he's* even. Well. Interested." His father would have said the words gingerly, with the tip of his tongue, as if by taking them too far inside his mouth he might be tainted himself.

"Sure."

"You don't mind?"

What the hell, he thought again. "Ask me anything."

"You really don't think I'm a horrible person?"

"That's what you want to ask me?"

"Yeah."

"Oh."

"What, is that weird?"

"No, no. I just expected—well, something else." She leaned back against the headrest, feigning indifference, he thought. They'd tried to clean up from the hike, dabbing their faces and arms with a moistened T-shirt Trevor had donated to the cause, but Cal had missed a streak of mud in front of her ear. "Hold still," said Matt. With the towelette from the seat pocket, he blotted away the mud. Cal held very still. He felt a wave of tenderness toward her. "No," he said. "I don't think you're horrible."

She was a little teary. "You don't understand what I did."

"We all did stuff."

"I lost touch with him. All through high school. We barely talked."

"I know."

"I lost those years." She exhaled a shuddering breath. "I didn't even know him. I don't know why I'm telling you this."

"You still knew him. You just knew an older version of him. An older layer. But it's like fresco. Even if it gets painted over, the first layer's part of the plaster, part of the wall. You knew him." But Matt ached for her. No matter what he said, the years were lost. There was only regret. "Let me tell you something." Could he? "Okay. It was June. Two months before. He'd been in and out of the hospital." When Matt got home from practice, he'd found his dad mixing sports drink, his cycling shoes clacking on the kitchen floor. "You got a call," said his dad. "The Serrano kid."

"On the home phone?"

"Your cell's dead, he said. And it's urgent."

Matt froze. "Urgent?"

His dad had his back to him. The sports drink foamed like a breaking wave. Surely his dad would face him if he had news to deliver. Matt had imagined this moment but he'd always thought he'd be the one to answer the phone. "You should come to the hospital," Professor Serrano would say. "Now?" "I think now would be best, yes."

"Wait," said Matt. "It was Jesse? Jesse himself?"

"He's got big plans for the two of you tonight. Tickets to a play."

Matt sank back against the cabinets. He hadn't realized how tense he'd been until every muscle loosened at once. He laughed. "A *play*?"

"That's what *I* said. 'A *play*?'"

Matt picked up the landline. "I'll call him back. Thanks."

"You gonna go?"

"Sure," said Matt. "Why wouldn't I?"

"Why wouldn't you?" His dad's voice was flinty. "'Yes, Jesse, anything you say, Jesse, I'll bend over, assume the position—'" He grabbed the bottles. "I'm off. Sixty miles on the docket. You have fun. Date night at the theater."

Matt had stared at the phone's keypad for some time

before he dialed. "It's *Arcadia*," said Jesse. "Tom Stoppard. This woman in my dad's department, she has two tickets but can't go, and my dad says he saw it years ago and I should invite you. He says it's about everything we like to talk about, time and math and poetry and chaos—"

"I can't," said Matt. "Can you go with Lillian? Or your dad?"

"Oh."

"I've got a match tomorrow. I've got to get some sleep. A late entry into this tournament. My coach, he's making me, he wants me to get more match play under my belt before the junior open—"

Matt could hear Jesse breathing, shallowly, rapidly, but he didn't think it was different from the way he always breathed now. "Well. I'm sure my dad will be happy to accompany me."

"Sorry," said Matt, "sorry, Jesse—"

"I understand," said Jesse. "And please. Allow me to wish you the best of luck."

Two more passengers boarded. They consulted their tickets and paused next to Cal and Matt. The woman, heels and jeans and flat-ironed hair, handed her bag to the man and sank into the aisle seat without thanking him. He put her bag in the overhead compartment and took a rolled-up magazine from his leather satchel.

"I've never seen such an empty plane," said the woman, her accent American. "What are the chances we're getting hijacked?" She angled her knees so the man could pass. He settled into his seat and opened the magazine. "Either it's a smuggling racket or we're taking a nosedive into the

Colosseum." The *Economist,* Matt saw. The woman sighed. "If you want to read," she told the man, "just tell me you want to read."

"I want to read."

She rolled her eyes across the aisle. Matt smiled politely. She half stood to catch the attention of a flight attendant, who obligingly teetered toward them on her stilettos. "Could we get some drinks here?" said the woman.

The attendant frowned. She couldn't have been much older than Matt.

"Drinks," the woman repeated. She mimed drinking. The attendant's face cleared.

"Ah! We depart. Then drinks."

"You have, like, five passengers. I think you have time to serve us drinks."

The attendant's mouth was open, her kohl-lined eyes wide. The makeup had to be part of the uniform, thought Matt.

"I'll have a glass of champagne. Babe? You want anything?" The man grunted no. "One champagne, then. Is that clear?"

The attendant obviously didn't understand a word. "Thank you," she said.

"Never mind. Okay. Never mind." The woman fluttered a hand, dismissing her. When the attendant left, she shook her head at Matt and Cal. "So much for service. That's one thing I can't stand about Europe. They say you don't tip so you can't expect much, but God."

Matt opened his mouth to mm-hmm, but Cal said, "What ees zis 'teep' you say?"

"Oh! I'm sorry. I thought you were American."

"American?" said Cal, looking horrified. "Oh no. No no no."

She took Matt's hand. "*Mon chéri!* I told you zis morning zat your clozing was not chic!"

"What are you, then?" said the woman.

"We are French," Cal said proudly. "We are Parisians. And you?"

"Oh, we're American." She was looking at Cal and Matt with a certain degree of envy. "We're from New York. Well, outside New York."

"We adore New York," Cal assured her. "We considered New York for zis trip—how do you call it, *mon chou*? Ze trip after ze wedding?"

"Ze 'oneymoon?" said Matt.

"*Exactement!* Ze moon of 'oney."

"We're honeymooning too! But aren't you—aren't you a little young to be married?"

"We French women know to take care of ze skin," said Cal. "Ze skin care, it ees ze fountain of youth. I am far older than I appear."

"You'll have to tell me your regimen."

"But no," said Cal, wagging her finger. "Zis ees a state secret. Protected information."

"Oh!" said the woman. She extended her hand across the aisle. "Well! I'm Melissa. Nice to meet you."

"Meeleesa." Cal shook the tips of her fingers. "I am Marie-Victoire Leblanc. And zis ees my 'usband, Antoine."

"*Enchanté,*" said Matt.

The plane took off. He let himself slip into his trance. "But ze American *chocolat,*" he heard Cal say, "it barely deserves ze name." He let his eyes flit closed but the green light of the plane diffused through his mind: avocado, pale leaves of jasmine. He'd been on a plane too when he'd finally read *Arcadia*. Last summer, last August, on his way home from a college visit. "We live in ze shadow of ze Eiffel Tower," Cal was saying. "Ze tourists are 'orrendous." His mom had driven him from the airport to the hospital. It was the last time. "Ah, *Paree*! My 'ome! Ze City of Light!" He had pulled the wooden chair close to the bed. "I read *Arcadia*," he'd said.

Jesse smiled, or attempted to smile. Matt tried to imagine himself in Jesse's body, but he knew it was impossible to understand the oppression of each breath, each motion. Jesse could not obey gravity enough. Lying down, he wanted to be lower; still, he wanted to be stiller.

"You were right," said Matt. "Everything we like to talk about."

"My dad said that."

"It's brilliant."

"It's okay, Matt."

Matt pushed aside the chair. He heard the echoes. "Your *best* friend, huh?" "Just the two of you?" "Aren't you a bit old to be sleeping over there all the time?" All the questions his father didn't want answered. "Who *are* you?" Standing by the bed, Matt paused, not out of hesitancy but because he knew the echoes were just that, vapor, illusion, and they'd go if he let them go. He climbed onto the bed. Regret, yes, forever and ever, but when regret sang without the lurching accompaniment of guilt, it sounded like grief. Like love. Wordlessly, Jesse adjusted his tubes. Matt slid his arm beneath him and Jesse rested his head in the crook of Matt's neck. You saved me, thought Matt. I could have been just like him and you saved me. He wanted to tell him, but he waited a moment too long, and Jesse's breathing slid into sleep. Without moving,

Matt craned down his eyes. Jesse's skin had once been brown and red but now it was gray and blue. His lips were cracked and his fingers, curled above the sheet, were as swollen as sausages. It was all right that he hadn't told him. Matt knew what he would have said. I didn't save you, Matt. It was your choice. It was always your choice.

"I thought Parisian women were snobby," the woman confided to Cal, "but you are *charming*! And such a beautiful couple, the two of you!"

Cal smiled modestly. *"Merci,"* she said. *"Merci beaucoup."*

CHAPTER TWENTY-THREE

Thea was in Rome, and she was in Rome for the *Pietà*. The word *pilgrimage* had tipped Lillian off. She had skipped Sunday dinners all year, but the week before they left for Europe, her mother appeared at the door of her room, an angular silhouette against the daylight from the hallway, and said, "Little girl, get out of bed and put on some decent clothing."

Lillian burrowed deeper into the comforter. She'd stopped using sheets. They were too much trouble. Her mattress had developed an indentation for her body, like a nest.

"You'll break your grandma's heart if she doesn't see you before you go."

"Momma. I'm sleeping. Go away."

Her mother marched to the window and drew the blinds. Lillian pulled the comforter over her head but she could still hear her say, "If you don't get out of bed, and now, you aren't setting foot on that airplane."

Lillian didn't mess with that tone. It was the tone of meaning it. She got out of bed.

In her grandmother's kitchen, Lillian was set to shaving carrots for the salad. They pushed her around, these women. You'd never guess it from the way they sat in the pews, narrow shoulders and bright bird eyes, hats at the same angle, back on the head and slightly askew. You'd never guess it from the way they bowed their heads before taking the Host on their tongues. (They didn't let the priest put it in their hands, not even the nervous young white guy who kept trying.) "Your momma tells me you're traveling," her grandmother said. "A pilgrimage to Europe. Lucky Lily. What I wouldn't give to see our *Pietà* before I die."

"You're not going to die. And we're not going to Rome. And it's not a pilgrimage."

"It is."

"Grandma. You know I don't go for that stuff anymore." The Mother of God where she did not belong, on a Bosnian mountainside and in a cave in the south of France and in the Spanish sky. "They're just stories."

Her grandmother checked the pot roast. "But you have the light of a question."

"What?"

"'A pilgrimage'"—she was using her quotation voice—"'is a journey taken in the light of a question.'"

Lillian said nothing, but shaving the carrots down to nubs, she thought, No. It was not a pilgrimage. All the things she might ask—*why* and *why him* and *why us*—were not questions so much as laments. But now, on the train to the Vatican, tying a red scarf around her head and giving the knot a decisive tug, she finally understood. Thea was the one on the pilgrimage, the one with the question: how could I have left him? And for someone haunted by Goethe and guilt and

Pietàs, that question led to only one place. Thea had given away her compass because she knew where she was facing, and she knew where she had to go.

Rome. Saint Peter's. The *Pietà*. There were *Pietàs* everywhere, of course. Arnold's study was full of them, painted in oil and carved from limewood, gilded on altarpieces and illuminated in books of hours, and sculpted from marble too, Michelangelo's unfinished Bandini in Florence and his spectral Rondanini in Milan. But Lillian and Jesse, her grandmother and her aunts and her mother, they all agreed there was one true *Pietà*. "Her face could melt the stoniest of hearts," her grandmother had said. "It is the omphalos. The center of the world."

The train slowed, nearing the Vatican station. Lillian's heart was beating fast. They hadn't yet found a place to sleep, but when she'd proposed starting at Saint Peter's, everyone had nodded. Cal was just going along with her, Lillian knew, and Trevor was going along with everyone. Matt thought her plan was illogical; he'd said as much in the parking lot. But knowledge, to Matt, was the last line in a proof, the result of kneading an equation through pages of penciled calculations, each step defensible and ordered, the last a tidy QED. Matt could not understand the leap of intuition, the flash of faith. Ben understood. Ben spoke the language of academia, theses and arguments, and Lillian the language of epiphany, but at root, they were the same.

They alighted at the station. Lillian was walking so quickly that she barely looked at the twin colonnades, the immense piazza, the basilica's façade. She was driven to the *Pietà*, the wind of all those stories at her back. In her mind the statue shone. After half a millennium of questions, it gave off its own light.

Fine, she thought. I guess this might be a pilgrimage after all.

Tourists teemed over the interior of the basilica like ants on a cake. The *Pietà* was to the right, tucked into a side chapel and fronted with bulletproof glass. Lillian bulldozed her way to the head of the horde. She was buffeted at all sides by beeps and shutters and flashes rebounding off the shield of glass. Next to her, a father wielded a video camera. "And Jared's kneeling before the world-renowned *Pietà*—*kneel*, Jared— and he's crossing himself—follow the cues, damn it—and, Jared, what are you asking Our Lady for?"

Lillian felt ill. For the first time, she thought, We might never find this woman.

She was glad when they went outside. They sat in the shade of the colonnade. She chose the top step when the others chose the lower one. Their backpack straps had left lines of sweat on their shirts. They *had* to find Thea, she had thought, and so they would. She groaned. Had that really been her reasoning? Hadn't she learned that the impossible didn't happen just because you hoped for it so hard? Miraculous cures, saintly visions, Holy Grails, Rings and Hallows and the Republic of Heaven: oh, the stories had led her astray. You could want something with all your heart and still it would not come true.

"Is anyone else having extreme déjà vu?" said Cal. "Like they've been here before?"

Lillian cast a glance at the massive piazza. An obelisk pierced the center. The cobblestones, curving in harmony with the colonnade, seemed to shimmer like the lines of a mirage. Officious pigeons bustled to and fro. "Not me."

"Trevor? Have we been here? Was I too young to remember?"

"We'd never been out of the country before this trip."

"Are you sure?"

"You think we were kidnapped?" he said. "Blindfolded, drugged, put on a plane?"

Cal subsided. After a minute, she said, "It's just so weird. It's so familiar."

"Pictures," said Lillian.

"Yeah," said Trevor. "I slept through an entire semester of art history—what genius scheduled slide shows in the dark for nine a.m., I ask you—but it's familiar even to me."

"I guess," said Cal.

Lillian propped her head in her hand. A moment of weakness, she told herself. Buck up. They would find Thea. They had to, because she'd promised. She rubbed the red scarf she'd tied over her hair. Her grandmother would have been appalled if she'd gone bareheaded. She could just hear her: "All that Christ and our Blessed Virgin have given you, and you can't cover your head in reverence before the *Pietà*?"

She had made Jesse the promise the same day he'd cut her hair. She'd glimpsed how sad he was, and she'd thought, I'll promise whatever he wants. She needed that silently keening child to go away; she needed *her* Jesse back, the boy who'd wooed her with a papier-mâché skunk, who'd been thrown out of English class because he couldn't stop laughing. At what? Something Mr. Carlisle had said, and he'd caught Lillian's eye, and he was done for. She remembered how he'd shaken, lips pursed, eyes watering, and how she'd looked sternly away but seconds later heard a sharp bleat of giggle erupt, and how, when Mr. Carlisle told him to shape up, he'd lost it, he'd doubled over and howled, the rest of the class laughing just to see him laugh. But what had been so funny? She couldn't remember and now it was gone. That was the worst part, she sometimes thought. The world they'd built for two had become as precarious as a dream, all those memories now dependent on her and her alone. Remember when they'd helped Ms. Garrett clean her room at the end of sophomore year? Remember? "You'll have to get the contractor bags from the walk-in closet," Ms. Garrett told them. It was a week after the quiz bowl bus. Lillian hunted for the bags while Jesse held the door open. She had floated through that week in a near-constant state of wonderment: that he was real, that he was hers. They had not yet kissed. She could not wait a second longer. "Come here," she said, and he let the door swing closed. She put her hands on his shoulders. It was pitch-black. He rested his lips on her cheek. She turned her mouth toward his and he pulled back.

"Wait," he said. "We can't kiss in the dark."

"What's wrong with it?"

"Nothing. But I can't kiss you for the first time in the dark. Not you. Our first kiss, I want to see your eyes."

These stories she would never tell another soul. They would remain inviolate. That was right. Still, she thought. It's lonely, this world. She rubbed her eyes. They should get up and find somewhere to sleep. The full-figured Mediterranean sun had not yet dropped behind the basilica, but it would soon. I won't forget you, she thought. Not in this lifetime or any other. No, she'd keep a headscarf at hand and she'd keep trying to muster some reverence for her Lady and her Lord, who had given and who had taken away.

"Where are we going to stay tonight?" said Cal. "Ben, we need your help."

He heaved a sigh. "*Now* you're asking." He was wearing a pair of aviator sunglasses that made him look far cooler than he was. A gift from Trevor, Lillian assumed.

"You know this city. I bet you have a plan in mind already."

"As a matter of fact, I do."

They traced the Tiber to Trastevere, and then trudged uphill. Last summer, Ben told them, he'd stayed at a student dormitory near the American Academy. "If we throw ourselves on Pina's mercy," he said, "she'll probably give us a place to sleep."

They climbed stairs to a piazza that overlooked the city, spires and squat domes and sunset-lit sprawl. Trevor drifted to a bench, but when Ben gave an irritated huff, he scurried back. They walked up a park road lined with plane trees and herms of men Lillian didn't recognize, and into a neighborhood of close, pink buildings.

Ben buzzed for entrance. The walk had taken nearly an hour. On the sidewalk, Lillian leaned her head on Cal's shoulder, and Cal stacked hers on top. "Pina!" said Ben. He broke into a storm of Italian. Lillian couldn't tell whether Pina was welcoming him or scolding him or both, but she ushered them into a wide classroom with two upright pianos. "The beds are all full," Ben told them, "but she's getting us blankets. And she says we have to bathe before we can even think about lying on her floors."

After her shower, Lillian returned to the classroom to find the desks pushed aside, the floor heaped with pillows and blankets. Cal's hair was swaddled in a huge blue towel. "You look like Marge Simpson," Lillian told her.

Cal peeled up the back of her shirt to display a brace of bruises. "Look what you did to me."

"Some of those are from the rocks."

"A few, maybe." Lillian saw Matt glance at Cal's back. He was already lying down, his hands underneath his head. Trevor, sprawled on his stomach, was scrolling through his phone, and Ben was invisible behind a map. "We'll need to try tour companies," Ben muttered, "and museums—"

"Universities," said Lillian, joining him. "Libraries. Churches."

She saw a flicker of hopelessness in Ben's eyes. He coughed. "We should develop a plan of attack, rank zones of the city in order of most likely to least—"

The map was a tangle of streets and alleys and tiny crosses. "There must be a hundred museums on there," said Cal.

"Not to mention archaeological areas," said Ben, "and private galleries—"

Lillian moved away. Tomorrow morning, she would be ready to tackle the search again; she would have to be. But not tonight. Cal followed, leaving Ben alone with his color-coded map tabs. She rubbed her head with the towel while Lillian spritzed her own hair. "What's that?" said Cal.

"Water, aloe vera gel, some almond oil. It moisturizes."

"Do you ever miss long hair? Those tiny braids?"

"Never." They'd made every pillow feel like wide-wale corduroy. "It's a good thing I don't have them anymore. Germany's not exactly hopping with braiding parlors."

"I saw one in Frankfurt. The sign said 'BLACK HAIR SALOON.'"

"Well, that inspires a lot of confidence," said Lillian. Cal giggled. "But no way there's one in small-town Bavaria. The whitest place I've ever been."

"Was that weird?"

"Uncomfortable," she said, "but not unexpected." When they'd stepped into the crowded Fiumicino airport, she'd felt the partial dissipation of a tension she'd barely noticed she'd been carrying. Her passport had been checked, even though they'd stayed within the Schengen zone, but she had shut her mouth and let it go. There was no other choice.

"I'd never have the courage to shave my head," said Cal, dragging a comb through her hair.

"Even at a saloon?"

"Even all liquored up. How'd you decide to do it?"

Lillian patted her hair. She'd kept it close-cropped all year, but over the trip it'd become what her natural-hair friends called a TWA: a teeny-weeny Afro. She liked it. "I'll tell you sometime."

"Come on, Lill, what happened?" Lillian shook her head, lips pressed together. Cal jabbed a bobby pin into her bun and brandished another at Lillian. "Let me play with your hair."

"There's not much to play with," she said, but she slid to sit in front of her. Cal massaged her scalp. Look at you two, Jesse would say. I told you so. "You can put in my conditioner," said Lillian.

"Jesse and I used to play beauty parlor," said Cal. "With my mom. She'd nap on the couch and as long as we didn't pull too hard, we could do anything we wanted."

"You're so lucky," said Lillian reflexively. "To have known him back then."

"Are you kidding?" said Cal. "You're the lucky one. You knew him in high school." She pushed her fingers deep into Lillian's scalp. Lillian let loose an involuntary sigh. She pictured herself in the plaid jumper she'd had to wear at her parish's tiny elementary school. She was walking down the streets of Berkeley. She was walking past him. Had there been a shiver of significance? She wished she could catch that girl. Get your act together, she'd say. Find this boy. Someday you will kill for these years. "Maybe we'd have hated each other," Jesse had said, shrugging. "No use in regrets." Easy for him to say.

His laugh pealed out of Cal, who was craning to see Lillian from the front. Lillian put up an exploratory hand. "What *are* those?" Her head felt like a cactus.

"Bobby pins." Cal burst out laughing again. "About fifty of them. My whole pack. You look like a porcupine."

"Thanks," said Lillian, amused.

"Appropriately spiky."

Now she laughed for real. Cal gave her a quick, shy smile. "Hey! Trevor!" Cal called. "Take a look!"

Trevor crawled across the field of blankets. "Too tired to get vertical," he explained. He palpated Lillian's hair. "You could fit an impressive amount of stuff in there."

"Another month and I won't have to carry a purse."

They turned off the overhead light, although light shone through the sliding doors to the courtyard; whether the moon or streetlamps, Lillian didn't know. She heard Trevor stop thrashing as if he'd been suddenly pinned by an invisible wrestler. She heard Ben's light snores. Matt, she suspected, was still staring at the ceiling. She turned her head to the side and saw Cal, out like a light, her mouth hanging open. The bobby pins were stacked like kindling between them. In its silk wrap on the pillow, her head felt smooth and shorn.

CHAPTER TWENTY-FOUR

"What time is it?" said Matt.

"Almost eleven," said Lillian, revolving her watch around her wrist.

"I'm already hungry," Cal moaned.

"We had breakfast a scant four hours ago," said Ben. "We've got a lot to do before lunch."

Trevor gazed at Lillian's watchband. Neat rounds of sunlight spun on the silver links like donuts on a conveyor belt. He was hungry too. They were sitting on the steps of some church in some piazza, which, in Trevor's view, was exactly how they'd spent every other break this week in Rome. He picked at his peeling sunburn while Ben riffled through his notebook. "We've got a major decision," said Ben. "Zone six or zone seventeen? Should we go east to the Via Nomentana, or stay here in the Piazza del Popolo environs?"

Trevor glanced around. His companions slumped in varying states of exhaustion, apathy, hunger, and hopelessness.

"Does *anyone* care?" Ben said peevishly.

"What'd you say, six or seventeen?" Trevor said. Ben didn't respond. A week after the pension hiccup, he was still barely speaking to Trevor. "Well, either one's good with me."

"Couldn't you have an opinion for once?" Cal snapped.

"I do. They're both fine, that's my opinion."

Cal exchanged an eye roll with Lillian.

"You're hangry," Trevor told his sister. "May I offer you a banana-flavored Twinkie, freshly filched from the breakfast buffet?"

Cal pretended to gag but unwrapped it. "Desperate times, desperate measures."

They had finally found a vacancy in a bed-and-breakfast on the Janiculum, though the room had just two double beds. Trevor had volunteered for the cot on the floor. He didn't mind. It took him back to beach vacations, when Ben and Cal would get the beds: Ben because the beach brought out the worst of his sensitive skin, heat rash and eczema, hives that flared up whenever a jellyfish jiggled a tentacle within fifty yards, and Cal because she was a girl. Thus the aunts decreed. On the floor, Trevor and Jesse would lay grand plans, narrating to each other the adventures of four cousins who grew up to live in the same house, a house with an indoor trampoline and a room made of pillows, with a fire pole instead of stairs. Even now, when the others had fallen still, Trevor could turn his head and see not bedposts nor the scalloped radiator but the dear silhouette. At times, he felt that Jesse was not far away at all.

"This isn't bad," said Cal with her mouth full. "Anyone want a bite?"

Trevor did. He had grown rather partial to banana-flavored pastries.

"I hate to trek all the way across the Villa Borghese," mused Ben, "although I should note there's a street called Viale Goethe—"

Trevor yawned. Cal shot him a dirty look. Didn't she see that the last thing they needed was another person weighing in on which zone, according to arcane and arbitrary algorithms, was slightly more likely to deliver up news of a woman who hadn't been located for three years? Didn't Cal see that if he hadn't been giving his all to the esprit de corps, they would have fallen apart long ago? He'd begun to stock his day pack with what he privately called the Wild Goose Therapy Kit: water, snacks, sunscreen, blister Band-Aids, a roll of toilet paper, a stale bun for amicable pigeons, a phrase book called *Street Italian* with lots of useful words, none of which Ben knew, and a variety of small toys guaranteed to raise spirits. He also kept a mental catalog of conversational gambits to employ when the topic veered too close to how screwed they were, how pointless this search had become. They were continually sweaty and sore of feet. They crossed off place after place from Ben's list but the list seemed interminable, Hydra-esque, growing even as they fought to subdue it, as they flashed her photograph at tour guides and church caretakers, as they found secretaries at museums and libraries and schools and asked to leave a message for the employee called Thea Vogel. It was becoming harder and harder to feign surprise at the response: "No Thea Vogel works here."

Had anyone else realized it was futile? He wasn't about to ask, that was for sure. That question would not go over well with this crowd. Though maybe, Trevor thought, it would provoke Ben into speaking to him. Nothing had worked, not even an innocent inquiry about how to pluralize your basic Italian noun. Ben spoke to Trevor only when necessary, which, now that Trevor had ceded him his phone, was hardly ever. "Can that contraption access an Italian dictionary?" Ben had said early in the week.

Trevor handed him the phone. "Keep it."

He hadn't checked his email since. Let Scott field his own wild ideas. Let Scott calculate the startling distance between the balance on the MasterCard and the minimum amount due. Let Scott face the calamity that was Plagueslist, the overdrawn accounts and the mounting bills and the unpaid freelancers—

Well. No need to think about *that*. Trevor wiped his upper lip and shook his damp shirt free of his back. The sun was harsh and white on the travertine. "Who's up for a morning gelato?"

"Zone six it is," said Ben. "But let's have a quick educational interlude." He consulted his *Blue Guide*. "We're on the steps of Santa Maria dei Miracoli. That one is Santa Maria in Montesanto, and up there's Santa Maria del Popolo."

"Three churches for Mary in one piazza?" said Trevor. "Laying it on a bit thick, aren't they?"

"In the center of the piazza, an obelisk, twenty-four meters high, celebrates the glories of Ramses II and Merneptah."

Cal jerked upright. "Trevor!"

"Who, me?"

"Who did that? What *is* that?"

"Transported to Rome by Augustus after the conquest of Egypt—"

"*Shit!*"

"Look," said Ben, "do you want to learn or not?"

Cal, jumping to her feet, examined the shoulder of her

T-shirt. She looked revolted. "A freaking pigeon just took a shit on me!"

Trevor peered upward. A self-satisfied pigeon squatted on the church's entablature. He caught Matt's eye and had to look away immediately.

"Shit!" Cal said again. She kicked the step.

Matt made a garbled noise. Trevor stared very hard at the obelisk.

"This is *vile!*"

"Don't think we're making a side trip home for you to change," Ben warned her.

"I'll go with you if you want," Trevor said. He wouldn't mind missing zone six.

Cal fluttered her hands and craned her head as far as possible from the greasy white splotch. "What should I *do*?"

"You want water?" Trevor peered into his day pack. "A premoistened towelette?"

"Won't be enough."

"Yeah," said Trevor, squinting at her shirt, "that was a well-fed pigeon, I must say—"

"Go dunk," said Matt, nodding toward the base of the obelisk, where lions spurted water into large basins.

Cal spun and marched toward the obelisk. They trailed after her. "So much for edification," muttered Ben, stowing the guidebook. Trevor had to laugh as Cal, without a second of hesitation, plunged her entire upper body into the fountain. Tourists stopped staring at the obelisk and started staring at her. She scrubbed at the spot underwater and emerged dripping.

"That felt so good." She wrung out her ponytail. "The water's icy. I'd recommend it."

Trevor ditched his day pack and stuck in his head. "Brilliant," he said, shaking off like a dog. Ben jumped back from the droplets, but Matt and Lillian looked intrigued. "Better than gelato," he told them.

"Together?" Matt said to Lillian.

"Okay. But I'm keeping my hair out."

They poised at the edge of the fountain. "You better take off your watch," said Matt.

"Good call." Lillian put it in her purse. "Ready?"

"Ready."

"On three!"

They hadn't bargained on the smell. Trevor wasn't the only one who had to give Cal a wide berth. "How about I treat you to a new shirt?" he suggested.

"Our budget would be thrilled to cover that," said Matt.

They set a rendezvous at the Porta Pia, and Trevor and Cal split off to head back to the clothing stores on the Via del Corso. "Phew," said Trevor. "Zone six was getting to me."

"The whole thing's getting to me," said Cal.

Did he dare broach the topic? "Thea—"

"We *know* she's here," said Cal. "We'll find her."

"Will we?"

Cal abruptly stopped. Trevor almost stumbled into her. A svelte woman in high boots gave them a dirty look. "If we don't believe that . . . ," said Cal.

She trailed off. He felt a rush of protectiveness for this little sister of his, cranky and sopping wet and smeared with pigeon poop. Ben wasn't speaking to him but Ben was solidly, comfortably alive. He and Ben were allowed to have a relationship that waxed and waned, that moved with time; Cal had only memories of Jesse. She would change, and he would not.

They went into a store called Mango. "I'll just grab something," she said. "Won't bother trying it on."

"I don't know about you," said Trevor, "but I don't see much point in hurrying back."

Cal cracked a smile.

"In fact, you could go on a whole shopping spree. Replace that dreadful wardrobe of yours—"

"I like my clothes," she said, scowling again.

Trevor scoped out a few shirts for her, and she went into a fitting room. He sat on a plush bench with bored men of several nationalities. "*Ciao,*" he said. "What's up?"

Cal emerged in a white shirt with large, decorative safety pins on the shoulders. "What do you think?"

"Well," said Trevor.

"Should I get it?"

"If you don't mind the slight resemblance to a diaper—"

She dove back into the fitting room.

"Or a toga," he told the guy next to him, who nodded solemnly and said, "*Sì, sì.*" Trevor offered him a gummy bear from the pack in the Wild Goose Therapy Kit. "*Sì!*"

Trevor bit off a bear's head and waited for Cal's next option, which was a short-sleeved button-down in a red-and-orange plaid. "I kind of like this," she said.

"I have two words for you," said Trevor. "Dad's bathrobe."

"Oh my God," said Cal, looking down in horror. "You're right."

"Good call," said a British guy once Cal disappeared. "That was hideous."

Trevor stretched expansively. "Cal's never had a sense of style."

"Your sister?"

"Yep. Little sister."

"She's lucky to have you."

"I've been telling her that all her life."

"She must agree. To bring you along as her fashion consultant—"

"Well, extenuating circumstances. You'll never guess what happened to her this morning." By the time Cal reappeared, he was squatting on the bench, squawking like a constipated pigeon. He had a large and admiring crowd. Cal glared at him.

"Oh, hi," he said. "There she is, our much-beleaguered heroine—wait! Cal! That one's nice!"

"Quite flattering," said the British guy.

"*Sì!*" said the Italian guy.

"Thanks, everyone," Cal said, rolling her eyes. "Let me just put on my old shirt so we can pay—"

"Don't bother," Trevor said quickly. "I'll take it." He held it with two fingers. "Nice chatting," he told his new friends. "Gummy bear for the road?"

They stood in line for the cash register. Trevor said, "How you doing?"

"Oh," said Cal, "I'm okay."

"You don't have to be okay." He took a deep breath. "Listen, Cal. I know this—Jesse—I know it's been hard for you."

"It's been hard for everyone."

"Well, sure."

"Not any harder for me."

"It's different for everyone," said Trevor. "It's not something you have to measure."

Cal's eyes were full, and her fists were clenched, but she didn't snap or stomp off. "Sometimes I think I don't even have the right to feel like this."

"Why not?"

"He wasn't my boyfriend. He wasn't my best friend. It'd been years since I'd seen him."

"He was your cousin," said Trevor. "Your cousin. Everything you feel, it all makes sense. When I think—if Ben died—" He could barely say it. "My heart would feel ripped out of my chest."

"But that's how we all feel."

"Yes," he said. "I guess it is."

They'd reached the front of the line. Cal's cheeks were flushed the color of her new tank top. She looked bright and beautiful and burdened and strong. She ripped off the price tag and handed it to the saleswoman. Trevor paid and then said, "*Signora?* Would you mind, um, disposing of this?"

"That's my shirt!" said Cal.

The saleswoman took it gingerly. "What should I do with it?"

"*Grazie,*" said Trevor. "Burn it."

"Solid work today, guys," Trevor said at the bus stop. "Lots of check marks in the ol' notebook."

"Check marks are bad, Trevor," said Cal. "Check marks mean no sign of her."

"Every place ruled out," he pronounced, "is one place closer to finding her." Well, he thought, technically that was so, but not when the world's hidey-holes and crannies, faced by a cadre of relatively resourceless adolescents, might as well be infinite. Pound infinity all you want, subtract from it, divide it, pummel it with fractional exponents, and it bounces right back, unchanged. Cal knew that too. She opened her mouth. Briskly, Trevor said, "Gelato, anyone?"

"I want real food, not gelato," said Cal.

"Think of it as an appetizer."

"It'd be better after dinner."

"We'll have it twice."

"I'm not eating gelato twice in one evening."

"Lighten up! YOLO!"

"Precisely why I don't want diabetes."

"Would you two shut up?" snapped Lillian.

Mortally offended, Cal stomped to the other side of the bus stop. "We *did* cover a lot of ground," said Trevor faintly. "And getting cussed out by that tour guide, that'll be a great story someday—"

Matt gave him a weak smile, but Ben's face was hidden by the Goethe and the girls had identical crossed-arm poses. Trevor let it rest.

The bus was packed, and they had to split up to find places to stand. More commuters and teenagers and tourists pushed on with every stop. Trevor liked riding the bus, which lumbered along like a rhinoceros, seemingly blind to the Smart cars and scooters that flittered across its path. He wouldn't mind giving Roman driving a shot. The city didn't even bother painting lane lines. "Maybe we should rent a car," he said to Cal, but she'd dozed off, gripping a pole. He made faces at a baby instead. *"Ciao, bambino!"*

"Bambina," said the mother.

"Oops, sorry, androgynous outfit—*ciao, bella bambina!"* He

hoped Ben could hear him. That was some proficient noun-adjective agreement he'd managed there.

The bus wheezed to a halt. "Hey!" Trevor heard. "Get *back* here!"

The voice was Lillian's. He craned over the crush to see. She was pushing off the bus, yelling at a tall, slender boy a few feet ahead of her. "Thief!" The other riders watched but did nothing. "He stole my purse!"

Trevor jumped to action. "Come on!" He saw Cal jolt awake as he vaulted out the rear door. The boy glanced back and took off down a narrow street. Trevor sprinted after him, his day pack juddering with every step. The boy's black cap wove in and out of the crowds. Trevor ran in hot pursuit, Lillian right behind, but the boy was quicker, more adept at dodging through the alley. Even before the street spilled into a teeming piazza, Trevor knew it was no good. He stopped and shaded his eyes. "I think we lost him."

Cal and Matt pulled up. Cal was limping severely. "What happened?" said Cal.

"He must have sliced the strap," said Lillian, furious. "I didn't feel a thing until the weight was off my shoulder. And by then he was out the door."

Ben arrived, puffing. "You got pickpocketed? Well, what did I tell you about carrying a purse?"

Trevor led them to the fountain in the middle of the piazza. They sat on its plinth and faced the Pantheon. The dome was invisible behind Agrippa's façade. "That kid!" spat Lillian. "How *dare* he steal from me!"

Trevor gave Cal a cautionary glance. Now was not the time to remark on how Lillian, perhaps, had it coming.

"What'd you have in there?" said Matt.

"A few euros. Lip gloss. My bus ticket. That's not the point. God, if I ever find him, I'm punching him out. I'm destroying him."

They sat glumly. Cal removed her sandal and massaged her heel, wincing.

"What a day," said Trevor. "Getting shat on, literally and figuratively."

"Too soon," Cal told him.

"And now we're half a mile from Piazza Venezia," said Ben. "Our transfer is probably leaving as we speak."

"Are you saying you want to go?" snarled Lillian. "Because I'm capable of walking without my purse."

"Hey, hey!" said Trevor. "Let's focus on the silver lining! I happen to know there's an *excellent* gelateria right around the corner from the Pantheon—"

"It's time for dinner, not gelato," said Cal.

"Yeah," said Matt, "what time *is* it?"

CHAPTER TWENTY-FIVE

Lillian had shrieked. It was a cry of anguish, of pure and bottomless grief, and then she had put her face in her hands and sobbed.

Cal didn't blame Trevor and Ben for decamping. There was not much that could be done. She and Matt sat on either side of Lillian and held her close between them, but how could they console her when her left wrist remained as raw and bare as a winter tree? Cal felt so bad for her that she could barely keep her eyes open. She fit her own body to Lillian's, aligning their legs and sides and heads, and held her as tightly as she could. Lillian's sobs were nearly silent but they shook her whole body.

Cal closed her eyes. She'd caught a glimpse of the boy as he'd darted off the bus. A lean, straight back. Alert eyes. Brown sideburns, a hat pulled low over his forehead. For an instant she'd thought—but no.

The piazza was crowded, but even the pigeons gave them a wide berth. Matt was crooning in Lillian's ear, *shh shh shh.*

Cal kept one arm wrapped around her and used the other to rub her back in rhythmic circles. It was instinct, she thought, to take her to infancy: to swaddle her, rock her, whisper white noise. Or maybe it was the womb they were trying to summon, a faint, wordless dream of a time when she had been protected beyond measure, the only sounds the inmost hums and throbs of her mother's body, a time when she had not even had to breathe. Last August, Cal had come home hungry and humming from preseason practice to see her parents at the kitchen table with no food or coffee. She'd hung up her keys and said, "Mile repeats, Mom, five of them! At 3K pace! It was insane!" Her father's hand shielded his eyes. "Sit down, honey," said her mother. They told her. Very calmly, she went upstairs and took the sheet from her bed and wrapped herself head to toe. Once she was in a tight parcel, she had carefully dropped into the crack between bed and wall. There she had fallen asleep.

She'd drifted off on the bus too. She'd been disoriented, just half awake, when she'd seen the thief, and that was why—well. She wouldn't put words to it. Lillian was composing herself, breathing more steadily. Don't be ridiculous, Cal told herself. A trick of stance.

Lillian gave one last shuddering exhale and sat upright. Matt took his arm off her back. Cal left hers draped around the curve of Lillian's waist, where the tapers of hip and rib cage met. "Well," said Lillian.

Cal glanced over. Even first thing in the morning, when Cal would have screwed-up eyes and a nest of hair and pillow creases all over her face, Lillian never looked anything but beautiful. But now her eyes, always heavy-lidded, were so swollen she had to squint. Sooty trails of makeup tracked down her cheeks and her nose was running. She rubbed her eyes with her fists. Cal didn't know what to say. She squeezed her waist, and Lillian briefly dipped her head onto her shoulder.

After a few minutes, Ben poked his head out of the Pantheon. When he saw that Lillian was calm, he joined them. "My condolences," he said to her.

"Thank you," she said, oddly formal.

Trevor returned with a cone of blue gelato. "*Puffo,* this flavor's called," he said. "So I asked what's *Puffo.* Turns out it means 'Smurf'!" His lips and tongue were a garish blue. "But how did those Italians figure out that Smurfs taste like black licorice? Anyone want a lick?"

"We need to stop." Matt spoke so suddenly that Cal knew he'd been thinking it for a while, the words twisting on his tongue. "This isn't good."

"But—" said Cal.

"We're not going to find her. And meanwhile, we're falling apart."

"But I want to know why she left." Cal felt her anger toward Thea rush back. She wanted to find her so she could put her on the rack, so she could drive in thumbscrews and force her to confess. "I want her to explain herself."

"You think she could?" said Matt. "Sometimes people stick around, and sometimes people leave. They don't always have good reasons. There might not *be* good reasons."

"But—" Cal said again. She didn't know why she was arguing to keep searching when for most of the trip all she'd wanted was to give up. "Lill. Tell them. Tell them how much he wanted us to find her."

"No," said Matt. "We've lost hope. We're trudging through.

We keep talking about what Jesse wanted, but he never would have wanted this."

"You know what he wanted?" said Lillian, and Cal had never heard her voice sound so cold. "You know what he *really* wanted? He wanted her to be Mary. He wanted to look at those ten thousand Madonnas like a Waldo book, to look and look until he found the Madonna who was his own."

"She's not Mary," said Ben.

"Of course she's not," said Lillian. "But that's what he wanted, and we wanted to give him that. He left us, he left us like this, he left us *bereft,* and still we wanted to protect him. To make him happy. So we bought it. We said, Okay, Jesse. You're right. She wouldn't have left you without a good reason. She's worth finding. She loved you."

"You're right," said Ben, looking shaken. "We bought it."

"And she didn't love him," said Matt. "Or maybe she did. But not like we did."

"Not like we do," said Lillian.

"You're absolutely right," said Ben. "I was fooled. Snookered. Bamboozled!"

"We fell for it," Lillian said heavily. "Just like he did."

"And I told him! You *heard* me tell him!" said Ben. "'Your mother is not Mary.' But look at us. We've got the Goethe like a Bible and those photographs like prayer cards and the compass like a relic. We're treating her like Mary. That's why we're in Rome. That's why we've made this—"

He paused. "Yes," said Lillian. "This pilgrimage."

"It's time to go home."

They were quiet for a long while. Cal leaned back on her palms and looked at the vast inscription: *Agrippa made this.*

They'd surrendered.

She had never truly believed this day would come. The prospect of home had shimmered so hazily that it had always seemed they'd return not with Thea but with Jesse. What else was this trip but a rescue mission? She would look up from the Pantheon and see instead the Plaza in Santa Fe, and Jesse would wriggle between two bushes, leap up, saunter toward them. Lillian would cling to his arm, and he'd joke with Trevor and slap Matt on the back, and Ben would hover, looking pleased. "I thought you might not make it back," Cal would tell him. Jesse would turn, tanned and strong. "Cal," he'd say. "Have some faith. Did you really think I'd let myself get caught?"

They would go to the airport first thing the next morning, they decided. With their open-ended tickets, they could stand by until seats were available.

It was seven-thirty by the time they got back to the Janiculum. They were too weary to face a restaurant, so Matt and Lillian stopped to buy a few kilos of *pizza al taglio*. "We'll go ahead and get that AC cranked up," said Trevor.

Cal trailed behind as Ben unlocked the street door. Their room was on the fifth floor. Cal was lagging. Her heel hurt every time it touched down, and she was so tired it took significant effort to lift her feet. They were almost to the top when Ben fell.

Cal heard his shoe slip off the worn marble step. He tumbled down the rest of the flight. He was in a heap on the landing. Trevor leapt down the stairs. "Ben!"

"Oof," he said, wincing. He'd landed terribly, right on his tailbone, one foot twisted beneath him and the other crashing into the wall.

"Are you okay?"

"I'm fine."

Trevor offered him a hand, but he ignored it and heaved himself up by the windowsill. He yelped as he put weight on his left foot. "Oh God." He gingerly lifted it.

"Your ankle?"

He tested it again and gasped in pain. He sank to the floor.

"That's the same one you twisted on Soiernspitze, right?" said Trevor. "I got this. Give me the keys." Ben's eyes were closed, his face drained of color, but he extracted the keys from his pocket. Trevor flipped them to Cal. "Get some ice. And the ACE bandage you brought for your heel. We'll take care of this, Ben."

When she returned, Trevor had peeled off Ben's shoe and sock. The ankle was already alarmingly swollen.

"We'll have to go to the hospital," Trevor told Cal. "I think it's broken."

"How do you know?"

Trevor gave her a rakish smile. "Plagueslist."

With the help of Google Translate, Trevor called a taxi. They supported Ben down the stairs. "We'll be back soon," said Trevor. "Don't worry. Modern medicine works miracles, I hear." He waved out the window, and the taxi pulled away. Cal slowly climbed the stairs again and drew shut the bolt on the empty room.

It felt strange to be alone. She sprawled across the bed without taking off her shoes. She would lie down for one minute. Matt and Lillian would be back soon. She just needed to rest her eyes.

She was back on that immense plain. The crowd thronged around her. They thrummed with anticipation. Whatever they were waiting for, it would happen soon. Cal felt a choking panic. She had to find him. She tugged the sleeve of a woman whose silver hair was swept into a French twist. "Have you seen him?" The woman gave a tinkling laugh and whispered in the ear of her tuxedoed companion. Her diamond earrings frosted over and winked. Of course they wouldn't heed her, dressed as she was in a stretchy black skort, a tank top, a bedraggled ponytail. She felt like a child. She looked down. She wore sandals, while they wore stilettos and polished oxfords. And beneath their elegant arches and pointed toe caps were the cobblestones of Saint Peter's Piazza. She realized it with no surprise, as if all along she'd secretly known where she was. Now that she thought to look, she could see the obelisk's needle and the statues atop the colonnade. In the distance was the miter of the great dome.

He was here. He was in this piazza. She would look until she found him. She would never give up. She scanned the beautiful crowd.

And there, a familiar golden sheen of hair, a face that shone out of the masses like a petal on a bough—

She was startled awake. A key in the door, the creak of the handle. She struggled to sit. It was Matt. He set the pizza on the desk and took off his backpack. "Sorry. Did I wake you up?"

Her words spilling over each other, she told him about the dream. "It's Saint Peter's. I didn't know till now. But I've been dreaming it just the way it is, Matt, all this time, even before we went there."

"And you saw her?"

"I always knew I was looking for someone. But I thought it was him."

A wild hope sprang onto Matt's face. He took her forearm. "Cal," he said, "maybe she's there."

"I think she is."

Cal had recognized Thea's face from the photographs and from her memory of Santa Fe, but also because of the rightness, the certainty. She knew her face because she knew what it would be like to see her own mother in the airport: *her* person among the nameless others, sun breaking through clouds.

"I think she's there now."

"You've got to catch her, Cal. Before she leaves again."

"Me?"

"Go. You're faster."

"I'm not faster."

"I wasn't letting you win, Cal. Run."

CHAPTER TWENTY-SIX

Ben heard Trevor talk to the driver as if he were listening through a glass pressed to a wall. His ankle was iced and wrapped, and Trevor held it in his lap to protect it from the jouncing of the uneven streets. The pain was bad. Ever since Trevor had said the word *broken,* Ben felt he could sense the space between the bones.

His memories of the past hour were jangled, spackled by pain, but he knew he hadn't made any of the arrangements that had gotten him into this taxi.

"Trevor?"

Trevor was humming a little tune. "Yeah?"

"Where are we going?"

"Um. It's a hospital. Something about margaritas. I bet you could use a margarita about now. I sure could, and I'm not even—"

"Ospedale Nuovo Regina Margherita," said the driver.

"What he said. They have a tourist emergency clinic."

"How did you know?"

"Oh, a bit of logistical legwork."

Trevor resumed his humming. The taxi jolted into a pot-hole, and Ben's ankle spasmed. He needed distraction. Over the past few weeks any spare moments had been devoted to the search for Thea, worrying about his evidence, rearranging his mental files—but no longer. He was appalled that he'd been so deluded. This was the whole reason he didn't read novels. Novels taught you to fool yourself. If you weren't careful, you'd find yourself believing in quests and Homeric heroes and gods made flesh. You'd believe that questions had answers, that art was theophany, that you could cast the net of narrative over the flotsam and jetsam of real life. No longer, thought Ben. Not again.

He watched the rush of stucco out the window. Pink and orange and dingy white. Every wall scummed over by graffiti. He wished he had his *Italienische Reise*. "Only in Rome is it possible to understand Rome," wrote Goethe. Ben strongly disagreed. He enjoyed the city's art, but he wished the idea behind Mussolini's EUR had caught on: a nice, clean suburb in which to house the Roman treasures.

He felt woozy. It was a hot Chicago summer, fifteen years back. Cal and Jesse toddled in the wading pool, diapers drooping, and brought Trevor plastic cups of pretend tea. "I hope you know why the water's so warm in there," Ben said from the edge. He didn't like the feel of air on his bare skin, so he never took off his shirt. "Urine, Trevor. It's urine." Rome was like that pool, he thought. It was pullulating with people, overheated, gross. When you showered, you'd see gray water go down the drain. Ben hated fording sidewalks, hated wading through churches full of tourists. The buses were always late, and the Vespas and trash trucks made a constant racket.

Why couldn't they transport the art away from the city? If only they'd give the job to him. He'd strip the Vatican and the Borghese and the Capitoline, he'd despoil the churches, and he'd gather everything in a single museum, lovely and sterile. He supposed he'd need to leave some things in situ— the Sistine Chapel, the Roman ruins—but he'd have replicas made. What was so important about seeing the "real thing," anyway? What made art "real"?

Maybe he fell asleep. He opened his eyes to Trevor gently lifting his ankle from his lap. "I didn't notice that the ice was melting onto my crotch," said Trevor. "I'm going to make a great impression on the nurses."

Ben struggled out of the taxi. "*Grazie,* man," Trevor said to the driver, tossing bills like confetti. "Here, have another." Ben had to turn away. Did Trevor think that since this money was colorful, it didn't count? He opened his mouth to say something, but his brain's speech center must have short-circuited. He had no words. Trevor put an arm around his shoulder. Ben leaned upon him and limped to the entrance.

After the X-ray, they were left alone in a curtained cubicle. Ben had regained his powers of speech; he had also taken several heavy-duty painkillers. Although he could feel his ankle throbbing, he was no longer sure it was attached to his body.

Trevor was poking around a shelf of medical supplies. "What happened to you?" said Ben from his mounted recliner.

"Huh?" Trevor found a latex glove, which he inflated and waggled at Ben's face. "Say *ciao* to Mr. Turkey."

Ben swatted it away. "You were competent. You took charge. You've never done that in your life."

"How would he know?" Trevor asked the turkey. "I'm very competent when it comes to inflating medical supplies, wouldn't you agree?"

The turkey nodded.

"Oh, *please*," said Ben.

The doctor entered. "Hello." Ben was half disappointed and half relieved to hear English. "Marco Ferrari."

"Awesome name," said Trevor.

Dr. Ferrari, who couldn't have been older than thirty, looked amused. He was stubbly, with a tiny patch of hair below his lower lip. "It's a common surname here."

"Still cool," said Trevor, experimentally stroking his own chin.

Ferrari projected the X-ray. "A football injury, I presume? Or a moto accident?"

"I slipped on a stairwell," said Ben.

"Nothing exciting, then."

Ben felt defensive. "It still hurts."

"Of course, of course." Ferrari took Ben's ankle in his hands.

"Do you see a lot of football injuries?" said Trevor.

"Many. That's why I chose orthopedics. If I cannot be a professional footballer, I can treat their wounds, eh?"

"So what was the Italian perspective on the David Villa broken leg?"

Ferrari laughed. A bad sign, thought Ben. What kind of orthopedist had such a cavalier attitude toward fractures?

"As a doctor, I am concerned for Villa, for Spain. He has been out for seven months now. But as an Italian, as a *tifo*, a fan—" Ferrari was now using his hands to gesticulate, not to examine Ben's ankle. "As a supporter of *gli azzurri*, our blue boys, I cannot say I was disappointed that Villa would be on the bench."

"Granted," said Trevor, "it didn't help much."

"No," said Ferrari mournfully.

"That final! What a terrible game!"

"I wept. Four to nil."

"Tragic," agreed Trevor.

Ben decided not to remind Trevor that he'd rooted for Spain. They'd been in Mittenwald, and he'd led the entire pub in a flamenco dance to celebrate the Italian defeat.

"We would have had a chance against Germany," said Trevor.

"Or Portugal," said Ferrari.

Ben coughed.

"Have you had ankle trouble before?" said Ferrari, unembarrassed.

"I twisted it a week ago. It hurt, but not like this."

"As I imagined. The ankle was already vulnerable." He pointed to gray lines on the X-ray. "You have a bimalleolar fracture. It's very unstable, and I'm worried that some of the medial ligaments are injured too."

Ben never liked to hear details about the inner workings of his body. He preferred to think of himself as a mind in a carton.

"Tonight," said Ferrari, "we will splint it. It's still too swollen for a cast, and we must ensure the bones align properly."

Ben felt queasy. This medical jargon was pushing him over the edge.

"Ideally, you will remain in the hospital for the weekend. I would like the joint to be elevated. Would it be possible to stay?"

"Sure," said Trevor. "Why not? We've got open-ended tickets."

"You are students?"

"Students—*and* entrepreneurs." Trevor handed Ferrari a card from his wallet. "Check it out. We've just launched an Italian-language interface."

"I love the Internet," said Ferrari. "Plah-goose-list?"

Ben closed his eyes while Trevor explained.

"I see," said Ferrari. "A social network?"

"Exactly."

"We Italians are enamored with the Facebook."

"Well, the Plagueslist is far better than the Facebook." Trevor thumped the recliner for emphasis. Ben flinched. "You'll love it. Interact with your patients, or recruit new ones. You should think about placing a banner ad on the orthopedics pages. Medicine has to enter the digital age, right?"

"It *must*," said Ferrari.

"You should set up an account. It's free!"

"I will." Ferrari carefully placed the business card in his wallet. "As soon as my shift ends. I will."

"Great."

"But first, I must splint this ankle. There's been some displacement, and I must perform what's called a reduction. A little shift, a little twist."

Ben kept his eyes firmly closed. He did not want to see those hand gestures.

"If we do not achieve alignment of the broken bones, all sorts of complications may arise."

"He'll never walk again?" said Trevor helpfully.

"Well, he may suffer from arthritis."

"You hear that, Benny? You don't want arthritis. You're practically a geezer already. If you get arthritis, you'll never get laid."

"Laid?" said Ferrari.

"Never mind," said Trevor.

Ben thought of Jean Lin. Perhaps the hospital sold postcards. He could tell her it was a football injury. They'd been kicking around, and he'd been tackled while heroically defending the basket. (Trevor could help him with the details.)

But—no. He would never lie, not on a postcard. Postcards were for the truth. Veiled truth, perhaps. Truth expressed in the most fustian of language. Yet in what other manner could he reveal his feelings? Deep-set as he was in formality and reserve, there were words he could not allow himself to use. But to his great good fortune, there were other languages. There were different grammars. There were more words. He would send this neat and frank girl postcards of affection, postcards of fondness, and they would betray the pull he felt, the tide he could not ignore.

The postcards he had sent to Jesse: they were always true. He had sent postcards of apology and postcards of regret. And here he could use that word, if only in his head, if only when the pain and the painkillers danced the tango, dipping sharply, making this moment seem surreal—not surreal, but *unreal*—he chortled at his malapropism—no, he did not have a Dalí-esque clock dripping around his body—he saw Trevor and Ferrari start at his laughter, and he waved. Precision of language was important. This was precise. To Jesse, he had sent postcards of love.

"Are you ready?" Ferrari said. "I will warn you. Despite the medication, this will hurt." He gripped Ben's swollen ankle.

"Here," said Trevor, giving Ben his hand. Ben squeezed. "Ouch. No, you're good. That's what it's there for."

"In my new Rome," Ben said, "one will pass over any art-historical periods one doesn't find appealing. For instance, I'll skip Impressionism. I admit its importance, yet I dislike it."

"Hold still," murmured Ferrari. "Keep him still."

"And my personal journey will include very little Mannerism."

"Shh," said Trevor. "It's okay."

"My museum." He was perfectly lucid, but he couldn't make them understand what he was saying. "You wouldn't have to go through it all. You could skip some parts."

"No, Ben," said Trevor. "It's going to suck, but listen. The only way out is through."

CHAPTER TWENTY-SEVEN

Cal ran. She careered down the stairs, swinging herself around the landings. She burst out the door. She leapt around an old woman tottering back from the fruit merchant's with an armful of blood oranges. She knew that if she kept heading north, kept running downhill, it would be impossible to miss the massive arms of the piazza.

Faces passed in a blur: shopkeepers pulling down their grates, commuters walking home, children bending from the sidewalk like grass before wind. Everyone stared. She was flying. She leaned from her ankles and drove her knees forward. Her strides were hungry. They wanted as much pavement as she could give them. To her left, the setting sun gilded the Janiculum and haloed the plane trees with thin coronets. To her right was the Piazzale Garibaldi's view of all Rome. The flower sellers stopped to watch her, and the couples kissing on the ledge. A man who had been bent over a book lifted his head. Even the heroes of the herms seemed to turn as she ran by. Her heart was beating out of her chest, her lungs were heaving, her legs and back were ripped with pain, and her heel did not hurt at all. She could not even remember which foot had once hurt.

Saint Peter's Piazza. She would find Thea there. She took Ben's shortcut through a parking garage. It was empty, eerie, the few cars bulging like hillocks from the concrete. The stairwell smelled of piss. She smacked the wall as she turned the corner, and she was so consumed, so single-minded, that she was not startled when the escalator, like a dormant dragon, sprang to life.

During her few minutes in the garage, day had swung to night. She ran down the middle of a narrow street. The buildings were high and close and gave the impression of a tunnel. She was not far now. She thought she had been running all out, but she found another speed, another gear. The pain was beyond belief. She was being wrenched apart. She was about to die.

At the end of the street, she saw the marble columns, the piazza's white arms, and she dove into their embrace. There was an iron fence and with one giant stride she hurdled it. She leapt down the stairs. She was in the piazza. She'd made it. She put her hands to her knees. Her vision swam with black dots. Her heartbeat pounded in her ears.

Now, where was Thea?

It wasn't crowded. Cal straightened and had to wait until the dizziness passed. She began to jog around the piazza. Her legs burned. The tourists were sparse and scattered. A wedding group was posing in front of the basilica, the sky billowing orange and purple behind them. There were some couples mooning about on the steps, and a few college kids taking selfies. Thea was nowhere among them.

Thea was not here.

What had she been *thinking*?

Cal's legs were quivering, and she slowed to a walk. She hadn't been thinking. She'd been dreaming, she'd been running. She trudged the piazza's ellipse. How had she believed she'd find her? She had thought she had resigned herself to failure at the Pantheon, but here she was again, hoping against hope. She'd truly believed she could jaunt out the door and follow the unmistakable, gleaming path to the grail. Once again, she'd been tricked. She'd fallen for the chicanery of stories. She had been a fool.

The cobblestones kneaded her feet. She had trouble keeping her balance, and her mouth tasted of iron. There were no guards in sight, so she stepped over the low fence that surrounded one of the fountains and splashed water on her face. Thea might not even be in Europe, thought Cal. She might be dead, and if she was alive, she had no idea they were searching for her. What a strange fact, the independence of these lives. Jesse had thought about her all the time but she had never known.

And pity fell on Cal like a tree. She had heard the creaks for some time, felt the battery of wind, but now the trunk splintered, now the crown fell, branches snapping, leaves sighing through the air. It was immense. She had to sit down and she stumbled to the railing around the fountain. She crossed her arms over her chest.

Oh, she thought. Oh, poor Thea. She had not known him and he had not known her.

Cal closed her eyes. She imagined him at her side, and that was all it took. He was laughing at her. He grasped her elbow and leaned close. How she loved him. "I was always here," he told her. She had been born to this love and she had chosen it with every whit of her being.

He took her hand and led her through the crowd. The people beamed at them. The woman with the diamond earrings clapped her hands twice in delight. "Look," she said to the man in the tuxedo, "the girl's figured it out."

"So she has." His eyes were like her earrings, twirling all the piazza's light into blithe and tiny winks.

"Look at them," the woman said. "Look at the pair of them."

"It took her long enough."

Jesse grinned at Cal. "I bet I'd have been faster."

"Where are we?" she said.

"You don't know?" He was as strong as he'd been in their childhood. His eyes were sparkling and his cheeks were pink and Cal knew that if she could see his heart, it would be as whole as her own. "Cal, we're home," he said. "This is the Land of Ten Thousand Madonnas."

She opened her eyes. Lillian was walking toward her. The spotlights trained on the fountain were gleaming on her cheekbones and forehead. In the rich light, her hair seemed almost golden. Cal rose and took both of Lillian's hands in her own.

"How did you know I was here?" said Lillian. "Did you come looking for me?"

"I dreamt it," said Cal.

"I had to see the *Pietà* one more time," said Lillian. "Did Matt tell you? We were walking toward the pizza place and I saw a rack of postcards and I had to come." She shrugged. "But the basilica was closed. I should have thought."

"Matt didn't tell me," said Cal. "I knew you were here. It was my dream." She laughed aloud. "He's okay, Lill. Jesse's okay." The thick, tremendous joy of it! It was as startling as the red of a blood orange, as sweet.

"I know," said Lillian. "He's okay. I don't know why but all of a sudden I believe it."

For the shortest of moments Cal felt herself poised at the point where the paradoxes met, where he was everywhere and nowhere. You are with me, she thought, and I will never lay my eyes upon you again. We seek mysteries far and wide and the greatest mystery of all is within. They turned to leave the piazza. Behind them, the sun set with arterial force, bleeding out all over the sky. Somewhere a thief tossed a cheap souvenir from Santa Fe. Somewhere Thea found a place to call home. The pigeons pecked at crumbs and the tourists took photographs and inside the locked basilica, behind the bulletproof glass, Mary held her son. The red sky surrendered to black.

An Excerpt from
THE JUVENILIA OF JESSE T. SERRANO

I'm scrawling this in my hospital bed, and though I've got the covers pulled up, it's impossible to forget about the tubes. I knew even back in Santa Fe that it would end this way, blood clots and organ failure, my body crumbling like an ancient wall, but nobody warned me that I'd look like the back of a stereo system. I hate this, Cal.

The tubes remind me of my own foolhardy, unshakable belief in the Choice of Achilles. I thought I'd ripped it out. I thought I'd put away childish things, myths and stories, lies. I thought I'd resigned myself, and I thought this notebook— this optimistically and ridiculously entitled *Juvenilia*, as if I'd have other, mature works—was the great apologia of my resignation. It would show my transformation from one who believed beyond belief and hoped past hope to one who nobly renounced it all. One who knows there is no Choice of Achilles; that there is, in fact, no choice.

But it's hard to shake off a belief. It feeds you. Your skin grows around it. It becomes a part of you. And all this time,

I was imagining I'd find glory *through* resignation. This note-book would be my testament, and the trip I planned would be my heroic deed. I'd go out with a bang, not a whimper.

I was a fool.

Now, now, at last, I'm ripping out this belief. I'm bleeding from that hole, and I bleed fast and hard, Cal; my capillaries are shot, my blood pressure's high. I'm done. I'm done with the Choice of Achilles. I *will* believe this: there was never a choice.

"You're the first person I've brought here who doesn't think the Land of Ten Thousand Madonnas is bizarre," I told Lill.

Even Matt still thinks it's weird. But Lill gets it. She makes the place feel normal. "My house is just as devoted to Mary," she said. "Minus the twenty thousand virginal eyeballs watching whatever you do." I liked hanging out at home with Lill even before I got so tired, so tired I don't want to go anywhere, so tired that even at rest my body feels ponderous, as if it's drowning by its own weight, as if I myself am the stones in my pockets, the cinder blocks chained to my feet.

No more whining.

Lill came over a few weeks ago so we could work together on our AP history assignment. The same teacher who had us color maps was now making us costume paper dolls for the First Ladies. We sat side by side at the kitchen table and followed a strict division of labor, skilled and unskilled: Lill paged through magazines, I snipped at her command. "Lill," I said, "I've got to tell you something."

She bookmarked a page with paisley culottes. "Oh?"

"Barbara Bush would never wear those."

"But I would. I'm multitasking."

"There's some stuff I wanted to do, Lill. Stuff I'm not going to get done."

"God. Am I going to have to volunteer at an animal clinic in your honor? Plant some trees? Shit like that?"

"Much less worthwhile," I assured her. "I want you to find my mother."

"That's the worst idea I've ever heard."

"I want you, you plural, to find her. I'll have all the details worked out by the time I bite it."

"Nobody's ever forced me to do anything so idiotic." She slapped shut the magazine. "And I'm including this First Lady Fashionista project."

My face grew hot. "You don't get it."

"Get what?"

"You don't get how important this is. You don't understand."

"You think I don't understand your weird obsession?"

I'd already spent hours on this notebook, and the non-refundable open-ended tickets had cost a fortune. I gripped the scissors.

"You think I don't understand your oedipal, masochistic, pathological fascination with a woman who doesn't give a shit about you?"

When I felt bad, really bad, mortal and forgettable, I imagined the six of them together, my cousins and my best friend and my girlfriend and my mother.

"Understand that you're fixating on your mom so you can forget you're about to die? Oh, I understand, Jesse Serrano. I understand."

I was enraged. This trip—and don't think I'm missing the

irony—this trip was what I was living for. In one swooping pounce, I grabbed a chunk of her hair, a handful of her long, thin braids, and held the scissors open around them. She froze.

"You wouldn't."

"I would."

"It took eight hours to get these."

"I would."

"You wouldn't dare."

I shut the blades.

It wasn't dramatic. The scissors were dull and the braids were tightly corded. And she could have stopped me. I wasn't some prime physical specimen; one shove and I'd have been gasping on the floor. Instead, she held stock-still. Two dusky spots of color burned through her cheeks. Her eyes glittered and she stared at me. How that girl can hold your gaze! I looked right back at her, and I cut them off. Six of them. Six of her braids, her pride and joy. She used to braid those braids, and whip them around, and pile them atop her head. She used to adorn them with beads and feathers and thrift-store brooches. They were like Medusa's snakes, as fearsome, as impressive, and I cut them off.

I chucked them onto the table. I was going for insouciance, but I was shaking. My vision's side curtains trembled, as if the stagehand were poised for the cue to pull them shut. I was dizzy. I closed my eyes and put down my head and took deep, heaving breaths. Blood was coursing through the Hole like whitewater. I did my visualization thing, even though I guess it was pretty futile. Building the wall. Plugging the Hole. After I don't know how long, I opened my eyes.

Lill was still staring at me. The stubs at her temple looked grotesque. They looked like an amputation. "I'm sorry," I said.

"This is the worst thing that's ever happened to me."

"Lill, I'm so sorry."

She moved to the floor in front of my chair. "Finish the job."

"Are you sure?"

"I'm sure."

I lifted the scissors. I had seen Lill angry, believe me, tantrums and tempers and scathing comments and cold, hateful wrath. She wasn't angry, not now. Her head was braced between my knees. She was sad. We could hear each individual hair splitting between the dull blades. It was a gritty sound, like rubbing a fistful of sand between your palms. It was the sound of a hole being carved into the center of her heart.

I cut them close. When I finished, I cupped her head with my hands. I could feel the bones of her skull. She put her own hands on top of mine, and we sat there for a long time. I thought, This is what it would be like to grow old with Lill.

Eventually, she pulled herself up to her chair. "How do I look?"

You know how she looked, Cal. Even with the knobbly cut, even with the part lines webbing her head like the mortar of cobblestones, she looked beautiful: vulnerable and invincible all at once.

"Lill," I managed.

"You have to talk to your dad about Thea."

"I don't want to."

"Why not?"

"I don't want to make him sad."

"That's why?"

I was scared. That was why.

"Talk to him," said Lill. "Promise me."

"Do *you* promise to find my mother? Do you promise to do everything you can?"

"I promise."

"Fine," I said. "Me too."

After dinner that night, I lay on the couch while Arnold read. It was quiet except for the gentle rasp of his pencil in the margins of his book. He'd recently put some hooks in the ceiling to hang postcards strung on fishing line. There was no more space on the living-room walls. Too many Assumptions, too many Madonnas enthroned.

"Don't you have homework?" he asked me.

"Did it."

"Don't you want to read, then?"

"I'm mesmerized by the MadonnaMobiles." The name bugged him, so I used it. "They shimmy in every draft of air."

"Ah," he said.

I gathered my gumption. "Dad. Why didn't you look for her?"

"For whom?"

He knew. I could tell by his immediate, forced nonchalance, by the way he didn't put down his pencil.

"For *her*. For Thea."

He frowned. I'd anticipated irritation, or grief, but not confusion. He wore the face he makes when a student asks something so obvious he assumes he's misinterpreting the question. "Because I didn't want to find her."

Now I was the one frowning. I'd thought he'd say something

about how she didn't want to be found, or he'd confess that he *had* looked for her, that she'd covered her tracks too well.

"But," I said, "but—"

"Yes?"

"You carried that photograph in your wallet." I'd have pulled it out of my own wallet but I'd already packed it up for Trevor. "The one where she's holding me, and she's glowing—"

"I didn't carry that photograph because of Thea," he said, puzzled.

"Then why?"

"Because of you," said Arnold. "Jesse. Of course. Because of you."

I don't remember what I said. "Oh," I think. "Okay." I watched the Madonnas quaver in the breeze from the open window. *Because of you.* It overturned how I'd narrated my entire story. *Because of you.* I thought of the phrase *love of your life,* and how I'd never seen much sense in it. A life has lots of loves, loves that shift with time and loves that persist, loves like stars in the wilderness, manifold and unchartable and sustaining. But now I knew: Thea was not the love of Arnold's life. I was the love of Arnold's life. And he was the love of mine.

And I knew my idea of looking for my mother was wrong. It was deeply wrong. The quest was built on a fault. I thought I would need to search the world to fill my Hole, I thought I'd need to look high and low, to comb the map, but the mystery's end has always been in my own home. I have Arnold and I have ten thousand Madonnas, and together they are all the mother I need.

Cal, can you imagine how my heart sank? I'm tired. I'm

tired and I can't do it over. The maps, the photographs, the tickets, the money. And this notebook. This arrogant notebook. How can you write when you don't know the first thing about yourself? I thought I was writing about my mother, but I flip back and now I can see. I was writing about my dad. Every story. Every single goddamn story. Arnold is the hero. Arnold is the grail. Arnold is the one who put in the untold, unsung hours. The finite time, the infinite love.

Cal.

I'm sorry.

I'm sorry for this misbegotten quest. And I'm sorry for leaving. I'm sorry, Cal, and, Cal, I hope you'll forgive me.

Arnold has tried to make the hospital room as cozy as possible. He brought my quilt, a yellow-orange thing that has always reminded me of Klimt's *Kiss,* and he brought a lamp, so I wouldn't have to read in the ugly white glare. The homey touches make it worse. It's harder to pretend this is only a weird interlude, that soon I'll go back to real life.

Lill visited me last night. She wasn't supposed to get on the bed, but she always did. We lay on our backs on top of the quilt. She gave me an earbud. One of my arms was slung up against the mottled patchwork and the other was warm against hers, and every song was right, low-key and lyrical and lovely. In the big black window, the lamp reflected a sharp triangle of light. I saw a hint of our profiles. I thought, Maybe they're right, the philosophers, and this is the cave and we're living a reflection, a dream. Maybe real life is yet to come. Maybe we're about to wake up.

Maybe not.

Lill's eyes were closed, but she was tense. I knew she was awake. I unbuckled my watch.

"Hey, Lill."

"Hey, Jesse."

"I want you to have this."

I expected her to fly out at me, but she extended her arm. I put it in her hand. She shook her head. I buckled it around her wrist. It was loose. She made her hand into a streamlined torpedo, to check, and it didn't fall off.

CHAPTER TWENTY-EIGHT

"'These paintings,'" Ben translated, "'are like friends with whom one has been long acquainted through correspondence and now sees face to face for the first time.'"

He arranged the bedcovers. His ankle was kept stable and elevated by a device that Trevor had engineered from a pillowcase, Styrofoam peanuts, and the drawstring of his basketball shorts. It was Sunday evening and they'd all gathered in the hospital room.

"Would you help me with something?" said Lillian.

"Depends on what," said Ben.

"He means, 'Certainly! I'd be happy to help!'" Trevor advised her.

"Depends," Ben repeated.

"It's a postal issue."

Ben perked up.

"Specifically, I need to mail two packages from Rome to Germany."

"Certainly," said Ben. "I'd be happy to help."

He suspected he knew the contents of the packages. Yesterday Lillian had given him his own copy of the *Italienische Reise,* which she and Cal and Matt had tracked down in a used-book store. He had been overcome. "I'll treasure this," he said, blinking.

"I know it's not the typical sickbed present," said Lillian.

He'd blinked again. The pain from his broken ankle, he presumed, could spontaneously stimulate the lacrimal glands. "Flowers! Balloons!" he scoffed. "Who would choose worthless ephemera over the immortal words of Johann Wolfgang von Goethe?"

Perhaps he'd ask Lillian if he could tuck in a note, a tasteful postcard, for Joachim Abend. Ben had found the *Italienische Reise* thanks to him, and it was now one of his favorite books. "At present," Goethe wrote, "I am so enthusiastic about Michelangelo that I have lost all my taste for Nature, since I cannot see her with the eye of genius as he did." That was exactly how Ben felt. He'd lost his taste for Nature long ago. He preferred instead to see her through the eyes of genius, through the eyes of Michelangelo and Goethe, of those who had sought, all their lives, to render the essence of flight.

He shut the book. It was far too loud to concentrate. "We ran this morning," Cal said. "And my heel didn't hurt."

"Must have been all in your head," said Trevor.

"It was *not.*"

"Uh-huh. Which is why they couldn't find anything on the X-ray."

She threw a banana peel at him. He draped it over his head like a lampshade and said, with a wave of his phone, "Attention, all. I've talked to the airline. Several times, actually.

They've got some cool people at their call center. Did you know it's monsoon season in Delhi right now?"

"The plan?" said Cal.

"Fiumicino to JFK to O'Hare," said Trevor. "And on to San Francisco for Matt and Lillian. Day after tomorrow."

"Nice work, man," said Matt. "Thanks for dealing with the logistics."

Trevor grinned. His sea-glass eyes gleamed. "It wasn't that hard. Not *nearly* as hard as I had been made to believe."

Ben chose to ignore the jab.

"Our invalid's getting his cast tomorrow morning. Then we'll have all day to take it easy and eat gelato."

"All day to sightsee, you mean," said Ben. A single day in Rome! He had to plan! What had the zones left out? Had his companions even visited the Colosseum? He flipped to the relevant passage. "It is so vast that the soul cannot retain its image," Goethe said. "Every time we return to it, we find it greater than before." Ben imagined strolling around the Colosseum's ellipse. He would fall into stride with a young man in breeches, a frock coat, a cravat. "Nowhere else," Goethe would say, "have I been so sensitive to the things of this world." Jesse had been hung up on text's drawbacks, on the imperfect and infinitesimal sliver of his consciousness represented by the *Juvenilia,* but to Ben, text bent time. Only in books could you flip forward and backward, revisit and linger and skim. Only in text could you wander the garden of another's thoughts.

They had read the fifth story in the *Juvenilia* on Friday night, when Trevor had finally gotten in touch with Matt at the bed-and-breakfast. "They're coming here," he told Ben.

"It's eleven. They won't be allowed in."

"I can pull a few strings. Cash in a few favors."

Ben didn't ask how Trevor had strings to pull when they'd been in the hospital for only three hours. Cal, Matt, and Lillian tiptoed into his room.

"Posh," said Matt. "A single."

"I told them to spare no expense," said Trevor. "Benny here doesn't have a temperament suited to a ward."

After they'd read Jesse's last story, they'd been silent, negotiating private, impossible conversations. In this world, Ben would tell him, text is about as close as you get to miracle. He never could have known his cousin like this in real life, where intimacy was always makeshift, minds always screened by bodies. In a way, Jesse's image was clearer and sharper than it had ever been.

Poor consolation, thought Ben.

Now Cal yawned. "Let's call it a night," said Matt. "You coming, Trevor?"

Trevor, stretching his back, made the yowl of a concupiscent cat. "I'll just sleep on the floor again. The casting's at eight, and I've got to hold our invalid's hand."

Ben was too tired to say something cutting. Plus, it was true.

"I'm just going to take a quick walk down the hall," said Trevor once the others had left.

"Sure," said Ben. Trevor had spent hours this weekend wandering the corridors. Probably staging puppet shows with a whole gang of latex turkeys, thought Ben. But he caught himself: he couldn't keep imagining him as a stock character. When Trevor returned from his constitutionals, he would perch on the windowsill and place calls to airlines, insurance companies, their increasingly fretful parents. Ben, lounging on the bed with Goethe, felt nary a frisson of envy. He'd wanted this all along. He could nearly forget the year wasn't 1787, that carriages weren't clacking down the streets outside.

Trevor would share one last guffaw with the other end of the phone. He'd prop his long legs on the rail of the hospital bed, and while he fiddled with syringes and tape, pilfered from who knows where, they'd have one of their long, meandering conversations. Was it compatibility, or was it because they'd grown up in lockstep? They had known each other for so long.

"When we came in," said Ben, "did you happen to notice whether the hospital has a gift shop?"

"Nope. Too busy dragging your incapacitated ass to the ER. Why?"

"Oh, nothing." A few minutes later, he said, "Do you think they sell postcards here?"

"You, good sir, are an idiot."

"I am not."

"Yeah, yeah, you speak a few languages, you graduated *summa cum laudo*—"

"*Laude*—"

"Are you intending to send a hospital postcard to that girl?"

"Well, but—"

"Are you sending yet another postcard to your crush?"

"She's not—"

"She is. Answer. Postcard. Yes or no."

"Fine. Yes. But—"

"You're an idiot."

"She likes postcards."

"Listen to me. This once, listen to me. Call her."

Ben took the phone and dialed. He knew her number by heart. Some things could not be mediated through the filter of art or correspondence. That was what he'd learned from Trevor. For everything else, there would always be postcards.

"Do not, under any circumstances, put weight on this ankle," the doctor said. They'd rustled up a pair of American-style crutches for him. "Use these for at least six weeks. It will be difficult, but you're a strong young man."

His armpits begged to differ as he tottered his way out of the hospital. The others were walking slowly, keeping pace with his lurches.

"Trevor!"

"Trevor!"

The name was called in an Italian accent, the *r*'s deeply rolled—"*Trrray-vorrr!*"

"Hang on," said Trevor. "Gotta bid farewell to my buddies."

The buddies streamed into the corridor, mobbing them. "It has been such a pleasure," said one old woman in a hospital gown.

"You have improved my life," said another, brandishing a cane.

"I have posted hundreds of pictures!"

"Wait," said Ben.

"We love Plah-goose-list."

"We adore it."

Ben craned to make out the Italian chatter humming beneath the English declarations. "Plah-goose-list! It is where I turn with my medical mysteries! No longer must I bother my children. My children have accounts as well! We do not know how we managed before!"

"You—" he said to Trevor.

Trevor was clasping hands like a politician. "Enjoy! Keep signing on! Tell all your friends!"

"We already have," another old woman assured him. "And we have told our friends to tell theirs!"

"It will be a virus," said another. "It will be bigger than cat videos."

"Friend me!" said Trevor. "I want to see all your medical problems."

He finally detached himself. A wet-eyed chorus gazed after them. Trevor casually smacked the wall to the beat of their footsteps.

"All those times you needed 'fresh air'?" demanded Ben when they turned the corner. "All those times you needed to 'take a little walk'?"

"Is it my fault I made some friends?"

"Friends!" said Cal. "Customers, more like!"

"Plagueslist is free," said Trevor. "We're not launching Plagueslist Premium till October. And it just so happens that its ideal demographic is old Italian ladies. I didn't even *try*. They're so into Plagueslist they quit tweeting."

"Here I thought you were hanging out in the hospital to keep me company," said Ben.

"And now we've made some big Italian blog. Technorati or something."

"That's not Italian!" yelped Ben. "That's *the*—"

"Oh, maybe that's why our traffic's spiked worldwide," said Trevor. "I was confused. I figured they might all have their phones set wrong."

Ben nearly tripped just thinking about it.

"Marco!" said Trevor as they neared the exit. "Yo, man."

"Buon giorno, Signor Ferrari," said Ben.

"Plagueslist!" he said to Trevor. "I'm obsessed. I'm addicted. Will you be my friend?"

"I'd be honored. Hey, you should get your patients to sign up."

"It is done. I hope you don't mind that I have reproduced your business card." Ferrari pulled a stack from his pocket.

"I should have known," said Ben as they continued. "You're brilliant."

"Hardly," said Trevor. "I'm just a guy with a dream."

To Ben's surprise, the modern Rome into which he stepped was not a disappointment. He felt sorry for thinking Rome smelly, or dirty, or disorganized with its treasures. You could never take the city out of the city. That was Goethe again. "Still the same soil, the same hill," he'd written. "Often even the same column or the same wall." Would Ben ever have an epiphany of his own, or would his thoughts always be brokered by books? Did originality exist? He did not know, but he thought he might know what book could help him figure it out.

And now he was crutching through Trastevere, now he was crossing the Tiber on the Ponte Sublicio. At this very spot, Horatius had defended the city from the invading Etruscans. Ben saw the place four-dimensionally, a place that slipped through time: the parvenu town and the imperial center, the deserted medieval Rome and the resurgent Rome of the Renaissance popes. He saw Goethe and Tischbein and Shelley and Keats; he saw Garibaldi, and Cavour; he saw Benito Mussolini and Ezra Pound. And he saw now. Now. Now. These were eternal, indivisible moments, elapsing as quickly as they came. They were written in water and they would never die.

He stopped halfway across the green Tiber. They were going to visit his favorite Caravaggio at Sant'Agostino, but he wasn't sure he could make it. His whole body ached. The sun was fierce. Sweat dripped down his back.

"Are you going to be okay?" asked Trevor.

"We could get a taxi," said Matt.

"Crutches are much harder than they seem," said Cal. "We always thought they'd be fun. We used to want to break our legs."

Ben didn't need to ask whom she meant by *we*.

"Someday," she said, "you won't even remember which foot used to hurt."

They were all stopped, and he realized they were waiting for an answer. Would he be okay? He closed his eyes. They ringed him, Trevor and Cal, Lillian and Matt, but also Jesse, and Goethe, and Michelangelo, and all the forgotten human beings who had crossed this bridge, whose moments piled on top of one another like postcards, weightless and translucent slices of existence in this world. Another moment slid by. He opened his eyes. "Yes," he said to Trevor, to them all. "Yes."

CHAPTER TWENTY-NINE

Matt surrendered to the drowsiness. He shut his eyes and half listened to the officialese, the way they shoehorned information about oxygen masks into the list of complimentary beverages. Was everyone lulled by the juxtaposition of "If this airplane loses power" with "We're pleased to serve tomato juice"? Was the bustle engineered for that very purpose, to drown out the liquid hiss of fear?

He'd lost it. He was awake again. He reached into his pocket for his squash ball. His tray table would have been the perfect surface for bouncing, but Ben sat in front of him.

"Restrain yourself," said Cal. "Nothing good can come of provoking Ben."

"True," said Matt. "He might start quoting Goethe again."

He flipped the ball from hand to hand. Squash seemed to belong to some distant past. It was as absurd as some of the stories Ben had told them about Rome: the dictator who'd marched on his own city, the pope who'd bankrupted the Vatican to build his own mausoleum. It was as circular. "I need to train," he told Cal.

"Me too," she said. "Preseason starts in four weeks. And I have to pack. My mom's probably already bought sixteen of those giant Tupperware bins—"

"Stop," Matt moaned. "I forgot college was a thing you had to pack for."

Trevor poked his nose between the seats in front of them. "Whippersnappers, calm the eff down."

"But we leave in *five weeks*—"

"I hate freshmen. You're not spending four years in Antarctica. You're moving to another city, which, I assure you, will be happy to sell you anything you've forgotten."

"But what about—"

"And nobody follows the summer training schedule."

"I hate seniors," said Cal.

"Here's a fun fact to cheer you up," said Trevor. "Every seven seconds, a new Plagueslist account is created."

"It's an epidemic," said Matt.

"Interesting marketing angle there," Trevor mused. "Co-opting the language of illness. I like it. Imagine a billboard at the entrance of every major hospital. PLAGUESLIST: CATCH THE BUG. What do you think?"

"Genius," Cal said dryly.

"Thank you," said Trevor. "I agree. And oh, is this bug contagious. We hit the million-user mark this morning."

"Who knew the world had so many lonely, diseased people?" said Ben.

"*You're* surprised?"

Ben tetchily returned to his croissant, which, Matt noticed, he was eating with no assistance from the coffee grinder. Trevor sighed in contentment. "I just wish I could tell my former self to stop freaking out."

The plane chased the sun west. The measures of time, the waxing and waning of light, were held suspended. Even the beautiful flight attendant drowsed on the jump seat, her head wobbling on her birdlike neck, lolling down, jolting up. Matt's hand loosened its grip, and the squash ball fell gently to the floor.

As they approached baggage claim in San Francisco, Matt felt a surge of nervousness. He tried to stay cool. He smoothed his hair, which now curled around his ears and the nape of his neck. "Lily!" he heard. She glided to a passel of women and was engulfed. Matt stood to the side. He nonchalantly scanned the crowd. He didn't want to seem eager or, worse, anxious. He'd emailed both his parents. Surely one of them would show up. Or he'd get a ride with Lillian. That'd be fine.

"My girl," he heard Lillian's tiny grandmother crooning, "my sweet girl—"

Lillian was crying into the stuffed bird that perched atop her grandmother's hat. Matt took a step back. He shouldn't interrupt. He watched the row of chauffeurs with their placards. He watched a girl in sandals and a messy topknot run laughing into the arms of a tattooed boy. He watched a man with a double stroller set up camp by the escalators. The children were unbuckled and given signs to hold. Matt craned to see the drawings: crayon hearts, quarter suns hugging the corners, stick figures with heads and legs and nothing in between. When their mother appeared, the children both burst into violent tears. "We did just fine," the man told her. "Of course you did," she said. She kissed him lightly on the lips. Matt swallowed and looked away. These greetings, these homecomings and reunions: they were too much. For a second you could believe that all people did was love each other and miss each other and count down the days till they were home again. Look at them. Look at how the desires of their innermost hearts walked off a plane and down an escalator and into their arms.

Matt focused on the baggage carousel. Someone tapped his shoulder and he spun around. "Your dad couldn't make it," said Professor Serrano, "and your sisters had a game that your mom couldn't miss, but I told her I'd be happy to—"

Matt dove in. He and Professor Serrano gripped each other's backs in a long, sturdy embrace. "My *dad!*" Jesse always said. Matt could hear his voice, the mix of mockery and delight. *"Arnold!"*

Your *dad,* Matt told him over Professor Serrano's shoulder.

Thank you, Jesse said back.

Matt slung his bag to his shoulders. "There's money left," he said. "It's yours. We don't need it anymore."

The crease between Professor Serrano's eyebrows deepened. "Did you do what you set out to do?"

"No," said Matt. "Yes."

"I thought so."

"There's a lot of money left."

"Well. I'm sure it'll come in handy someday."

"You could move."

Professor Serrano regarded him. You could never tell whether he was thinking deeply or spacing out. "Maybe I will," he said. "Maybe I will."

How natural it felt to follow him to his car. Professor Serrano seemed the sort to hunch over the wheel, but today he drove expansively, his shoulders thrown back. A single photograph, the size of a playing card, hung from the rearview mirror. Matt expected it to be a Madonna, but as soon as he gave it a tap to rotate it toward him, he knew it would be a snapshot of Jesse. He was right. Jesse's arms were flung wide, his head thrown back. He embraced the spacious sky.

The thread lazily spun, and the photograph trembled. Matt felt his throat tighten. "Thanks for the ride," he said.

"Anytime," said Professor Serrano.

CHAPTER THIRTY

There was her mother. There was her father. Cal sprinted toward them, not caring that her backpack lurched against her head with every stride, not caring that other travelers were giving her sidelong smirks. It felt so good to run.

She hugged them. "Your heel!" said her mother.

"Mom," said Trevor. "Mom, look at this." He pulled up his shirt. He was wearing the money belt.

"He put that on in customs," said Cal.

"Did not," said Trevor.

"Did too."

"Children," sighed their mother.

Ben swung toward them on his crutches. Aunt Janice shrieked. "My son! I send my hale and hearty son to Europe and *this* is what's returned to me!" She smothered him in a hug. One of the crutches hit the floor.

"Mother," said Ben, disengaging, "I'm *fine*."

"How could they allow you to walk all the way from the gate?"

"I'm perfectly capable of locomotion, Mother."

"Too capable," muttered Trevor. If Ben's crutches had dampened his enthusiasm for sightseeing, it was not by much. "One short day in Rome!" he'd chanted all day yesterday. By noon, they had visited several churches and the ancient Forum. They headed down the open boulevard of the Via dei Fori Imperiali to see the Colosseum.

"Maybe we should spend the afternoon on the Spanish Steps," suggested Trevor. "Soaking in the ambience, savoring some top-notch gelato—"

"'I am not here simply to have a good time,'" Ben intoned, "'but to devote myself to the noble objects about me.' Goethe."

"It's a freaking reincarnation," said Matt.

"All the noble objects look the same to me," said Trevor. "Painted ceilings. Simpering statues. Doors, columns, Latin crap."

Ben sputtered.

"Overturned pillars. Moss-grown crumbles. Heaps of old rocks."

"The grandeur of Rome is wasted on you," Ben told him. He suddenly stopped and leaned over the railing at the side of the road. "Behold! The Forum Transitorium!"

The five of them beheld the overturned pillars, the moss-grown crumbles, and the heaps of old rocks.

"Imagine," said Ben in an ethereal tone. "Nerva himself walked here. You can just *see* him."

"Ooh, where?" said Trevor. He squealed. "Ahh! Crutched in the crotch!"

"Nice one, Ben," said Lillian.

Cal grinned at her. She loved the way Lillian dressed.

Fishnet stockings and a gauzy skirt that looked like the plumage of a peacock. A black shirt, a newsboy cap.

"See," Ben told Trevor, "*Cal* is delighted by the imperial fora."

They continued down the road. Cal and Lillian walked together toward the distant lacework of the Colosseum. Behind them, Trevor and Matt were discussing soccer. "What I don't understand," Ben said loudly, "is that you don't give a fig about the Julio-Claudians, but you'll lap up the most insignificant detail about this Ronaldo Messi person—"

Lillian sighed. "Can we do something to tune them out?"

"Tell me a story," said Cal. "Tell me a story about you and Jesse."

"I never tell those stories."

"I've noticed." Cal was tempted to relent but she thought, Girl, where's that backbone? "Come on. One story. You have a million, don't you?"

"Yeah."

"So tell me one."

"Fine," said Lillian. "If you insist." She wants to, thought Cal. Lillian and I, we don't do anything we don't want to do. The wide street had been cut like a swath through a field, and they both kept their eyes on the tiered arches of the Colosseum, looming at its end. "Well," said Lillian, "here's one. I had to write a personal essay for junior English. Something I could maybe use for a college app. And it felt so fake. Summarizing myself in five hundred words, bragging without obviously bragging."

"Pretending you've learned and changed and shit," said Cal.

"Exactly," said Lillian. "And I got blocked. Beyond blocked.

I'd type, like, 'My summer job at Camp Sunshine taught me about working with autistic children, but it also taught me about myself,' and I'd actually feel sick. It was due the next day. So I go over to the Land of Ten Thousand Madonnas, just to procrastinate more, and he can see how tense I am, and he says, 'Okay, time to spill,' and I blurt out the whole story. Even though it was embarrassing. You know how he could write."

"I know."

"I figured he'd make me leave so I could get it done, but instead he said, 'I need your help.' Arnold had been ragging on him about his clothes. Justifiably, I might add. So he said, 'Will you take me thrift-shopping?'"

Cal listened, and she smelled the musty secondhand-shop detergent. She thumbed through the racks, seeing the clothes through Lillian's eyes: they shone out to her, the shirts that would make Jesse look like himself, rakish and handsome. They wanted to be chosen. Meanwhile, Jesse asked her questions. By the time they left, he had two new plaid shirts, three dollars each, and a pair of jeans he liked so much he wore them out of the store. Lillian had an essay. All she had to do was write it down. Walking along the sidewalk, they held hands and swung them back and forth. They couldn't stop laughing and they couldn't keep their eyes off each other. Lillian thought, He is the most beautiful boy in the world.

"That's a good story," said Cal.

"They're all good stories."

"I'd listen to more. If you want to tell them."

"Yes," said Lillian, "I think I do."

Trevor never knocked. "Holy shit," he said, peering into Cal's bedroom. "What *happened*? Did you pipe-bomb your own closet?"

"Looks like it, doesn't it?" Cal said glumly. "I'm packing for college."

"Let me guess. You decided to do the job properly. Now everything you own is on the floor—"

"Or the bed—"

"And you wish you'd never started." Trevor used his toe to investigate one of the piles. "Get rid of all this shit. A travel chess set? You hate chess."

"Someday I'm going to turn noble and cerebral—"

"A four-by-four-by-four Rubik's Cube? Like you'll ever be smart enough to solve that. Are those econ notes? You took *notes* in econ? I took naps." Trevor tapped his forehead. "This great entrepreneurial mind didn't need conventional economic wisdom."

Cal rolled her eyes. "What should I do with my science fair board?"

" 'Research Question,' " Trevor read from the board. " 'What is the effect of bleach on rosebushes?' Wait. Cal. Is *that* what happened to Dad's—"

"Don't tell," she said quickly.

"Ha!" Trevor crowed. "Eternal blackmail! Anyway, dudette, you don't want to empty out your room. Mom'll put her treadmill in here. It'll reek of sweat." He sniffed. "Granted, you have that problem already."

"What am I supposed to do instead?"

Trevor gathered an armload. "We'll stuff everything back in the closet."

An hour later, Cal found the turquoise egg. All summer she'd thought she must have lost it, but there it was, nestled in an old running shoe, as smooth and cool as it'd been in Santa Fe. It was girded by elliptical striae like the growth rings of a tree. Her hands must not have grown much, because it still fit perfectly within her palm.

"You got that with Jesse?" said Trevor.

"Yeah." She set it on her bedside table. "Want to go burn some econ notes?"

"Actually, can I take a look at those?"

The next morning, Cal woke up at five. She lay in bed for a minute, but it was already noon in Rome. Her favorite purple shorts were clean, at the top of the laundry basket. She tiptoed out the door and laced her shoes on the front stoop. She loved running before dawn. She loved the downy gray light and the mist smoldering from the lake. She would glint with sweat and clarity just as the light hit the water. Her hamstrings were stiff for the first few blocks and she felt jangly, unoiled, but by the time she reached the lakefront path, she had snapped into the run. A light film of moisture appeared on her forehead and arms. Her feet ticked against the pavement, *one* two three four, breath! Her knees bent, her hips swung, her shoulders swayed, her arms pumped.

Look, Jesse, she thought. Look what I can do.

She thought about him all the time.

The path hummed with runners, the sun rose, and Cal stopped thinking. She ran with nothing to remember, nothing to fear.

The Last Page of
THE JUVENILIA OF JESSE T. SERRANO

Cal. Here you are. Here's your infinitesimal slice of the consciousness of Jesse T. Serrano, former human being.

Do you remember Santa Fe, Cal?

Of course you remember Santa Fe.

"Which would you choose?" I asked you. "A long, quiet life, or a short, heroic one?"

"Both," you said.

Pigeon *and* dinosaur.

I keep saying there's no Choice, and what I've meant is that you can't choose: you have no right or ability to select one of the two alternatives. But I didn't go far enough. There's no Choice because the Choice itself is wrong. It's a false dilemma. The alternatives are not alternatives at all. Long versus short, quiet versus heroic: they're the same. In the scope of infinity, in a universe with no edge, human history is a flare and human consciousness is a blink. All lives are short and all lives are quiet.

But all lives are glorious too, Cal. To live! To live like a human! You are ordinary and extraordinary all at once. You have a heart that contracts and relaxes and beats out your moments. You are alive and you know you are alive. Your too-short time is long enough.

Long, short, humdrum, heroic: toss those considerations aside. Nothing to choose there. But we do have a choice. We *do*. Is consciousness a tragedy or a miracle? Does nothing matter, or does everything matter? That's the choice. That's the real choice.

And I've chosen. My cousin, my match, listen to me and tell them all. Tell Trevor and Ben and Matt and Lill. Tell my father. Tell the ten thousand Madonnas, each and every one.

I am Jesse, and I have a choice, and I choose everything.

ACKNOWLEDGMENTS

The writing of this novel relied upon good books and good people. Lest I write another novel, please imagine "and many more" after both lists.

Books first: Jaroslav Pelikan's *Mary Through the Centuries;* Joseph Campbell's *The Hero with a Thousand Faces;* Paul Elie's *The Life You Save May Be Your Own;* Johann Wolfgang von Goethe's *Italian Journey,* translated by W. H. Auden and Elizabeth Mayer; Alta Macadam's *Blue Guide Rome;* Richard Russo's *Empire Falls;* essays by E. M. Forster, Søren Kierkegaard, Ann Patchett, and Bertrand Russell. And the *Iliad,* forever and ever, amen.

Now, the people. Thanks to my teachers, especially Larry Dean, John Hick, Roger Lerch, Jane Levin, and Joseph Solodow. Thanks to my friends, especially Allison, Ariel, Ben, Emery, Jasmine, Libby, Rita, Sarah, Sasha, and Will. Thanks to my aunts, uncles, and cousins, especially Liz, Frank, Clare, Steve, Nancy, Ed, Ida, Ellie, Henry, Andy, Arna, Alexander, Charles, and, always, George.

Thank you, my dear brothers, Spencer, Derek, Peter, and Henry, and thank you, my sweet sisters, Lucy, Emma, and Rebecca. You are great—terrible, yes, but great. For these seven, I have you to thank, Ellen and Charlie, as well as for all the dinners and all the Boggle, for cardiological facts I probably messed up, for succor and sangfroid and love.

I'm thankful for the support of those who employed me while I wrote this book, Joseph-Beth Booksellers and Ogichi Daa Kwe. The Public Library of Cincinnati and Hamilton

County has provided both sanctuary and proof that nickel fines add up to quite shocking sums. Thanks to Sibongile Sithe and Gruschen Veldtman. Thanks to Alison Impey, Artie Bennett, Sue Cohan, and the whole team at Random House. My deep thanks to Kelly Delaney for her gracious, dedicated work.

Erin Clarke, editor and visionary, and Uwe Stender, agent and champion: I cannot express how grateful I am to work with you.

With books, with people, I am fortunate beyond measure.